D0068491

Estelle Ryan

The

Gauguin Connection

The Gauguin Connection

A Genevieve Lenard Novel

By Estelle Ryan

First published 2012

Acknowledgements

Anna J Kutor, for your unending and unconditional support. Jola, for being my personal cheerleader. Linette, for being the best sister anyone can ask for. Moeks, for your faith in me. Wilhelm and Kasia, for valuable friendship and fabulous photos. Paula and Kamila for suffering through the first ten chapters with me and your support. RJ Locksley for the second edit. Ania B, Krystina, Maggie, Julie, Kasia, the B(l)ogsusters and Jane for all your interest and support.

Dedication

To Charlene.

Chapter ONE

"Pleased to meet you, Ms. Lenard." The stranger held out his hand expectantly. His rumpled overcoat and the dark circles under his eyes gave the impression that he hadn't slept in days. Even his voice sounded exhausted, despite the crisp British accent. The tightened muscles of his unshaven jaw, his stiff neck and pursed lips sent a very obvious message.

"It's Doctor Lenard." I kept my hand to myself. "And you're not."

"Not what?" The dishevelled stranger pulled his hand back. His lips moved from a simple disagreeable pucker to a full-on sneer.

"Not pleased to meet me." I had lost count of how many times I had witnessed the corners of someone's lips drawn toward the ears to produce a sneering dimple in the cheeks. The vast majority of those expressions had been aimed at me.

"Genevieve, play nice." Phillip Rousseau's voice carried enough warning to pull my focus from the angry man. Despite his French background, Phillip pronounced my name in a manner more familiar to English speakers. I had insisted on that. It might be thought as callow, but it was my small rebellion against a pretentious sophistication forced on me from birth.

Phillip had been my boss for six years and none of his non-verbal cues or voice inflections was unknown to me. At present he was annoyed by my lack of sociability. He moved from behind the conference table. For a moment I thought he was going to position himself between me and the other man. Most people couldn't handle me and some outright avoided me, but somehow I had never managed to rattle Phillip. Or rather, never managed to rattle him too much.

Since my first day in this exclusive insurance company, he had also taken on the role of a buffer between me and the other staff. Something I was sincerely grateful for. I didn't like working with other people.

My boss came to stand next to me, far enough that I didn't feel crowded, but close enough for me to smell his expensive aftershave. As usual he was wearing a bespoke suit with a price tag that could feed a medium-sized African family for a year.

The stranger was studying me. My immaculate appearance, all the way down to my matching handbag, was not endearing me to him. Phillip should be glad that I possessed enough restraint to not comment on the man's lack of grooming in this elegant conference room. At least I had made some effort this morning with my appearance in an attempt to blend in. I doubted the stranger had made an effort in decades.

Ignoring the guest, I lifted an eyebrow at Phillip. "What am I doing here?"

"Okay, everyone, let's start over. Nicer." Phillip gave both me and the stranger warning looks and sighed. "Genevieve, this is Colonel Manfred Millard. He is the Deputy Chief Executive for Strategy at the EDA."

"The European Defence Agency?"

"You've heard of us." A surprised lilt changed Colonel Millard's statement into a question.

I gave him an impatient look. He was stating the obvious, so I moved on. "What is the EDA doing here, Phillip?"

"Let's sit down and discuss this." As the CEO of one of the most prestigious insurance companies in Europe, Phillip was a master in mediation and negotiation. Competencies I admired but had no desire to emulate. At times his unending patience frustrated me beyond my limits and I had a suspicion that today was going to be one of those days. Phillip pointed to the chairs at the far end of the conference table, where folders and piles of documents lay open. Phillip and Colonel Millard must have been here for a while.

I moved to the chair Phillip indicated to me. Both men sat down and Phillip started organising some of the documents into a folder. A photo lying on top of another pile of official looking reports caught my eye. The moment I focussed on it, I knew I had made a mistake. A monumental mistake. The photo was sucking me into its depravity. Into its sadness. Its wrongness.

It was clearly a crime scene photo with markers pointing out things I had no interest in learning more about. A young girl, dressed in loose-fitting pants, a colourful tie-dye T-shirt and a bright-green spring coat spread open under her, was lying on the ground. If it weren't for the hole in her forehead and the pool of blood framing her head like an evil halo, she would've looked peacefully asleep.

My heart was pounding in my skull and my breathing had become alarmingly shallow. Focussing on the simple task of inhaling and exhaling became a near-insurmountable undertaking. The blood surrounding the unfortunate victim's head kept drawing me back into the photo with a strength greater than the last two decades of training I had forced on myself. I could feel the warm stickiness of the girl's blood between my fingertips. There had been days that I hadn't wanted to train my mind, but the thought of feeling like I did at this very moment was what had motivated me to search, study, train and focus. A lot of good it was doing me now. I couldn't snap out of this.

"What's wrong with her?" The contemptuous stranger's voice reached me through the thick muddiness in my head.

"Oh, dear." I barely heard Phillip's whisper, but a second later he was next to me, mercifully not touching me. "Genevieve, sit down. Come now. Two steps to your left. Slowly does it. The chair is right behind you. There you go."

I focussed on my own gasping breaths and Phillip's calm

voice. If I held on for long enough, the black void threatening my peripheral vision might disappear. If I fought it, maybe it would not close in on me until the darkness swallowed me and spat me out hours later, unaware of what had occurred.

"I'm going to look in your handbag for your sheets. Stay with me, Genevieve."

I was genuinely glad that I had confided in Phillip the day my handbag had fallen off the chair, spilling its contents. The embarrassment of that day was nothing compared to what I was facing right now. I heard a rustle in my handbag and then the magical empty music staff paper appeared in front of me. "Here's a pencil as well. Manny and I will give you a moment."

Like a man having travelled in the desert for days would reach for a bottle of water, I grabbed the pencil and drew an accolade, connecting four staves, preparing it for the composition for four violins. I loved the elegance of the G-clef and took care drawing it with perfection. I barely heard the half whispered conversation taking place next to me.

"What's wrong with her, Phillip?"

"She has some form of autism. Writing Mozart's compositions calms her."

"Why does she need calming?"

"Manny"—Phillip sounded exasperated—"she saw the photo."

"Oh." There was a pause. "Do you really think she is the best person for this job?"

"Without a doubt. How long have you known me?"

"I don't know. Thirty years?"

"Thirty-four years this December. And how many people do I trust?"

There was a long silence. "I don't think you totally trust anyone."

"I trust Genevieve. There is not an ounce of deceit in her. She's the only one for this job."

"How long have you known her?"

"She started working for me six years ago. I met her at the opening of an exhibition. She was standing at a sculpture close to me while I was discussing business with a potential client. Unsolicited she walked up to me and told me that this man was lying to me and most likely was planning to defraud my company. I hired her on the spot."

"Why have you not told me about her?"

"For what reason? Are you interested in all my staff? The guy who services our coffee machines?"

"No need to get testy, Phillip. Just tell me more about her."

"Her speciality is reading body language. Whenever we have a claim that seems dubious, we video the interview and she views it. Not once has she been wrong in her assessments. She doesn't only read people and situations to the point where it feels like sorcery, she also notices patterns. When she's not viewing footage, she goes through claims and policies, and has picked up seven cases of fraud when our specialists and our extremely expensive software programmes had failed to pick anything up. She has single-handedly saved my company more than fifteen million euros."

I was a page and a half into the Adagio of Mozart's String Quartet No.1 in G major. I would need another page and a half to finish this movement, but already I felt considerably more in control. My breathing had almost returned to normal and the threatening blackness had receded.

Manny's shocked response to Phillip's explanation nearly elicited a smile. A few more bars and I would be in control enough to join in their conversation. And savour the fact that the man who had so easily disregarded me now spoke with grudging respect.

"She looks so normal though."

"Manny, hold your tongue. She's not deaf. People with a high-functioning form of autism like Genevieve work among us all the time. A lot of people go undiagnosed and never receive the help and support they need. They just become marginalised as strange or eccentric."

"Are you preaching to me?"

"Yes, he is and he should." I squared the two sheets of handwritten music and carefully placed it next to me, aligning it to the edge of the conference table. I would finish the last page later.

"My apologies. I didn't mean to offend you." The EDA official lifted his hands in a pacifying gesture of surrender. His increased blink rate indicated that he was truly troubled.

"Most people are ignorant about a lot of things. I've come to accept it."

His eyebrows shot up.

"Genevieve, we need your help," interrupted Phillip.

"Actually, *I* need your help." Manny squared his shoulders and jutted his chin. "I have a sensitive problem at work and don't know who to trust."

"Your work is defence. How can I possibly be of help? I work with art and insurance."

"You work with patterns, body language and deception spotting. Those are the skills I need."

I manipulated my body in such a way that Manny could receive all the signals possible to let him know I was not interested. I pointed my feet to the door, looked askance at him through narrowed eyes and blocked my body with my right hand on my left shoulder in a miniature body-hug.

"Manny, maybe you would allow me to explain the situation to Genevieve?" Phillip's deep voice brought the tension in the room down a notch. Manny sighed and I unblocked my body. I would never dream of showing Phillip such disrespect.

"Please, explain to her." Manny sat back, splaying his legs in front of him.

"Genevieve." Phillip waited until I looked at him before he

continued. "Manny and I have been friends for—"

"Thirty-four years. I heard you."

"I know." He gave Manny a quick reprimanding glance and continued. "Of the few people I trust—"

"You said that you trust me."

"That is true. You are the only person I trust implicitly. There are, however, a few other people I trust and Manny is one of those. He's one of the good guys."

"Oh." If Phillip declared Manny a good guy, I would accept that. I wouldn't have to like it, but accept it I would. My extensive studies had prepared me in many ways for understanding the human psyche and behaviour, and reading all the subtle nuances of non-verbal communication. But until the day Phillip had employed me, I'd only had academic knowledge.

It was Phillip, through tremendous patience, who had introduced me to the more real-life applications of that knowledge, including the confusing concept of good and bad guys. His earlier declaration of unconditional trust in me moved me in a way I had not yet experienced. Being brought up by parents who had been agonisingly embarrassed by me, I had never known acceptance or trust until six years ago. It still jarred me.

Phillip inhaled and exhaled very slowly before he continued. "Manny came to me for assistance and I would like to help him. But to do that I need *your* help."

"For what?"

"This case." He pointed at the files, which had been closed so the offending photos were out of sight. "A girl was murdered four weeks ago. It's very unfortunate that you had to see the photo, but at least now you know."

I took a shaky breath and nodded for Phillip to continue when he lifted an enquiring eyebrow. I distanced myself from the story and listened with an objective ear, another skill I had acquired out of necessity.

"Patrolling police officers noticed a large man searching through what appeared to be a pile of rags in an alley."

"Where did this happen?" I asked.

"Here in Strasbourg. The police officers became suspicious of the man in the alley. So they went closer and that's when they saw that the pile of rags was in actual fact a dead girl. The man was searching through her clothing for something. The moment he saw the officers, he ran, but they caught up with him. When he realised that there was no escape, he pulled out his gun and shot himself."

"Then the murder case is closed. What is the bigger problem?"

Manny sat up in his chair and copied Phillip's neutral tone. "The murderer's fingerprints identified him as a Russian tourist who had entered Europe through Spain on a supposed holiday. That was three days before the murder. It has since been discovered that he had hired a car under another name. He had all the legal documents for that identity. We followed his progress to France through the petrol stations where he filled up and the hotels he paid for with the credit card under the other name."

"And I assume that identity theft and credit card fraud are still not the biggest of your concerns."

"You assume correctly." Manny looked at Phillip. "She's really bright, this one."

"Yes, I'm bright. So why are you here? Why am I here? I would much rather be in my viewing room." I raised my chin a fraction and looked at Phillip. "I did not appreciate the way I was summoned here."

Manny gave a snort of laughter. The vexed look Phillip gave him sobered him instantly. "The murderer's weapon is one of the reasons we are here. The gun he shot the girl and himself with was stolen from a Eurocorps cache."

I lifted one shoulder in a half-shrug. "That is cause for an internal investigation. By Eurocorps. Why is the EDA involved?"

"I will explain that later." A frown marred Manny's tired face and he rubbed his neck a few times. "Eurocorps does have an ongoing investigation into the weapons theft."

"And you are stressed about this investigation. Why?"

"Isn't it obvious?"

"No. What is obvious is that you don't feel very confident about the weapons theft investigation. Using only a limited amount of deductive powers, I dare to conclude that there is an internal problem. You"—I pointed at Manny and narrowed my eyes—"suspect someone in either your agency or in Eurocorps. Most likely someone in a very high position."

Manny stared at me with shock clearly written on his face.

"I told you she was good." Phillip's voice held a hint of pride.

"Eurocorps didn't even know that the weapon was stolen until the local police entered the murder weapon's serial number into the system. It set off an alarm, which led to the discovery that a large number of weapons are not where they're supposed to be." He cleared his throat. "Even worse, Eurocorps doesn't even know when exactly these weapons disappeared."

"They don't keep track of what they have in their warehouses?"

"Of course they do." His angry answer bounced off the conference room's walls. For a moment Manny focussed on a painting on the opposite side of the room. He continued in a more modulated tone. "It would seem that someone ordered the stock-take to be postponed in that specific warehouse."

"And the only person with the authority to do so would be someone much higher up the chain of command." I added.

"Exactly. It's been a very long time since the last check. That means we can only hope that these are the only weapons that were taken." His answer tapered off as if he regretted sharing this much information.

"I assume that you also don't know if they were taken all at once or systematically over time." I accepted Manny's squinted eyes as an affirmative, albeit angry, answer. I turned to Phillip. "This man does not trust me. And yet both of you want me to get involved in this case in a manner that has not been clearly stated to me."

"Maybe she's right." Manny turned his torso away from me toward Phillip. I was hard pushed to not laugh at the unconscious, yet blatant, display of dislike. "Maybe she should not be involved. This is after all hugely sensitive information that requires a high level of security clearance."

"Who else are you going to ask?" A coldness sharpened Phillip's question.

Unfortunately, I was familiar with that tone. Phillip didn't know he used it when he ran out of patience and was about to lay down the law. A law that was expected to be followed unchallenged. One I usually challenged.

"Well—"

"There is no one else, Manny," interrupted Phillip. "You came to me as a last resort. Don't think for one minute that I feel flattered that you are here. You are desperate and you have nowhere else to go. You came here because you know that I can be trusted, right?"

Manny nodded, his lips sucked in, totally disappearing from his face.

"If you trust me, you should trust my judgement. I say Genevieve is the only person for this job and that should be enough for you."

A loaded silence hung in the conference room. It was only through years of training and experience that I knew to wait patiently for the outcome. I used this time to evaluate Manny's body language and read his internal struggle as clearly as if it were written on a billboard. I knew even before Manny spoke that he was going to accept my help. It was in his body language. Logic also dictated that this was his best option. Yet his visible discomfort with me was reason enough for him to hesitate. Fair enough.

"Fine," he said with an inelegant sigh. "Tell her the rest."

The quick appearance of Phillip's tongue between his lips made me smile. My boss was pleased with himself for winning this round. He turned to me and frowned at my anomalous friendliness. "What?"

"I'm just thinking—"

"Never mind, I don't want to know." Most times when he asked he got annoyed with my answers. "Back to the case."

"I haven't agreed to be part of this." I still felt shaken from the photo and my episode. If this case was going to bring back involuntary behaviours that hadn't been part of my life for more years than I cared to remember, I wasn't interested.

"Not you too. Just listen to the rest and then you can make a decision. The two of you are worse than dealing with spoiled trust-fund babies. There wasn't much of an investigation into the murder, since the murderer was in the morgue with his victim. One detective, though, was curious about what the Russian was looking for when he was searching the victim and decided to go through the girl's belongings with a fine-tooth comb."

"Why would a comb help?"

"Genevieve," Phillip answered in the slow voice he used when he was trying to stay patient with my inexhaustible questions, "it is just a manner of speaking. He searched her belongings very thoroughly."

"He found something," I stated. The excited lift in Phillip's voice had been my cue. Why couldn't people just get to the point? The need people had for a dramatic build-up was a source of great frustration to me.

"A strip from a canvas was carefully sewn into the hem of her coat."

"What canvas?"

"That's not of importance now."

"I disagree."

Phillip closed his eyes for the time it took him to take a calming breath. "It is a strip cut from the right-hand side of the Still Life, The White Bowl."

"Which artist?"

"Paul Gauguin."

My mind was racing. The moment all the pieces fell into place I glared at Phillip. "That piece is insured by us, by Rousseau & Rousseau."

"Yes, we insured that artwork seven years ago for a client who is extremely private about his art collection. Why he never reported it stolen I would really like to find out."

"Why weren't you going to tell me about this?"

"I was going to tell you about this once Manny left."

"Oh." I suddenly understood and nodded towards the other man who was quietly assessing us. "You didn't want him to think that you were more interested in the artwork than in helping him solve his insider problem."

The moment the *procerus* muscles between Phillip's eyes pulled both his eyebrows lower and together, I knew I should've held my tongue. Manny's laughter saved me from another sermon on censoring myself. I liked him a little bit more.

"She's got you there, old friend." For the first time since I had laid eyes on him, Manny's facial muscles relaxed. "I don't blame you for your concern. And just to set the record straight, I did not come to you as a last resort. When that fragment led me to you, I considered it to be a godsend. I know that you have an incredible fraud detection department and that your investigators can teach most law enforcement agencies a few things."

"How did this land on your desk, Manny?"

I silently applauded Phillip for his question and waited eagerly for the answer. Manny looked like he was arguing with himself. We waited. His brow smoothed as he straightened his shoulders.

"The commander of the Multinational Command Support Brigade at Eurocorps headquarters is a long-time friend of mine. We served together in an investigation division for a few years. I was visiting him and his wife when he got the call about the weapon used in the murder. Eurocorps has been co-operating with the Strasbourg police, but they have gotten nowhere in four weeks. He phoned me last week and asked if I knew an outsider who could help."

"Why an outsider?" Against my will I was becoming intrigued.

"The storage of light weapons for Eurocorps headquarters' personnel is also under my friend's command. That is why he was contacted when the police connected the weapon to Eurocorps. He started looking into it and that's when he discovered the disappearance of weapons. He also discovered that the inventory had been tampered with. It seemed to have been done at random in the last five years. That is when he first suspected someone powerful enough to interfere with our stock-taking system. It's the only explanation for how it had gone undetected for such a long time. The system is highly secured, accessed by a select few." He sighed heavily. "Eurocorps just recovered from a scandal three years ago. He didn't want to draw any attention to a suspicion that might come to nothing."

"What suspicion is that?"

"Nothing good. The involvement of a Russian murderer, an artwork and a Eurocorps weapon do not point to anything good. Some years ago a clerk working in the budget and finance department of Eurocorps noticed irregularities in the books. He went to the Deputy Chief of Staff Training and Resources and reported what he had seen. Immediately he was escorted from the building and subsequently fired for insubordination. What the deputy didn't know was that the clerk had copied all the files for himself. He sent them to three major news agencies, pointing the finger at the deputy and a few enthusiastic helpers. This caused an in-depth investigation, proving that the deputy had been siphoning funds from Eurocorps for years."

"Greed, one of man's greatest weaknesses." Humans disgusted me.

Manny nodded. "By the time this came out into the open, it was four years after the deputy chief had left and the EDA was only a year old. It took Eurocorps three years of layoffs and rigorous PR to recover some of the ground it had lost in the public eye. It was shocking how many soldiers had allowed greed to destroy their morals. Leon transferred from the EDA to Eurocorps and was instrumental in rebuilding its reputation."

"Who's Leon?" I asked.

"Oh, he's the Deputy Chief of Staff for Training and Resources at Eurocorps. Major-General Leon Hofmann."

This was interesting, but I was getting impatient. "The suspicion?"

"When Leon started looking into this weapons theft, he discovered something else. Every time there had been any tampering, at that same period there was a joint EDA-Eurocorps meeting or conference here in Strasbourg. The coincidence of the stock-take manipulation at the same time as EDA-Eurocorps meetings makes both of us wonder if there are insiders on both sides."

"And if an investigation was to start at one of the agencies, the other might get wind of it."

"Hence the need for an outsider." Manny was the only other person, aside from myself, whom I had ever heard use the word 'hence'. I liked him a fraction more. He cleared his throat and faced Phillip. "I trust you with this."

Phillip waved away the sentiment. "Are you sure about an insider in your office?"

"Unfortunately yes. The Head agrees with me about this."

"Who knows that you're asking for our assistance?" Phillip asked.

"Only Sarah Crichton, the Head of the EDA, Frederique Dutoit, our Chief Executive and Leon. To quote the Chief, 'I want this annoying case to close as soon as possible'."

"As soon as possible or as thoroughly as possible?" I had experience enough to know that those two concepts were more often than not worlds apart.

"The Chief wants it closed as soon as possible."

"And you?" I asked.

Manny took a moment to answer. "I want this bastard caught and locked up for a long time. I despise people who use their positions of power to further their own agendas. Especially when their agendas lead to this." He pushed the closed folders far away from him. His anger and earlier displeasure at the whole situation won him points in my book. It was indeed a very interesting case and my curiosity was piqued. For a few moments all three of us contemplated the situation.

"Thank you for trusting me with this." I knew how difficult it could be for people to trust and also knew that I should be honoured by Manny's trust. Even when it was begrudging. "I need time."

"You what?" Manny's eyebrows drew closer and the corners of his mouth pulled down. He looked at Phillip. "She what?"

"Genevieve—"

I got up. "It was interesting to meet you, Colonel Millard."

I picked up the sheets of handwritten music, slung my handbag over my shoulder and walked out of the conference room. I needed the safety of my viewing room filled with monitors where I could control the speed and frequency of the behaviour of the people on the screens. In the conference room, human behaviour was all too real. I preferred keeping it confined inside the monitors. In real life, people's behaviour disconcerted me far too much and far too often.

The expensive carpets in the corridor muted the staccato of my medium-sized heels and I was glad that the other office staff seldom frequented this corridor. The last thing I wanted was to produce a social smile and force myself to practice small talk. I needed a moment alone. At least I was honest enough with myself to acknowledge that my behaviour at this moment was pure avoidance. I was running away.

Change had never been easy for me and Phillip's cantankerous friend was about to throw my safe routine completely off its tracks. I liked coming into the office every day at the same time, spending exactly eight hours in my viewing room and then reversing my morning commute home. The predictability of working with contested insurance claims was safe. Guns, murders and Russians were different. Interesting, but different, and therefore unsettling.

The secured wooden door to my viewing room whooshed silently open when it recognised the swipe of my key card. I entered the safe familiarity of the air-conditioned room.

I wasted no time walking to my viewing station and sat down in my chair. My handbag still hung on my shoulder and I awkwardly pulled my arm from the sling before I placed the bag on the floor next to me. I knew that I only had a few minutes before the door would open and Phillip would follow me in. There was no mistaking the nose-flare, narrowed eyes and other intention cues when I had left. He was going to come into my haven and disrupt my life by demanding my co-operation.

Even though I did not want to work on this case, it wouldn't take much to convince me otherwise. Phillip was very good at convincing me to do things I didn't want to do. So, what I needed now was a moment to determine how I was going to do this on my terms. Especially if I was to work with Manny and all the complications his personality type would pose to my uncomplicated life.

For a short while I allowed myself the calming feel of my hands rubbing my upper arms. No sooner had I straightened my shoulders and composed myself when the door silently whooshed open. Phillip walked in, shoulders back, chin lifted and eyes focussed solely on me. Behind him Manny followed, contempt warring with doubt on his face.

Chapter TWO

"How long have you been working for me?"

"Six years."

"Have I ever demanded anything from you?"

"All the time."

Phillip's eyebrows lifted and then formed a frown in a silent question.

"The positioning of your feet demands that I hurry up and finish when you're in a rush and I'm explaining something. Your inner and outer frontalis, your orbicularis oculi—"

"My what?"

"The muscles on your forehead and around your eyes demand that I explain more, that I stop talking, that I—"

"You've made your point, Genevieve." Phillip ignored Manny's snort behind him and pinched the bridge of his nose. "What I meant was, have I ever demanded you to do any kind of work, any specific work here?"

"No."

"You've given her carte blanche?" Manny glared at both of us.

"I told you that I trust her." He turned his narrowed eyes to me again. "Do you think I would ask you to do something that would put your life in danger?"

I took a moment to seriously consider this. "No."

"You had to think about this?"

"Of course. Why would I give you an answer if I am not sure of the truthfulness of it?"

"We're digressing." Phillip put his hands on his hips. "I've never demanded anything from you, giving you the freedom to do things your way. You've proved yourself over and over to be very responsible with that freedom. So much so that I am now reluctant to be this insistent, but I do insist."

"Okay."

"Really, Genevi—" Phillip's argument broke off and he tilted his head to one side. "I beg your pardon?"

"It's an interesting case. A challenge." I looked at Manny. "I have conditions, though."

"No. Really?" Manny sounded disbelieving.

"Yes, really. Why would I say this if it's not real?"

"He was being sarcastic." Phillip glanced at Manny. "She doesn't get sarcasm or jokes. What are your conditions, Genevieve?"

"I need full access to all the files."

Manny started shaking his head even before he spoke. "You can't have full access to the files."

"Then I can't help you."

"You don't understand. To view these files you need to have a very high security clearance."

"So get it for me."

"It's not that easy. Ask me what you would like to know and I will give you as much as possible."

It was simply not an acceptable option, but I knew that I would have to prove it. "How many weapons were stolen?"

"So far the count has reached eight hundred and thirty-seven."

My eyebrows lifted and Phillip whistled softly.

"Were there any unique, out-of-the-ordinary weapons taken? What about very common weapons?"

Manny looked very unhappy being on the receiving end of so many questions. "About three hundred SIG 226 nine-millimetre pistols were taken."

"What exactly are those?" I was going to have to learn more, much more, about weapons.

"It's a service pistol very popular with special forces in many countries, from the US army to Polish special forces to a counter-terrorist unit in Greece."

"How many of the total guns taken were handguns?"

"I don't have the exact numbers on me right now. The weapons stored at headquarters are mostly light weapons. The majority of those stolen would be handguns, I suppose."

"You suppose?" I infused a healthy amount of annoyance into my voice. "How many stolen were assault rifles? How many sniper rifles? If there were sniper rifles stolen, when were they stolen? In the beginning, the middle or were they the last to disappear? These rifles, are there many people who would be able to effectively put them to use?"

"Genevieve," warned Phillip.

"Oh, but I'm not done. If most of the weapons were handguns, was there a specific gun favoured? Or were most the SIG's? Are these guns popular with certain groups like gangs or more organised groups? Once I have some of these answers I would need to check into lists of names associated with these guns and groups. Then I would have to compile a list of artefacts being stolen in areas targeted by these—"

"Stop." Manny lifted his hands in a gesture both of surrender and resistance. "We've already had our best guys look into some of these questions."

"But they didn't get anywhere?"

"No."

"Since you don't trust them to look into it any further and come up with unbiased information, not influenced or corrupted by those you suspect, you'd do a lot better giving me access."

Manny closed his eyes and shook his head, undoubtedly waging another internal war.

"Maybe Genevieve can tell you a little more about how she does things here. To set your mind at ease." Phillip looked pointedly at all the monitors and equipment he had installed for me without questioning a single request. The room was completely soundproofed, not allowing the top of the range sound system to reach beyond the room. Against the wall facing me were ten of the highest definition monitors on the market, arranged in an almost semi-circle for easier viewing.

Usually I had at least six of the large monitors running at the same time, each isolating a certain feature of the person being read. I liked having the other monitors available in case I needed to bring up another clip for comparison or have a document open for viewing. Now they were all dark.

In front of these monitors was a long wooden table running the length of the wall with three keyboards, three carefully placed notepads and three pencils neatly aligned to the notepads. Three antique-looking filing cabinets covered one wall and carefully chosen paintings decorated the remaining space. I was fully aware that anyone looking at my workspace would be able to see my need for organised surroundings. One might even go as far as wondering if I suffered from obsessive compulsive behaviour. I knew that I was only a few obsessions short of OCB and was thankful that I had missed out on that particular oddity. As it was, I had enough to deal with, including the two men in my viewing room.

The last thing I wanted to do at that moment was explain to Manny the complex process of reading someone's non-verbal cues. Or how I went about looking for patterns in seemingly innocuous data. Everything in me rebelled against Phillip's suggestion. But the knowledge of how important a high-profile case like this was to him held me in check.

"She can show me another time." Manny broke the silence and turned to me. "I'll give you a copy of all the files that Phillip and I went through earlier."

A small shiver ran down my back with the memory of the photo of the dead girl. I stiffened my spine and strengthened my resolve. There had been many difficult situations in my life that I had never thought I would overcome. This was going to be an opportunity for me to prove to myself that I could cope with a challenge as dark as this one. "What about the rest?"

"The rest?"

"You know very well that those files alone would not suffice. I will need more."

"I have an EDA computer in my car. I'll give you a password and make sure that the IT guys set it up for you to have enough access to EDA files."

"What do you mean 'enough'?" My question caused a deep frown between Manny's eyes.

Phillip jumped in quickly. "Why don't we start with the files and the computer? Manny, you can give Genevieve enough access for her to start. Genevieve, when you find that you need more information than is available, we can revisit this issue."

"Agreed." That sounded like a logical solution. "Where would you like me to start?"

"I'm familiar with the weapons theft, so I'll continue working on that."

"On your own?"

"No. I'm co-operating with Leon. There are also still a few people I know I can trust. Together we will look into the theft. For now I would like for you to focus on the artefact. I really want to know why it was so important that a girl got killed over it. But more than that, I would truly like to know what the connection is between the girl, the artefact, the Russian killer and the Eurocorps weapons. I hope that the connection between them will point us to the insiders."

"And I would like to know why our client didn't report that piece missing." Phillip sounded perturbed about this.

"Bring me the files and the computer and I'll have something for you by—" I closed my eyes to access the calendar in my head. "Today is Tuesday. I'll have something for you by the end of the week."

"If you have anything earlier—"

"We'll let you know," finished Phillip. "How are we going to work out the agreement between our two entities?"

"Between the EDA and you guys? The Head doesn't want Rousseau & Rousseau to be officially connected to anything."

"I don't know if I can agree to that."

"Phillip, this is more than just business. This is about catching someone who is abusing his position of power. The Head and Leon have both assured me that once we've concluded this, Rousseau & Rousseau will be on the receiving end of a lot of business from the EDA and, with Leon's influence, Eurocorps."

"You think I can get that in ink?" Phillip sounded increasingly less impressed with the direction this discussion had taken.

"That would make this official. It would create a paper trail."

"And that might alert Manny's insider." I almost smiled at Phillip's displeased frown and Manny's surprise that I agreed with them. "If we want to find the connection between all these things and Manny's insiders, it makes perfect sense to not announce our co-operation."

"They are not my insiders."

"They're working for your agencies and, for all we know, working directly under you. Of course they're yours."

"I'm not going to get into this." He turned to Phillip. "The Head is as good as her word, Phillip. Since taking over, she's kept every single promise she's made."

"I suppose that will have to be good enough for me. For now."

"Good. Now, if you give me a few minutes, I'll go get that computer."

Phillip called for an assistant to accompany Manny through all the security doors in and out of our offices.

"He's really one of the good guys." Phillip rested his hip

against the long table once we were alone in the viewing room. It took all my self-control to not physically remove him from invading my space like that. Instead I took a deep breath, reminding myself that he too would leave soon and my viewing room would be my own again.

"It's evident."

"You were reading him?"

I just looked at Phillip. After all this time, he should have known that I read everyone.

"What did you see?"

"He's sincere. He believes in what he does."

"That would be Manny's essence." His eyes lost focus. "I remember a time when we were both young and full of dreams. I used to tell him that one day he would become a superhero."

"Superheroes don't exist."

Phillip's expression sobered and he gave me a quick smile. "Indeed that is true. So Manny became the next best thing."

"The Deputy Chief Executive of Strategy at the EDA?"

"Someone fighting for what is right."

"How does that make it the next best thing to being a superhero?"

Phillip looked relieved when there was a knock at the door before it whooshed open and Manny came through carrying a black leather case.

"Phillip, can I have a moment alone with Ms Lenard?"

"Of course. I have a few phone calls to make." Phillip gave a slight nod and left me with Manny.

"Well." He moved around the viewing room trying to look comfortable, but his entire body communicated his discomfort. He lifted his hand to presumably run it over the artful workmanship of the filing cabinets.

"Please don't touch that." I hated when people were in my space. They always wanted to touch my things and then I had to clean their oily fingerprints.

Manny withdrew his hand. "Phillip trusts you. He knows you. I don't. I don't know anything about this thing that you have."

"What thing?"

"Your"—he waved his hand towards me and then let it drop limply next to him—"autism."

"I was never really diagnosed with autism. People just like to label me that way so that I make more sense to them."

"What were you diagnosed as?"

"Many things." I was not going to tell him all the tests and psychological probing I had gone through. "You can also choose to believe that I have high functioning autism."

Manny looked intrigued and moved closer to me. "You don't believe that you have high functioning autism?"

"It doesn't matter what I believe."

"To me it does. If we are going to work together, I need to know who it is that I'm trusting."

"I appreciate that you need to know this, but I'm not going to become your best friend, Colonel Millard. Working together on this case really only requires your trust in my skills and my discretion. Both of which you will have full access to."

Manny studied me for a long time. I didn't flinch. "You are a very strange individual, Ms Lenard."

"So I have been told."

"Just one more question." He swallowed his discomfort. "Do I need to be careful what I say or do in case you, you know, go all weird again?"

"Go all weird?" If I wasn't still shaken by the uncharacteristic lapse of my control, I would've smiled. "I can guarantee you it won't happen again. And you don't have to tiptoe around me. I'm much less delicate that most people think."

The corner of Manny's mouth quirked into an almost-smile. He reached into the black leather case and took out a black laptop.

"Okay, then. This is the EDA computer. I don't know what the IT guys did to it, but they claim it is unhackable." He opened the laptop and waited for it to boot up. It took him ten minutes to take me through all the passwords. It took me only once to memorise both twenty-six-digit passwords. I was impressed with the layered security on the computer and told Manny so.

"Yes, my guys are some of the best. You will have access to much of our database and all the files on this case. We update these files every day as new information comes in. Please take all precautions with this computer."

I ignored the insulting warning, but Manny obviously wasn't going to let it go.

"Ms Lenard—"

"Enough with the miss. Call me Doctor Lenard or Genevieve."

"Okay." He drew out the word as if unsure which option to choose in case it was the wrong one. "Doc, it is really important that no one else has access to this computer. You can't allow anyone else to work on it or leave it unattended at any time."

"Colonel Millard, please don't insult my intelligence. I fully comprehend the significance of being in possession of this computer."

"Good. Fine. Okay."

I waited for him to continue. He didn't. His blinking increased, indicating discomfort or a stressful thought process. Maybe both. The third time he swallowed heavily, I lost my patience. "Oh, for goodness' sake, just say it."

His lips thinned. "This is sensitive information."

"We've already established that."

"Well, yes." He took a bracing breath. "This might not be of relevance, but the murderer said something before he shot himself. Actually, he shouted it. He was speaking broken French with a strong accent, so the officers were not sure of everything they heard. The autopsy showed traces of an antipsychotic drug. It would seem that he was being treated for schizophrenia, but had gone off his meds for some time. This might just be a lunatic's rantings."

"Get to the point."

"According to the officers he shouted, 'The red will end all twenty-seven daffodils. We will just have to sit back and watch. No one will escape the red who is all-powerful'."

"You're right, it sounds like the rantings of an insane man," I said. "Or it could be a very bad translation."

"I'm repeating it word for word, just like the officers noted it down. He shouted it over and over before he killed himself."

"No need to get defensive, Colonel Millard."

He sighed. "I'm in a position I don't like to be in, working with people I don't know, so forgive me if I'm a bit out of sorts."

He did not sound or look repentant at all. But he did look stressed. I relented. "I'll think about these rantings and see if I can find some meaning in it. Maybe 'red' is a euphemism or a codeword for something. 'Twenty-seven' might also have a different meaning as might 'daffodils'. He could've used the word order of his native tongue, which could change all the words around."

"Those are a lot of maybes."

"Applicable to three very incoherent sentences." I leaned back in my chair. "Is there anything else?"

"Yes. Call me Manny." He turned and walked to the door, twice looking back at the laptop lying open on my table. "We'll be in touch."

"Goodbye, Manny." I watched him heave another sigh before he left and wondered what he was going to say to Phillip. There was, however, no point in speculating about his issues and complaints now. The challenge was much too alluring to waste time and energy on Manny's ill-placed worries. Already I had a

Chapter THREE

"Genevieve!" The shock in Phillip's voice caused me to drag my eyes away from the computer. I had just made yet another connection and was becoming increasingly excited.

I turned to Phillip, who was standing in the viewing room doorway, looking bewildered. "What?"

"My God, how long have you been here?" He moved into the viewing room, looking around with not a small amount of concern. I inhaled sharply to tell him that it was none of his business, but reality rushed towards me like a freight train.

"Since we last spoke."

"Since Tuesday?" He shook his head as if he had received a hard blow to his skull. "You have been here for the last two days."

The ten-year-old girl in me, being berated by her embarrassed mother, threatened to hang her head in shame. Fortunately, decades of discipline came to the fore. I straightened my shoulders and blinked slowly. "I lost track of time."

"It seems a bit more than that." He dragged a chair closer and sat down far enough from me to make me wonder if he was respecting my personal space or whether I smelled like I had locked myself in the same room for the last forty-eight hours. I looked at my usually immaculate workspace and could understand the frown marring Phillip's face.

The long desk was covered in over a dozen coffee mugs, chocolate wrappers and crumpled sheets of paper. I took a bracing breath before I could look down at my outfit. My white silk shirt looked like it had been lying at the bottom of the laundry bin for a week. A few stray coffee drops had stained my light green skirt. I didn't even want to think about the unattractive mascara rings that undoubtedly were lying under my eyes. Not once in my adult life had I allowed myself to reach this point. I pushed away the shame to make place for self-aimed anger.

"I need to clean up." How had I failed myself twice in so many days? First the episode with the photo and now this. It was unacceptable.

"That can wait. Tell me what's happening with you."

"Do I have to?"

"Please."

I really didn't want to. The sincere concern pulling at Phillip's face was the only reason I even considered telling him. He had been the first person in my life who cared to understand me instead of trying to change me. I closed my eyes for a long moment until I found the courage to look at him. "I used to be like this all the time until I was about ten years old. I would get interested in something and completely lose touch with reality. It is called hyperfocus. I would just focus on my new favourite topic and nothing else existed. My nannies didn't know what to do, and since it kept me quiet they didn't try to get me out of this zone. It was only when my mother found out that there was hell to pay." And there hell to pay. Every time.

"But it stopped when you were ten?"

"Yes. That was when I... are you sure you want to hear this?" It was boring and irrelevant to all the interesting things I had discovered.

"Yes, please."

"Fine. I was ten when my parents had another one of their diplomatic dinners. It was one of my better days and I was observing everyone. That was when I realised how everyone was acting falsely and lying with almost every word that left their mouths. I decided that if that was what it took to get my parents' approval, I would learn to pretend just like everyone else. It wasn't difficult to imitate everyone's behaviour. It was a game for me, something that I considered a challenge and fun. Soon my parents thought that I had grown out of whatever it was that had ailed me before. What they didn't realise was that I was no longer myself. I was them, their friends, everyone else but me."

Phillip shook his head in anger like he had the only other time that I had told him about my childhood. "And that is why you studied psychology, body language and all of that."

"Yes. That helped me understand why people had such a need to pretend. Why people were so good at it."

"And now you know how to behave like everyone else."

"Oh, I mastered that skill long before I graduated. It makes people more comfortable. It's simpler." And I hated it.

"So why don't you behave like that around me?"

I thought about it. "You don't need me to be like you."

My answer seemed to surprise Phillip, but he quickly recovered. "I do, however, need you to go home and rest."

I barely refrained from uttering a self-berating grunt. "I will. But first I have to show you what I've discovered."

"I assume that you've found something very interesting."

"Why would you assume that?"

"If you hadn't, you wouldn't still be here."

I gave him a quick smile for his rationale and turned to the monitors. "They are all one man."

"Who are?"

"The poets." I organised my discoveries to be displayed on the screens for easy show and tell.

"What poets?" Phillip sounded bemused. "I think you should start at the beginning and tell me as if I am not as intelligent as you."

"But you aren't." The moment the uncensored words left my mouth, I knew it was a faux pas. I slowly turned to Phillip, only to see him clench his teeth so hard that his cheeks were bulging.

"Just tell me from the beginning."

"Right. The beginning." I really had to watch my mouth. "I decided to look more deeply into that piece of Gauguin that was discovered on the murdered girl. Our information says that the painting Still Life, The White Bowl was stolen during the Second World War and had been on Interpol's list of stolen artworks. It was discovered by a Mister Henry Vaughan in 2004. This Mister Vaughan is an art historian who helped a friend move into an old mansion the friend had purchased. In the attic they discovered this painting. It was very fortunate that Mister Vaughan was at hand to identify what it was and make sure that it went back to its rightful owners. And it did, but only after proving provenance and a vigorous authentication process. A year later it was sold at an auction to our client."

"I know all of this. What was strange about it?" When it came to artwork that had been stolen during any war, Phillip was paranoid about its authenticity and rightful provenance.

"There is no such person as Henry Vaughan, the art historian."

"Are you sure?"

I ignored his inane question. Of course I was sure. I had not only used my usual internet sources to check the existence of this man, I had also used an EDA database search, not that it did much good. All I got were people with this name not matching any other of the parameters. "There is also no trace of any work record for this man."

"Interesting."

"If you look at this article"—I pointed to one of the monitors and zoomed in on the text—"you'll see quite an impressive resume that he gave to the journalist. It no doubt gave him more credibility for this article and also for the find."

"I remember reading this interview. He was extremely knowledgeable about the Cloisonnism and Primitivism eras in which Gauguin worked."

I made a sound of disbelief. "What is interesting about his resume in this article is that there is no mention of any specific institution where he studied or worked. I spent a lot of time searching for anything else on him and found nothing. Not a published paper, not another interview, nothing. It was as if he only existed for this one occasion."

"Why would he appear in the public eye only once and then disappear?" Phillip's eyes widened. "Maybe he died."

"No, I also checked that. Lacking any other avenues, I decided to see what other artefacts were discovered and returned to their owners and that was when things got interesting. Look at this."

I used all ten monitors to display more than a dozen different newspaper clippings.

"These are artefacts that were stolen during some conflict in the last century or so. There were so many that it took me hours to sift through them to get to these particular ones. In these articles the artefacts were discovered by a man who claimed to be a museum curator, an amateur archaeologist, a gallery owner"—I pointed to all the different articles—"an art dealer and in this one, an art restorer."

Phillip was staring intently at the monitors. "All very interesting. It is wonderful that these owners got their art back. I don't see anything suspicious in this."

"The museum curator's name is Edward Taylor, the archaeologist is William Strode, the gallery owner is Isaac Watts, the art dealer is John Milton and the art restorer is Sydney Goddphin." I finished on a triumphant note and looked expectantly at Phillip. He slowly turned to me with a blank expression. My shoulders slumped. "You don't know who they are."

"No, Genevieve, I don't."

"Every single one of them was an English poet who lived in the seventeenth century." I could barely sit still with the excitement bubbling in me. "Can't you see? The probability of all of these men discovering stolen pieces having names of seventeenth-century poets is incalculable. It simply would not happen."

"And that led you to believe that this is the same person."

"Yes!" I all but shouted and took a calming breath. "What I haven't been able to figure out is his agenda."

"It would seem clear to me. He reappropriates artworks that were illegally taken from the owners."

"True. But who is he working for? I couldn't find anyone fitting his description working for any agencies."

Phillip narrowed his eyes at the screens. "I see only three photos in these articles."

"Unfortunately there aren't any more photos of this man, these men. Only the three photos here."

"None of these photos really show his face." A sly smile pulled at the corners of his mouth. "Clever bastard."

"But these three photos are enough for me to believe that this is the same man."

"I don't know, Genevieve." He tilted his head and narrowed his eyes. "The men in those articles look mighty different from each other."

"Look at their noses and their mouths." I reached for a laser pointer and aimed it at the perfectly shaped male lips in each photo. "This is the same man. We can puff out our cheeks and try to draw attention away from our eyes with glasses and contact lenses, but we can't change the shape of our lips. Or our noses. At least not without the help of a professional makeup artist."

We spent a full minute in silence studying the photos. I was reliving the burst of excitement that had cannoned through me when I had made this discovery. Almost as if to myself I said, "These articles date back five years. I'm sure that there are many more discoveries and poets if I looked."

"But why would you look? What is this man's connection to

the case apart from being the one who identified the artefact?"

"Talking about the artefact, did you find out why your client didn't report the artefact stolen?"

"I haven't been able to get in touch with him," grunted Phillip. "He tends to go off the grid for weeks on end and then it's impossible to reach him."

"Which means we don't know if or when the painting was stolen."

"Correct."

"Hmm, that might be a problem."

"It is obvious to me that it would be a problem, but why do you think it's a problem?"

"So far I've found six different poets who discovered another thirteen artefacts. See these three cases?" I pointed to three different screens. "Here the poet declared the stolen artefact a forgery. In each case it caused huge controversies since all three of these pieces were authenticated."

"By whom?"

"By different and very reputable entities. One of the artefacts alone was authenticated by a museum, a university and an independent archaeologist."

"This is not good. Not good at all."

"No, it's not. It leads me to believe that the poet-man not only recovers artefacts, he also has some ability to identify fakes. After his very public declaration that they were forgeries, they were once again tested and were found to be extremely good replicas of the originals."

"Okay," he said very slowly. "How is all this connected?"

"I don't know yet. But I know it is connected. I've found more art murders."

Phillips blinked at my quick change of topic. "Art murders?"

"Well, murders involving artists."

"And what does this have to do with our current case?" Phillip looked like he was having a hard time keeping up with me, so I slowed down a bit. I had after all had forty-eight hours to connect all the dots in my mind.

"The girl in the photo is most likely an artist."

"What makes you think that?"

"While I was looking for more discoveries by poets, I was looking through a lot of newspapers online. In one of the newspapers I noticed a small report about a murder, which made me think again of the girl." An involuntary shudder rippled through me. "Manny said that she was killed with a Eurocorps weapon, one typically used by agents. Also one on the list of the stolen weapons. So I phoned Jacques."

"I'm afraid to ask. Who's Jacques?"

"The detective we worked with last year on the arson case."

"Please tell me you didn't give him any of this information. Manny couldn't emphasise enough how important confidentiality was." Phillip sounded like someone was strangling him. Strong distress caused his throat muscles to constrict.

"I only asked him if he could find out if there were any open cases in France and the rest of Europe with a SIG 226 nine-millimetre as the murder weapon."

"And he didn't ask you why you wanted to know?"

"Of course he did."

"And?"

"I lied to him." I was so proud about this achievement that my voice lifted with this admission. "I told him that I'm working on the side for a private investigator and that he asked me to do some research into this."

"And he believed you?"

"After some time." I'd had to use all my learned skills of deception to convince Jacques, but it hadn't taken too long. Not only did people lie easily, they just as quickly believed a lie.

"Oh, dear. I don't want to know the details. Just tell me what you found out."

"Well, he told me that there are two unsolved murders in France, one in Italy and two in Greece where this type of weapon was used. The cases happened four to seven years ago and there's been no reason to connect them whatsoever. I told Jacques that I was wrong and there obviously was no connection. I even managed to sound very disappointed."

"Genevieve, lying is not something to be so proud of."

"It is. It's only the second time this year that I've lied, so I'm very proud that I was so believable."

Phillip shook his head with a half-smile, but quickly sobered. "Tell me more about these murders."

"Well, once I had this information, it was really easy to find out the rest. All five victims were artists. And not just any artists. They were highly regarded in their fields."

"What fields?"

"This is another interesting anomaly. If there was a serial killer in Europe, he might have chosen something more fitting to a type. The only thing these people have in common is that they were artists. Their age, gender, social status, everything differs so greatly that it is difficult to imagine that this could be the work of a serial killer. Not one of the artists specialised in the same field. One was fantastic at the restoration of Renaissance art, the other was a sculptor, the other specialised in bronzes and the other one was a graphic designer. I think the last one was skilled in watercolours from the Romantic era, especially Turner's works. They came from different countries, so why a serial killer would or could find them doesn't make sense at all."

"A serial killer with a Eurocorps weapon."

"That is another reason that makes me think it's not a serial killer. These murders were all committed with the same type of weapon, but not the same weapon. I'm sure if Manny requested the ballistic reports of these cases, he would be able to match it to the stolen Eurocorps weapons."

"I'll be sure to tell him about this."

"You can also ask him why it is that the other cases didn't register that they were Eurocorps weapons."

"Maybe because the data was only entered in a local database. Or maybe these weapons weren't Eurocorps'."

"Oh, they were. Of that I'm convinced."

"Genevieve, how can you be so convinced of your theory when most of it is conjecture?"

"It is not conjecture." How dare he insult me like that? "I would never form a theory without the relevant information."

"That's just it. You don't have enough information to make this a viable theory."

"How can you not see it?" The censure in my voice caused Phillip to lift his eyebrows in a warning. Even though he was the only person totally accepting of who I was, I still couldn't expect him to accept my intolerance of being challenged by those of lesser intellect. I took a deep breath and modulated my tone. "How can I explain this to you? I've gathered all these pieces of a puzzle. Putting it together can do no other than form this specific picture."

"A picture that includes numerous murders on the continent with Eurocorps weapons. Manny will be so pleased."

"Why would he be pleased? I would think he would be outraged at this." It only took a look at Phillip's face for realisation to dawn. "Oh, you were being sarcastic. I'm sure that Manny will not be pleased with this information either, but he did ask us to look into this."

"Actually he asked us to find the connection between the girl and the painting."

"And the connection between that, the Russian murderer and the EDA weapons." I could recall every conversation verbatim, to most people's utter frustration.

"Let's assume that the girl is an artist. How does that connect her to the Gauguin painting?"

"I don't know that yet."

"And let's assume the girl and the artefact are connected. How does that connect her to the poets?"

"Apart from the fact that it was the poet who discovered this artwork?" I gave it a moment's thought to remember which connection I had not explained yet. "I didn't mention the fact that there were poets and discoveries in the same areas as where three of the five unsolved murders took place, did I?"

Phillip only looked at me, waiting for me to continue.

"Going through all those local newspapers' archives proved to be very enlightening. I discovered all sorts of interesting things. Did you know that in 2005 a hundred and twenty-one people died in a plane crash in Greece?"

"Does this have anything to do with the case?"

"No, it doesn't." I sighed at my own digression before going on with the determination to stay on point. "A month before the second Greek murder, William Strode, the archaeologist, discovered a long-lost Van Gogh." I took a moment to locate the specific article on one of the monitors and zoomed in on it. "This is one of the cases where he declared it to be a forgery. In one of the French cases, another poet declared the artwork to be a forgery and it was soon followed by a murder. I couldn't find any connection with him and the three other unsolved murders. What I do know is that this poet-man is somehow involved. To say that he's involved in the murders would indeed be conjecture, but the fact that he's the one discovering these pieces and then exposing the forgeries makes me wonder how he fits into all of this. There are simply too many threads connecting him to call it any kind of coincidence."

"Not that you would ever call anything coincidence." Phillip sat back in the chair, pinching his chin. I gave him time to process all the information I had bombarded him with. I had a lot of respect for how his mind worked. When it came to business and people, he far outranked me in natural skill. I could see patterns and make connections like the ones I had just made. Phillip would add the human element that I, even with my extensive training, sometimes missed. The silence stretched on. Just when I once again became aware of my embarrassing dishevelled state, Phillip spoke. "Manny told me about the things the killer shouted. Have you come up with any theories?"

"No. To be honest, I haven't given the twenty-seven daffodils and the all-powerful red much thought."

"Maybe you should. I've looked at it every which way and it still sounds like rubbish." He glanced at the monitors. "I have quite a lot to tell Manny. I'll meet with him today while you go home and rest."

"Yes, I need to go home." I needed to stand in the shower for an hour and wash away the zone I had been in. "While you speak to Manny, tell him to work harder at finding the girl's identity."

"I'm sure he and the local police have worked really hard in identifying the girl, Genevieve." He lowered his head and gave me a warning look. "While you're at home, do whatever you need to do to tune back into your social skills. Manny is not one to take too kindly to your special brand of honesty."

I disagreed with him on that point, but kept my own counsel. The way I had read Manny, I strongly believed that he would prefer my total honesty, even if he did not always find it, or me for that matter, agreeable or likeable.

After another two warnings that I was to go home and rest, Phillip left me alone in the viewing room to face the mess I found myself in.

With a heavy sigh I gathered the coffee mugs to take them to the kitchen. It took another hour to tidy my viewing room enough to allow the cleaning crew to come in later and clean it to my exact specifications. All the while I berated myself for allowing this case to get the better of all the years of discipline.

Once I got into my little city car, I decided that I had had enough of the self-flagellation. As with most other experiences, I would consciously look at this as a lesson on how to, or in this case how not to, handle certain situations life threw at me. I had worked extremely hard in the six years that I had been with Rousseau & Rousseau to establish stability and control in my life. It should not have come as a surprise to me that I could not always be in control. I should have been prepared to handle such an unexpected situation better. The predictable stability in my life had made me lazy and unprepared. That would have to change.

I turned my car into the parking space under my apartment building and got out with a sigh of relief. The soothing spray of my shower would help me plot out how I would handle such a situation differently, were one to come up again. Hopefully the unexpected photo that triggered my almost blackout and then the zoning out were the last of these unwanted behaviours. Waiting for the elevator to whisk me up to my apartment, I was determined to regain every ounce of control.

It had been almost a novelty after so many years to once again feel the darkness closing in on me. I had forgotten what it was like to feel the whole world recede and just lose myself in that dark space, not aware of any of my actions. Fortunately I had been able to keep myself from complete surrender to that darkness. Even still, it was certainly not something that I wanted to repeat any time soon.

I opened the door to my large loft apartment, relief to be in my safe haven washing over me. This was the place where I was totally in control.

I locked the five locks on my heavy front door and turned to the kitchen. My usual homecoming ritual of a cup of herbal tea before I took a shower would go a long way in helping me regain total control. My apartment had been a find that I still relished in. The spacious airy rooms with windows on both sides, large enough to bathe all the wooden finishing in natural light, always made me feel at peace. That and the fact that there was no one to move anything out of place or to leave their grimy fingerprints on the impeccable surfaces.

I walked through the long open-space living area, single-minded in my focus on making tea. The front half of my apartment was divided into four quarters. Directly to the left of the front door were two comfortable sofas facing a good-sized balcony on one side and a wall-length bookshelf on the other. Next to that was the dining area. The wall separating my bedroom and the dining area was the only wall in the living area covered in paintings and masks. All the other walls were covered in books.

The kitchen was directly opposite the dining area. I stepped into the immaculate space without as much as a glance at the reading area behind me. All I wanted was to switch the cold kettle on to boil the water for my tea. Why was it then that a thin wisp of steam was coming out of the kettle? And why was there an aroma of camomile tea in my apartment? A cold hand of awareness clamped around my heart.

"Hello, Genevieve."

Chapter FOUR

I had no air in my lungs to scream in horror when I turned to the reading area to face the voice that had intruded in my safe space. I also had no time to consider my own safety. Not when the darkness was closing in faster than it had two days before. I barely had the presence of mind to pull my handbag from my shoulder and dig out empty music sheets and a pencil with stiff fingers. In the very far background I heard a concerned voice calling me, but it was not strong enough to pull me back. Only the music sheets in my hand and the notes floating around in my head were real. Nothing else.

How I made it to the dining table I had no idea, nor did it matter how long I was there. As long as I was focussing on Mozart's Piano Concerto No. 5 in D major, the darkness stayed peripheral. It closed in on me the moment I allowed my attention to be drawn to the other person speaking softly to me, moving around my apartment as if searching for something and then placing more empty music sheets in front of me.

I pushed the knowledge of his invading presence in my apartment out of my mind and focussed on the purity of the music notes on the sheets. In many of his letters Mozart mentioned that this Concerto had been his favourite. It was mine too. I loved his use of trumpets and timpani in the first and last movements. The horns, oboes and strings that served as the piano's support were perfect. It was pure, safe, in harmony. I had to focus on this to regain my own harmony.

Slowly my mind returned to my apartment and back into my body. The threatening darkness had moved away, but the stranger was still in my apartment. I shook this knowledge off and looked at the table. The music sheets were neatly arranged next to each other, in two rows, from one side of the long wooden dining table to the other. There were twenty sheets. I had written a lot.

Still not completely back in control, I chose to finish the second movement, the Andante, giving myself time to assess my situation. Writing Mozart not only helped me through moments like this, it was also the most effective way for me to think things through. I never had any problems memorising the compositions and must have written each of Mozart's works at least twice in my life. Others I had written countless times. This work especially had helped me several times to come up with solutions to seemingly impossible situations. Like the one in my apartment.

For some unfathomable reason he was still in my apartment. Who was he and what was he doing here? I didn't want to chance looking at him in case he would think that I was available for conversation or maybe some more sinister activity he had in mind.

I had completed seven years of self-defence training, combining different disciplines to enable a woman to defend herself in all kinds of situations. All the years of training flooded my mind. I would have to assess my assailant to best determine what form of defence I might need, yet I was reluctant to look away from my safe music papers.

"I made you a cup of tea." The intruder spoke quietly a few feet away from me. He had a deep voice and spoke with smooth confidence. My favourite teacup filled with camomile tea appeared next to my left hand. A strong hand made the fine porcelain cup and saucer look even more fragile. A quick glance revealed muscular forearms partially hidden by the pushed-up sleeves of a black sweater. "It looked as if you drink a lot of this tea, so I hope that I assumed correctly that you might like a cup."

The temptation to look at the rest of the man was hard to resist, but I wanted more time to analyse my situation. The gentleness in his voice did not alert me to any violent intent, but he might just be trying to create a false sense of safety before he pounced. I almost laughed at my unprofessional analysis. Never had I used the word 'pounce' in any of the profiles I had created.

According to the twenty-four sheets of music in front of me, I estimated that I had been writing for at least three hours. Questions started gnawing at me. I finished the last notes, drew the bold double bar line to indicate the end of the second movement, and stilled the nagging questions in my mind.

I looked up from the table and found the intruder.

The unwelcome fiend was in my reading chair, a chair no one but I had ever used. He was immersed in a newspaper. My newspaper.

He appeared in his mid-thirties, maybe a few years older than me. Taller than average, he had the build of a gymnast. Very muscular, but not bulky. This was important to know in case I had to defend myself. His dark brown hair was just a bit too long to qualify as short. It looked finger-combed, a bit messy. Stylists needed a lot of product and time to give male models that look.

His square jaw was darkened by stubble and his skin had the tone of someone who had just returned from a Mediterranean holiday. The fingers holding my newspaper were long, the nails neatly clipped. Everything about him stated relaxed elegance, from his quality dark clothes to his demeanour.

His crossed ankles and relaxed torso showed that he had no concerns about his safety. Not like I did. I studied him intently for any cue that he might be a threat to me. I found none. I did, however, sense something familiar about him.

"Who are you?"

"Oh, hello." He looked up from my newspaper that I now

would not be able to read. He had destroyed the creases. "Glad to have you back."

"Who are you?" I maintained an even tone, not willing to let him see any more vulnerability than he had already witnessed.

"You have a cool collection of artwork here." He got out of my chair and walked to the wall behind me. I had chosen and bought the fourteen masks that took up a quarter of the wall after extensive research and consideration.

I took the time to assess him further as he passed me. I would have to be quick and smart to get the better of him physically. He was light on his feet and moved with the kind of grace attributed to boxers, gymnasts and athletes. And thieves.

His English was flawless with no accent to place him in any particular region. I continued watching him for possible clues to his identity or purpose in my apartment while he perused my collection.

"I especially like this Inca funerary mask from Peru. Ah, Peru. I loved travelling there."

I refused to be drawn in into his reminiscing, but I was dying to know how he was able to identify that mask. It could've been from any South American country.

The way he held his body while facing my favourite mask oozed self-confidence. I was looking at a man who very seldom tasted failure. It seemed not to have made him arrogant, but rather self-assured, if not overconfident. And he was trying to distract me from my question. So I waited.

It didn't take too long for him to turn back to me with a half-smile. "Do you really have the IQ of a genius?"

I clenched my teeth to refrain from responding. I had watched enough interviews to know that one should never reveal too much about oneself. Nor did I think it prudent to be pulled into a conversation with someone who had broken into one's house.

"Who are you?" I asked again in the same controlled tone.

"What happened earlier? It looked like you had some kind of autistic blackout."

That was it. I had had enough of people asking me about my state of mind. And I was bored with explaining it to complete strangers. I pushed my chair back with uncharacteristic force and placed both my hands flat on the surface of the dining table. "I am going to have a shower. The bedroom and bathroom doors are reinforced, so don't even think to enter. When I come out, you will not be here."

"And if I am?"

I straightened myself slowly to my full average height and gave him my most severe gaze. For a few seconds we were locked in a battle of fixed stares before I turned around without a word and walked to my bedroom as if the matter was settled. I knew that it was all but settled, but I was not going to allow some common criminal who had broken into my sanctuary to dictate the direction of any conversation.

My security paranoia in a very safe city at last became useful as I bolted my bedroom door. Only after I turned the third lock did I allow myself to slump against the door. How he had managed to enter my secure apartment was a mystery that I would have to solve before I went to bed. Wherever the gap in my security was, it had to be filled, else I would never have another good night's rest.

He hadn't seemed to have any harmful intent and I could only hope that he would respond to my warning gaze and leave. I shook my head as I made my way to my bathroom. The way I had read him, I knew that he was still going to be in my apartment when I finished my shower.

The desired half an hour under the spray of a hot shower was cut short with the uncomfortable knowledge of a stranger on the other side of the wall waiting for me. At least I was comforted by the fact that there was no way he could penetrate the two steel-reinforced doors leading to my bathroom. I went through my routine as quickly as possible and felt much better by the time I pushed my fingers through my short, dark brown hair to give it a natural messy look.

In my bedroom, I gave myself a last inspection in the mirror and approved. My dark jeans fitted my slim legs snugly, but gave me enough room to manoeuvre in case of a physical altercation. The dark brown boots would do some serious damage if they connected to any part of the human body. I inhaled deeply and on the exhale relaxed the muscles around my eyes so that my emerald-green eyes wouldn't look so disturbed. Once I was satisfied with the image in the mirror, I unlocked the door, fully expecting the intruder to still be there.

I found him perusing the floor-to-ceiling bookshelf in the reading area. He had a first-edition Kipling in his hand and was paging through it with unadulterated awe etched on his face. How could a common criminal appreciate art and literature like this? The same sense of familiarity pulled at my consciousness. I inched closer.

"You have exquisite taste, Jenny." He must have sensed my presence, because he only looked up from the book after he had spoken. And he had shortened my name. "Your art collection is small, but chosen with an obvious eye for quality and substance. Your music taste is an interesting jump between genres, but this"—he pointed to the books—"this is something I would give my big toe for."

"Why would you—" I stopped myself from inquiring why he would sacrifice a digit, knowing that it probably was one of those senseless things people said. "Why don't you just give me your name?"

He carefully replaced the book and even managed to align it the right distance from the edge of the shelf before he turned to me. "If I give you my name, will you sit down with me and have a conversation?"

"Why would I want to do that? You broke into my apartment

and have overstayed your welcome by a few hours."

"I would consider it a huge favour." His smile used all those facial muscles indicating insincerity. Most likely he used it to charm his way around other hapless victims. This was the first time that I felt him to be a threat. I moved away from him to a small wooden table I had bought from a Cambodian art dealer.

"What are you doing?"

"Phoning the police."

"I'm afraid that won't work."

Without taking my eyes off him, I picked up the receiver of my home phone only to be met with a dead instrument in my hand. I shook it slightly towards him. "What have you done?"

"Played it safe." Surprisingly he looked apologetic. "I've also switched on a scrambler that won't allow you any reception on your mobile phone."

My life had been in such controlled harmony until two days ago. Now I had to deal with a lapse not only in my carefully cultivated control, but also in my home security. All of this had started with that blasted Manny and his case. Not being one to believe in coincidence, I was leaning towards the intruder's visit having something to do with the photo and Manny's case.

"I don't want to frighten you, Jenny." The intruder turned his palms outwards, but it was the true concern on his face that had me convinced. This time.

Using a shortened version of my name grated on my nerves. I desperately wanted to release all the pent-up frustration of the last few days in a lecture about respecting people's names. But this might not be the wisest move. I considered all my options and sighed. "Your name and then we talk."

"Fantastic." He took a step closer and stretched out his hand in introduction, but immediately stopped when I stiffened. His hand floated to his side. "Sorry. My name is Colin Frey."

The little time I had already spent with this intruder had been enough for me to have established a baseline. This enabled me to know that at that very moment he was telling the truth. I replaced the dead receiver and gave my reading chair a look of disgust. I stepped to the left and sat down on one of the two wingback chairs that completed my seating arrangement in the reading area. Colin took his place again in my chair, much to my dismay. I would have to disinfect my entire apartment.

"What do you want, Mister Frey?"

"Colin, please." He looked unsure how to continue.

"Please just state your business so that you can leave."

"You work for Rousseau & Rousseau. It is not quite stated what you do there, but it seems that you're working in the fraud detection department."

"Your business, Mister Frey." I was not going to allow him the pleasure of drawing information out of me. I studied every movement of his facial muscles and found my eyes continuously drawn to his lips.

"Please call me Colin." One corner of his mouth lifted in a self-deprecating smile and the penny dropped.

"You are him!" I sat up in my chair, eyebrows raised and my heart racing. "You are the poet-man."

Colin closed his eyes, which was as much as an admission. "How did you know?"

"Your lips. They are the same lips as those of Sydney Goddphin, John Milton and Isaac Watts."

"How do you know?" He shook his head. "Those photos in the newspapers. I knew they were going to come and bite me in the arse one day."

"How far back does this go?" I forgot all my previous concerns. The man in front of me was much more fascinating than any safety concerns. "I only looked back five years, but I have a feeling that you've been doing this much longer."

"I would prefer to not implicate myself at this very moment." He rubbed his wrists as if he could feel handcuffs tightening. "But I must admit that in all the time the poets have been in existence, no one has once even come close to making any connection."

"How did you know that I had made the connection?" Wasn't the EDA computer supposed to be secure?

"You did a Google search."

"Surely my Google search didn't make direct contact with you."

"Actually it did. I'm telling you too much, Jenny." He rubbed his hand once over his face. "But I need to know that you are taking me seriously."

"Seriously about what?" I had so many questions. "Why are you here? How did you get in? My apartment is supposed to be secure."

"It really wasn't that difficult. Top-floor apartments are always easy to breach."

"Are you telling me that you do this frequently?"

Shock registered on his face. "I'm definitely telling you too much."

"Just tell me how you got into my apartment." I had to know. Or else I wouldn't be able to move on.

"Through the ceiling in the guest bathroom. It was a tight fit, but easy enough. I could also have come through the window if it wasn't full daylight."

"Or you could've knocked on my front door."

"Would you have opened it?" He smiled when I looked at him askance. "Thought so. Jenny, why did you do this search into the poets?"

"You know that I work for an insurance company, so surely you had to come to some conclusion."

He had just successfully managed to shift my attention from my unanswered question. Unknown to him, I had watched hundreds of interviews and had learned valuable lessons. Like when a fraud suspect started asking his own questions, much could be gleaned from those questions. For now I would allow him to take the lead. It might prove to be very informative.

"Of course I have a hypothesis, but I would rather hear from you why these poets interested you."

I didn't want to tell him anything that wasn't public knowledge. I chose my words with care. "The stolen art. That was what drew my attention. I'm working on this case involving an artwork that was stolen during the Second World War and then retrieved. You were the one who identified it. One thing led to another until I found too many names of seventeenth-century poets discovering stolen artwork. I don't believe in coincidence so I came to the conclusion that it could be the same man."

"Which artwork?"

"Pardon?" I knew what he was asking, but needed time to consider my answer. Not only did he appear to be an accomplished burglar, he also had a way of manipulating the conversation that showed a higher intellect. That intrigued me.

"Which artwork is part of the case that you are looking into?"

"Um... I can't tell you that, Miste—"

"Colin."

"Colin." I took a deep breath. The topic needed to be changed if I was to continue keeping Manny's confidence. "Who do you work for?"

"Who says I'm working?"

I lifted one eyebrow and glared at him. "You're the one who quoted my IQ. Don't underestimate me."

"I would never make that mistake. No one has ever gotten me to talk so much about myself."

"Not that you've said much." Something clicked into place. "Your name. You don't tell people your real name."

"I'm not admitting that it's my real name."

"Your face tells me it is." It was interesting that someone who for obvious reasons would not trust anyone chose to trust me. "Tell me, why do you steal these pieces back?"

"I've never admitted to stealing anything."

"True. But we both know that you're the one stealing back these art pieces, some of which were thought lost forever."

"Were they?" He held up his hands when I frowned. His avoidance was becoming annoying. "Okay, okay. So those pieces are valuable, but I'm not here to talk about that."

"Then tell me why you are here." Even though I was desperately curious about his motives behind re-appropriating those artworks, this was a much more pressing issue.

"Why are you looking into Gauguin's *Still Life, The White Bowl*?"

"I can't tell you that."

"Is that the piece of artwork the police had found on the dead girl?"

"I can't tell you that," I repeated, but this time my voice sounded breathless. How was it possible that he knew about the piece of the painting found on the girl? "And stop answering my questions with questions."

"I know it is a lot to ask of you, but I need you to trust me."

A disbelieving sound escaped my lips. "I don't know you. All I know about you is that you've broken into my apartment, have stolen back a lot of art pieces and seem to know a lot about a lot. Can you give me any rational reason why I would trust you, an obvious criminal? Or why I would tell you anything at all?"

"Your life is in danger."

The stark statement hung between us. I found myself mentally writing a few bars of the third movement of Mozart's Piano Concerto No. 5 in D major. I would not allow any more shocking statements, photos or bits of information to steal my control. After a few short bars I asked, "In danger from whom?"

"You're not the only one who cannot reveal information. There are also things that I cannot tell you. We will have to get to know each other better for that kind of trust."

"That's not going to happen."

"What? Getting to know each other or trusting each other?" His smile was quick. A sober expression took over his face. "If you are looking into the murder of that girl who hid a piece of the Gauguin, you need to be very careful of any and all association with the EDA."

Cold fear constricted my throat. Who was this man? How did he know about the EDA? Manny had said that only himself, Leon, the Chief and the Head of the EDA knew about Phillip's and my involvement.

"Aha," Colin said in a knowing tone. "You are working with the EDA."

"I did not say that." I couldn't believe that I had fallen for this amateur test. He had simply thrown that statement out into the air to see how I was going to react and react I did. I might as well have told him everything I knew.

He leaned forward, resting his elbows on his knees and letting his hands dangle. "I cannot emphasise enough how dangerous this is."

"How would you know? Does this have anything to do with the artists who got murdered?"

It looked like I had shot him with a stun gun. "How do you know about that?"

This was a job for Phillip with his excellent people and negotiation skills. The two of us were attacking each other with information and successfully shocking each other into admissions that should not be voiced at all. I had to delve very deep into my psychology training to find the right way to deal with this.

"Okay, stop. We are walking in circles and it's leading nowhere. I don't owe you any kind of trust since you are the one who entered my home uninvited. If you want me to listen to you or answer any more questions, you will have to tell me your true purpose for being here." I did not have to try to put severity into my voice and expression. I had never been this serious about anything.

"Fair enough. I suppose lying is not an option since I know that you are an expert at detecting deception."

I did not move a single muscle in my face. I did, however, want to roll my eyes and raise my upper lip in disgust. He was still stalling, but I knew that I could outwait him.

He breathed a tired chuckle in surrender. "Fine. I came here to find out who you are. I was curious about the person who had uncovered such a well-constructed secret. I also wanted to warn, or scare, you away from this case. But I have changed my mind."

"Have you now?" I was reading his every muscle movement. Holding on to a poker face was nigh-on impossible. We always gave away clues as to what was going on inside our heads. So far Colin had been truthful. Uncomfortable, but truthful.

"Yes, I think that you are exactly what I need. Before you get upset, let me explain. I don't have access to law enforcement like you do." His smile was wry. "For obvious reasons. A lot of bad things have been happening for a long time and someone needs to stop it. Unfortunately, a lot of those bad things are done by people in law enforcement. That is why I think you're perfect."

"I'm an outsider." It was like listening to Manny all over again. I wondered if the thief and the respected EDA deputy chief would find it as amusing as I that they had something in common.

"Exactly. Already you know much more about this than anyone else. I believe that you are the one who could put the pieces together to stop this." I was surprised to see that he truly believed this. "You already have connected... um... the poets to a lot of artworks. Surely you have found connections between forged works, stolen art and the murders?"

I took my time to answer. "We can both agree that we know things that should not be shared. Why don't you start by telling me everything that you can share?"

"Just for the record, I'm the only one sharing at the moment. It should show you my willingness to trust you and also the ominous nature of this situation." He waited for a reaction, but when I didn't even blink, he just smiled and continued. "Do you know about the EDA connection with these murders?"

It had become clear that Colin knew nothing of Eurocorps' connection to all this. I thought about all those stolen weapons, but immediately remembered Manny's frantic warnings to keep this confidential. I still hadn't decided to trust this thief.

"What connection?" I asked.

"I haven't figured out all the details." The *levator labii superioris* muscle on the side of his nose raised his upper lip in disgust. "The connection goes very high. And that is honestly all I know. There are a lot of fragments of information that I am trying to use to come up with a viable theory. About the EDA, I don't have anything but a long list of coincidences and a healthy dose of suspicion."

"Are you a conspiracy theorist?"

He burst out in rich laughter and for a moment the stress lines on his face lifted. "I never thought of myself as one. Not until this came along."

"What makes you suspect the EDA? What are the co-incidences that you're talking about?"

"How many artist deaths have you found?" He yet again countered with a question and I hesitated to answer him. Could I trust a criminal with information that was easily obtainable on the internet? What would Phillip do in a negotiation like this? "Genevieve?"

"Five." It tore me in pieces to say that one word.

"I know of thirteen. I suppose that you only looked at Western Europe."

"Thirteen? All of them artists?" I decided not to ask him if he had any knowledge of murders in the last four years. That would reveal the limited scope of my research and the frustrating mystery of why I couldn't find any more murders in the last four years.

"Some of them amateurs, some professional, but all of them must have some connection other than being murdered."

"The EDA?" I reminded him.

"Oh yes, the coincidences. I first became aware of the EDA's presence when a friend of mine disappeared."

"Your friend was an artist?"

"Yes. It was in 2006. A few weeks later his body was found floating in the Danube river about twenty kilometres outside Budapest." His voice was controlled, but the *masseter* muscle bulging in his lower jaw spoke of his anger. "At that time there was a large defence meeting held in Budapest with very little publicity. The EDA was present at this meeting. That in itself made me suspicious."

"But how do you connect the EDA to this? I'm sorry to say this, Colin, but your conclusion has no factual base. It is all total conjecture."

"I told you it is only my suspicion. It's just that at four more murders, the EDA also happened to be in the same city." He looked at his watch and grimaced. "I have to go soon. It's a pity. I would've loved to sit and talk much longer. We have much to discuss. Jenny, I can't tell you how glad I am that I have found you."

"Glad?"

"After all these years of leaving anonymous tips at numerous police stations, at last there might be someone who could put a stop to this senseless killing of great talent. None of the other investigators or agencies ever took it to be a real threat. And it was not like I could walk in and try to convince them. At least now I have you."

"You do not have me." Each word was slowly pushed through my teeth. No one laid claim to me. It was detestable.

"Oh, I think I do. You are untainted by all that power, bureaucracy and traditional thinking. You're also intrigued by the connections." He moved to the edge of my reading chair and rested his hands on his knees as if ready to push himself up. "You will come up with the necessary physical evidence and connections to catch the bad guys and end this."

"Bad guys?" I had to smile at his use of that term. "Aren't you a bad guy?"

"You know that I'm not." He spoke with total confidence in his good character. I narrowed my eyes and considered this. He interrupted my pondering with concern pulling the corners of his mouth down. "I don't know how, but the EDA is up to their necks in this. Why else would there be so many forgeries and deaths in all the places that the EDA can be found?"

"Conjecture. They are the European Defence Agency. Of course you're going to find their presence throughout Europe."

"Maybe." He thought for a moment. "Have you looked into the Russian guy who killed the girl? Have you looked for a Russian connection?"

"A Russian connection? Is there one?"

"Find it," was the only answer he gave me after a staring at me for a long while. "There is also a lot more about that girl than meets the eye. You should see what you can find out about her. While you are at it, look into ships too."

"Ships?" This man was infuriating me now with all his cryptic suggestions. The Russians, the girl, ships. Why could people never just say something straight out? He had told me a lot, yet I felt like I had only received the first four words of a paragraph. Not one sentence was complete. It was confusing, frustrating and deliciously challenging.

He got up and turned to the guest bathroom, ignoring my question. "I really have to go. It was wonderful meeting you. It's going to be fun working with you."

I jumped up from my chair and glared at him. "There will absolutely be no working together. Do you really think that I will work with you?"

"Of course. You're going to need me." He started walking away from me. "Walk me out."

I was hard pressed to not go on the offence and attack him with some of my self-defence training. It would release a lot of the residual anger whirling around in me. I managed to breathe through it. "The front door is in the other direction, Colin."

"I know," he said over his shoulder. "I'm going to leave the way I came in."

I followed him to the guest bathroom at the back of my apartment and gasped at the gaping hole in the ceiling where he had removed the cover leading to the ventilation system.

"Don't worry. I'll put this back so neatly, you won't even know that I've been here." He effortlessly lifted himself into the man-sized hole, disappeared for a moment and then peeked back. "Don't bother securing this entrance. There are at least another six ways that I can enter your apartment."

"You could always just ring the doorbell."

"You would never open the door for me." He gave me a genuine smile. "It's really been a pleasure, Jenny."

His head disappeared into the darkness of the ventilation system. A moment later the cover closed the hole and it was as if there hadn't been a thief in my home. An intruder insisting on my trust and co-operation.

"My name is Genevieve," I said to the bathroom ceiling. A shudder rolled through me and I walked back to the living area. The only evidence that he'd been in my apartment was the untouched cup of camomile tea on the dining room table. And the ruined newspaper in the reading area. I took the cup to the kitchen and carefully looked around. There wasn't even a stray fingerprint on the marble counters. They were as spotless as when I had left my apartment two days ago. Not that it mattered. I had an overwhelming urge to clean my whole apartment from top to bottom, scrubbing away any possible trace of Colin Frey's presence.

Episodes like I had experienced the last few days reminded me that regardless of all my knowledge and training, I was still vulnerable to losing control. It humbled me. I looked through the kitchen cupboard with its neatly organised cleaning products and chose a few to start my cleaning spree.

While I was putting on a fresh pair of rubber gloves, I accepted the fact that the only part in me rebelling against the case and all its elements was my intense and instant dislike of change. My fear of change was constantly at war with the cerebral parts of me. This was no exception. The excitement of finding new connections and patterns barely overrode that fear. But above all, I had given my word to Phillip and Manny. I never went back on my word.

But was I going to invite a criminal into my life? I had enough confidence in my abilities to believe that I could find the pattern and make the necessary connections without his help. I took the soft cloth that I kept especially for marble surfaces from its holder and started to polish the kitchen counter.

A small smile pulled at my mouth. When I needed to have something stolen, or reappropriated as he called it, I would ask for Colin Frey's help. Until then, I was going to look for those six possible entry points and make sure that they were secured.

Chapter FIVE

I sat back in my chair and stared at the bank of monitors in front of me. I felt like pulling at my hair in frustration, but settled for a deep sigh.

It was noon and I had been at it for five hours. After a restless night, I had left my sparkling apartment very early to start my search for some connection with the girl. The EDA database had proved to be completely useless and no matter which approach I took, I couldn't find anything to connect the girl to the poets, the EDA or even the Gauguin. Not having her name made for a very short search.

There had to be something else. I hated to admit that I had allowed Colin and all his cryptic clues to influence my usual manner of working things out. The balance that I had managed to find between my natural way of working and the input of my education and experience had stood me in good stead until now. Why would I change that?

With a decisive change of posture, I cleared the monitors and my mind. Leaning my head back, I closed my eyes. Without anyone there to pull my thoughts into another direction, where would I look next? I went through the list. The girl had led nowhere, so that was out. I had found out everything possible about the Gauguin, including its connection to Colin. The weapons were not my concern at the moment, not while Manny and his friend continued their investigation. Again Colin had managed to sneak in here, connecting himself with his suspicions. The Russian murderer was of no real interest to me, but Colin insisted that there was a connection. Then there were the ships that Colin had hinted at. And the Russian connection that only he seemed to know about. I groaned. All I had received from Colin was frustrating non-clues.

My eyes flew open and I frowned. The one thing connecting all the dots I had just listed was not a thing; it was a person. Colin. And that was the thread I was going to pull until I could unravel this mystery. My fingers hovered over the computer keyboard while I decided which of the clues to follow first.

It felt like only an hour later when the door to my viewing room whooshed open.

"You haven't eaten today." Phillip walked in with a plastic bag emitting the mouth-watering smell of Chinese takeaway.

"It's not healthy food."

"And we both love it." He smiled knowingly when I rushed to put a large sheet of paper on the desk. I might love Chinese takeout, but it left horrid grease stains. Taking care to use no other space than the large sheet, he unpacked enough little boxes to feed a party of five. "I thought I would get a big enough selection for whatever you were in the mood for."

My stomach chose that moment to growl its need for sustenance. I opened a few of the small boxes and smiled. "Ah, chicken lo mein. Perfect. Thank you, Phillip."

He took his time to choose his meal, dragged a chair closer and sat down with a tired sigh. "It's been a hard day."

"What's the time?" I broke apart the chopsticks and started eating the greasy chicken dish.

"It's three o'clock." He looked up from his food. "How are you doing?"

"I've discovered quite a few things." I noticed Phillip shaking his head. "Oh, you mean how am I doing after the last few days. I'm fine. I'm focussed again, so you don't have to worry about me."

"But I do. You've been here since six-thirty this morning and you haven't taken a break."

"You're checking up on me." I hated that I had once again lost track of time. The knowledge that Phillip was keeping an eye on me also didn't sit well with me. I hoped that the stabbing pain in my heart region didn't show on my face. "Don't you trust me anymore? That whole episode won't happen again. I promise."

"Of course I trust you. And I don't care if you have another episode, as you call it. At least we know how to handle it. All I care about is that you look after yourself. I don't want you to lock yourself in here again for two days." His voice was gruff.

"Well, that won't happen again either." I pointed at my computer. "I set an alarm for eating and going home. I decided to skip lunch today, but the moment it is time to go home, I'm going home."

Phillip chuckled. "Only you would do that."

"What? Set an alarm? It's a logical solution." We ate in companionable silence for a while, until a ping from my computer sounded through the viewing room. "I hope that is my manifests."

"What manifests?"

I turned to my computer and opened my email inbox. "Oh, it is an email from Manny."

"You emailed Manny?" Suddenly Phillip was sitting up in his chair, sounding troubled.

"Yes," I answered absently while I waited for the email to open. My computer was too slow. I seriously had to consider upgrading it. "I wanted to get all the shipping manifests from Russia to Europe."

"Why?" He sounded even more troubled.

"Oh. Manny seems to be using sarcasm again. Does that mean he's angry? And he says that he can't give them to me." I didn't understand this.

Phillip sighed heavily. "Let me have a look at that email." He looked at one of the wall monitors when I put the email up there.

It took him longer than necessary to read through it before he sat back in his chair with closed eyes.

"What?"

"I think you should allow me to do all the communication from now on."

"Did I make a faux pas?" It would be the only explanation why Phillip would suggest this intervention.

"Writing to someone who barely knows you and struggles to trust you that you expect all shipping manifests in your inbox by the end of the day is not a good way to encourage friendly co-operation. And you didn't even say hello or goodbye."

"It's superfluous." The moment I said it, I realised how wrong it was and lifted both my hands, palms up. "You're right. I wasn't thinking. I was just so busy working through all the possible links that I didn't take the moment it needed to be more polite. I'm sorry."

"No wonder Manny got his hackles raised. I'll take care of this."

"Thank you, Phillip." He always protected the world from me.

"So, tell me about the ships."

"That is a possible lead that I want to follow up on."

"Why? How do ships fit into this? And ships from Russia to Europe?"

"Um…" My breathing became much shallower and I had to focus not to touch my throat in a pacifying gesture. "I received a tip."

"Genevieve, it is not like you to not answer a question concisely. What happened?"

"The poet broke into my house." The words just poured out of me and the relief of telling the truth was tremendous. I relayed all the details of Colin's visit including the six hours of cleaning that had followed. Throughout my rushed report of what took place, Phillip looked increasingly distressed until I felt compelled to stop. "What's wrong?"

"What's wrong?" His voice shook with controlled emotion. "What's wrong? A thief broke into your apartment and sat down to have a chat with you is what's wrong. You couldn't phone the police is what's wrong. You allowed him to stay in your apartment is what's wrong."

"I read him. I could see that he wasn't there to do me physical harm." I wondered if I had made a mistake telling Phillip. He was uncommonly upset.

"Genevieve, your confidence in your abilities is well placed, but in a situation like this you should always run."

"But then I would not have learned so much. His visit might have been unsolicited and unwelcome, but it was enlightening. He said quite a few things that helped me find some new information today."

"I can't believe I'm going to ask, but how did that thief help?"

"Well, he said something that made me think he'd been stealing back art for at least eleven years, so that is how far back I've looked. There are most likely more, but the ones I found were reported in the media. The owners were all very grateful. So far I've found reports of forty-seven artefacts discovered, recovered, identified and magically resurfacing."

"Forty-seven?" Phillip's eyebrows almost touched his receding hairline.

"Yes. Some of them had reportedly been stolen during some or another conflict and others in robberies. He seems to be stealing back artworks and delivering them to their rightful owners."

"A modern-day Robin Hood."

"What a wonderful analogy." My momentary smile was quickly replaced by a frown. "But he's still a thief."

"True. But didn't he also say that a few of those works were forgeries?"

"Not many of the works that he recovered. Most of those seemed to be the authentic pieces." I turned to my computer, changed a few windows until I found the right one and put it on one of the large wall monitors. "On fifteen occasions, as you'll see here, he said the pieces were forgeries and he was right each time."

"Then he must have an incredible eye for a fake."

"I don't think he's a professional expert. Maybe he's developed his discernment because he's a criminal. Maybe he forges some artefacts himself and that's how he can recognise this."

"You should ask him when you see him again," Phillip said absently.

"I will not see him again." The mere thought of that criminal breaking into my apartment again and lounging in my reading chair outraged me. "I told him that he was not to return at all. Ever."

"Calm down, Genevieve. It was a careless comment."

I took a calming breath. "He also told me about thirteen deaths of artists that he knows about."

"Thirteen?"

"Yes. I followed that line for a while, but couldn't find anything more. I think that I should tell Manny to look deeper into that."

"I will tell Manny." It was an order.

"Of course. I will just offend him." I sighed. "Also tell him to get the ballistic information on these cases."

"He was one of the best military investigators in his day, Genevieve. Trust him to do his job."

I made a noncommittal sound. "I decided to look for more artwork with the reasoning that maybe the poets had recovered even more works. Then I started seeing another pattern. A different pattern. A lot of previously lost and stolen artworks mysteriously turned up at auctions. These works were not all lost during a period of conflict. It is a combination of heists, single burglaries, long-lost pieces and so on. These were sold at art auctions held by very reputable auction houses." I named a few of the auction houses.

"I've recommended a few of those to clients." He swallowed a few times. "Genevieve, are we in trouble?"

"What do you mean?"

"I mean you are finding artworks that had been insured by companies similar to ours. Artworks that were authenticated by the same institutions we use. Artworks that are forgeries. I'm beginning to worry about the pieces that we're insuring."

"I haven't found anything from Rousseau & Rousseau yet, but the way it looks, there's a high probability that something we've insured might be a forgery."

"We always worked with that risk. I just hoped it would never actually happen. Tell me what else you've found."

"I started looking for reports on how these pieces were found, but none of those connected to Colin. They all just mysteriously appeared."

"Interesting. But is there a connection between all of this and our case? You, *we*, can't afford to be wasting time on whimsical searches."

I gasped. "Whimsical? How could you say this is whimsical? Of course there is a connection."

"Okay. Then tell me more about the mysteriously rediscovered artworks that are not connected to your thief."

"He's not mine." I exhaled angrily through my nose and waved my hands in the air as if to remove this topic from our conversation. "What I discovered was that during interviews, a few of the owners said that their artworks were found by private investigators. This came up in eight different cases. None of them wanted to name the agency or investigator working for them. I found that extremely strange. Not many people are so private that they don't want to let on who worked for them. There are people like that, but statistically it is improbable that such a large number of the people interviewed would be equally secretive about who had found the art for them."

"And you don't think it is the poet?"

"Colin? No, he's not involved in this."

"Why not?"

"For a start, he would have been too busy stealing back his own artworks to be doing this work as well. It wasn't even worth thinking about further."

"I don't follow your logic."

Often I had to explain my reasoning to others. Every time it was exhausting to simplify my logic enough to make it understandable. "I did a lot of cross-checking. While the poet was in one country, these specific art pieces were discovered in another country. And Colin exposes forgeries, he doesn't sell them."

Phillip thought about this. "Weren't those forgeries he named of high quality?"

"Indeed, they were. They were masterpieces in their own right. Many of them passed the authentication process with flying colours."

"If they were sold as reproductions, they most likely would've fetched a very healthy sum on the open market."

"Most likely."

"But since they are sold as the real thing, it makes it an unforgivable crime. It seems like dumb luck that none of the pieces we've insured have been discovered to be forgeries so far."

"There is no such thing as dumb luck." A look at his lowered eyebrows made me realise that my comment had annoyed him. "Sorry. To return to my previous topic, I started looking for investigators or agencies in the cities and areas where these pieces turned up, but could find none. At least not anyone who specialised in finding missing art. Some of these people talked about the private investigator being local, yet I couldn't find anyone or any agency registered locally. Again, it wouldn't have been uncommon, but it stood out as a highly unlikely coincidence when it happened in each and every case."

"I have to agree with you on that." He sounded reluctant. "I'm still hoping for a connection here, Genevieve. You seem to have strayed from the original case."

I stared at the wall monitors for a few moments while collecting my thoughts. "There is a connection. I know it." I turned to Phillip. "Please give me more time to pursue all the clues that Colin gave me."

"How sure are you about the connections?"

"When have I ever had a suspicion that turned out to be nothing?"

"Hmm. Point taken. Next question. How sure are you about Colin?"

It took me a moment to reply. "As much as it pains me to admit this about a thief, I believe he was being straightforward with me."

"Genevieve, you have to be sure about this. Having this thug know your address is not safe. You should really consider phoning the police."

"He is definitely not a thug. The Russian murderer was a thug. Colin is, well, he is suave."

"Suave, as in James Bond suave? I never had you pegged as a romantic."

"Are you out to insult me today? First you call my search whimsical and now you call me a romantic. My assessment of Colin was purely professional. How could you even think any different?"

Phillip did not answer me for almost a minute. He stood up and faced me. "I did not mean to offend you. There are moments that I forget what an extraordinary person you are. You know, law enforcement agencies often make use of criminals to help them solve cases. Maybe you should consider asking this Colin for his help."

"Never!" The denial exploded through my whole system. "He's everything I abhor. There is a reason why society has laws. Anyone thinking he is above the law shows a clear lack of respect. I will not invite that kind of behaviour and mentality into my life. No way."

A small smile pulled at the corner of his mouth. "Never say never."

"He so much as suggested that we'll be working together and I told him in no uncertain terms that we will not be working together."

Just as Phillip started to say something, the cell phone in his hand started ringing. He gave the screen a quick glance and moved towards the door. "I have to take this."

My acceptance or an answer was not required, so I returned to my computer. There was a lot more research to be done. Five minutes later Phillip was back in my viewing room with his cell phone still against his ear, speaking into it.

"Yes, I'm with her now. Just hold on a moment." He pressed the phone against the front of his suit jacket. "It's Manny. He wants to speak to both of us."

"Please tell me you didn't say anything about Colin," I whispered urgently.

"I was planning on doing that. Why shouldn't I?"

"Phillip, please." I didn't need the added complication of Manny's opinion about Colin's visit. For all I knew, he would want me to welcome Colin back into my apartment so that he could arrest him.

"Give me one good reason not to tell him."

I needed to tell Phillip my true reason, but was loath to. I had seldom felt as conflicted as this. Colin was, after all, a criminal. Yet the man who had seen something in me no one else had deserved an honest answer. "He challenges me. He intrigues me. And I know I can learn from him. If Manny finds out about Colin, he will take him away from me."

Some time back I had greatly offended Phillip when I had bemoaned the lack of interesting people in my life. Once he had moved past the unintentional insult, he had understood that for me most people were tediously predictable. For me most people held no mystery. Not Colin.

Phillip shook his head. "You had to go and pick the only reason why I wouldn't tell him."

An insistent sound penetrated the confines of Phillip's jacket. It was the voice of an irate Manny calling to us. Phillip gave a wry smile and with a nod put Manny on speaker.

"Answer me! You bloody—"

"Manny, you're on speaker," Phillip said, quickly interrupting any further tirade.

"Oh. Why did you make me wait so long?" His voice dripped with suspicion.

"Genevieve and I had to clarify something."

"To do with the case?"

"With another issue." Technically he wasn't lying and I wished that this kind of quick thinking came naturally to me. I was simply not a good liar. Which was why I was so proud of my success with Jacques.

"Oh," Manny said again and cleared his throat. "Well then, hello, Doc."

"Hello, Manny."

"Yes. Well." His inappropriate response made me smile. Time away had not made him any more comfortable with me. He cleared his throat again. "I received more test results from the autopsy on the girl."

"Have you identified her yet?" I knew that the girl's identity was a key that would lead to many new avenues to pursue.

"No. My people are working on it, as well as the local police, but no one has found anything yet."

"You've had four weeks. How can you not have found anything?"

"What Genevieve wants to say"—Phillip gave me a warning glare—"is that the girl's identity will answer a lot of questions."

"I know that." By the sound of Manny's voice, I was sure his face was red, his cheeks puffed, a vein popping out on his forehead and his hands balled in tight fists. "May I continue with the results?"

"Please do." I guessed he was being sarcastic again.

"In the first autopsy report, the doctor said that she had had"—there was a rustle of papers—"carpal tunnel syndrome. The doc reckoned that she had done some repetitive work with her hands."

"It is a very painful condition for anyone to have. All that pressure on the median nerve," I said.

"What's the median nerve?" Phillip looked interested.

"It's the nerve that makes the thumb side of the hand feel and move. The area in the wrist where the nerve enters the hand is called the carpal tunnel. When there is excessive pressure, from typing, writing, painting or any other work involving the hands, it causes swelling in this area, which pinches the nerve."

"You just had to go and ask," Manny groaned.

"She was rather young for this." I ignored him. "It usually appears in people over thirty. Did the doctor say how bad it was?"

More papers rustled through the speaker of the cell phone. "I can't see anything in the report here. I'll have to ask him. Is it important?"

"Most likely not. Knowing this is enough. But that was in the first report. What did the new results render?"

"Render?" Manny said the word as if trying it for the first time. "It rendered a lot of different chemicals deeply embedded in the folds of her skin. Deep enough to make the scientist-people believe that she was working with this stuff every day."

"What stuff? Could you please be more factual?" I turned away from another one of Phillip's warning glances. I needed as many facts as possible if I were to prove that a connection between it all, a pattern, existed.

"I can't even pronounce half of the stuff, so I'll just put it on the network and you can access it from your EDA computer. But the scientist-people told me that all those chemicals combined pointed to materials that artists would use, especially painters."

"I knew it." I couldn't keep the triumph out of my voice.

"You knew what? Phillip, what did she know? What didn't you tell me? No, *why* didn't you tell me?" It sounded like Manny was ready to climb through the phone.

"Manny, she didn't know anything. Yesterday she did a lot of research and found some things that made her suspect that the girl was an artist."

"What things?"

"Just a few rather unspecific things." To my own ears I sounded like I was lying. I really didn't want to tell Manny about the murdered artists. That would lead to questions that could not be answered without mentioning certain poets who declared artworks forgeries. With only my facial expressions I appealed to Phillip to support me in this. When he didn't look particularly impressed, I mouthed the words, "Please trust me."

He rolled his eyes and turned his head away from me. "She just had a hunch. Since there was no evidence to back it up I didn't consider telling you about it."

"Are the ships from Russia also a hunch?" Manny sounded justifiably suspicious.

"Yes."

"Hmph." There was a long, pregnant silence on the phone. "I'll send you what I managed to get at such short notice. I don't suggest you print this out. You'll destroy an entire forest. Would it be too much to ask for a report on all you've unearthed so far?"

"I'll get Genevieve to send it to you as soon as possible."

"I understand that it's late Friday afternoon, but could I have it by tomorrow?"

"To do what with?" I immediately regretted my quick mouth.

"To investigate." He broke the last word into sharply enunciated syllables.

"No problem. I'll send it." My grimace brought a smile to Phillip's face.

"And I will come in on Monday so that we can discuss the report and also any new discoveries you might make over the weekend."

"I'm not going to work this weekend." I took great exception at the tone Manny used to deliver what should have been a request. "I've already put an immense number of hours into this case. I need a weekend to relax."

Phillip's eyes stretched at my uncharacteristic need for relaxation. "Maybe you could make an exception this weekend, Genevieve. I'm sure Manny would like us to make more progress than they've managed. Of course you'll be compensated for this."

"Only because you asked, I will do it." I moved closer and addressed the cell phone. "I don't take orders from anyone."

There was a long silence. Phillip switched the speakerphone off and left the viewing room, most likely to placate Manny. I shook my head at the complexities of social and professional relations and waited for Phillip to return. I didn't have to wait very long.

"Did you have to provoke him like that?"

"I only spoke my mind."

"Which in Manny's world is extreme provocation even on a good day." He sat down with a sigh. "What are you going to put in your report?"

"Everything I have found so far with the exception of the poets and the murdered artists." It was much easier to be deceptive in writing.

"Don't you think he ought to know about the artists? You were the one who pointed out that they had been murdered with Eurocorps weapons."

"And you were the one who pointed out that we had no proof that those were Eurocorps weapons."

"Genevieve." My name held the frustrated acceptance that he was fighting a losing battle.

"Give me this weekend. I will send the report to Manny tonight and work on the rest over the weekend. He's sending me the ship information. Hopefully between that and some other ideas I have, I will be able to give him more on Monday."

"You have until Monday. When Manny arrives here on Monday you are going to tell him everything that you've discovered so far." He stopped me with a lifted hand when I wanted to speak. "This is not a simple art fraud case, Genevieve. There has been the murder of this girl and, if you are correct, many more murders. We are working under the greatest confidence looking into a possible case of the abuse of power in the EDA and Eurocorps. For the love of God, there is even the theft of who knows how many weapons."

"Eight hundred and thirty-seven. That they know of."

"What?" Phillip looked disoriented. His eyes widened with comprehension and if possible he looked even more serious. "Oh, yes, of course. What I'm trying to get through to you is that this is different. You can't look at it as one of our usual cases. Please, for my sake, be careful. I didn't anticipate this case to be dangerous."

"Phillip," I said with a frown, "it started with a murder. How could you possibly think that it was not dangerous?"

"You're right." He looked defeated. "And if I had the smallest hope that it would do any good, I would try to take you off this case. But I know you too well. You've got your teeth into this and won't let go. At least just promise me if that thief comes around this weekend, you'll be careful. Don't hesitate to scream and run. Give me your word."

Knowing how much stock Phillip placed in my word, I thought about this carefully before committing myself to anything. "Agreed. I give you my word that I will be careful. If anything happens that could possibly put my life in danger, I will first phone you, then the police."

"You do that," he said gruffly and got out of his chair. Suddenly he looked every one of his sixty-one years. "And take care of yourself this weekend. Do something other than just work on this case."

"No promises on that one." I was glad to see my comment tease a tired smile from him. "But I promise to take regular breaks, sleep and deliver something on Monday."

Phillip only uttered a grunt and left the viewing room without a backward glance. The silence of the soundproof room surrounded me like a well-worn coat. This room and my apartment in a leafy and quiet area were the two places where I felt the safest. The noise of city traffic completely overwhelmed me and even the sound of a few colleagues chatting in the kitchen sometimes proved too much for my sound sensitivity.

I turned back to my computer, deciding whether to finish what I had started here or to pack everything up and continue at home. After a complex fifteen-minute debate with myself, I settled on working at home and began collecting everything I would need to take with me. While I performed this mindless task, my mind wandered to Colin. I had warned him to never enter my apartment again. Yet my ability to read people had been inerrant on so many occasions that I knew I was going to have to face him again sometime soon. Everything about him communicated unlimited self-confidence and pertinacity.

At least I had the half-hour commute home to work on a strategy to handle him. With a man who had eluded authorities for more than a decade, I knew that I needed a plan. I wanted him to comprehend that I would never work or even associate with a criminal. Even if his motives were noble and said criminal intrigued me.

Chapter SIX

"Nothing. Again you give me nothing." I glared at the three computers on my dining room table, neatly arranged in a semi-circle. It was late Sunday afternoon and I had spent my entire weekend at my dining room table, on an uncomfortable chair, going through the shipping data Manny had sent me. Of course the email delivering the data was rife with sarcasm. He had ended his email with an order to not lose focus with my quixotic look into the ships. I made a point of counting how many times he referred to me 'wasting my time' with this. It was eight.

Neither he nor the Chief had been impressed with my report, a report heavily edited to not even hint at Colin's involvement. The thought of Colin triggered a strange emotion in me and it took me a few seconds to identify it. Disappointment. I did not often experience that emotion since I had very few expectations of other people. My training had given me the exceptional skill to predict people's behaviour and reactions, which protected me from disappointment.

The fact that Colin caused this intrigued me. Against all my expectations, the thief had not broken into my apartment again. I realised that I had actually been looking forward to the challenge of sparring with him again. That specific realisation irked me and I returned my attention to the notepad. I supported a paperless office environment, but I did my best thinking when I put pencil to paper. Not until I looked, really looked, at the notepad did I realise how many notes I had scribbled over the course of the weekend.

On the top page were the three sentences the Russian murderer had shouted. In neat blocks I had rearranged the words in six different ways. My first attempt was to translate it to Russian, a language I loved for its melodious richness. Of the six attempts, the first made the most sense, yet it made no sense at all. I traced the Russian lettering with my index finger, but nothing revealing was forthcoming.

The top page was the least of the riddles I was currently facing. I lifted a couple of sheets and stopped at the third page to look at it more intently. On it were all the players in this mystery that Manny had brought to our doors—the murdered girl who still had no identity, the Gauguin painting, the Russian murderer, the stolen Eurocorps weapons, the suspected EDA and Eurocorps insiders, the ships and the unknown Russian connection. I had written all these in a circle around the page and had drawn blocks around each item, separating them.

Now I was at a loss. I had made such negligible progress in forty-eight hours. What else could I enter into the search parameters to give me more results? Results that could solve this mystery.

"It's all that thief's fault." Irrationally, I wanted to blame Colin for my unproductive weekend. He was the one who had sent me on this ship witch-hunt. Yet, I was the one who followed that trail. Now I was stuck. And annoyed with myself. My mind felt bruised from forcing it to look for different approaches. I couldn't believe that I was contemplating it, but I realised that I might need Colin's help. "If he ever sets foot in my place again, I will tell him how much I despise him."

"I really hope you are not talking about me, Jenny."

I shrieked. No other word would be apt to describe my undignified reaction. I closed my eyes for a second to regain control. When I opened them to glare at Colin, I allowed all the annoyance burning in my stomach to seep into my voice. "How did you get in?"

The art reappropriator was lounging in my reading chair. How had he walked past me without me noticing? His denim-clad legs were stretched out in front of him, crossed at the ankles. This high-comfort position was not lost on me. He felt confident and safe. It annoyed me even more. While I was studying him, he simply sighed and tilted his head to the side with an amused smile. "Superglue? Really, Jenny, you should've known that was not going to keep me out."

"Genevieve. My name is Genevieve. And I didn't have anything else to seal the windows with." I stopped abruptly when I realised I was justifying myself. "Why did you not just ring the doorbell?"

His only response was one lifted eyebrow and a sideways glance. "Moving on. Why are you so frustrated?"

"Because you are in my apartment. Again. Without an invitation. Again." I got up and walked to the kitchen. Almost imperceptible footsteps alerted me to Colin following me.

He groaned. "That's not quite what I meant by moving on."

I spun around, ready to give him an earful, but didn't get the chance.

"Let's not hash through our last arguments again, Jenny." He winced at my fierce look. "Genevieve. I've had a few days to think this over and have made a decision. I'm totally committed to working with you and finding out who the bastards are who killed my... these artists. Wait. Before you argue again. I know that one of your main arguments is that you can't trust me. So, as a show of my trust in you, I will give you this."

He reached into his designer charcoal jacket. Out came a folded piece of paper that he held out to me. I looked at the white paper as if it was a snake ready to strike. "What is that?"

"My trust in you." He shook it towards me. "Please take it before I change my mind. I've never given anyone this."

I took a moment to move past my distrust of this man and read him. The piece of paper in his hand quivered very lightly, indicating a surge of neurotransmitters and hormones. Most likely adrenalin, causing the uncontrollable quivering of his hands. Why was he stressed, nervous? There was no trace of any deception to be read on his face. Combined, all of these unmanipulatable cues led me to only one conclusion. He was being truthful about never having trusted anyone with whatever was on that piece of paper. This made the accomplished criminal infinitely nervous.

Without a word, I reached out to take the piece of paper. I realised that with this gesture I had just sealed an agreement with a criminal. I had accepted his trust and in return had given some of mine. I took the paper and wondered how this piece of pulped, pressed wood was going to change my life.

"Open it."

I looked up from the piece of paper in my hand and regarded Colin.

"Oh, stop reading me. Just open it or I'm taking it back." He pulled his arms closer to his body and his eyes narrowed. He was exhibiting signs of discomfort with his decision to trust me and my hesitation to see what was on the paper. It gave me no pleasure to cause him such discomfort, but it went a long way to soothe my mind.

I unfolded the sheet of paper. On it were written, in strong masculine handwriting, five addresses, one of them in Strasbourg.

"What are these?"

He swallowed and then looked me straight in the eye. "My homes. All of them."

"Your homes," I repeated while trying to find the significance of this gesture. "Oh. Wow. Oh."

"It's not so many homes. Most of them are rather rustic."

"I doubt that. But that is not why I am surprised." I refolded the piece of paper and unconsciously pressed it against my heart. "You're willing to trust me, a complete stranger, with your freedom?"

"That is how much I want to catch these bastards."

"I'm working with…"

"… the EDA. Yes, I know that. I have a theory that you're working with Millard. Aha, you blinked. So, you are working with him. Good. He's an irritating arsehole, but he's good."

"You know Manny?"

"Let's just say that our paths have crossed a few times."

"Translated, that means that either he arrested you or almost arrested you." The piece of paper was still clutched to my chest. I closed my fist around it and then held it between us. "I don't understand your trust."

"You need something that will assure you that I'm not playing games and I gave it to you."

"But why me?" Not many things confounded me, but Colin's absolute trust had my mind reeling. People didn't trust me. They felt uncomfortable around me and were even scared of me. Very few liked me. But trust?

"Because I know you will never use this"—he nodded at my fist—"against me. Not unless I betray your trust."

I thought about this. "That's correct. Would you like some coffee?"

Colin blinked his surprise and then awarded me with a smile that reached deep into his eyes. "I would like that very much."

We stood in companionable silence for the time it took the coffee machine to drip out two cups of coffee. By offering him a cup of coffee, I had agreed to co-operating with a criminal. I did not know when exactly I was going to regret this decision, but I knew it was going to be soon. I handed Colin one of the cups. "Milk? Sugar?"

"Black is fine." He followed me to the dining room table. "So, what have you found so far?"

I hesitated for a moment. Was I really going to trust a criminal with my findings when I didn't even trust Manny with them? Colin's pointed look at the paper that was still in my hand made up my mind. I opened the piece of paper again, looked at the five addresses for a full minute and handed him back the page.

"Now what?" His eyes narrowed with anger.

"Calm down, Colin. I memorised your addresses." I tapped with my index finger on my temple. "Once it's in here, it stays. I don't want the responsibility of it on paper in my home."

"Oh. Okay." The folded piece of paper disappeared into his jacket pocket.

"Let's sit down." I pointed to the chair next to mine and cringed slightly when he moved closer to look at the computer screens. I leaned away from him. "What is your interest in this case?"

"To stop the senseless murders of artists."

I pushed my chair away from him, crossed my arms and glared at him. "Your main motivation for being involved in this is not to stop murders."

"What do you know?" He mirrored my body language by also crossing his arms.

"Every time you talk about it, I see remorse. You are feeling guilty about something. What?"

He bit down hard and swallowed a few times before he answered. "I feel responsible."

"How?"

"It was only after the seventh time that I became suspicious." He smiled sadly. "As you know, I exposed forgeries whenever I found one. It was seven times too late when I realised that soon after my reports…"

"… an artist was murdered," I finished softly. Guilt and regret were deeply etched on his face. It had no rational basis. "You could not have known."

"Maybe not in the beginning. But once I had noticed the murders, I should've immediately made the connection and stopped."

"Did you stop?"

"I did. Too late."

"Have there been more murders since you stopped pointing out forgeries?"

Colin frowned and blinked a few times. "Yes."

"Well, there you have it."

"Are you always this rational?"

"Yes."

I followed his thought process by watching the different expressions moving over his face. The last was relief. "Thank you."

"No thanks needed. It's simple logic." I pointed at the computer screens. "Let me show you what I have so far."

I moved a bit closer to the computers, which put me closer to him. From the corner of my eye I saw him take a sip of his coffee and he moved to place the cup on the table. I stopped him with a quick hand and a voice that came out too stern. "Please use the coaster."

Colin's hand stopped mid-air. With a slight smile he took the coaster I offered and placed his cup on it with care. "Why three computers?"

"It helps." Not even Phillip knew that it helped me to have as many things visually in front of me as possible. My auditory memory had never been my strength. It was my visual memory, my visualisation of patterns that awarded me the reputation I had acquired. I was not about to explain this to Colin. In the next fifteen minutes I did, however, explain to him exactly what I had found in the last few days. I told him about the mysteriously recovered artwork and the non-existent private investigators.

"Then I started checking through all the shipping info," I said.

"You have details on shipping?" Colin leaned closer. Again I leaned away.

"Manny sent me the shipping info for the last five years.

It's an incredible amount of data. It lists all the types of ships, the companies that own these ships, even the manifests for each voyage."

"From your earlier frustration, I assume you didn't find anything?"

"Of course I did." The audacity to suggest otherwise drew my eyebrows together. "Just not as much as I hoped."

"Okay," he said slowly, as if careful not to offend me. Again. "What did you find?"

"When I entered the forty-seven miraculously discovered artworks, three of those were registered on the shipping manifests."

Colin's eyes widened. "Which ones?"

"A Degas pastel, a Gustav Klimt painting and an Amedeo Modigliani sculpture."

"Valuable stuff."

"But that's not the most interesting." My voice changed pitch as I became excited again with my meagre discoveries. "The Degas was shipped on a general cargo ship from St Petersburg to Rotterdam on 17 August 2009. The ship was called *Derbent* and belonged to a Russian shipping company. The final destination for the Degas was to be in France."

Colin started shifting in his chair. "Yes?"

"Don't get bored. The details here are important," I said. "The same Degas was mysteriously found by a private investigator in May of 2009. A newspaper article stated that the owner, Monsieur Villines, was delighted when his private investigator tracked the Degas down in France. The journalist wrote that Monsieur Villines had had tears in his eyes when he said that for months he sat with it in his villa in the south of France, overwhelmed by having it back. The article continued by saying that even though the owner was delighted at the artwork's recovery, his dire financial situation caused by the international financial crisis called for him to sell it at an auction.

The auction was held in late November."

"Wait." Colin held up both hands and closed his eyes. I assumed he was going through the facts he had just heard. I saw the exact moment all the pieces fell into place. His eye shot open. "How was it possible for this Monsieur Villines to have his Degas returned in May when it was shipped to him three months later?"

"A very good question. One that I don't have an answer to. I found the same with the Klimt and Modigliani. The discovery dates and shipping dates don't make sense." I glanced at my notepad, thinking of the other connections. That was when Colin noticed my notepad. I didn't even have a chance to stop him from taking it, he snatched it so quickly. Thief.

"What have we here? Your notes?"

"I will tell you everything that's written down. Please give it back to me." I reached for it, but he pulled it farther away from me without taking his eyes off my notes. He turned the pages and slowly perused each page, squinting every so often.

"You might have to interpret some of it. Wait. What's this?" He placed the notepad on the table, still holding it in his possession. He pointed at the first page with my attempts to make sense of the Russian murderer's last words.

"Manny's going to kill me." I closed my eyes and sighed. "If you ever tell anyone else this, I will give Manny all five of those addresses and a very detailed description of everything I know about you."

"Understood."

He listened intently as I explained the girl's murder and rantings of the Russian before he killed himself. Colin stared at the page for a long time. "You speak Russian. A woman of many talents."

My eyes widened. "You studied the page and that's all you have to say?"

"Well, it's the only thing that makes sense." He shrugged at the notepad. "The daffodils and the all-powerful red is muddled nonsense."

"What if it isn't? What if it's key to understanding all of this?" I tapped on the notepad.

"Maybe." He didn't sound convinced. He turned the page, found nothing of interest and turned to the third page, the page with all the different pieces of this puzzle listed in a circle. His eyes widened. "Explain, please. Especially the stolen Eurocorps weapons."

I gave him the short version of how the events had led to the discovery of the missing Eurocorps weapons and its tenuous connection to the EDA. "And they still don't know the exact number of weapons stolen."

Colin whistled softly. "This is even worse than I'd thought."

"I've told you all that I know. Tell me what exactly you suspected."

"I didn't quite manage to make sense of the deaths, except that they were somehow connected. I was also convinced that the EDA was involved. I never suspected Eurocorps. I thought this was simply an official of the EDA with his finger in an art fraud pie."

"I don't understand what you are saying. Please use normal English."

"But I was." He tilted his head. "You're not very good with euphemisms, are you?"

"No." For the sake of speeding up our conversation, I admitted this weakness. I didn't like doing it.

"Okay. Normal English." There was no verbal or non-verbal censure. He simply accepted this particular oddity of mine, the same way he did not show any judgement of my episode during our first meeting. "I thought that some EDA official, someone quite high up, was involved in art fraud. I thought that he was using his power, influence and connections to ship the pieces. Somehow he—"

"How do you know it's a man?" I interrupted him.

"Gross assumption. It could be a woman, but I doubt it. This is mostly a man's game."

"A game?"

"A gentlemen's game. Art crimes are almost exclusively non-violent. It is rather about outwitting the system, the fraud detection systems, the investigators, the security in the homes, galleries and museums where the pieces are. It's about beating the authentication processes. And, of course, the money. But it's not about violence. That is why the deaths of some, let's just call them friends, caught my attention. We all have an incredible love for the arts. Some have an equally strong love for money, but very few, if any, are in it for violence. The power comes from the outwitting."

"Interesting." I had never spoken to a criminal before. To have a first-hand insight into the workings of their minds captivated my interest. "But look at this page. You say this alleged EDA official was shipping the art. There is no line drawn between the shipping and the dead artists. I haven't found any connection."

"But you have lines between the girl and the weapons, the girl and the dead artists, and the forgeries and the ships." He stopped suddenly. "Tell me about the forgeries and the ships. How are they connected?"

"I searched the shipping database for any links to the mysteriously discovered artworks and got three connections I told you about. The Degas, Klimt and Modigliani."

"What other connections did you search for?"

"I entered all the art listed on Interpol's website, but didn't get any other hits. That was when you overheard me."

"You were angry with me." There was a smile in his voice.

"You started this whole shipping search disaster. It feels like I have wasted this whole weekend searching through the shipping database for nothing."

"Not nothing. You got three art connections."

"Yes," I almost shouted. "Only three. It's nothing to be proud of. I need more search parameters. I need more connections."

Colin leaned back in his chair and rested his head against the high back. He closed his eyes and for a moment I thought he might be falling asleep. His eyes flew open. "What about the girl? Have you entered her name?"

"We don't know her name yet."

He rolled his eyes. "Sometimes the police are so embarrassingly incompetent. I'll bet you a thousand pounds that I'll have her name by tomorrow."

"I don't bet and I have no use for pounds. In case you haven't noticed, you're in France. We use euros."

"Pounds, euros, it's all the same to me," he said dismissively. One of his homes was in England, so I supposed it really was all the same to him. I saw his mind working, most likely on a strategy to ascertain the murdered girl's identity. "What about the Russian who killed her?"

"I don't even want to know how you know this." The fact that he knew so much about the investigation and my involvement was jarring. "Manny told me that they had identified the Russian as a tourist who had entered Europe, but he never gave me the guy's name. It will be here somewhere. Just a moment."

I turned to the EDA computer and started searching through the case file to see if the Russian's name was there.

"Is that an EDA computer?"

"Yes," I answered absently.

"With full access?"

"Not full, but enough for now." I located the page with information on the Russian and perused it. Then a thought struck me and I turned sharply to Colin. "You are at no time to work on, switch on, open or even touch this computer. Have I made myself clear?"

"As a bell."

"Excuse me?"

"You made yourself clear."

I turned back to the computer, knowing that I had made myself clear, but that Colin most likely was not going to heed the limits. My attention was drawn away from this concern to the second paragraph on the page. "Here. It says that he had three different identities on him, but after liaising with Russia, they got his real identity."

"Russia liaised? That's a surprise."

"Russia is not all bad."

Colin made a rude sound. "Not in my experience. If they liaised, it was only to create the image of goodwill and co-operation."

"Do you want to argue about this or hear the murderer's name?" I was hard pushed to not start a political debate. I had a soft spot for Russia. It was a country rich with history and culture. True, it had a tumultuous past and present, but the people at heart were wonderfully generous. It was the elite few who were corrupt to the core.

"Who was he?"

"Nikolay Chulkov. He also travelled under two other identities."

"Put his name in the shipping search."

I did that and waited. Nothing. I sighed despondently.

"What about his other identities? Try them."

The next identity didn't give any result, but the third, Sergey Kruchenykh, was going to help us draw another line between the boxes on my notepad page.

"I can't believe it worked." I felt like I had just won a Nobel prize and smiled brilliantly at Colin. "We have another connection."

He was also smiling. "Follow that link."

"Okay, here it is. He was working on the ship *Trojka* in

October 2007. The ship left the port of St Petersburg and stopped in Gdansk, Poland before it continued on."

"How many ships did he work on?"

"He was only on that one voyage."

"Isn't that a bit strange?"

"I certainly think so. Why would anyone work on a ship only once?"

"Maybe he suffered from sea sickness and had to give up his new career." Colin smiled and I assumed he was being witty.

"Maybe. But I think it is unlikely."

Colin sobered. "Of course. Draw a line."

"What? Oh. Yes." I paged back until I found all the items listed and drew a line between the 'Russian murderer' box and the 'ships' box. "What's next?"

I accessed the personnel records on the EDA computer and ran the names of the permanent staff against the manifests. The people who cooperated with the EDA were not listed and it would be nigh-on impossible to find those thousands of names. With Colin's help we got as many names as possible from Eurocorps' website and did the same. With no results. I grunted in frustration and slumped in my chair.

Colin stared at the notepad in front of me for a while and then tapped on one of the boxes with a long finger. "What about the non-existent private investigators?"

"Let's see." I entered each of the eight private investigators' names, but none of them resulted in anything. "If there is a connection between the Russian murderer and the ships, then there must be some kind of connection between the ships and the girl."

"We need to know who she is," Colin stated quietly. "What do you know about her?"

"She was most likely an artist, a painter. The coroner put her in her early twenties, in good health when she was murdered."

"Once we have her identity, I'm convinced it will lead us to the ships and the Russians."

"What is your problem with the Russians?" I couldn't tolerate his hateful tone any more.

"Don't get me started. They are a bunch of ruthless criminals."

"I have an idiom for this!" I felt enormously proud of myself. "You are the pot calling the kettle black."

Colin surprised me by laughing. "Brilliant. Of course, I would not consider myself as ruthless."

"But you would consider yourself a criminal?"

"I admit to nothing." There was still a smile in his voice, but he was serious.

"Since we are talking about your crimes—"

"We are not."

"—I have a few questions for you," I continued without acknowledging his denial. "How did you know those artworks were forgeries?"

"Aw, Jenny. If I tell you that, I might as well hand a written statement in at the police station." He sighed. A moment passed while I just stared at him. He sighed again. "There are certain methods used when forging an artwork. Sometimes it was a hint of a method I know about that made me suspicious. Sometimes it was the signature of a forger I knew. Forgers are sometimes better artists than the artists themselves. It takes incredible skill to copy a piece of art so that it not only resembles it in appearance but also in age and chemical composition. Forgers often are required to have an extensive knowledge of art as well as geography, history and chemistry."

"And you know all this?"

Colin took a deep, deciding breath. "Yes. I'm considered to be one of the best."

I considered his tone of voice and studied his face to see if he was being truthful or sarcastic. I settled on the former. "Do you forge artworks?"

"I think I have trusted you with enough incriminating details for one day, Jenny." His use of this version of my name was an obvious ploy to vex me enough to discontinue any further questioning. It almost worked.

"I will respect it for today. But only because I realise the risk you are taking by trusting me. Not because you are disrespecting me by not calling me by my true name."

"You just seem much more a Jenny to me than a Genevieve." He leaned back in his chair. "A Genevieve is all stuck up and artificial. Jenny is soft, gentle and very real."

"You think of me as soft?" I didn't even bother to hide my shock.

"Of course. Doesn't everyone else?"

Nobody had ever shown enough interest in me to attribute such adjectives to me. Maybe Jenny was not such a bad name after all. The corners of my mouth pulled down at that silly thought. "I don't know nor do I care what others think about me. Shall we continue searching for more connections tonight?"

He smiled at my quick change of topic. "No. I think we've done quite well."

"There is one more thing I'll do." I opened the file with the shipping companies. "I want to see if there is any connection between the ship carrying the Degas and the ship Nikolay Chulkov worked on. Maybe I'll even find more ships."

"You're going to make another list?" The smile pulling at the corners of his eyes didn't indicate any malice in his question.

"Yes."

"I'm sure all your lists will come in handy soon. Already they've helped." He got up from his chair. "While you're doing that, I'm going to find out who our girl is."

"How do you plan to do that? Oh, wait, don't tell me. I shouldn't have asked."

Colin smiled. "Don't worry. There won't be too many criminal activities involved."

"I told you, I don't want to know." I stood up and looked at him earnestly. "It's really difficult for me to work with you."

"With me?"

"Not you as a person. That's quite easy." Much to my surprise. I had never worked well with anyone before and I had just spent five hours without once feeling the panic from human closeness eating at me. "It's working with a criminal that goes against everything that I believe in."

"Then maybe it's time to change what you believe in."

I made a noncommittal sound. I hated change but knew it was essential to my own growth and development. Change made me feel terrifyingly unsafe. But it had brought me bit by bit out of the very small world I used to live in. I was the first to acknowledge that my world was still miniscule compared to Colin's.

For me though, it was a proud achievement to have proved everyone wrong—everyone being my parents. They had been convinced that I was going to be some computer scientist who never left the basement. Someone who never had contact with the outside world. I had proven them wrong. My world was much larger than a basement and I was in contact with the world, even if the contact was feeble at times. But maybe it was time to widen my horizons.

"Well, okay," Colin said when I didn't respond any further. "I'll see you tomorrow then. Hopefully with the girl's identity."

"I suppose I shouldn't bother suggesting that you use the front door."

"You're welcome to suggest it."

"But you'll still use your own means of entering and exiting."

His smile brought warmth to his eyes. The man was a menace. I couldn't deny that he was a fascinating and attractive man, but he was still a criminal. And that was a chasm between us that would prevent me from even considering a friendship with him. This tentative working arrangement was as far as I was going to enlarge my world.

I followed him to my home office and narrowed my eyes at the sight that met me. I was furious.

"There's a footprint on my windowsill."

He looked surprised. "I'm not Superman. I didn't fly in here, Jenny."

"If you're going to continue breaking in, you're going to have to start cleaning up after yourself."

"I thought that I did quite a good job cleaning up the superglue remnants." He gave me another dazzling smile. "Just keep the windows locked, not glued. I'll find my way in."

He hoisted himself effortlessly onto my windowsill and disappeared into the night before I could object any further. I immediately fetched my cleaning products and once the windowsill was yet again spotless, I placed a brilliant white towel on the marble windowsill. At least a towel was easier to clean.

A quick glance at the clock and I decided to get a good night's sleep. Tomorrow was Monday. I could look into the owners of the shipping companies at the office before the meeting with Manny. That was really not something I was looking forward to. The EDA deputy chief was an intolerant boar. At least Phillip would be there to play his usual role as a buffer and translator. I switched off the lights around the dining room and wondered how I was going to convince Phillip to not tell Manny about Colin and his involvement. I didn't even know if I was going to tell Phillip that Colin now knew everything. I cringed to think what his reaction would be.

Chapter SEVEN

"We have to tell Manny."

Phillip was resolute in his position. He had been waiting for me and the moment I had stepped into out of the elevator, he had guided me into his office. I was reporting on my progress and he didn't seem too pleased. His lips were drawn in thin lines and he was using his stern voice. "I can't believe I condoned this. This Colin Frey is a criminal, for the love of God."

"I know that, Phillip. You suggested that I should work with him."

"It was a careless comment." He was exasperated. "I distinctly remember also telling you to phone the police, or me, or preferably both. Why didn't you do that?"

"He wasn't a threat. He isn't a threat. As a matter of fact, he was the one who suggested that I look for any connections with the Russian murderer." At least I had been able to impress Phillip with the connections I had made over the weekend. He was particularly interested in the three artworks that I had discovered on the shipping data.

"Genevieve, we have to tell Manny."

"No, we don't. He'll want to arrest Colin and I think that Colin can really help us. He seems to be very driven to find out who's responsible for this whole situation." Why I defended the thief was beyond me. He annoyed me, tested my belief system and made me desperately want to get rid of him. Now I was championing him.

"That is yet another reason to be concerned. Being that driven probably means that he is emotionally invested somewhere in this whole tangle. That is never a good thing. Oh, hell." His expletive took me aback. Phillip wasn't one for crass language. He was too cultured for that. "Last week we only had one murdered girl, one Russian murderer, a stolen artefact and stolen weapons. This week we have a full-blown conspiracy."

I had shown him my notepad and it came as no surprise that he was aghast when he saw the page with all the boxes. The fact that the boxes and the lines were multiplying had brought deep furrows to his brow. His face exhibited all the classic cues of distress and it was getting worse the more we talked.

"I think I should go and see if I can make any more progress with the owners of the shipping companies."

"Oh, dear lord." He shook his head. "You'd better put all this in a nice presentation before one o'clock."

"One o'clock?"

"Manny will be here then."

I barely refrained from groaning out loud. I only nodded and left Phillip in his office to tend to matters he would find less stressful.

From the first day I had stepped into his office, it was obvious that he loved the stress that came with his job. If there were not enough new clients, works of art that needed authentication or the possibility of a fraudulent claims, he became listless. The smallest hint of a problem and he thrived.

This case, however, did not have that effect on him, I mused as I entered my viewing room. While this case intrigued me, he seemed genuinely distressed by it all. He hadn't said it this morning, but I had read regret on his face and was wondering if he regretted agreeing to help Manny with this case or whether he regretted getting me involved. I set my computer bag on the long desk and took out both my work and the EDA computer. It was time to look for more connections.

A few hours later Phillip's assistant cautiously entered the viewing room. It was a rarity that Angelique even spoke to me, so I was surprised to see her in the doorway. She was a formidable woman in her early fifties with a husband of thirty years and three adult children. Not once had I seen Angelique back down for even the brashest of executives, yet she always appeared uncomfortable when she had to speak to me.

"I hope I'm not disturbing you." She spoke as if she was addressing a caged tigress. Her non-threatening body language showed her intent to not startle me into some unpredictable behaviour. "Phillip asked me to call you to his office. He wants to speak to you before Monsieur Millard comes."

"Thank you, Angelique. I will be there in five minutes." I didn't have the energy nor the desire to make the older lady feel more comfortable in my presence. During the last six years, we had been polite to each other, but never familiar. I preferred this.

"I'll tell him." She left as quietly as she had entered. It gave me the chance to quickly print out my presentation. There was no way that Manny could disapprove of my progress today. The last few hours had been productive. Very productive.

I switched off all the computers, made sure everything was straightened, put the printouts in my handbag and left the viewing room. Angelique jumped up from behind her large mahogany desk to open the door to Phillip's office.

"He's waiting for you. I put your coffee on his desk."

"Thank you very much, Angelique." I realised that our conversations had always been limited to these exchanges. This prompted me to give Angelique a warm smile which only confounded the older woman.

"Come in, come in." Phillip's voice from behind his desk drew me into the room. He was looking at me with a mixture of expectation and dread. "So, did you find anything?"

"Oh, yes, I did." Excitement brightened my voice. I quickly

walked to one of the leather chairs facing his desk and sat down. "You will not believe this."

"Oh, dear." He did not sound excited at all. As a matter of fact, he sounded downright apprehensive. He glanced at his gold wristwatch. "We have at most twenty minutes before Manny comes. The more I know, the better I can present it to Manny."

As I reached into my handbag for the presentation, a happy tune started playing somewhere in the office. I looked up from my handbag and gave Phillip an annoyed glance. "What is that?"

"A cell phone." It was the tone he used when he thought I was being brilliantly daft. "And it's coming from your handbag."

"Nobody ever phones me." I put my hand back into the bag and came out with my smartphone. It was indeed where the irritating tune came from. I carefully put my handbag on the floor and held the phone as if it were a live hand grenade.

"I didn't know you had a phone." Phillip was clearly surprised. "Aren't you going to answer it?"

I looked at the screen and nearly threw the phone against the wall. I swiped the screen to answer. "You put your photo on my phone?"

"Hello, Jenny." Colin's charming voice answered my outrage.

"Don't hello me. How did you get my number? And when did you put your number on my phone? With a photo!"

"How did you like the ring tone? It's Lady Gaga."

"I know of no such lady." I modulated my tone to a cold whisper. Phillip looked very concerned and stood up to move around his desk towards me. I shook my head to stop him. "I'm blocking this number and resealing my windows. With industrial glue."

"Wait!" he called as I started to move the instrument away from my ear. "I know who the dead girl is."

I slapped the smartphone back against my ear. "What? Who? How?"

"Come downstairs and I'll show you."

"I'm not in my apartment."

"I know that." He chuckled. "Come on down. I'm waiting for you in front of the building."

Before I could pepper him with more questions, he disconnected and I was standing with a silent smartphone in my hand. I brought the instrument down slowly and glared at it. "I'm going to kill that… that common criminal."

Phillip stormed around his desk and reached for my phone, but I snatched it out of his reach. "Genevieve, what did he say? What did he want?"

The better question was how Colin had known where I was. I was most definitely going to confront him with that as soon as I laid eyes on him. The thought of that annoying, overconfident thief waiting outside for me was, however, infinitely more appealing than meeting with Manny. Why that was, I was not about to explain to myself with my Freudian background. Instead, I picked my handbag off the floor and put the smartphone in its designated pocket. "I have to go."

"What? You can't go now. Manny is going to be here in ten minutes." He reached for my arm, but I sidestepped him with a frown on my face. Phillip knew I hated to be touched. He was uncharacteristically concerned. "Genevieve, please. Where are you going?"

I stopped at the entrance to his office and turned around. "Please don't tell Manny anything, Phillip. Not a thing."

"How can you expect me to do that when you won't even tell me where you are going or what Colin said to you?"

"He found the identity of the murdered girl. I'm going to meet him now." I thought for a moment. "Tell Manny that I'm following up on a lead and will be able to give him an exhaustive report tomorrow. I'm sure that this girl's identity will open a whole new line of connections for us."

"God help us all," was Phillip's response. I gave him a quick smile and turned to leave. As I walked past Angelique's desk, Phillip's voice followed me. "I want your number, Genevieve."

I shot Angelique a guilty smile and hurried to the elevators. Even though the elevator doors opened less than a minute later, it felt like an eternity. The trip down four floors took equally long and it was with great impatience that I walked past the security desk to the front door. Hitching my handbag over my shoulder, I pushed open the heavy wooden door of the historic building and stepped into a bright sunny day.

The weather in Strasbourg often pushed the mercury past tolerable and today was one of those days. I reached into my handbag for my sunglasses. Once my eyes were protected from the bright sunlight, I started looking around for Colin.

A full minute later I had scoured the street in front of the building and still couldn't see Colin anywhere. Rousseau & Rousseau's offices were on a quiet street with buildings housing corporations that didn't require foot traffic. There were therefore never many people passing the buildings, not even in tourist season. Today was no exception.

Across the street, a young mother was pushing her infant in a stroller and to my left was an elderly couple slowly making their way towards the shopping district. The only other person I could see was a distinguished-looking gentleman leaning heavily on his cane. His gray hair was mussed as if he'd pushed his hands through it numerous times. Despite the high temperature, he was wearing a three-piece suit that dated from a few decades ago, but still looked very sharp. Every step he took towards me looked like it caused him great discomfort.

"We'd better go. I just saw Millard driving around the block looking for parking."

I gaped at the old man with Colin's voice. It could not be. As I had done with the three photos of the poets, I only recognised him once I focussed on his mouth. "You're good. Really good."

"Why, thank you, young lady." The smile that lit up his face took decades off his artificially aged image and he looked much more like the thief who consistently annoyed me. He reached me and put his free arm through mine. What was it with men touching me today? I tried to pull away from this unexpected physical contact, but he held on tighter. "It will look more natural if you aid me when we rush to my car. We don't have much time before Millard will drive down here again."

I pushed down my intense dislike for physical contact and started walking. "Where is your car?"

"It's the red Toyota down there." He lifted his hand from my arm to point to a car about fifty meters ahead before he rested his hand lightly on my arm. The heat from his hand burned on my skin. I swallowed hard against the discomfort tightening its fingers around my throat and started imagining Mozart's Symphony No. 9 in C major. In my mind I drew the accolade, the clefs and first notes on a clear music score sheet. A few steps later my breathing deepened and the tension left my body.

"You have to teach me to do that thing."

"What thing?"

"The thing you just did. I could feel you calm down and relax."

We reached the car and Colin pulled his arm from mine. He reached into his retro pants pocket and came out with a remote control for the car. A soft pop sounded and the doors were unlocked. He opened the passenger door and waited for me to get in before he slowly walked around to the driver's side. I watched with a mixture of admiration and annoyance as he stayed in character even when there was no one else on the street. He settled in next to me and put his cane on the back seat. "I'm serious about you teaching me your relaxation technique."

"If I am going to teach you anything, Mister Frey, it will be to not break into my home, my life, my handbag and my cell phone."

"Oh, that." He pulled out of the parking space and drove down the one-way street. "I suppose you want me to explain."

I didn't consider it necessary to answer him and just glared at him. He turned into a main street before he glanced at me and winced.

"You're pissed. Okay, it was the first time we met. You were busy writing your music and I had nothing else to do."

"So you went through my handbag?" My cell phone very seldom left its designated pocket in my handbag.

"Yes. I thought it would be a good thing for me to get to know you better. When I saw your phone I realised how important it would be for us to be able to contact each other since we were going to be working together."

"How could you have made such an assumption? I hadn't even agreed to work with you then."

"I knew you would."

"You have an inflated sense of confidence."

"Thank you, young lady," he said with the same charming smile as earlier.

I didn't understand why he would think of my observation as a compliment. I took a few deep breaths and mentally wrote a few more bars of Mozart. He was not going to get me to lose my hard-won control.

"You don't have any contacts on your phone." Colin glanced at me before he swiftly changed lanes and accelerated to catch the green traffic light.

"Please slow down." I pulled at the seatbelt to ensure that it was tight against my body. "I'm sure there is no reason for us to be rushing there."

"I wasn't rushing." He sounded surprised, but did slow down a fraction. "Why aren't there other contacts on your phone?"

"Because I don't phone anyone with it. Please don't tailgate."

Colin's laughter filled the car. "You are a backseat driver. Who would've thought."

"I'm not driving nor am I in the backseat." I was too concerned with Colin's abandoned manner of driving to pay attention to idioms and nuances.

He must've sensed my genuine discomfort, because he slowed down enough to allow some distance between us and the white station wagon in front of us. I relaxed a fraction against the seat.

"Did you find any more connections?"

I was glad for a topic to take my attention away from his driving. "Yes. I found something very odd."

"And?" he prompted when I didn't elaborate.

"While I was looking for connections between the three ships that shipped those artefacts and other cargo ships, I noticed a most peculiar pattern. They're all singularly owned." My triumphant pronouncement was met with silence. I closed my eyes briefly. Why did I continue to forget that I had to explain things more clearly? "Most shipping companies own more than one ship. As a matter of fact, some of them have quite an impressive number of vessels registered."

Colin was driving too fast again. He glanced at me when I stopped talking. He must have noticed the tension around my mouth because he slowed down. "At this speed, it'll take us hours to get there."

I dismissed his complaint. "I first looked at the owner of the ship with the Klimt, then the owner of the ship with the Degas. Something didn't fit, so I searched some more. I found another four shipping companies like these two. All six companies own only one ship."

"Are you telling me that there are six shipping companies, each owning only one ship?"

"Why are you repeating what I just told you?" I waved away this redundant line of thought. "The Degas, Klimt and Modigliani were each on these kind of ships."

"All three?"

"Yes," I said with exaggerated patience. "I haven't had enough time to find out who owns these shipping companies. Maybe they are also connected."

"Well, you can draw another line now."

"Oh. Yes, of course. Between the ships and the art." We sat in silence for a few moments. I wondered how much information I could get on each shipping company from the EDA files. My thoughts wandered to the murdered artists. "Tell me about the girl."

"Only if you tell me why you have a smartphone, but never use it to phone people. Why you have no contact numbers on it." The professional makeup had aged him a few decades. The added wrinkles around his eyes and mouth made him a very handsome older man, but also made it difficult to read micro-expressions. Without that, I had mostly his tone of voice and his words to guide me. I decided that he was not going to give me anything unless I gave something first. Working with this man was infuriating and stimulating at the same time. Most definitely it was not dull.

"It is an extremely useful tool. People are so enamoured with their phones nowadays that it doesn't look strange when I'm sitting in a café working on my phone. Most people would be checking their emails, updating those social networking things or playing some silly games."

"So what is it that you do with your smartphone when you are in a café?" Colin sounded suspicious.

"I record people." I ignored the surprised sound he made and stared resolutely through the windscreen. He had asked and I was going to answer, but he'd better not judge me. "I downloaded this wonderful application that immediately sends the footage to my computer so that I can analyse it later."

"Why would you want to analyse it?"

"The more I study people, the better I become. When people interact in a public environment like a café, it is rather disconcerting to observe how intimate their behaviour can be. But that gives me hours of great footage. By analysing it, I hone my skills."

There was a long moment of silence. "You're a fascinating woman, Jenny."

I had no response to that. I moved on. "Tell me about the girl."

We slowed down and turned into the street leading to the university. "She was an art student. Her name was Danielle Rioux. She studied here and we are going to speak to her roommate."

I balked at that. "I don't speak to people."

"You're speaking to me," he said, unruffled, while parking the car in one of the few available spaces on the street. "If you prefer, I'll do the talking and you can just observe."

"I think that would be prudent." We got out of the car and I started walking towards the university, but stopped when I realised Colin wasn't next to me.

"We're going to her apartment first. It's this way." He was again leaning heavily on his cane and put his hand out for my assistance. I stared at his hand for a long moment. With a sigh I walked towards him and allowed him to put his arm through mine.

"How did you find her?" I ignored the feel of his hand on my arm, focussing instead on the case.

"Um"—he adjusted his bodyweight so he was leaning more on the cane—"I know someone."

"Someone?"

"A computer someone." We walked a few steps in silence. "She can find anyone anywhere."

I groaned out loud. "Did you break the law finding this girl?"

"Isn't it more important that we actually did find her and not how we found her?" He stopped in front of an old building. On the scuffed wooden door was a plaque announcing that this student house was under video surveillance. Colin turned to me. "She lived here on the third floor. Her roommate is expecting us."

A group of noisy students exploded out of the door, cutting off any more objections I had. I really didn't like this gray area of life that I had stumbled into. My life had been clear-cut until five days ago; things were black and white. There were right and wrong, acceptable and unacceptable categories for situations and people. Criminals were an entity that never ventured into any positive category and I most definitely did not associate with them. Now I was about to enter a student house with a well-disguised thief.

The last student passed us with a loud whoop and Colin used his cane to stop the door from slamming shut. With difficulty appropriate to his faked age, he opened the door. "After you, young lady."

I considered him for a moment and then, exasperated, squeezed past him into the bright entrance hall. He followed me in. I moved away from him when he reached for my arm. He acknowledged my gesture with a small smile and a nod.

"We can take the elevator. I'm too old for the stairs."

We waited for the elevator car to arrive. "Are you sure that Danielle was her real name?"

"A very good question." He thought about it for a while. "I'm pretty sure it was her real name. Francine would've found other identities if there had been any."

"Is Francine your computer someone?"

Colin looked at me in surprise. Before he could respond, the elevator arrived and the doors unlocked. I opened the antiquated doors and entered the car first, thinking about Colin's reaction. It appeared to me he was surprised that he had told me this computer person's name. My expertise told me that it could only be interpreted as trust and that I should feel honoured to be trusted by someone as cautious as this cunning thief. I did feel something, but it was relief rather than honour. I placed that interesting insight in the back of my mind to take out later and dissect.

We arrived on the third floor and I switched on my non-verbal reading skills.

I was about to learn more about the girl in the photo.

Chapter EIGHT

Danielle's roommate was an unassuming young woman, petite in size with large green eyes hidden behind studious glasses. She had opened the door on Colin's third knock. "Professor Dryden. Please come in."

I gave Colin a fierce look that he completely ignored. Really? A false name? Now I could add making me an accessory to falsifying an identity to his many sins.

He leaned even harder on his cane and, to my further outrage, spoke with a voice hoarse from age, smoking and whiskey. "Miss Paschal. Thank you so much for meeting with us. This is my esteemed colleague, Doctor Genevieve Lenard."

Miss Paschal held the door wide open and smiled at me. "It's a pleasure to meet you, Doctor Lenard. The professor said he would be bringing someone along. Please forgive the mess. I'm writing exams at the moment and don't have much time for housekeeping."

Colin and I stepped into the tiny apartment. He made a show of assuring the student that we were not here to inspect the living space. I thought it was a good thing we weren't. The girl would spectacularly fail an apartment inspection. The entrance hall could be no more than four square metres, but most of that space was taken up by an overflowing coat tree, a mound of shoes and a bicycle. The panic of such messiness sat in my throat like a large piece of dry bread.

Four doors led from the entrance. To the right was a bedroom with books and a laptop carelessly strewn across a large unmade bed. Straight ahead was a bathroom door and the open door next to it led to the kitchen. A bolt of horror shot through my system as I looked into that room. The health department would declare that small space a public hazard. I quickly turned my head towards the room to the left that Miss Paschal was showing us to.

"This is Danielle's room. I haven't touched anything, even though she still has my green coat and I've wanted to wear it a few times."

The image of the bright green coat spread underneath Danielle and the blood pooled around her head rushed into my mind. I hastily suppressed it and followed Colin into the room. Unlike the crammed entrance, the room was spacious. It was sparsely decorated, but clearly with a very artistic hand. The single bed was covered with a colourful duvet and on the walls hung paintings that looked like original masterpieces. I made mental notes of everything I saw.

I ignored Colin's small talk with the student. I wanted to learn more about the dead girl and right now I could read a lot by just looking at Danielle's room. The roommate could be observed later. When I looked around the room, it quickly became noticeable that there was a distinct lack of personal effects. There were no photos of family members, pets, boyfriends or even girlfriends.

I turned towards Colin and the girl, and interrupted their chit-chat about how Miss Paschal wished she had artistic talents. "Where did Danielle do her work?"

The young woman blinked nervously and looked at Colin. "She studied at the university and did some of her assignments there. But she told me that her boyfriend had given her studio space at his work."

"Tell me more about her boyfriend." Colin spoke with a gentleness the student responded to. I didn't need his quick glare to know that the girl felt uncomfortable with me. Her body language was screaming it. I shrugged mentally and paid close attention.

"I don't know much about him. Danielle is very private." She cleared her throat. "Actually, she is a bit strange. A few times she disappeared for a week or so, but never for this long. Do you know where she is?"

I narrowed my eyes. Colin hadn't told her that her roommate had been murdered. I did not want to be the one who delivered such news and waited for Colin to answer.

"No, dear." He had built a rapport with this girl at an amazing speed and I could not help but admire that. "All we know is that she is an amazing artist and our foundation would like to get in contact with her. We would love to co-operate with her. Maybe fund some of her studies."

"I don't think she needs money. Not now. The first few months we shared the apartment, she was broke most of the time. We used to joke about living on bread and water for the duration of our studies and how we could sell it as a trendy diet. Then she met her boyfriend and everything changed. I asked her if she had won the lottery or received a scholarship, but she didn't want to speak about it. She has enough money now to focus only on her studies and her art. A few times she even helped me out. Should I be getting worried about her?"

"I don't know, dear." There was compassion in Colin's voice and face. It had to come from his knowledge of where Danielle truly was. "It sounds like you are good friends. Where did she meet her boyfriend?"

"I don't remember. Let me think." Miss Paschal placed her fingers on her lips for a few moments and then her eyebrows lifted. "It was after her holiday. Oh, that is quite a story."

Colin responded to the sudden brightness in her voice with a warm smile. "Tell us about it."

"She won a cruise on the Baltic Sea. I don't remember anyone ever being so happy to win anything. She couldn't even remember entering the competition. It was a three-week cruise last summer and that is where she met this guy."

"Do you remember his name?" Colin asked softly.

"Danielle never introduced us. Like I said, she is very private. I just call him Russ."

"Russ?"

"Oh, he has the most delicious Russian accent. His French is really good, but combined with that accent, he sounds so sexy. And he is really good-looking too."

"Do you maybe know how we can get in touch with him? Maybe he knows where Danielle is."

"Oh, no. I spoke to him only three times and it was just in passing. I'm beginning to worry about her now. If I think about it, she has been acting a bit strangely the last while."

"Really?" Colin sounded sincerely concerned.

"Yes. She was spending a lot more time at her studio than at the university. When I asked her about it, she said that she was working on a project for someone and once it was done, she was going to move out of the studio. She didn't want to tell me any more than that, but that day she looked really unhappy."

"Do you know where her studio is?"

The roommate was looking increasingly distressed. "No, I don't know that either. It seems like I really don't know anything about Danielle. Oh, God, I hope she is okay."

"Don't worry too much, dear. Rather think about your studies and your exams. I'm sure that Danielle is somewhere safe." Colin's words seemed to calm the girl. He chatted to her for another five minutes about her studies. By the time he followed me out of the apartment, the student was once again consumed with exam stress.

We continued in silence until we were outside in the sun. He put his arm through mine and leaned on me. I glared at him. "How could you just lie to her like that?"

"I did not want to be the one who told her that her friend was murdered." He sounded aghast. "And from a practical point of view, we are not supposed to be here."

"Oh, lordy." I stopped midstride. "Phillip is going to be so displeased."

Colin gave a rude snort and pulled me so that we were walking towards the university again. "I don't think Phillip will be your biggest problem."

"My problem? Good lord, I'm going to bear the brunt of this, aren't I?" I had not even considered this when I had offered him that blasted cup of coffee and with that my trust and co-operation. "And it's Manny who's going to be shouting at me."

"I'm afraid you are right."

I wrote a few more bars of Mozart's 9th on the music sheet that necessity had placed in my mind this morning. Knowing Colin was helping me brush up on all my Mozart. "Are you just going to leave me to deal with this alone?"

"For now." His soft-spoken cryptic answer did not invite any argument. "What do you think about the cruise ship boyfriend?"

"I think that now I have another box in my notepad that will need lines."

"Dollars to doughnuts the cruise ship they were on is also singularly owned."

"I don't understand."

Colin looked at me with surprise. "You don't? Oh, the dollars to doughnuts thing. That only means that I'm willing to bet that the cruise ship that Danielle met her boyfriend on belongs to a company with only one ship on its books."

"Oh. Well, it was a good guess, but I'll have to do proper research to have concrete proof. Why doughnuts?"

"I really don't know." He laughed. We crossed the street and walked into the university campus. "Where did you study?"

"I'm sure you know."

"But I would like for you to tell me."

I stiffened when he didn't deny having knowledge about my education. "I studied in Oxford, Tokyo and the Paris Descartes University."

"One of the most prestigious universities when it comes to psychology. I already know your French is flawless. Do you speak Japanese?"

I started to answer, but stopped myself. "No, you must first give me information about yourself. That is how co-operation works."

"Very well." With Colin's artificial old-age walking, we were making slow progress through the beautiful campus. We were following the signs leading us to the library. "I spent a lot of time on campuses like this, but I was never a registered student."

"So what did you do at the universities?"

"Studied, of course. My childhood was not very academic, so I never would have qualified for university, but I wanted to learn."

He had even stolen his education. "What did you study?"

"History, art, art history, world politics. I even dabbled a bit in philosophy. Here we are." He led me up a stone staircase and into the cool interior of the library.

"Who are we going to see now?"

"Danielle's professor. She told me she would be waiting for us here." We walked into a large room and the hushed reverence of literature surrounded us. I loved libraries. Colin leaned closer to me and whispered, "Over there."

I pulled away from his closeness, followed his glance and saw a middle-aged woman sitting at one of the long dark wooden tables. She looked like she had stepped out of a Seventies magazine aimed at the hippies of that era. Her gray-streaked hair fell below her waist, both her wrists were adorned with mismatched bracelets and her colourful dress perfected the image. When we stopped at her table, she looked up and welcoming wrinkles formed in the corners of her eyes.

"You must be Professor Dryden. Please sit down." Sympathy

softened her face even more when Colin lowered himself painfully onto a chair. I wanted to hit him.

"Thank you, Professor Benoit." He awarded her the same smile that had won the roommate over. "And thank you for making the time to meet with us. This is my colleague, Doctor Lenard."

The hippie professor beamed at us. "It's such a pleasure to meet you. Paul couldn't talk enough about your unparalleled knowledge when it comes to art restoration."

"Oh please, Profess—"

"Please call me Jeannette," she interrupted.

"Jeannette." Colin's voice oozed warm friendship. I was in awe. I was witnessing a con artist at work and couldn't stop myself from being caught up in the skill it took. None of my book knowledge had prepared me for the artistry in deceiving someone so smoothly.

Colin was talking again. "I assume that Paul didn't tell you about our scholarship programme? Well, we are in the fortunate position of sponsoring a select few students and Danielle—Miss Rioux—has caught our eye."

"Yes. Yes." Concern marred the older woman's face. "After your phone call, I started wondering why I haven't seen her in a while. I decided to look Danielle up at administration and it seems that she has dropped out."

"Dropped out?"

"Yes. The head of administration showed me an email they received from Danielle, informing the university that she will no longer be attending classes here."

"When was this?"

"About three weeks ago. It really is a loss. She has the makings of a great artist. You know, one of the few great ones." Tears formed in her eyes and her lips thinned as she tried to control her emotions.

Despite the heavy makeup, Colin's distress was strong enough to be displayed clearly. He was not mourning her absence at the university, of that I was sure. It was her senseless death that pulled the corners of his mouth down. "You are right, it is a great loss."

"What was she working on?" I knew I wasn't supposed to speak, but someone needed to break the sadness that had settled at the table.

"Oh." The hippie professor dabbed lightly at her eyes and took a stuttering breath. "She was good in most disciplines, but it is painting that she excels at. She has the right touch for it. And she so loves Post-Impressionism and Cloisonnism. The artists of that time inspire her with their adventurous attempt at doing things differently. That was the time for the -isms. One day she told me that she thought she was born in the wrong time. I could easily believe it. I don't understand why she decided to quit."

"I saw one of her works that greatly resembled Gauguin," Colin said quietly

The professor and I both looked at him in surprise.

"Oh yes, she said that Paul Gauguin was her greatest inspiration. She loves all his works, but it is his paintings especially that she can't get enough of. Once she showed me the beginnings of a painting that she was working on privately. It was far from finished, but I was sure that it would've been an exact replica of Gauguin's Two Tahitian Women. She was a master in the making."

I inhaled sharply and looked at Colin. His slight nose-flare, constricted pupils and narrowed eyes revealed that he was as interested and excited by this new development as I was. Colin gently questioned the professor for a few more minutes, but gained nothing else.

"Thank you so much for your time, Jeannette. It is truly a pity that we've missed the opportunity to work with Miss Rioux."

We all stood up and the professor smiled warmly. "No, it

was my pleasure to meet such an esteemed colleague of Paul's. The next time you find yourself in Strasbourg, please come and visit again."

After a few more pleasantries, we slowly made our way to his car.

"Wow." Colin broke the stunned silence between us. "Would you believe that? She used Gauguin as inspiration and the professor even saw the beginnings of a copy. Then she's murdered and a piece of a Gauguin is found on her? What are the odds of this happening?"

"I don't think that we can calculate the odds here." I noticed a slight relaxation of his *orbicularis oculi* muscles, taking away the stress that had been evident around his eyes during the two conversations. One corner of his mouth lifted. Understanding dawned on me. "Oh, it was a rhetorical question. Well, I have a real question for you."

"Shoot."

"Who? What?"

"Shoot with your question, Jenny." There was laughter in his voice.

"Oh. If you are Professor Dryden, what is your first name?"

"Care to guess?" The car was a few feet away and he stopped. After fumbling in his pocket like an old man would, he came out with his wallet and found his identity card. I reached for it, but he held it back. "Guess."

"John. You are pretending to be John Dryden, the British poet who lived until 1700." I grabbed the laminated card out of his hand, glanced at it and shook it angrily at him. "This is fraud, Colin."

"John, dear. My name is John." With that he shuffled to the car and folded his body painfully into the driver's seat.

It was with no small amount of agitation that I got into the car. "You can't continue doing this, Colin. It is illegal and I will have no part in it."

"Is your ID forged?"

"No, of course not. And what does that have to do—"

"Do you have anything else that is forged? Did I provide you with anything illegal?"

"No."

"Well then. You have no part in anything." He pulled into the street with a quick smile. "Not that I'm admitting to any illegal activity, of course."

I didn't like being in this gray area. It was much easier to think of all the information we had just gleaned, so I forced my thoughts to stay on topic. I couldn't wait to get to my computers and add cruise ships, especially those on Baltic cruises, to the search and see what came of it. And to think that of all the folders I had received from Manny, I hadn't even considered opening the cruise ships folder.

It was hard to decide what to do first. Maybe I would cross-reference all the names of the fictional private investigators with the cruise ships. I thought of all my lists and how I would just start with one list and cross-reference the whole lot of them.

"Genevieve!" Colin's voice bounced around the interior of the car. He had the same tone of voice and look on his face as Phillip when he had been calling my name for some time without any reaction from me.

"What?"

"Where were you?"

"Here. Sitting next to you." What an inane question.

"That is not what I meant. Obviously your mind had taken you to another place. That is the place I'm interested in."

"Oh. I was just thinking about everything we've learned today."

"Quite something, right?"

"Quite."

There was a long silence. "Are you going to tell me what you were thinking specifically?"

"No."

Colin laughed softly. "Did you notice the paintings on Danielle's wall?"

"Of course I did."

"Did you recognise any of them?"

"No. Did you?" I was not an art expert. I had, however, learned a lot in the six years that I worked at Rousseau & Rousseau. The different eras in art rolled off my tongue as easily as all the facial muscles controlling our expressions. It was only the most costly artists, those whose paintings we insured, whom I was more familiar with. I would never claim to be able to recite a chronological list of their paintings though. Something told me that Colin could.

"With the exception of one, they were all Gauguins." He quickly glanced at me. "Really good Gauguins."

"Oh, dear. It seems that she was a forger."

"It would seem so." He stopped at a red light. "Where do you want to go now?"

"Back to the office."

"It's past five already. Why don't I drop you off at your apartment?"

"It's that late already?" I looked at my watch with amazement. I had been acutely aware of the time until Manny and Colin entered my life. That I had not noticed how much time had passed attested to how completely engrossed I was in this case. "At least Phillip won't be in the office. He's most likely raring to lecture me. Again."

"Does that mean you still want to return to the office?"

"Yes, please. And do slow down. It's not necessary to race through the streets like this. I don't mind if it takes a bit longer to reach the office."

"I'm not racing." But he did slow down and maintained a reasonable speed and distance from the other vehicles until we reached Rousseau & Rousseau's office building. He double-parked in front of the large building and turned to me. "I'll contact you tomorrow to find out if you've drawn any more lines."

I got out of the car and leaned back in. "Please use the front door."

"Aw, Jenny. That would be so boring." Not even the layers of makeup could hide the merriment on his face. He was having too much fun with this.

I slammed the door with unnecessary force. Psychology had taught me that reacting to his actions the way I did only encouraged him. I simply did not have it in me to ignore his grating behaviour. If only he hadn't proved himself to be so useful. And resourceful.

I silently bemoaned my bad luck all the way into my viewing room. Only after the door slid closed did I realise that Phillip hadn't been waiting for me at the reception desk. He was, very possibly, at some or another important function, playing the social games required for the survival of businesses. With a sigh of pure contentment for not having to play those games, I switched on my computers and opened the folder with the cruise ships.

Three hours later, all I had to show for my efforts was the beginnings of a headache. I had managed only to discover that the list of cruise ships was long. It proved to be quite a challenge to cross-reference anything with that folder. The format of the cruise ships file was not searchable and I had to draw on all of my computer skills to change that. Even though I loved technology and its use in streamlining actions that previously would have been laborious, I had never taken enough interest to advance my knowledge to the level of a specialist.

When the files were compatible, I looked at my watch and decided to call it a night. I would make an early start of it in the morning. I predicted that I would first have the inevitable argument with Phillip before I would be able to continue this search. Meticulously I saved all that I had done, shut down the computers and was in my car shortly before nine o'clock. If my luck held, I could enjoy a leisurely soak in the tub and be in bed long before midnight.

Chapter NINE

I was outside my front door, ready to get inside and shut the world out. A sound from inside my apartment caused me to tilt my head. Nothing. I was sure that I had heard something inside, but now I thought that I was just spooked by the last five days' excitement. I aimed the first key at the top keyhole when I heard a noise again. My hand stopped midair and I listened intently.

The unbelievable audacity of that man. No matter how useful he had proven himself to be, Colin was out. Out of my apartment, out of my life and, if I could arrange it, out of the country. The noise he was now creating inside my apartment meant that I was going to spend the rest of my evening cleaning up instead of mulling over the case allowing my mind to free-associate.

Something crashed to the ground with shattering loudness and a frown formed between my eyes. With speed born from habit, I had the five locks unlocked and the door open in under five seconds. The comfort of working for Phillip for the last six years had lowered my guard. The true nature of the human race had only been evident on the ten monitors in my viewing room. I had very effectively isolated myself from human interaction.

In the last few days, I had rediscovered my determination to not lose control, to not give in to the darkness that threatened to cloud over my brain in extremely stressful situations. I had fallen back into the habit of reading people, in particular Colin, and so staying fully in control of myself. The limit of my control was now being tested as I stared in horror at the scene in front of me.

My usually immaculate apartment looked as if a tornado had blasted through it. I took a few disbelieving steps into the chaos.

"Well, what do we have here?" An unfamiliar voice spoke behind me and I heard the front door close with an ominous click.

Already facing the destruction of my apartment, I had my mind set on analysing the situation. I felt in no imminent threat of an episode. Losing my patience was a distinct possibility though.

I swung around and glared at a very large man looming in front of me. He was in my reading area; books were scattered at his feet. My precious books. A deep anger burned in me. His all-black criminal attire, which included a facemask and gloves, infuriated me even more. "What the hell are you doing in my apartment?"

Only his eyes were visible through the slits in the mask, meaning that I wouldn't be able to read him. I could, however, still see the slight lift of his eyebrows indicating his surprise. It took me less than two seconds to memorise what I could see of his appearance and shelve it for future analysis.

"Where are your computers?" His voice was gravelly, but it was his German accent that made it particularly memorable. Another bit of information I shelved.

My training dictated that calming a situation down was preferable to having to defend oneself in a physically violent manner. "There is a safe in my bedroom."

"We've found it. You must open it." Another voice spoke from behind me. His English was heavily accented with Russian. For the first time I felt more than just a hint of apprehension. One man I might have been able to defend myself against, but two? One being Russian did not particularly help the shiver of panic that went through my nervous system. Immediately Colin's question about the Russian connection to this case came to my mind. I swallowed and forced my mind away from thoughts that could only lead to panic. I needed to be productive, needed to read and analyse. That was the only way I was going to survive this.

My focus shifted to the importance of memorising what I could about these intruders. I manoeuvred myself so that my back was towards the windows and I was facing both of them. They were dressed completely in black. Movement from the kitchen drew my eye and to my utter disbelief another masked man clad in black walked towards us. He was followed by a fourth.

"We haven't found anything else." The third man addressed the German in Spanish-accented English.

"Nothing?" There was facial muscle movement behind his mask, but I could not see enough to make an accurate reading. His gravelly voice, however, was displeased.

"She must be hiding it. It must be in the safe." The clipped accusation came from the Russian. I forced myself to calm my breathing. I hoped that if I co-operated, they would not turn violent on me. The Russian's body language indicated that he was spoiling for a physical confrontation and I knew I probably would not live through it.

The Spaniard and the fourth man joined us. I noticed that the German and the Spaniard were dressed in exactly the same outfits. Their cargo pants, black boots and long-sleeved shirts looked as if they were part of a uniform. Silver duct tape formed crude crosses on both shoulders and one sleeve. It took me a moment to realise that they were trying to conceal an insignia of some sort. My mind was racing to piece together as much as I could as fast as possible.

Then I came to a crashing realisation. There was no doubt in my mind that they all had to be military. The stealth with which they moved, the rigid confidence coming from the core of their torsos and even the way they spoke were specific to a select group of people. Even though only two of the intruders wore the same outfits, it was clear that the four of them worked as a team. Of that I was sure. Their awareness of each other and confidence in each other's movements testified to that. I had observed the same phenomenon numerous times while analysing group dynamics in my sheltered viewing room.

They formed a semi-circle in front of me without a word to each other. Their postures were not of a placating nature, but rather indicated that they were ready for action. These four men were warriors.

"Open the safe," the Russian growled at me.

I tucked my elbows into my sides, at the same time exposing the insides of my arms in a non-threatening gesture. "Of course. You can take anything you want. Just please don't break anything else."

The fourth masked man was a bit shorter than the rest, but he made me think of a panther. There was something feline about his movements. He looked me straight in the eye when my gaze turned to his face. The tiny muscles under his eyes contracted a millisecond before he picked up a clay bowl I had purchased while travelling in Kenya and dropped it to the floor. The sound of it shattering on my wooden floor sent a shudder through my body. The men laughed. I closed my eyes and suppressed a groan. The sacrifice of one of my favourite pieces had confirmed my suspicions. These men were bullies and such personality types revelled in doing exactly what was begged of them not to.

"Go, bitch. Open that safe. Else I break every fucking thing in this place." The fourth man's voice was deep and would be well suited for radio if it were not for the cold malice in it. It was the accent, however, that I filed away with all the others. His Russian accent confirmed that two of the four men in my apartment were from Russia. Another shudder went down my spine.

If they were indeed military, which I believed they were, it brought a few questions to the fore. Why would an international military team be ransacking my apartment? There was absolutely nothing of value to them here. The only possible reason was the case Manny had brought to us.

I had no more time to analyse the four men or their agenda. The German took a step closer to me and with the flat of his hand against my back shoved me none too gently towards my bedroom. I stumbled forward and pushed down the panic that surfaced with that physical contact. So far I had kept the darkness at bay with anger, rational observation and analysis. Even though I could feel panic gathering strength to overwhelm me, I resolutely refused to give in to it. The bullies would never have the pleasure of seeing me at my most vulnerable.

My mind was equal parts reeling at the chaos and hungry for more information to enable me to understand what was going on. The latter would prove to be more useful in the future, so I gathered my wits and my balance and walked to my bedroom.

"What do you want with my computer? There is nothing special on it. I only use it to surf the internet." Maybe I could find out why they were here or what they were looking for.

"Shut up!" The short Russian's voice cracked through my apartment and I flinched. He was walking next to me and a quick glance at him was enough for me to see that every muscle in his body was coiled for attack. I was the only one he would aim his attack at. With that amount of aggression, I would not be able to defend myself. Quietly I led them to my bedroom, my sanctuary.

A protesting fury burned inside my stomach. I had taken every precaution possible to keep myself and my space safe from intruders. The extra locks on my front door, the strong doors to my bedroom and bathroom, and the extra locks on them. Even the top-of-the-line safe was there to keep my personal documents and laptop safe. I had had it installed in a hidey hole behind a wooden panel that looked like it was a part of my antique wardrobe. No one was supposed to have found the safe. These men had taken away my sense of safety and that was going to take time to recover from.

I stood in front of the carved oak wardrobe and bit down hard on my teeth. They had broken the wooden panel to reveal the safe behind it. All they had needed to do was push the hidden button under the first drawer inside the wardrobe. Instead they had used excessive force, which left the panel shattered and most of the wood lying at my feet.

The four men had followed me into my bedroom. The airy, spacious room that had been my haven now felt crowded. Refusing to allow that feeling to overwhelm me, I opened my senses to observe the large military men looming over me. The way they positioned their bodies indicated that the German was the team leader. They were waiting on him to direct their actions.

"Open it, bitch," the short Russian spat. He didn't wait for any orders, nor did he give me time to react. Before I could lift my hand to punch in the twenty-four-digit code, he grabbed me by the hair and slammed my face against the wardrobe.

I was stunned. Never in my life had I faced any physical threat or abuse. The sharp pain that shot through my cheekbone brought on a thankful thought that my face connected with wood rather than the unyielding hardness of my bedroom walls. I didn't feel or hear bone breaking, which might have been the case had it been the wall the Russian had chosen for his show of force.

It was interesting that I could feel so detached to the pain in my face and my scalp where he still had his hand in my hair. While I was thinking that it surprised me that my hair was actually long enough to be grabbed so tightly, I heard the two Russians quietly arguing. Intent on listening to the tone they were using, I also managed to understand them.

The short Russian who still had me by the hair, pulled me

roughly away from the wardrobe. I was slammed a second time against the wardrobe when the German gave a gravelly order. "Enough. Let her open it."

I was suddenly free. Having had my head slammed against the wardrobe made me light-headed and I put a hand against the wood to steady myself. It only took a second to regain my equilibrium and I straightened my spine. They would not win. The darkness would not win.

My head was throbbing and my hands went up to inspect the damage. One hand massaged my scalp while the other went to my face. My cheek was painfully tender to the touch. I touched my eyebrow and my fingertips came away wet and sticky.

"If you don't open that safe, I will hand you over to these gentleman and leave you to them." The German's threat kept the shock of my blood on my fingers at bay.

"I'll open it." It would have taken a deaf person to not hear the fear in my voice. I blinked a few times and took a deep breath. I could do this. My fingers were still wet from my blood and I wiped my hand on my pants. I looked at the keypad of my safe and my mind went blank. The twenty-four digits that had automatically come to me in the past now eluded me.

"Is there a problem?" the Spaniard asked.

"Um, no. I just need a moment."

"You don't have a moment. Do it now!" It was the first time the German had raised his voice and I felt the power of it. I nodded my head emphatically and immediately regretted the movement. The darkness responded to the sharp pain in my head.

I closed my mind to the whispered conversation behind me and called up my favourite Mozart serenade, No. 7 in D major. Three bars into the serenade, the darkness had receded and the twenty-four digits were once again accessible.

While the men were furiously communicating behind me, I entered the digits. I hadn't wiped all the blood off my fingertips and I noticed dispassionately that there were red smudges on the keypad. The safe opened with a soft click, which silenced the conversation behind me. "It's open. Take what you want."

The German pushed me roughly away from the wardrobe and reached into the safe. He pulled out my computer and handed it to the Spaniard who slipped it into a black backpack. Impatiently he paged through my personal documents before he tossed them to the floor. "Where is it?"

"Where is what?" I hated the quiver in my voice. I didn't want to lose control. I didn't want to be scared. I didn't want these men in my apartment, but I was scared and they were here. But I wasn't going to lose control.

"The computer, bitch." The short Russian grabbed me by my arm this time.

Later I tried to recall what exactly had happened and my memory failed me. All I remembered was the frantic struggle that ensued. I recalled being blind with fury for all that had happened and my self-defence training kicking in. I remembered connecting my fist and elbows with a few body parts. And how the jarring pain shot to my head with each hit.

I hit, kicked, screamed and scratched until one of the men had me in a grip so tight I couldn't move. It turned out to be the taller Russian holding me. He was behind me, one arm tight around my throat and the other hooked around the front of my left arm, bending it painfully backwards and gripping my right arm in a bruising fist. My arms were trapped between our bodies. He had one leg around the front of both my legs so that I had zero balance and was being held up by his arm around my neck. Not even in lovemaking had I ever been so taken over by another body. Every inch of me was touching his body.

I immediately brought the serenade back into the forefront of my mind. Colin's arm through mine was one thing. This kind of physical contact was infinitely more than I could bear. When the Russian spoke again it was filtered by Mozart.

And very close to my ear. "Where is the other computer?"

"This is the only one I have."

"Liar!" His arm around my throat tightened with intent, but the German's voice stopped him.

"Quiet!"

The sudden silence in my bedroom was broken only by hard breathing. Mine was from the fight for survival, but I suspected theirs was from anger. The three men exhibited body language associated with annoyance and anger. I focussed on that and my breathing calmed.

"Do you hear something?" the short Russian asked.

"I said quiet!" The German was looking towards the front door. Then I also heard it. A man was calling my name in a manner familiar and loving. I had never heard that voice before. I also heard a light scratching noise.

"He's picking the locks." The German looked at the Russian holding me. "Did you lock all of them?"

"Yes." His answer rumbled against my back. I mentally wrote a few more bars of Mozart.

"We have three minutes at most. Are we sure there is nothing else to be found here?"

They all assented that they had searched every inch of my apartment and had found nothing else hidden. I listened to them through the calming sounds of Mozart. Hearing what they were saying was enough. I committed every word to memory, every nuance, every inflection. I didn't have the strength, physically or otherwise, to understand or analyse it. That would have to wait for later.

"What are we going to do with her? We can't take her now. We'll have to leave through the windows." The tall Russian was still holding me in a death grip. I was going to be badly bruised.

"Inject her." The German looked at the Spaniard. "Do you have it ready?"

"Yes, it's here. Just hold her still."

"What? What are you going to do?" What were they going to inject into my system? I didn't want to die. I didn't deserve to die. Not by the hands of thugs breaking into my apartment.

"Now listen very carefully to me, Doctor Lenard." The German moved to stand so close that I had to lift my head to see his eyes. "We know who you are; we obviously know where you live. You are to stop putting your nose where it doesn't belong."

"Where is that?" My question brought angry muscle contractions to his eyes.

"If you need me to spell it out for you, then you are not half as clever as I've been told." His tight whisper frightened me even more than his previous threat. "Stay away from this. You are to forget about your investigation. You are to forget about our little visit. Am I clear?"

I opened my mouth to answer, but screamed when a sharp needle entered the triceps of my left arm. I struggled against the Russian's hold, but he held me firm until the needle pulled out.

"How long?" The German was looking at the Spaniard who was putting the syringe in his backpack. He took out a tablet-looking device and stepped closer to me.

"She should be out in thirty seconds."

"Good. And she'll be out until morning?"

"Yes."

The Russian released his hold on me and I found myself standing on unsteady legs. I lowered myself to the floor and wondered if I looked as disoriented as I felt. Feeling in my lower limbs was slowly disappearing and my hands were tingling. I lifted one hand and stared at it. It was fascinating to be able to move my fingers and not feel it at all.

My hand was roughly taken by the Spaniard. My fingers touched something smooth and cool before my hand was thrown down. I couldn't lift it again.

I wanted to laugh at the realisation that I was drugged. Genevieve Lenard, renowned expert in non-verbal communication, was high. I frowned with concentration, memorising what I was experiencing. This might be the only time that I would have the opportunity to observe myself drugged. Definitely worth remembering.

My cerebral acuity was not yet as strongly affected and I put all my energy into mentally recording everything. My drugged experience as well as the muted conversation of the intruders as they were set to leave my apartment were carefully filed away. It might have been two minutes or it might have been longer, but I was very pleased with what I had observed. As a deep lethargy took over my body, I didn't even know that I had collapsed on my bedroom floor. My only concern was whether I would remember everything once I woke up.

The last thing I saw, and filed away, was a giant storming into my bedroom and kneeling next to me. He was calling my name, but I couldn't respond. Awareness slipped away from me just as he placed a gentle hand on my tender cheek and swore.

Chapter TEN

Consciousness came to me slowly. First, I became aware of the pain in my face. My cheek was throbbing and the cut on my eyebrow stung. My eyelids were too heavy to lift. I assumed the drug had not yet fully worked its way out of my system. Fortunately, I had four more senses with which to assess my current situation.

An attempt to lift my hand so I could inspect my injuries came to nothing. Even though I was awake, I was not able to move. I did not know where I was, but someone close to me was moaning pitifully. After a few seconds, I realised that I was the one moaning.

"Colin," an unknown male voice very close to me called out, "she's waking up."

My entire body jerked. Not another attack. Please. My panicked breathing sounded loud in my ears and did nothing for the pain in my face. I forced Mozart past the panic and felt its soothing effects within seconds. Then I started doing what I did best. Reading and analysing.

It took me only a few moments to register that the deep, hoarse voice next to me had sounded concerned. And he had called for Colin. I opened my eyes with Herculean effort and was relieved to be looking at the walls of my own bedroom. My head felt like it was split open, but I forced myself to look around. I frowned slightly as I tried to remember whether there hadn't been more devastation in my bedroom. It seemed as if someone had cleaned up. The last I remembered I had been on the bedroom floor. Now I was lying on my bed.

I took a bracing breath and turned my head to the left, towards the window. Next to my bed, on one of my dining-room chairs, was a man large enough to cause concern for the legs of the chair. So this was the giant whose presence had chased away those thugs. His feet were firmly planted on the floor and he was leaning forward with his elbows on his knees. My eyes roamed over his canvas pants, his loose-fitting cotton shirt, all the way up to his face. An ugly scar starting from his left temple and zigzagging to his jaw marred his strong features. His *orbicularis oculi* contracted, muscles causing him to squint. He was looking at me as if I were an unknown specimen in a Petri dish.

My eyes were now wide open in a combination of surprise and interest. I was in an absurd scenario, lying half-paralysed in bed and scrutinising the man just as he was scrutinising me. He seemed to be one solid bulk of muscle. Combined with his shaved head, the ugly scar and his scarred hands, he made a very intimidating picture. Yet his upturned palms, relaxed shoulders and the concern in his eyes did not induce panic. This fear-inspiring man staring intently at me did not project a single non-verbal cue leading me to think that he was aggressive.

"Colin?" I managed to squeeze the word through my vocal cords. It came out scratchy and for some reason caused more pain in my bruised cheek. My mind was starting to function at its usual speed and numerous questions were nagging at me. Who was this hulking man? Why had he called Colin? Was the thief here? If so, where was he and why was he here?

"I'm here, Jenny." Colin's deep voice spoke from the doorway. I heard him walk in before I managed to turn my head. He stood by the side of the bed for a moment before he lowered himself gently onto the mattress next to me. "How're you feeling?"

"Lame."

"Did you say lame or pain?"

"Both." I only mouthed the word. Nausea was the latest addition to the physical ailments pulling at me. I took four shallow breaths to keep the pain and nausea at bay.

"I'm not surprised. It looks like you had quite the battle in here, young lady." He smiled when I rolled my eyes at him. Since talking was proving to be too big a challenge at that moment, I looked pointedly at the large man silently watching me before I looked questioningly at Colin.

"She was shooting the breeze with her eyes, dude. That's sick." I had no idea what the man had just said, but I did take note of his voice. It was raspy, as if he had damaged it from overuse. That, and his unidentifiable accent, added even more to his intimidating image. He did, however, sound amused.

"Jenny, I would like for you to meet Vinnie. Vinnie, Jenny." Colin gave Vinnie a warning look. "Vinnie is here to help us."

"Genevieve." I was fighting a losing battle.

"Nah, you're a Jen." Vinnie turned his attention to Colin. "She's too small to be a Genevieve. Definitely a Jen."

"I'm not small." Not only did I have more uninvited guests, they also insisted on insulting me. The annoyance with them gave me enough strength to try and lift myself onto my elbows. "What's the time?"

"Don't get up. Just lie there for a moment." Colin glanced at his wristwatch. "It's just past six."

"In the morning?"

"Yup," Vinnie said. "You've been out cold the whole evening. Ol' Colin and I housewifed a bit while you were catching your zees."

I stared at the man sitting next to my bed. There was an uncomfortable silence and I turned to Colin. "I don't understand a word he just said."

"Don't mind Vinnie. He's harmless." Colin chuckled again when Vinnie snorted and I looked at him with obvious disbelief. "Vinnie here spent a few years with his family in America and he fell in love with the slang they use over there. He's also created a few of his own special words."

"Why is he here?" I was feeling stronger by the minute and also increasingly annoyed. "No, why are *you* here?"

"Like I said," Colin said slowly as if talking to a child. "Vinnie is here to help us. I came as soon as I realised something was wrong. I phoned Vinnie and he managed to get here before me."

"Yes, I found you on the floor, out for the count," Vinnie said. "The place was trashed and at first I thought you were pushing up daisies, but then I saw you oxygenating."

I looked at Colin.

"He said he found you unconscious on the floor. Your apartment was destroyed and he thought you were dead, but then he saw you breathing." His eyes narrowed. "Who was here, Jenny?"

I lifted myself higher against the pillows. A big mistake. The room started to spin and the nausea returned in full force. It took me a full minute of working on a Mozart minuet to regain some level of normalcy. I opened my eyes to see Vinnie striding toward me. In his hands were a few empty music staff sheets and a pencil. He handed them to Colin and stood back, looking unsure.

"You told him?" My voice shook with fury and my eyebrow stung when I frowned. Writing Mozart as a way to cope was private. Only a handful of people knew about this and I resented anyone knowing unless I chose to tell them. I would never have told Colin, but he had witnessed it. But this giant knowing? It was unacceptable.

"Jenny, please don't get angry. You're still recovering. I'm just trying to help." Concern and guilt strained Colin's voice. "I should never have dragged you into this case."

"You didn't ask me to help. Manny and Phillip asked me to work on this case." I looked uncomfortably at Vinnie, who was leaning casually against the wall. This was not a topic for open conversation. "What you did was insert yourself into my life and into this case without giving me much of a choice. You did not drag me into this case, you cretin."

A muffled cough drew my eyes to Vinnie, but he had recovered from whatever caused his discomfort. I did, however, notice the relaxed lines around his eyes and the slight lift of the corners of his mouth. He thought this was funny. That annoyed me even more.

"Jenny." Colin held both his hands up, palms out. "Before you get very angry and chase me out of your apartment again, we need to talk about this."

"What is there to talk about? You've once again broken into my apartment."

"I didn't technically break in this time. Vinnie opened the door for me."

"That's even worse! You brought another criminal"—I quickly glanced at Vinnie—"no offence, into my home."

"She knows I'm a criminal?" Vinnie's raspy voice was low in its threat towards Colin.

"She guessed, but you've just confirmed it."

"Oh." A warm smile transformed his face. "You're good, Jen-girl. Colin told me you were a whiz, but I thought he was blowing smoke."

I didn't even try to understand or respond to what Vinnie had said. I knew that aiming my anger at Colin and his friend was irrational, but I hadn't had enough time yet to deal with the remnants of the panic from the night before. And I ached all over. "I need to be alone."

"No." Colin's immediate answer surprised me in its vehemence. "You're not going to be alone. I would love to talk you out of working on this case, but somehow I know that won't be possible. Since neither Phillip nor Millard seem to realise how dangerous it is for you, I'll take your safety into my hands. No, don't you dare argue with me, Genevieve Lenard. Until we have closed this case nice and tight, you will not be alone for one second."

"Colin, I cannot." The idea of constant company brought the suppressed panic to the fore. "You're not even supposed to be on this case. And now this man also knows things no one else is supposed to know. This won't work."

"Jen, hon." Vinnie moved away from the wall, but didn't crowd in on me. "My aunt Theresa is my father's youngest sister. He has three sisters and two brothers, you know. Ah, his middle sister really makes a mean chilli con carne. Anyhoo, Theresa is agoraphobic. I have seen what it is like for people who are special like that when things get too much. I used to stay with her some holidays, so I know what to do and what not to do. I promise you won't even know I'm here."

"He?" I was relieved that the large man had spoken normal English, but I didn't want him in my space all the time. I didn't want him in my space at all. "You're leaving me with him?"

"Hey. I'm not that bad. I can even cook." Vinnie didn't look in the least offended.

"It's true, Jenny. Vinnie is a killer-cook."

"A killer-cook?"

"Just a manner of speaking." The look that Colin gave Vinnie was one of apology and guilt. By using a euphemism, Colin had just unwittingly given a secret of Vinnie's away. "He will be here when I can't. He will make sure that nothing like this happens again."

There was no going back on my agreement to let Colin work with me on this case. I wouldn't dream of breaking my word, even though I had regretted it a few times before and at least a dozen times in the last five minutes. What I didn't want was a very large man in my apartment, messing up my kitchen, my neat world. That would distract me immensely. After last night I needed to focus on making connections. I wanted to hand Manny his case back as soon as possible. That would rid me of all these new complications in my life.

My thoughts of how to avoid change were interrupted by

Vinnie quite loudly clearing his throat. "I think I'll go fix us all breakfast. What chow do you fancy, Jen?"

"English?" I understood each individual word, but had no idea what Vinnie tried to communicate.

"Will scrambled eggs and toast be okay for you?" Colin asked.

"I don't want breakfast."

"She'll have scrambled eggs and toast. Thanks, Vin."

"No problemo, dude." Vinnie was already halfway to the kitchen, no doubt going to mess up any surface that the thugs last night hadn't already spoiled.

My thoughts returned to the previous night's events and another question turned up. "Colin, how did you know that something was wrong last night?"

"I'm psychic?" he offered, but grimaced when I glowered at him. He looked decidedly uncomfortable.

"Just tell me. I know I'm not going to like the answer, but you knew to come and I am glad that you are here."

Colin's eyebrows raised at my admission. Then he closed his eyes and sighed. "I planted a bug."

"A bug? What does an insect have to do with this?"

Colin let out a long groan. "It's a colloquialism for a small electronic listening device."

"A what?" I was horrified. "You've been listening in on me? That's perverse. When did you put that device in my apartment?"

"The first day when you were writing music"—he pointed to the music sheets between us on the bed—"I kept myself busy. Please don't get up. You're still too pale, Jenny. Just lie back against the pillows and I'll tell you everything."

I glared at him, but dizziness combined with the nausea left me with little choice. I settled back stiffly and waited for him to continue. If that heinous invasion of privacy had not been the reason that Vinnie had chased off the thugs, I would never have forgiven him for it.

"While you were writing music I started looking around. At

that time I only knew the basics about you and was curious. And I didn't know if you could be trusted. I wanted to find out who this woman was who figured my poets out when no one else had managed to do so. You were writing for a very long time. Do you know how much you can tell about a person by the books on their shelves and the art on the walls?"

I didn't answer this question, by now familiar with his technique to derail conversations. Of course he was right and I wondered what impression he had formed about me from my books and art. But I was too angry with him to say anything. I just pursed my lips tighter and continued glaring at him.

"I suppose you do know." He sighed. "Your books and art intrigued me. It showed a highly intelligent woman with varied interests. When I first came here, I had a whole plan to send you into a different direction. But your apartment, your music selection and especially your books convinced me that you might just be the one. No one else had been willing to listen to me before and I had no solid proof that I could convince them to take a closer look. But I knew that you would."

"How could you know that from my music, books and art?"

"That all showed me that you are someone who likes to get the whole picture. You don't have just one genre of music, nor do you only have books on one religion. It was clear to me that you try to understand the whole picture and that was what I knew we needed."

"But you don't trust me. You planted a surveillance device," I accused him.

"Of course I didn't trust you at first. That is only one reason why I planted the bug. The other reason was that I wanted to know whatever you discovered and maybe talked about." He held up his hands when I inhaled to argue. "I know, I know. It is a violation of your privacy and so forth. In my defence, I only planted devices in your living area and study. Not even I would go as low as listening in on your bedroom activity. But I am truly not sorry I did it."

"You heard the men in my apartment." I chose to ignore the humiliating thought of him listening to me singing Happy Birthday while I brushed my teeth.

"Yes. At first I was surprised that you got home so soon. I thought that you would've worked much later and then just accepted that you had come home earlier and were cleaning or something."

"They were breaking things and throwing things around. How could you think I was cleaning?"

"People do all sorts of strange things in private." He shrugged. "But it was when I heard you come in and speak that I realised something was very wrong."

"And you phoned Vinnie."

"When he got inside—"

"Did he break in?"

"He had to pick your front door locks. You can't be angry about that. It was that noise that chased the guys away. So, when he got inside you were unconscious on the floor, but the bastards were gone. How many were there?"

"Four." A shudder went through me and I looked longingly at the music sheets. "They hit me, Colin."

"I know, Jenny. I'm very sorry about this." He reached out and gently put his hand on mine. Never before had someone's unsolicited touch not made me cringe. His touch was warm and light. I looked at his strong fingers covering both my hands where they were clutched on my lap. Having this thief in my space at this moment made me feel safer. Even though I was still incensed.

"Don't think that I'm easily going to forgive you for planting a listening device in my living area." I lifted my eyes to his and knew that there was not much annoyance expressed on my face. I was going to forgive the thief.

"I'll remember that." He smiled and removed his hand. "Why don't you have a shower? When you're done we can have breakfast and you can tell us exactly what happened."

"Us?"

"I've told Vinnie everything, so don't bother fighting about this."

"Colin!" How many more horrors was he going to impart on me before breakfast? "You gave your word that you wouldn't tell anyone."

"Vinnie isn't just anyone, Jenny. And this is really an exceptional situation."

"I don't care who he is to you. You shouldn't have told him."

Colin was unrepentant. "There are very few people in this world worth trusting, Jenny. Vinnie is one of those people. We've walked a very long road together and I trust him with my life."

"Just because you trust him doesn't mean that he should know anything about this case. You know the kind of sensitive information we're working with."

"And he will take that to his grave." There was only implacable belief in Colin's voice and face. "Please think about this in the shower. If you reason with yourself, I'm convinced that you will see the sense in having Vinnie around for protection."

I shook my head and swung my legs off the bed. A shower was so far the only acceptable suggestion Colin had made today. Most of the dizziness and nausea was gone and I was convinced a shower would take care of the rest.

I ignored Colin's pleas to consider everything he had said and walked slowly to the bathroom. As much as I hated to admit it, Colin did have a point. I locked the door behind me, then stepped out of my clothes and into the shower.

A week ago I had had enough sense to realise that I was going to need Colin's help. I had asked for it and he had proved himself helpful. Until last week I had thought travelling alone to foreign countries had been an unequalled achievement for me. It had taken months of planning, self-motivation and

Mozart before I could even buy a plane ticket. Every leg of the trip had been a panic-laced experience, the completion of each an incalculably proud moment.

But this? Yesterday I had been so proud of my open-mindedness to be co-operating with Colin. I had entered a new journey, one of travelling through a world of gray zones. The difference between this and my previous odysseys was that I hadn't had time to plan. It constantly felt like I was catching up, not planning ahead. I was a planner.

Just as I had caught up and accepted the reality of travelling through gray zones, I was thrown into another gray area. One that required me to entrust a giant of a criminal with my physical well-being. I tilted my head back to let the stream of water flow over my face and wash away the last grogginess of the drugs.

Did I trust Colin? The answer came to me almost instantaneously. Yes.

Did I trust him enough to take his word that Vinnie was trustworthy?

I shampooed my hair while sorting through every bit of physical, intellectual and psychological information to reach clarity in my mind. I had reached a turning point and I needed to decide in which direction to go. I wanted to make the right decision, but I wanted to make it before I went out to face the two men waiting for me.

Chapter ELEVEN

I walked into the living area with strong strides. I knew what I wanted to do and I had decided what needed to be said. All those carefully thought-out demands deserted me the moment I looked around.

"You cleaned." The shock was clear in my voice.

In the kitchen both men whirled around with surprise on their faces. I walked to the tall bookshelves to confirm what I found hard to believe. I distinctly remembered my books lying scattered on the floor. Said books were back on the shelves, not in the exact order that they had been in, but very close. They were almost perfectly aligned, but I would rearrange them. The effort, though, did not go unappreciated.

Further inspection showed me that everything that had carelessly been thrown on the floor had been picked up and placed in a logical place. Even the broken African bowl shards had been cleaned off the floor. I was grateful for that, but knew that hours of cleaning and rearranging were ahead of me.

"I didn't hear you." Vinnie spoke from the kitchen and I turned to them. The giant was wearing an apron and didn't look happy. "Why didn't I hear you? I always hear everybody."

"Are you feeling better?" Colin picked up two plates piled high with food. He left the kitchen and put the plates on the dining room table. I frowned at the table, then saw the placemats protecting the polished surface. I had been ready to battle the two of them, but the thoughtfulness the two criminals had shown me robbed me of my fight. I was touched.

"I'm feeling much better, thank you."

Colin moved around the table and stopped in front of me. He leaned a bit forward to inspect my face closely. "You look better. Better colour and your eyes are not so glassy any more."

Feeling uncomfortable under such scrutiny, I moved away and gave a look towards the kitchen. The time had come for me to face the horror of having strangers work in my kitchen.

I looked again. "Oh my God. It's clean."

Vinnie smiled at me from the stove where he was making more scrambled eggs. "My auntie Helen was a neat freak. When I was seven, I stayed with her for two years. A lovely woman, but by gad, she had a thing about a clean kitchen. I suppose that stayed with me."

I walked into my open-plan kitchen with lifted eyebrows. Last night those thugs had spilled most of the contents of my fridge on the kitchen counters, on the floor and against the tiled walls. There was no evidence of that now. I had never had any knick-knacks on my kitchen counters to start with, and they were now as uncluttered and clean as when I had left my apartment the day before. Except for the kettle. The angle wasn't quite right. I quickly remedied that and when I turned, both men were watching me.

"I, um, thank you."

"Aw, Jen-girl," Vinnie crooned, "don't look so sad. It was my pleasure to help such a pretty lady as you. Now, let me just take these plates to the table and we can eat. Colin, bring the coffee, dude."

We settled at the table and I smiled. If anyone had told me a week ago that I was going to have breakfast with two criminals, I would have taken great exception to that. Yet here I was, sitting at my table, feeling strangely comfortable in the presence of these two rather intimidating men.

I gave them a few minutes to start their breakfast before I spoke. "I've made a decision."

Both men looked up from their plates. Vinnie had curiosity

written on his face, but Colin looked wary. Maybe he thought my declaration might not be good news.

"Since both of you so ungraciously pushed yourselves into my apartment and into my life, you have forfeited any right you even think you might have to tell me what to do. In the last week I've had my fill of arrogant men and their opinions about me. I'm not helpless nor am I mentally incapacitated. No, let me finish." I held up my hand firmly when Colin looked like he wanted to go on the defence. I really needed to say what I had planned. "I have high-functioning autistic spectrum disorder that sometimes gets the best of me. The last week has been very trying and has caused some of my control to slip. It won't happen again."

"But it might?" Colin interrupted me quietly.

"Yes, it might, but let's work on the assumption that it won't happen again." I really was not planning to rewrite every single one of Mozart's compositions. Or having another episode. "Here is what I decided. You are here. You cannot unlearn what you know about this case. We cannot turn back time, so we'll have to find a way to work this thing out together. But, and this is a big but, you will not tell me what to do. You will not treat me like a delicate little blossom. You will not take over my life. Colin, you are right. It makes sense for Vinnie to be my bodyguard. Vinnie, if it is acceptable to you, you can move in, but you will adhere to my house rules."

"Yes, ma'am." If I wasn't so determined to make them see how serious I was, I might have appreciated Vinnie's expression more. The large man looked like a ten-year-old getting a tongue-lashing from his mother.

"You can stay in the spare bedroom. For the duration of your stay, you will keep the door closed at all times, so that I can't see into the room. You will clean up after yourself. You will speak normal English to me so that I can understand you. You can drive me to and from work, but you will not go in with me. You will not go anywhere with us when Colin is with me. One of you at a time is enough. When I am in my study or bedroom and the door is closed, you are not to disturb me. Understood?"

"Yes, ma'am." Vinnie swallowed. "If there is an emergency—"

"You're more than welcome to disturb me, but only in a true emergency." I wavered. "Maybe we should define what a true emergency is. I don't want you to disturb me for something inane."

Colin looked thoroughly amused. "I'm sure that won't be necessary. Vinnie here will only disturb you with life-and-death emergencies. Right, big guy?"

"Right."

This felt surreal. I had made my decisions based on the facts as I had them. Colin had trusted me with not one, but all of his home addresses. I knew that he knew that I would not think twice about handing that information over to the authorities if he betrayed me. Or if Vinnie betrayed me. With that much power in my hand, I could not convince myself that he would have brought Vinnie into my life and into this case if he didn't have full confidence in his friend.

I did not have that kind of confidence in either of them, but I had unshakable confidence in my ability to read people. It was this ability that had helped me make this decision. Not that it was an easy decision. I trusted Colin and decided to trust his judgement concerning his friend.

"Colin." I turned my gaze on the thief. His amusement disappeared. Apprehension was written all over his face now. I felt immensely empowered by intimidating two criminals. "You will stop treating me like I'm going to fracture into tiny little pieces. You will not, under any circumstances, tell anyone else about this case or bring anyone else into it."

"It might happen that we'll need more help, Jenny."

"No one else, Colin. Take it or leave it."

His lips thinned while we glared at each other. I knew the exact moment I had won the stare-down. He blinked and exhaled angrily. "I'll take it. For now."

I was going to argue the point further, but decided against it. "Since Vinnie will be with me, there is no more need for any listening devices. You will remove them from my apartment. All of them."

"Agreed. Anything else?"

"Yes. If you placed those devices, does that mean that you know how to find others? Ones that aren't yours?"

"I've already checked your apartment for other bugs," Vinnie said past a mouthful of toast.

"We did that right after we determined that you would be okay," Colin explained. "The way those guys disappeared made me think that they were professionals, so we searched your apartment."

"Did you find anything?"

"No."

"Are you sure?" The thought had come to me in the shower and it really disturbed me that people meaning me harm could be listening in on my life. Colin listening in on my life was an unacceptable invasion of my privacy, but somehow I didn't mind it as much. What had my life come to that I was actually asking about surveillance devices in my apartment?

"As sure as death and taxes."

I stared at Vinnie.

"I meant that I'm one hundred percent sure."

"Thank you." Maybe I should buy a slang dictionary. But I didn't think it would be a sufficient aid, not with Vinnie's language. We continued eating in silence for a few minutes. "Could you now please tell me why you didn't phone an ambulance? How were you able to ascertain that I was going to be okay?"

Neither man had the decency to look guilty. Colin spoke. "I

overheard the men talk when they were leaving. They seemed to have an argument about the injection they had given you. They were arguing about your weight and that the dosage might have been too much. That is when the Spaniard said that Midazolam was not lethal in that dosage. You might just sleep an extra two hours. They were, however, hoping that it would affect your memory. I know about the drug and knew that they had no reason to be lying, so you were going to be okay. How's your memory?"

I narrowed my eyes and focussed on my recollection of the previous night's events. "It seems to be fine. I remember everything, I just feel groggy. What is Midazolam?"

"It's a fast-acting drug, potent in its sedation. It's quite common, but should have worked out of your system much sooner than it has. It could be the muscle-relaxing qualities that made you sleep so soundly."

It had been an extremely restful sleep, despite the slight headache. I didn't want to know how Colin came to know so much about Midazolam.

We were not done with the previous topic though. "What was the other reason?"

"For not phoning an ambulance? Surely you can guess. If the emergency services were in your apartment and had seen the way it looked, the police would've gotten involved."

"And how were you and Vinnie going to explain your presence here? Right?"

"Right." There was a long silence while it seemed they were waiting for me to respond.

"Well, you made a very logical decision." I couldn't fault them for those reasons.

"Tell us what happened," Colin said.

"How much detail do you want?" I often bored people with the detail in my observations. Knowing how much was expected, I could censor myself.

"Everything," Vinnie said before he put an impossibly heaped fork of scrambled eggs in his mouth.

I told them in the finest detail everything from my suspicions that Colin was making a mess to opening the door and later being shoved by the German. "He was the leader of the group. They were deferring to him the whole time. The two Russians had very aggressive body language, even more so than the other two."

"Wait," Vinnie interrupted. "How do you know all these things? You can tell that the German was the leader by his body language?"

"No, by the way the others were positioning their bodies and waiting on him for their cues."

"But how do you know all this?"

"I read people."

"What does that mean?" Vinnie leaned forward.

"It means that our faces, our bodies, give away all our secrets. I know what every muscle movement in your body is saying. These are limbic responses." I saw the blank look in Vinnie's eyes. "It is the most basic part of our brains, and it controls the most basic of our responses."

Without any indication what I was about to do, I picked up the basket with baguette slices and threw it at Vinnie. His reaction was as expected. First, his eyebrows lifted and his eyes enlarged with shock a millisecond before he reached out and caught the basket. One slice hopped out of the basket and rolled away from the table. For the purpose of this illustration, I didn't mind the breadcrumbs or the bread on the floor. I was going to clean my entire apartment tonight in any case.

"Hey! What was that for?"

"To show you a limbic response. We have no control over these responses. Even someone like me with expert knowledge can't control it. Sure, there are certain responses that I can attempt to control, but if you were to throw that basket at me without me reading any cues of what was about to happen, I would most likely have done the same. No, actually I think I might have ducked."

"You're an expert in this?"

"I'm rated as the third most proficient in this field." I noticed the surprise in his eyes. "Third in the world."

"I told you she was smart." The pride in Colin's voice didn't make sense to me. Why would he be proud of me? I was nobody to him.

"So you can read me? And Colin?" Vinnie's whole demeanour screamed of his unease and he shifted in his seat. I smiled at his attempt to reach a neutral position. His stiff arms placed on the table only served to confirm his discomfort.

"Yes, but let's get back to the topic." I didn't want all that focus on me. I told them the rest. "I read these men and learned quite a lot. Like I said, the German was the leader. The shorter Russian was a very aggressive man and the taller one didn't speak much. The Spaniard was the one who injected me."

"Bastard." Vinnie spat the word out.

"Their accents and their teamwork made me wonder who they could be working for."

"You said that two of them wore the exact same outfit?" Colin asked.

"Yes. I'm convinced it was a uniform of some kind. The other two had similar outfits, but not like the uniforms. The two with the uniforms had covered up the insignias on their sleeves with duct tape. When I was fighting with them, I managed to pull the tape from one of their sleeves. I got a good look at it." Then, as if to myself, I said, "I will have to search on the internet for that logo. I have never seen anything like it before."

"Could these idiots have been from Eurocorps?" Vinnie had eaten all his food and was looking around for more. He turned, shrugged at the baguette slice on the floor, picked it up and placed it on his plate after half-heartedly blowing at it. How uncivilised.

"I doubt it. Russia isn't part of Eurocorps, so how could they be on the same team? Only the Spaniard and the German could be in Eurocorps. Hey." Colin sat up with a sudden realisation. "Maybe their logo is one of Eurocorps' units."

"That is very possible, but I don't know the units. I'll have to ask Manny about this. There is also the question of why they were here." I only managed half the portion of scrambled eggs on my plate and pushed it away. I reached for my coffee mug. "They said that they were looking for my computer, but I can't believe that it was only that. Why would they tear up my entire apartment for a computer? What do they think is on it?"

"It's an intimidation technique." Vinnie sounded completely convinced about this. He looked longingly at my half-empty plate. "May I finish this?"

I felt unsure about this level of familiarity. Nobody had ever eaten off my plate. "Um. Sure."

His eyes lit up and he pulled the plate closer. "Thanks, Jen-girl."

"Why do you say it was an intimidation technique?" I asked him.

"I…" He coughed and tried again for neutral body language. "It has been done many times and is apparently very successful."

"You've used it before."

It looked like Vinnie was going to have some sort of facial seizure. I took pity on him. "Vinnie, I'm exceptionally good at reading people. There isn't much that you can hide from me. If you prefer, I will keep all my observations to myself."

Colin was quiet throughout this and I suddenly wondered why he never appeared uncomfortable with my intellect or observations. It was quiet around the table while Vinnie took a long sip of coffee, obviously weighing his options.

"This is very strange for me," he admitted.

"Welcome to the last week of my life. I have a thief as a partner and a giant as a bodyguard." I sounded as despondent as I felt. Why they thought it funny, I didn't know, but both men chuckled.

"I suppose that makes us even then." Vinnie smiled warmly at me. "I think this is going to be a lot of fun, Jen-girl. I'll keep you safe and you can teach me a few things about reading people."

"Does this mean that I can speak freely?"

Vinnie nodded, but Colin was the one who answered. "It's settled then. Jenny, have you given any thought about how these men knew about you? Did they let on that they knew about me?"

"I thought about this and honestly have no idea how they knew about my involvement. Only a handful of people know that I'm working on this case. But then again, you tracked me down, so it couldn't have been so difficult." I really didn't like that idea. As much as I loved the age of technology and information at one's fingertips, it gave the bad guys too much to work with.

"Getting your address is easy enough. What concerns me is that they were asking about your computer. What do they think is on there?"

"I don't know. I don't like to speculate."

"I would like to speculate," Vinnie said and promptly continued. "I think that one of these crooks in the EDA or Eurocorps discovered that there was an investigation going on and wanted to find out what you've discovered so far."

"The men who were here last night are most definitely not Manny's insiders," I declared. "With everything that we have uncovered so far, I have to agree with Manny that his insiders are in top positions. These guys were soldiers, not top management, not officers."

"Which only means that they were sent here by the insiders to find out what you know."

"Oh, I don't know." I really didn't feel comfortable with this kind of wild speculation. I would rather stay with facts, observations and everything that I had so carefully memorised last night. A memory surfaced. "Oh my God! I totally forgot about this."

"About what?" Colin sat up straighter and moved a bit closer to me.

"Last night while I was trying to remember the code to my safe, I overheard the Russians arguing. They said something that stuck with me. And later, just before the guys left, they repeated the same thing. They said someone was not going to be pleased with the lack of success they had had in my apartment. The name they used for this someone sounded like Peerosh."

"Like what?" Vinnie's whole face crinkled in concentration.

"Peerosh," I repeated. "It stuck with me because I could hear the fear in their voices when they spoke about this man."

"You're sure it was a man?" Colin asked. The air was now tense around the table.

"Yes. The one Russian told the other that Peerosh was going to have one of his screaming fits when they told him what took place here. And when they left, I heard the Spaniard say that Peerosh would want an immediate report and asked the German what they were going to tell him. Both times they used masculine personal pronouns."

"Was that all they said?"

I closed my eyes to recall those terrifying moments. My eyes shot open. "The German was angry at the two who were speaking Russian. He said that he would be the one to deal with Peerosh. Then the Spaniard said they should all just relax. Peerosh had big plans for the flower house."

"The flower house?" Vinnie asked. "That's just weird. I wonder what kind of plans they were talking about."

"None of it made sense to me, but I am very certain of what I heard."

"Peerosh?" Colin whispered to himself. He leaned back in his chair and closed his eyes. He repeated the word a few times before he sat up and looked at Vinnie. "You remember when we were in Budapest a few years ago?"

"That time when we—"

"Yes, that time," Colin interrupted him. "You loved the red pepper paste."

"*Piros magyar etterem.*" Vinnie turned to me with a dreamy expression. "Oh, Jen-girl. It's the most wonderful thing to cook with. Traditionally the Hungarians put it in soups or use it in preparing meat dishes. They even use it as a condiment. You have to try it."

Colin waved Vinnie's enthusiastic recommendations away. "*Piros* is the Hungarian word for red, written differently, but pronounced peerosh. Jenny, remember I told you about my friend being killed in Budapest in 2006? Maybe there is a connection. Maybe the insider's nickname is Piros."

"Those are a lot of maybes." I didn't like maybes.

"Check the EDA database for that word." He spelled it for me. "Maybe something will come of it."

"Another maybe." A niggling feeling kept pulling at my subconscious. The moment Vinnie had started with his explanation something had registered. "Oh my! Red is Piros."

"Yes?" Colin drew out the word, asking for elaboration.

"Red. Piros. Red." How could they not see it? I wished I had my computers, especially my notepad. "Colin, do you remember the top page of my notepad?"

He frowned. "That's the page with the Russian murderer's rantings."

"Yes. Nikolay Chulkov shouted that the red will end all twenty-seven daffodils. No one will escape the red." I was so excited, my face flushed. "What if he wasn't saying 'the red', but Red. As in the name Red. Piros. This guy was Russian. There are no definite or indefinite articles in Russian. So when he translated it to French, he might have used articles when he shouldn't have."

"But who would be named Red?" Vinnie asked.

"Piros," I corrected. "These thugs were speaking English, but they used a Hungarian word."

"If that's the correct word," Colin interjected.

His logic stole some of my excitement. "True. But, if that's the case, then we have a strong connection between the murder of Danielle, the other artists, the thugs who broke into my place and this Piros."

"How are you going to verify it?" Colin asked.

"I don't know yet." I glanced at my watch and winced. "I have to go. It's already past eight and I have a lot of work to do today."

"What are you going to look into today?" Colin asked.

"Yesterday I couldn't check the cruise ships properly, so I'll do that today. And of course I'll have a look at this Piros person."

Vinnie got up and started clearing the table. "Let me just get this and we can go."

"Oh. Yes, of course." How could I have forgotten that I now had a driver and personal bodyguard?

"Jenny, please be careful."

I turned to Colin to dismiss his worries, but stopped myself on the inhale. Concern was etched on his face. I didn't know how to feel about this, nor was I equipped to deal with such sincere concern. When I spoke my voice sounded strained. "I will. You too."

Chapter TWELVE

This case was the most exciting thing that I had ever faced. Apart from my innate dislike for change, the intellectual challenge was fast proving to outweigh all my fears.

I had been in my viewing room for the last three hours looking into cargo and cruise ships. My expanded search had rendered thirteen cargo ships and seven cruise ships owned by a shipping company with only one ship in its fleet. This pattern was outrageously suspicious. So engrossed was I in following the latest connection that I didn't even hear Phillip enter the room until he spoke.

"Where's your car?"

I started and turned to him, thinking of a lie. I couldn't come up with anything but the truth. "I didn't come in my car today."

"Then how did you get here?" I should've expected Phillip to be suspicious of a change in my routine. He leaned in closer. I knew the exact moment that he noticed my injuries. "Good God! Genevieve, what happened?"

I closed my eyes. Typical blocking behaviour when someone did not want to face something unpleasant or was trying to create a distance from something. I definitely did not want to discuss this with Phillip.

"Genevieve." He sounded calmer, but also angrier. "Look at me."

I realised that I was sitting, like a cowardly child, with my eyes closed. I slowly opened one eye. My uninjured eye. Phillip was leaning in close enough for me to feel the puffs of his breathing on my face. I opened my other eye. The depth of the concern he exhibited was disconcerting. I steeled myself against it and leaned away from him. "I'm okay. I have a bad headache, but I'm okay."

"Did that criminal do this to you?" His eyes were locked on the cut above my eyebrow. We had decided this morning that the cut didn't need professional attention and I had put two butterfly plasters on it to pull the skin together.

"Colin?" My voice was two pitches higher. What a ridiculous accusation. Colin might have been many things, but violent he was not. "He would never do this. As a matter of fact, he's the one who stopped it."

Phillip dragged a chair closer and sat down heavily opposite me. "Genevieve, you can't continue like this. I won't allow it."

"I'm on this case because you, as my boss, ordered me to do it."

"I know." He dragged his hand over his face and took a deep breath. "Tell me what happened."

"I would prefer not to."

"As your boss"—he looked me straight in the eye—"and as your friend I'd prefer that you do."

"I'm not going to tell you everything, not yet."

His gaze focussed on my lifted chin. He called it my obstinate look. "Tell me what you can."

I sighed with relief. I didn't know if I wanted Phillip to know of Vinnie's involvement. How long I could keep this from the man I always told everything was yet to be determined. So I told him about the previous evening, carefully censoring out Vinnie's involvement.

"And Colin found you drugged in your apartment and didn't phone an ambulance?" He was outraged.

My head was throbbing and I didn't have the energy to placate him.

"It wasn't necessary and I don't want to fight about this."

"Oh, Genevieve." Phillip sounded tired. "You are going to be the death of me yet."

"I don't plan to kill you, Phillip." My logical comment made him laugh. I wasn't trying to be funny.

"Your co-operation in this case and with Colin might." He waved the topic away with a weak gesture. "Don't even think about convincing me otherwise. We are telling Manny about the attack."

"I agree. I would also like to ask him about the insignia that I saw on the one man's sleeve."

"Is this all you can tell me?"

"The most important parts, yes."

"How did Colin know something was wrong?"

"I would rather not discuss anything else, Phillip." Knowing Phillip, he might just phone the police, the military and Interpol if he knew that Colin had placed a listening device in my apartment. Fortunately, Phillip accepted my answer. Had he pushed, I would've told him. I was glad he didn't push.

"I will phone Manny and find out when we can meet. He is out of town today, so hopefully it will be tomorrow." He sat back in his chair. "Where did you disappear to yesterday?"

"Oh, yes." So much had happened since my rude exit from Phillip's office, I had almost forgotten. I told him everything about Danielle, her boyfriend and the cruise they had met on. I put the presentation that I had prepared for yesterday's meeting on the screens. Most of it he already knew.

"Did you find anything on the ship manifests that Manny sent you?"

"Yes. Three of the recovered artworks were on cargo ships owned by companies that only own one ship."

"That is more than just a coincidence."

"There is no such thing as coincidence." I told him the rest of what I had discovered about the ships. "Now I'm looking into the cruise ship connection. I started to cross-check all my lists with the cruise ships. Maybe there is a connection with the dead artists, the private investigators, the miraculously rediscovered artworks and the other shipping companies. I will let you know when I find any more connections."

"Your report so far will most definitely please Manny. This is much more than I expected. If you find a connection with the cruise ships… well, that would just add another complication to an already complicated case."

I agreed with him. This was a case with so many different elements it made me think of a pendulum clock. All these separate gears, springs and weights were somehow connected. Then there was the power source, either a weight on a cord that turned the pulley or a mainspring. Without that power source, none of the parts would be of any use. They wouldn't move, wouldn't make the clock work. What, or who, the power source was in this case, I had no idea. I also didn't know whether it was just one source. This bothered me greatly.

I had to have been quiet for a long time, because Phillip looked concerned and asked, "What?"

"I'm missing something, Phillip. A vital part. The part that moves, that manipulates all the others."

"Explain?"

I gave him my pendulum clock analogy and felt very proud of using it. "All these elements are separate. There must be a central element that connects all these artists, artworks, ships and so forth. The power source that makes it all connect and work. This is eluding me."

"And frustrating you." Phillip knew me well.

"Greatly. That is why I keep digging to find more connections. Somewhere these connections will have to cross paths and that will lead me to the person holding this all together."

"The person controlling all this."

"Assuming it is one person," I said. We were quiet again for a short while, lost in our own thoughts. I broke the silence, following the direction my thoughts were going in. "Is there something happening between Russia and the EDA or Eurocorps at the moment that we know about?"

Phillip took his time to think about this. "Manny is the best person to ask, but I would say that the most obvious contention between Europe and Russia in the last decade or so has been natural gas. There are also the ongoing disagreements about the construction of the highways being built. The North-South and East-West highways."

"Ah, yes. The eternal struggle for power. If humans aren't fighting for power over territory, it is for resources, accessibility or some other reason. But in the end it all leads to a desire for power." As much as we like to think we have evolved, we haven't. These struggles are as old as time. A question was burning in me. "I know that you trust Manny, but I just need to know. Are you very sure that he didn't by accident tell someone about my involvement?"

"One hundred percent." His answer came without any doubt. "It must be from someone else who has access. That is why we need to tell Manny about this attack."

"I'm not arguing about this. I also think that he needs to know that the people he thinks he can trust might not be trustworthy."

"What has the world come to?"

"The world has always been like this. It's human nature."

"That is a very bleak look on life, Genevieve."

"I don't think it is. It's just realistic. There has always been war. Whether the reasons were economic, religious, territorial or racial, it's been there. And will be there. The same way with people's desire for power. It has always led and will always lead to espionage, betrayal and other forms of treason. Usually, it is the people who are at the bottom level of the pyramid who are the most sincere, the kindest and the closest to goodness we can find."

"Can't argue with you there." He sighed. "You're going to have to apologise to Manny."

"Why?" Immediately I was on defence. I had done nothing wrong. Or had I?

"For walking out on the meeting yesterday."

"Oh yes, that."

"He was very unhappy."

"More than usual?" My question elicited a bark of laughter from Phillip.

"Much more. As a matter of fact, he was furious. He felt that you were dismissing him and this case as something of lesser interest. I didn't tell him about Colin, but he knows that I'm hiding something. Don't underestimate Manny's insight and intellect, Genevieve. He looks disorganised and scatter-brained, but he has a sharper mind than most people I know."

"I knew that the first time we met."

Phillip looked very serious. "You know that at some point you will have to tell Manny about Colin."

"I know."

"Why don't you want to?" he asked gently.

"I don't want Manny to take him away from me."

"This is the second time you've said this. Do you realise that you sound like a little girl who found a puppy and wants to keep it?"

"I would prefer a comparison to a scientist who discovered a new species of butterfly." Phillip was right. Colin was not a puppy or a butterfly that I could keep. My throat was dry and my voice scratchy. "It's just that he makes me feel."

"Feel what?" Phillip asked carefully.

"Much more than ever before." I looked down at my hands and admitted softly, "I've not once flinched when he touched me."

"He touches you?"

"Twice he got my attention by touching my arm." It took me a moment to realise why Phillip looked relieved. I was indignant. "You think I'm a virgin? I'll have you know that when I put my mind to it, I find a man's touch quite pleasurable."

"Stop right there. Please." This was the first time in six years that I had managed to make Phillip uncomfortable.

"Too much information? I'm sorry. My comfort around Colin is quite disconcerting for me. I suppose it's made me defensive." I had so many new emotions to analyse.

"Why do you feel so comfortable with him?"

"I trust him." My statement came out as a whisper. Phillip drew in a sharp breath, but I stopped him with a lifted hand. "I know. It even surprised me. But it is the way it is. I don't want to fight with you about Colin. As a matter of fact, I would really appreciate your support."

"Oh, Genevieve, you've always had my support."

"And your worry." I got a wry smile from him.

"And my trust. I know that you would never in a million years associate with someone you didn't feel safe with. I have always trusted your judgement and will do so in this case as well. But only as far as Colin's character goes. I need you to trust me as well."

"I do."

"Then trust me to handle Manny. Trust me to tell him that you went against his and my wishes and got outside help involved. I will convince him that you would never do anything to jeopardise the case. That you acted in the interest of solving this as quickly, accurately and cleanly as possible."

"You think you could convince him of all that?" Disbelief weighed heavily on my voice. "I read him, Phillip, and I saw that he is extremely cynical."

"We've been friends for longer than you've been alive. I'll bring him around."

Phillip was a top-class negotiator and could make people see his point in an effortless few sentences. Yet it took a conscious effort from me to nod my head in agreement. Immediately Phillip's demeanour lifted and he awarded me a relaxed smile.

"Fantastic. If you could email me this report"—he pointed to the monitors where the report was still on display—"I will forward it to Manny. He can read through it and I'll try to set up a meeting for tomorrow."

I was not looking forward to meeting with Manny. Even though he was an interesting subject to read, I found the thought of being the focus of his displeasure hugely unappetising.

The last few minutes with Phillip brought to my mind once again why I so much enjoyed his presence. Never had he discounted my opinions and he had always been open to discussing, debating, negotiating and settling issues with me. It was that trust in me that helped me make an instant decision. "I have a bodyguard."

"You have a what?" It must have been his cultured upbringing that prevented him from shouting at me.

"A bodyguard and driver, to be precise. He's a friend of Colin's and will keep me safe."

"And you're okay with this?"

"Well, not really. I have someone with me all the time and I'm not used to it. It does, however, make me feel safer. It's also quite amazing how much extra thinking time I have now that I don't have to drive."

"This bodyguard doesn't speak to you?"

"He does, but I just ignore him most of the time."

Phillip snorted inelegantly, but recovered quickly. "When did this happen?"

"Colin organised it last night after the attack. We had a huge argument about it at first."

"I'm sure you did." I didn't know why Phillip was smiling.

"He did give me a very valid argument and I conceded. Even though I still don't particularly like the idea."

"Who is this bodyguard?"

"A friend of Colin's." Phillip did not look happy with my hedging. "Before you get angry with me, I read him and made very sure about him before I agreed to it. I'm as sure as I can be that he can be trusted."

My boss and friend did not look convinced. "If he's Colin's friend, it might be a good assumption that he's also a criminal."

"He can be trusted, Phillip. Colin has a vested interest in this case and wouldn't have brought someone who cannot be relied upon." I was defending Colin and Vinnie now? What had my uncomplicated life come to?

"So I'm not the only one concerned for your safety?"

"Oh no. Colin was quite vocal. I didn't have much choice in it." As I talked, I realised that Phillip's question was sarcastic and I frowned at him. "Are you being nasty to me?"

He sighed. "No, I'm just worried. I've regretted agreeing to help Manny almost from the first day. This was only supposed to be a paper investigation, not anything closely resembling what it has turned into."

"Let's not waste time on regrets. It's unproductive." I was getting bored with this thread of the conversation. "I still have a lot of the shipping manifests to go through. The sooner I get back to it, the quicker I might find some connections that will help us finish this."

Phillip stood with a smile. "That is me being dismissed. I will handle Manny. You just make sure that you have that criminal and your bodyguard under control."

"What about Manny's friend at Eurocorps? Have you met him?"

"Not yet. I would like to meet him." He straightened his already erect posture even more. "I would also like for you to meet him."

"To read him."

"Yes. I trust Manny to know whether someone is clean, but I would like to make sure."

"Maybe he could join us tomorrow when we meet with Manny?"

Phillip smiled. "For someone so adept at reading facial expressions, you're not very good at hiding them. Your distaste at the thought of this meeting is written in capital letters on your face."

I didn't have a response except to sigh.

"I'll speak to Manny and see if Leon can join us tomorrow. You have to be at that meeting, Genevieve. Don't run out again."

I shook my head, which brought on a sharp pain, reminding me that I had recently been attacked. "I'll be there. I want to speak to Manny and also meet his friend."

"You really shouldn't be here." Concern narrowed his eyes. "Go home, Genevieve. Rest."

"I can't. There is too much to do."

"At least work from home. Take the computers. And tell Colin to keep an eye on you so that you won't overwork yourself." His eyes widened with a sudden memory. "Your cell phone. I want your number."

"I never use the phone, Phillip." At least not until Colin had decided it was acceptable to steal into my life.

"I'm not going to budge on this. I want your number."

With not a small amount of resentment I wrote down my number on a post-it note and handed it to Phillip.

"Go home. If I come back in ten minutes, I want to see this room empty." His face and tone of voice brooked no argument. In all honesty, I didn't want to argue.

"Okay. I'll go home. Please email me or phone my landline if you find anything new. I really don't want to use my cell phone."

Phillip just shook his head and moved to the door. "I'll let you know what time our meeting is with Manny and Leon tomorrow. Take it easy, Genevieve."

I watched him leave my viewing room and turned to the monitors. His visit had interrupted my momentum. The ache around my eye and Phillip's order made it easier for me to get ready to work from home. Maybe it wasn't such a bad idea. I saved and closed the documents I had been working on, packed my work computer and the EDA computer and walked to the elevators.

Vinnie would be waiting for me in the car in front of the building. When he had dropped me off, he had promised not to move from that spot and I knew that he was not going to break his word. I reached the front door and on a bracing inhale opened it. Vinnie was leaning against my car, tapping away on his smartphone. As if sensing me, he looked up and his whole face lit up with a smile.

"Howdy, Jen-girl." He pushed away from the car. "What's up? We're going home?"

"I'm going to work from home." I moved around him to the passenger door, scared that he might hug me. His familiarity and openness was disconcerting.

"Okey-dokey." He folded his gigantic body into my little city car and turned the ignition. "Tomorrow we're taking my car. This little toy is far too uncomfortable for me to spend a day in."

I made a noncommittal sound and settled back into the seat. While Vinnie chattered away about the people he noticed on the street in front of the office building, I allowed my mind to wander. I loved this time of the year in Europe. The beginning of the summer holidays saw the end of serious traffic congestion, shops crowded with bargain-hunting students and parks filled with them carousing. The city would start to empty now as people headed off to seaside resorts. This left me free to go for long runs through the many beautiful parks in Strasbourg without feeling as if I was wading through throngs of people.

I continued to ignore Vinnie's monologue. We were driving on one of my favourite medieval streets, trees separating the street from the river on the left, historic buildings on the right with happy flowerboxes adorning petite balconies. We crossed the bridge leading to my apartment and I sighed with contentment. The view of the riverside, which was especially spectacular all lit up at night, pleased my sense of the aesthetic.

My street was a few intersections ahead and my mind floated back to the case. I didn't plan on wasting time at home. As soon as I got there I wanted to get back into looking for patterns and connections with the cruise ships. I had already noticed two

Chapter THIRTEEN

"Dinner will be ready in twenty minutes." Vinnie's voice interrupted my concentration and I glared at him. He lifted his hands defensively. "Just saying. You've been at those computers for the last four hours and barely moved. It's time you took a break."

"Go away, Vinnie." It was the eleventh time I had shooed him away in the last four hours. He had been pestering me to take breaks, drink tea, lie down or stretch my muscles since I opened the computers on the dining room table. He was the worst nagging bodyguard anyone had ever had the fortune to have.

He just gave me a warm smile and walked back to the kitchen. Something mouth-watering was cooking on the stove. It smelled better than any Italian restaurant I had ever been to. He might just live up to his reputation.

I was surprised how non-intrusive I was finding his presence. Though he had the body of a wrestler, he moved with surprising grace. So quietly that I often lost track of where he was in my apartment.

While I was engrossed in my research, he had cleaned up all the broken bits and pieces that had escaped his first clean-up and tried to organise my space. I appreciated his efforts, but was hard pushed not to jump up every time he put something down at a wrong angle. Eventually we had agreed that he would just clean up and I would position everything later. Now I wanted to focus on finding more information, because I had reached a dead end.

This was beyond frustrating. I was going to have to ask for

Colin's help. Again. I had found this pattern and I needed another set of eyes and, to my greatest disgust, expected Colin to take me past my own law-abiding limitations.

"Hello, Jenny." Colin's deep voice startled me out of my thoughts.

"How did you get in?"

His lifted left eyebrow was the only answer I got.

"I have a front door."

"It's not as much fun." There was a smile in his voice and Vinnie chuckled in the kitchen. I closed my eyes and took a calming breath. I was not going to let these two men anger me. Colin pulled a chair closer and sat down. As usual he was close enough for me to feel his body heat, but not too close to crowd me. "What's new?"

"Tell me about art auctions at sea." I walked closer and sat down next to him, facing my computers.

He looked at me for a few seconds before he answered. "What makes you think I know about art auctions at sea?"

"The question you just asked me." Really. Did people not realise how much they revealed when they avoided questions? "And the probability that you have run across this in your past criminal activities."

"Why don't you just call a spade a spade?"

I was well acquainted with this particular expression. "Are you denying that you have a past in crime?"

"She's got you there, dude."

Vinnie appeared next to me with arms full of crockery. "Where are we going to eat?"

"I'll move the computers to the other side of the table and you can set up on this side." My computers were arranged in the centre of my long dining room table and were taking up too much space.

"If you could do that now, please. The food is almost done."

"Nice duds, Vin." Colin stood up and gave me room to rearrange my workspace.

"Thanks, dude." Vinnie looked down at the floral apron that he had dug out of a linen cupboard. I vaguely remembered receiving it as a holiday gift from someone. Since I seldom cooked anything that could splatter, I had placed it in the linen cupboard and promptly forgotten about it. The angry flowers on the hard material made me thankful that I had never fully opened that gift. Somehow Vinnie's size made the flowers look less intimidating.

It took less than five minutes to set the table and be seated with steaming plates of delicious-looking fettuccini. The first few mouthfuls were followed by compliments from Colin and me and beaming smiles from Vinnie. It didn't take long for Colin to get back on topic. "Art auctions at sea are a tricky business. You see, it is a no man's land. The admiralty law is in power, but there are a lot of gray areas. No specific country's laws apply while you are at sea. Mostly, if a forged artwork is sold at sea, or someone is conned at sea, the individual does not have much power. In the last five years there have been many scandals involving art auctions at sea. But still they are mostly swept under the rug. Um, kept quiet."

"So if a stolen artefact is sold at an art auction at sea, we might never know about it?"

"Exactly."

"How big is the market for such auctions?"

"Oh, Jen-girl." Vinnie dabbed daintily at his mouth with a white napkin. "Art sold on the black market is in humungous demand. Colin here is the expert, but even a redneck like me knows about this."

"Your neck isn't red. Are you referring to the subculture in America of unskilled, uneducated, inbred communities? You can't possibly come from such a community, Vinnie. You exhibit none of the typical traits. I know. I read up on that socioeconomic group once."

There was a stunned silence around the table. Vinnie glanced at Colin before both of them burst out laughing. I looked at them in confusion.

"My bad, Jen-girl." Vinnie was still chuckling. "I mean, my mistake. What I meant was that someone as unsophisticated as I knows about the high demand for stolen art."

"Oh. Okay."

"Jenny." Colin sobered, but the lines around his eyes were still relaxed. "We didn't laugh at you. Your black-and-white rationality is just so refreshing that it made us laugh. Until I met you, I didn't realise just how many things we say that mean something completely different."

"Is that why people laugh at things I say?"

"Possibly." Colin wanted to say something else, but Vinnie was faster.

"Jen-girl, I would never laugh at you for any other reason. You are the most interesting, intelligent, wonderful woman I've ever met. Apart from my mother, of course."

At that moment I realised that they were feeling guilty for laughing at something I had said. Usually people laughed from shock at something I said and then they would turn away in discomfort. These two men were trying to apologise and make me feel more comfortable. I didn't know how I felt about it, so I moved back to safer territory.

"I found thirty-three ships singularly owned," I said. "Twenty-three cargo ships and ten cruise ships. All of these ships are smaller in size. The cruise ships interested me more, so I researched them on the internet. They cater mostly to the affluent. Their cruises offer excessive luxury and are shockingly priced."

"There certainly are enough billionaires in Russia to afford these cruises," Vinnie groused.

"But that isn't the best part." I was restless with excitement.

"All of these companies are owned by the same two entities."

"No way." Vinnie leaned back in his chair.

"Who?" Colin asked.

"Kozlevich ZAO owns a ninety-nine percent share of all thirty-three companies. The other one percent belongs to a private holder."

"That's strange. Did you find out who this private holder is?"

"Unfortunately not." It had been a frustrating and fruitless search. "I also don't know who owns Kozlevich ZAO."

"What does the ZAO stand for?" Colin asked.

"It is a Russian closed joint-stock company. The shares in Kozlevich are held by a limited number of shareholders." My brow contracted in a scowl. "I found limited information about the cruise ships Kozlevich owns. Of the ten cruise ships, all of them advertised their art auctions as a coveted activity. These cruise ships are noticeably similar in size, design, routes, offers and marketing."

"Quite the researcher, aintcha?" Vinnie looked at me with something akin to awe.

"Were any specific paintings listed?" Colin asked.

"I was just going to start looking into it."

"This is one of the easiest ways of moving black-market art. Have you thought of what happens to the money gained from the auctions? Who holds the coffers?"

"Not yet," I admitted reluctantly.

Vinnie pushed his chair back. "Would you like anything else to eat or can I clear the table?"

I looked down with surprise at my empty plate and realised that I had just emptied a very large serving of fettuccini. "Vinnie, this was delicious. Thank you so much."

"My pleasure." He took my plate and stacked Colin's on it. "You two can bicker about the case on full stomachs now. I will clean up and find something to do while you two save the art world."

"Thanks, Vin," Colin said. "You make a very pretty housewife. Do you want to darn my socks?"

"Fuck off, dude." Strangely, there was no malice when Vinnie growled at Colin before stomping into the kitchen. I had never witnessed this kind of interplay between males. It had been intensively discussed during my studies and I even knew a few euphemisms related to male bonding rituals. I just didn't know how to use them appropriately in conversation and I didn't want to be laughed at again. So once again, I returned to a safe topic.

"Shall we check for more connections?" I was already moving to my computers and wasn't surprised to find Colin sitting down next to me moments later.

"Let's make that list of artworks sold at these auctions." Colin's suggestion was sensible and I returned to all the websites I had been to. When I reached for a pen to write down the art pieces, Colin was ready with my personal laptop. I took a shaky breath before I started naming first the paintings and then the sculptures I had found. Having another person work on my laptop was a first for me.

After an hour, I glanced at his progress and was satisfied that he had listed everything neatly. It took us another two hours before we were satisfied that we had exhausted all possible avenues of finding artworks that had been on offer or had been sold at these auctions. We had gone through promotional brochures, forums, shipping manifests and a few art collector websites that Colin directed me to.

Five hundred and thirty-nine works of art were listed. I was impressed. Any reputable auction house would be delighted to auction off so many valuable pieces. Very few of the artworks were from unknown artists. I stared at the computers, seeing nothing. There was a connection calling to me, but I just couldn't catch it. I inhaled deeply and reached for a Mozart sonata in my mind. It only took seven bars of mentally written music. "Oh my!"

I ignored Colin's impatient questions next to me, grabbed my personal laptop from him and started hitting the keys. Once I set the search parameters, I leaned back in my chair and waited. Colin was still making unhappy noises next to me, but I couldn't let him distract me now. I knew something was going to click in my brain. It didn't take long.

"Look at this!" I leaned closer to the computer screens and suddenly realised that Colin was sitting so close to me that our shoulders were touching. I subtly moved a bit to my right to make more space for him to look at the computer monitors.

"What am I looking at, Jenny?"

"This." I pointed at the screen with my index finger. "Another connection."

"Woman, if you don't tell me right now what I'm looking at, I'm going to pour honey all over the inside of your fridge."

I swung towards him in horror. "You would never do something so malicious to me."

"Refuse to tell me what you've found and you'll see just how malicious I can get."

I started speaking very quickly. "Most of what I read about the art auctions at sea seemed to be very innocent. A few of the forums made me think that the people who attended had no idea that the art sold there might be illegal."

"Are we sure that all the artworks were illegal?"

"Of course not. I've just taken the five hundred and thirty-nine artworks from these auctions that we have listed and searched for connections with the list of miraculously recovered artworks." My voice was rising with excitement and I pointed at the screen again. "Look. Of the forty-seven miraculously recovered artworks, I have found twenty-nine that were sold at these auctions. Twenty-nine, Colin. Twenty-nine!"

Colin smiled. "We have more lines that we can draw between the boxes."

I pulled my notepad closer. "First we have to draw another box for the art auctions. This connects to the recovered artworks, which by default connects to the non-existent private investigators. It also connects to the cruise ships, which then connects to Danielle, her boyfriend and Nikolay Chulkov."

Vinnie's deep voice started singing from the sitting area. I looked over and saw him lounging in one of my sofas, reading a newspaper. He was singing some song about the hip bone connected to the thigh bone and I frowned at him in irritation. Colin's chuckle next to me indicated that Vinnie might be making an attempt at humour, so I refrained from asking him to desist from his off-key singing.

I looked at my computer screen. A colourful promotional brochure advertised an art auction on a once-in-a-lifetime cruise. People were so gullible. There were not many products in life that could not be bought again. I changed the window to look at another brochure. More of the same promises and breathtaking photos. I changed the window again.

Colin's body stiffened next to me so suddenly that I anticipated an attack. "What's wrong?"

"Go back to the…" He grunted in frustration. "Oh, just let me do it."

I watched bemused and a bit annoyed as he moved into my personal space and started tapping away on the two computers. I leaned away to give him more space, or rather to give myself more space.

"There!" Colin stared wide-eyed at my work laptop screen. "I knew it."

I realised how disagreeable it was to be left out of someone's line of thought. "Colin, please tell me."

"I'm willing to bet my freedom that these bastards are using charity organisations to wash their dirty money." Anger put a strain on his voice. How come a thief was getting angry at someone laundering money? My attention was brought back to the screens with him tapping lightly on one. "In these promotional brochures they state that three percent of the money changing hands will be donated to the Foundation for Development of Sustainable Education. What does this mean?"

"What does what mean?"

"Development of Sustainable Education? It seems like one of those silly names chosen to cover a multitude of sins." He shook his head and changed the screen to show another brochure. On this one, he had to zoom in on the bottom left-hand corner to read the fine print. "The same here, although they don't state the percentage."

"How on earth did you notice that small writing?" I was in awe.

"I have a very practiced eye, Jenny." His smile was pure evil. "It's useful in my job."

For the first time in my life I actually snorted. His job? The man did not have a job. Or did he? My thoughts were leading me to niggling suspicions about Colin and his so-called life of crime. The more time I was spending with him, the more convinced I became that he was not the criminal he had led me to believe.

"Jenny, come back to earth." Colin touched my wrist lightly to get my attention. "What are you thinking?"

"That you…" I stopped myself just in time. "I don't want to talk about it."

"Okay." He drew out the word with wariness in his voice and around his eyes. "Shall we see how many more charity connections we can find?"

I readily agreed and we divided the search areas. For the next half an hour we worked in silence, he on my work computer and I on the EDA computer. My eyes were growing wider in astonishment.

"What have you got so far?" he asked.

"I went through all the marketing for these cruises that I could find. At some point each one of the ten cruise ships advertised their three-percent donation to this Foundation.

What did you find?"

"I did an internet search on the Foundation. It has quite an extensive website with loads of programmes listed."

"Where are they based?"

"Patience, Jenny." He smiled. "The charity was founded in Hungary nineteen years ago. At first it was purely a charity focussing on helping the disadvantaged by distributing food and other aid."

"That was just after communism ended."

"Yup. When Hungary joined the European Union in 2004, the Foundation immediately applied for EU funding and has expanded its work into the southern parts of Russia. There seem to be quite a few cross-border programmes with Russia as one of the partners."

"See? Russia is not all bad."

"We'll just have to agree to disagree on this point. More about this foundation." He pointed at the computer screen. At least this time he didn't touch it. I was going to have to clean all my computer monitors tonight. Colin liked to touch everything. "Since it is such an old charity organisation, they have a number of high-profile individuals involved. You can look through all their programmes later, but the handful I've checked seems to be huge and complex. I've noticed that there are quite a few individuals donating large sums to this foundation too."

"We need to check into all the Foundation's finances. I'll get Phillip to ask Manny to do that."

Colin was looking at the gallery of photos from the Foundation's website. There were photos of gala evenings with beautiful people in beautiful clothes, photos of keys to small houses being given to families, streets being renovated and more along that line. Most photos had descriptions of the events being shown, complete with the names of everyone in the pictures. My attention was caught by one of the photos. The muscles in my back tensed.

"Wait, go back."

"Which one?"

"The previous gala photo."

Colin clicked back two photos and looked at me. "Something I should zoom in on?"

"I'm looking at the names of the guests photographed."

The script wasn't big enough to read from where we were sitting. Colin moved in closer and started reading out loud. "Selina Kowalska, supermodel; Leon Hofmann, Deputy Chief of Staff, Eurocorps; Sarah Crichton, Head of the EDA; Tomasz Kubanov, philanthropist; Manfred Millard, Deputy Chief Executive for Strategy, EDA; Janus Kutor, actor."

I gasped at the mention of Leon and Manny's names being read out loud.

"Jenny, they're all here. Manny, the head of the EDA, and this person from Eurocorps. There are simply too many people involved in this thing for it to be a coincidence."

"I don't believe in coincidences," I said absently. My brain was on overdrive. "Leon Hofmann is Manny's Eurocorps connection."

"I beg your pardon?" Colin started to rise from his chair, but sat back down.

I repeated myself, much slower this time.

"Yet you don't think Manny is involved?"

Even though I knew the answer, I still took time to think about it for the umpteenth time. "I'm as sure of him as I am of you."

My answer brought an annoyed frown to Colin's brow. "What does that mean?"

"I read you, Colin. Both you and Vinnie. If I were not convinced that you two intended no harm, I would never have allowed either of you in my life." The rustle of newspaper being moved pulled my eyes to the living area. Vinnie was watching me with stunning intensity. "The same goes for Manny. I don't know this Leon person, but I'm convinced that

Manny is a good man. I might not like him, but I know that his interest in this case is pure."

A look passed between the two men and I was convinced that it had something to do with Manny and Colin. I really wanted to find out what past those two shared. For now, my concern was this photo on my computer screen. "I'm meeting with Manny tomorrow and will ask him about this."

"Forgive me if I don't trust him at all." Vinnie sounded put out.

"Why don't you trust him, Vinnie?"

"Here it says that it was the annual Foundation ball two years ago. Give me a moment," Colin interrupted. He gave Vinnie a warning glance, who responded by picking up the newspaper, pretending interest. Colin turned his attention back to the computer and opened another window to start a Google search. I decided to let the topic drop. For now. Vinnie, Colin and Manny's past could wait.

"From what I can see here, this gala is quite the event every year. It's reported in most of the important newspapers. All the major players in the EU community are invited. It used to be held in Budapest until seven years ago. Since then it's been moved here."

"Where here?" I moved closer to look at the screen.

"Here, as in Strasbourg. The last seven years the annual gala event has taken place in La Maison Russie. The address is in a very old, very rich area. Oh, my." He looked surprised. "Not only do they usually have some popular musician entertain the guests, but they also have auctions. Art auctions."

"No shit." The newspaper lay forgotten on Vinnie's lap. "Doesn't La Maison Russie mean the Russian House?"

"Yup. Interesting, isn't it?" Colin answered.

"Go back to the photo." Something was bothering me. Colin changed screens and waited for further instructions. My mind was racing, trying to get to whatever was nudging my memory. "Read the names again. Only the ones that are not EU-related."

"Selina Kowalska, supermodel; Tomasz Kubanov, philan-thropist; Janus Kutor, actor." Colin zoomed in on the photo. The supermodel was stunning in her beauty, and the actor was a good-looking middle-aged man. Kubanov's face was mostly hidden by the supermodel's hairdo.

"I don't see anything strange." My frustrated sigh was drowned by a hard, insistent knock at my front door. The instant change in both men was disconcerting. Vinnie's face changed to a hardness that in all honesty scared me a little. I was glad he was on my side. Colin's whole body became quiet, reminding me of a large cat watching its prey.

"Expecting someone, Jenny?" Even his voice was quiet.

"No." I glanced at my watch. It was just past eleven. We had been working most of the afternoon and night.

"Take her into the back, dude. I'll get the door." Vinnie was already walking to the front door.

I was about to offer to see if I knew the visitor, but Colin touched my elbow, lifting me out of my chair. His touch was light, but firm. The fact that I didn't mind being touched by him consumed my thoughts so much that I was surprised to find myself in my bedroom with Colin, who closed and locked the door.

Loud voices reached us through the bedroom door. I groaned out loud when I recognized the visitor's voice and reached for the first lock. This was not going to be fun.

Chapter **FOURTEEN**

The sight that greeted me in the front of my apartment would have been comical, had it not been Phillip and Vinnie facing each other off. Literally. Vinnie's body served as a human wall, preventing Phillip from entering my apartment. I had to stand to the side to see my boss and was surprised to witness a different side of the normally controlled corporate leader.

Phillip had pulled himself up to his full height, which meant that his nose reached Vinnie's throat. My giant bodyguard had lowered his head and was standing nose to nose with my boss and friend who I had trusted more and for longer than anyone else.

"Let me in."

"Nah, old-timer. You can just turn around and go back to listening to opera and smoking your pipe."

Phillip's eyes widened. Even I was taken aback that Vinnie would know about Phillip's private habits. Had he spied on my boss?

"Where is she?" Phillip didn't take his eyes off Vinnie.

"She's where she is." There was ice in Vinnie's voice.

"I'm here, Phillip." I stepped forward and glared at Vinnie. "Let him in."

Vinnie didn't move. He looked at Phillip for another threatening five seconds before he turned his eyes to me. "Are you sure about this, Jen-girl? He doesn't seem very friendly."

"He's only responding to your animosity. This is my home and you will not treat my friends like this." Looking up at Vinnie at this close proximity emphasised his head-and-a-half advantage over me. I lowered my voice and ordered Vinnie with as much authority as I could muster, "Let him in and be nice."

"Yes, ma'am." Vinnie stepped aside with a textbook insincere smile aimed at Phillip. "Please come in."

Phillip did not look intimidated in the least. As a matter of fact, he looked taller than usual and much more forceful. This case was bringing out different sides to all of us. He ignored Vinnie as if he was the help and walked straight to me. "Are you okay?"

"I'm fine."

"Are you sure?" He glanced back where Vinnie was closing the door.

I was tempted to roll my eyes. "I'm fine, Phillip. Vinnie is my bodyguard."

"*This* is your bodyguard?" Phillip's voice raised.

This time I did roll my eyes. "Vinnie, meet Phillip. Phillip, Vinnie."

The two men glared at each other. It was a fascinating study in male behaviour. Here were two alpha male personalities weighing the other's threat to the territory. Were they primates in the jungle, they might have started beating their chests. Apparently Vinnie decided that Phillip had passed some kind of test, moved closer and held out his hand. "Pleased to meet you."

"I don't know about that." Even though Phillip took Vinnie's hand in a quick shake, his rudeness took me aback. His corporate behaviour had always been smooth. Now he seemed much more on edge. "Are you a criminal?"

Vinnie's entire expression froze. His neck muscles stiffened, his eyes were fixed on Phillip and his jaw muscles tightened. He addressed me without taking his eyes off my boss. "Are your friends always this rude, Jen-girl?"

"Enough. Both of you. If you can't be civil to each other, you can both leave." Really. I had had enough of this posturing and male intimidation. I turned away from the two men and started walking to my bedroom. Then I realised that Colin was most likely still in there, no doubt avoiding making his identity known to Phillip. The spare bedroom was invaded by Vinnie and my study had also been taken over by my two criminal protectors. Nowhere in my apartment was safe for me to go.

My indecision on where to go slowed my steps until I came to a standstill next to the dining room table. When Phillip spoke, his voice was a few feet behind me. "Genevieve, can we please talk?"

I turned around. Vinnie was still standing at the door, looking ready to physically remove Phillip from my apartment. The latter took a step closer, the forcefulness on his face replaced by concern. All this male silliness was because of concern. The behaviour of this gender was at times utterly ridiculous. I sighed.

"Let's sit in the living area. Vinnie, would you give us some privacy, please?"

"I'll make tea." Vinnie walked past us to the kitchen and I knew that he was going to listen in on this conversation. There wasn't going to be any privacy. I ushered Phillip towards the front door and into the living space to the right. As I settled into the sofa Vinnie had earlier occupied, Phillip tensed. He was looking around my apartment.

"You didn't tell me that they brought so much destruction."

I looked at the scratched furniture, my books that still needed to be properly arranged and the empty spaces where ornaments used to be. They were now somewhere in a garbage container. "My apartment was pretty well destroyed by the time they left. Vinnie and Colin cleaned up."

Phillip threw a doubting look towards the kitchen. "He cleans?"

"Surprisingly well."

He moved quietly to the sofa and sat down next to me, leaving enough space for my comfort. "Genevieve, this is turning out all wrong. I'm really worried."

"We've been over this." And I was bored having the same

conversations all the time. "Can't we just avoid this conversation and work on what is really important?"

"No." His tone held a finality that made me sigh. We were going to have this conversation. Vinnie chose that moment to bring a tray with tea and cookies. He placed it on the coffee table and gave me a searching look.

"Thanks, Vinnie." I made sure that my smile reached my eyes. He was annoying me, but his concern was sincere. "I'm okay for now."

"You'll shout if you need me."

"It won't be necessary." The orbicularis oculi muscles around Vinnie's eyes contracted to harden the expression in his eyes. I sighed for the eighth time. There was only one way to get rid of him. "Fine, I'll shout if I need you."

He gave Phillip a last unfriendly look and walked to the back of my apartment, towards my bedroom. I didn't even want to think about him and Colin together in my sanctuary. Instead I got up and, after choosing my favourite Ella Fitzgerald CD, placed it in the player and turned the music louder than I usually would.

"I thought you trusted him," Phillip said when I sat down.

"You mean the loud music?" When he nodded, I smiled. I poured us each a cup of tea and handed Phillip his before I took mine and settled into a more comfortable position. "I trust them both, but that doesn't give them the right to listen in on my conversations."

"What do you mean them?"

Oh, damn. I didn't even try to lie. "Colin is in my bedroom."

"They're both here?" Phillip's voice rose above the music and he inhaled deeply when I frowned at him. "I want to meet him."

"I don't think he wants to meet you. If he did, he would've been out here with Vinnie."

"Genevieve, there are some things you don't know."

"There are a lot of things I don't know." For instance, how to build a computer virus. I also didn't know all the species of animals on this planet of ours. Nor did I know who the most influential people in the fashion industry were. Until recently I hadn't known about Kwaito, a music genre specific to South Africa.

"That's not what I mean." His sharp answer brought me back to the present conversation. "There are some things you don't know about Colin."

"I should think so. I've only known him for a short time." The exasperated look in Phillip's eyes gave me pause. I took a moment to absorb what he had said. "Do you mean that he might be pretending to be something he's not?"

Phillip glanced towards my bedroom door and dropped his voice a few decibels. "I have discovered some things about him."

I stopped him with my hand in the air. "I know that Colin has had a life of crime, Phillip. There is much about his… um… work that I find disconcerting, but he is a man I trust. He's proven himself to me."

"He is keeping things from you. He is—"

"No. I'm not going to argue any further with you about his involvement. Or Vinnie's for that matter. They are helping me and I trust them. Let me rather tell you what we've discovered."

After a few moments of Phillip searching my face for something, he conceded. "What have you found?"

I told him about the cruise ships, each belonging to a company, and the odd ownership thereof. All the while he listened intently, sipping his tea. Mine was getting cold. I also told him of the auctions on these ships and the legal gray area auctions at sea enjoyed, but it was the EU charity that really caught his attention.

"I've never heard of the Foundation for Development of Sustainable Education."

"Well, it's been around for almost twenty years."

"And you say that the Foundation is connected to ten cruise ships."

"That we have found so far."

"I wonder if Manny knows about this."

"He most definitely knows about the Foundation. He's on a photo on their website. He attended a gala function and is on the photo with his friend, Leon Hofmann, the head of the EDA and also Tomasz Kubanov."

"The Russian philanthropist?"

"You know him?" I asked.

"I only know of him. He's Russia's Oprah Winfrey, Angelina Jolie, Bono."

"I don't know who they are."

"Of course you don't." Phillip smiled and was silent for a long time. "We'll ask Manny about this tomorrow when we meet. I sent him your report and we can discuss it tomorrow, together with all this new information."

I placed my untouched cup of tea on the coffee table and turned to Phillip. "Why did you come tonight?"

My question must have interrupted his thoughts, because he looked confused for a second. "Oh. Oh, yes! How could I have forgotten?"

"Forgotten what?"

He dug into the inner breast pocket of his suit jacket. "This." He handed me a photo. "Danielle's roommate, Anna... Anna..."

"Anna Paschal?" In my mind's eye I could see the exam-stressed student in her messy apartment, worried about her roommate.

"Yes, her. Well, she came into the office this afternoon and brought this photo. She said that she had forgotten that Danielle had given it to her. It's a photo of her and her boyfriend on the cruise where they met."

I looked at the photo and saw a happy and very much alive Danielle smiling up at a good-looking man. He was tall, in his early thirties, with Mediterranean features. His facial expression immediately caught my eye. He was looking down at Danielle, his *orbicularis oculi* muscles tightened, exhibiting intent. What his intention was would be pure speculation, but sexual it was not. None of his other non-verbal cues communicated sexual interest. The rest of his body confirmed the intent showed by his constricted pupils.

His right hand on his hip, left arm draped over Danielle, and feet firmly planted were signs of a strong, territorial display. Nothing in his body displayed comfort or infatuation, whereas Danielle was clearly smitten. She was leaning into him, her arms thrown around his torso and her neck totally exposed while looking up at him. Where everything in her expression was soft, he was as hard as marble. Righteous indignation rose in me for the abuse of such innocent trust.

"What do you see?" Phillip's voice reached me through the fog of the thousand words this picture was telling me.

"A girl who trusted a calculating, hard man. Do we know who he is?"

"Not yet. I scanned and emailed the photo to Manny. Hopefully one of their databases will identify this man."

"If he's the one who caused her death, I hope he spends the rest of his life in prison." I looked up from the photo and stifled a yawn. This caused worry lines to crease Phillip's brow and he stood up.

"You're tired. Really, Genevieve, you need to take better care of yourself." After a few more warnings from him to eat enough, rest and not go into the office too early, Phillip left. I made sure all the locks on the front door were in place and then turned the music down.

"You can come out."

Immediately Colin and Vinnie exited my bedroom and made their way to the kitchen where I was putting the cups and saucers in the dishwasher.

"Loud music? Really, Jenny." Colin sounded annoyed. I stood up from the dishwasher and was surprised to see real anger pulling at his facial muscles. He was standing in front of me, hands on his hips with his thumbs facing back, a clear communication that he was not pleased. "You told me that you trusted me."

"I do."

He moved closer, more confrontational, glaring down at me. "Then why the music?"

I sighed. "Colin, you don't intimidate me with your dominant display of vexation."

"My domi—" His indignant response was interrupted by Vinnie's laughter.

"Oh, that's rich. Dude, she nailed you." Vinnie was shaking with mirth. The corners of my mouth lifted in response. Not that I found anything funny. It was simply a pleasure to not be totally immersed by seriousness.

Colin didn't seem to appreciate this moment as much. His brow was lowered and deep lines formed a frown of displeasure. Should I apologise?

"I didn't mean to offend you, Colin." This only deepened his frown, so I tried another tactic. I was truly not good at this. But I was really good at honesty. "I knew that Phillip was going to argue with me about Vinnie's presence and I didn't want you to overhear something that would cause another show of male behaviour. As fascinating as I find men beating their chests, I don't know how to referee that and didn't want it in my apartment."

Different sounds of annoyance were uttered by both men and I threw my hands in the air. "That's it. I don't know how to communicate with you when you are like this. I'm going to bed."

I started walking towards my bedroom, but the men were blocking my exit out of the kitchen area. They didn't move and I stopped in front of them with an angry huff and a lifted eyebrow. We stared at each other for a few long heartbeats. My brain was working overtime, trying to figure out how to deal with this. How on earth did people have relationships when no one was willing to listen to the other person's honesty?

"Can we sit down and talk about this?" Colin broke the standoff with his quiet question.

"Are you going to listen to me or get angry at everything I say?"

He inhaled to answer me, thought better of it and pressed his lips together. A second later he stepped aside. "Let's sit down. I'll listen as long as you also listen."

"I always listen."

"And always argue back."

Vinnie found this funny and chuckled quietly as he followed us to the living area. We all settled in the sofas and I gave them the highlights of Phillip's visit. When I mentioned the photo, both men leaned forward.

"Let me see the photo." Colin held out his hand. I picked it up from the coffee table next to me and handed it to him. He studied it for a while before he handed it to Vinnie. We discussed what was visible on the photo, but came to no conclusions. It would be up to Manny and his people to identify this man.

"Dude, you could ask Francine," Vinnie suggested. "You know how good she is with finding things, info, people."

"Let Jenny first speak to Manny tomorrow. If he isn't able to get the man's name, then we can contact Francine."

"Right on, dude." Vinnie leaned back in the chair, happy with Colin's solution. A pensive silence descended on us and Phillip's words of warning came back to me. After a while I felt Colin's eyes on me and looked at him.

"What's bothering you, Jenny? What are you not telling us?"

I studied his face for any tell-tale signs of deception, malice or animosity. I found none of that. What I did take note of was how he waited out my scrutiny with a quiet calm. Either I was completely mistaken and he was a psychopath. Or he was comfortable with himself and with me, allowing me to read him until I reached a conclusion. Which I did.

"He told me that you're not telling me everything, that there are things that I don't know about you."

"There's a lot you don't know about me."

"I know that."

"My favourite colour is blue," he said. I didn't understand why he would tell me this, but surmised it might have some social significance, so I smiled politely. This had him chuckling softly. "Never mind. Jenny, any time you have a question about or for me, just ask. I'll be as honest as possible."

"You can only be honest or not."

Vinnie snorted and Colin groaned. "Okay, then I will be totally honest, but will only tell you what I can."

There was not a single sign of deception to be seen. No one was that good at lying. "Thank you."

"Same goes for me, Jen-girl," Vinnie said. There was a smile in his voice. "Although this whole honesty thing is totally new for me."

I took a few moments to think this over and then decided that there were a few answers I wanted. "Can I ask you something now?"

Colin looked at me askance. "Okay."

"Are you working for the EDA?"

His lips twitched with humour. "Most definitely not."

"Eurocorps?"

"Jenny, you're the one who accused me of being a criminal from the moment we met. How can you think that I'm working for these guys?"

"You're not answering my question." Which was an answer in itself.

Colin sighed. "I'm not working for Eurocorps."

"What is your connection to Manny?"

"What makes you think there is a connection?"

I ignored Vinnie's soft gasp. And focussed on the numerous cues Colin was exhibiting, telling me exactly how uncomfortable he was. "Answering my question with a question is a diversion far beneath your intellect, Colin."

"Manfred Millard is a person I am not fond of, Jenny. This is one of those cases where I want to be honest with you, but I can't tell you everything."

"But you have a connection?"

"Yes." That one word carried a wealth of information. His lips drawing sideways to produce a sneering dimple in his cheek showed me that there was no love lost between the two men. Whatever the event was that connected Manny and Colin it did not produce happy memories. Hissing the word through his teeth only reiterated my reading of his face.

"I would really like to know."

"Maybe one day I will tell you."

"Okay."

My silent acceptance surprised him. Then he smiled at me with relief and gratefulness. Apparently, this was a sensitive topic for the man portraying himself as unaffected by the world.

He was not. I settled back into the sofa and allowed my mind to wander over the day's discoveries. I couldn't find any new links that we might have overlooked, so I turned my attention to the two men sitting with me in contemplative silence.

I took a mental step back and looked at the three of us lounging on my sofas. Vinnie was taking up most of the space of the sofa facing the bookshelf, while Colin and I were on opposite ends of the sofa facing the balcony. The body language all around communicated high comfort, trust and goodwill.

It astounded me that two people exhibited such cues while in my presence. Never, to my knowledge, had I had that effect on anyone before. Was this what friendship was like? People comfortable in each other's presence. Was I comfortable in their presence?

Before I could analyse this question, Colin spoke. "It just doesn't make sense."

"What, dude?" Vinnie rearranged himself to sit a bit more upright.

"The forgeries." He was sitting with his eyes closed and spoke as if to himself. "There must be someone facilitating the forgeries being sold at the auctions at sea."

"Please explain," I said.

"There are so many varied artworks. So far we have almost fifty artworks that were miraculously recovered by private investigators who do not exist. Of those fifty works we have paintings in all kinds of media—statues, bronzes, different eras, different everything." He opened his eyes and looked at me. "There is not one single forger able to reach so wide in this range. Not one."

"And you know all of them?"

"All the ones able to forge works at this level."

Vinnie's gasp drew my eye. He was clearly surprised that Colin would tell me this and therefore almost implicate him via association.

I looked back at Colin. "How do you know them?"

"That is not important now. What is important is that I believe there are quite a few forgers working on this. That is the only way I can explain this varied portfolio of works."

"Dude, do you actually think that would happen? You know how stiff the competition is out there. I can't imagine a group of forgers forming a union and co-operating." Vinnie paused a second and tilted his head. "Unless the money is good."

"The money is never good enough. Not for something like this."

"Something like what?" I asked.

"I don't know yet. It just doesn't make sense."

I couldn't see us uncovering any revealing clues tonight, so I pushed myself out of the sofa. "I'm going to bed."

"Rest up and we'll speak about our discoveries tomorrow evening."

"Nighty-night, Jen-girl. Don't worry about a thing. I'll clean up after Colin here as soon as he gets his messy ass home."

Chapter FIFTEEN

"She's what?" Manny's outraged voice greeted me as I entered the empty pub. I sighed and walked deeper into the badly lit room. Even though these places were usually rife with interesting subjects to study for non-verbal communication, I very seldom ventured into pubs. There were simply too many places I couldn't bear to touch. Too many unnamed and unthinkable germs.

I slowed my steps and looked around. At least this place didn't look too shabby. Booths lined the back and side walls, and worn wooden tables and chairs filled the remaining space. The bar ran along the entire wall to my right. Unsurprisingly, the pub was devoid of customers at this early hour in the morning. A young man was scrubbing the tiled floor leading to the back with suspicious enthusiasm. A slight sniff informed my olfactory senses that a lot of cleaning products were used this morning. It marginally eased my germ phobia.

The knowledge of what I was about to walk into made me stop next to a stained table. Generally, I preferred to avoid confrontations at all costs. Since Manny had exploded into my life, every day had been filled with confrontation. I swallowed hard and tried to gather the calm needed to face the men waiting for me. Phillip had phoned me earlier and told me that Leon wanted to meet with us, but not at anyone's office. He was very wary of somebody seeing us enter his office or him entering our building. It made sense.

Rock music blared through the speakers overhead and I sighed. An hour in this place and I was going to have a headache. Another reason I didn't frequent these types of establishments. I supposed that it was a good place to have a covert meeting. No one could eavesdrop on a conversation without looking obvious doing it. Not that there was anyone here to eavesdrop. Only one booth against the back wall was occupied. I could only see the top of Phillip's head. I assumed Manny was slumped in the seat across from him. I could still hear Manny complaining about something.

Vinnie had driven me to the pub, grumbling about it being like a bad spy movie. It took the threat of introducing him to Leon and all the other law enforcement people I knew to make him wait outside for me.

I frowned at myself. Standing here was only avoiding the inevitable. I pulled my shoulders back and walked to the booth against the back wall.

"Good morning." I placed my computer bag with both the EDA and my work computer on the bench next to Phillip. Manny was indeed slumped on the opposite bench. I glared at the plastic-covered seat before I carefully lowered myself onto it. Phillip looked his crisp professional self. In contrast Manny looked like a pile of dirty laundry. As usual.

"Haven't you just been the busy bee," grumbled Manny.

"I beg your pardon?" I took out my work computer with my latest report on it and wondered what bees had to do with me. I opened the computer and switched it on. If I focussed on work, I could avoid thinking of the sticky substance under my shoe.

"I've been updating Manny on some of your findings, Genevieve." Phillip smiled at me. "Good morning."

I returned his smile, but my facial muscles lost their friendliness when I looked at Manny. He was oozing animosity.

"Why does Phillip not want to tell me all the details about your attack, Miss Lenard?"

"*Doctor* Lenard or Genevieve," I said pointedly and waited for Manny to acknowledge. The frumpy man wanted to bring me down a peg or two, but I was not going to let him reduce me to a 'Miss'.

We stared at each other for a good minute. It gave me time to do a more accurate reading of the agent's face and I came to a startling realisation.

"You're worried about me." The words rushed out of my mouth unchecked.

He ignored my declaration. "Tell me everything about your attack and your attackers."

I looked at Phillip only to see amusement. I shrugged mentally and told Manny everything except for Colin and Vinnie's involvement. I stated that friends helped me. Of course he noticed something was amiss. "You are being just as cagey about the story as Phillip. What are you not telling me?"

"Something that I don't want you to know."

He sneered at my obvious answer and went straight to the heart of it. "Who are these friends of yours who came to your rescue?"

I swallowed nervously and looked at Phillip for help. He wasn't in a haste to be my buffer. I wondered why.

"No, missy, Phillip is not going to help you out here today. It's just you and me, and I want to know who these people are. Is one of them the outsider Phillip just told me about?"

I sucked in both my lips and bit down on them. I did not want to talk. The whole truth about Colin and Vinnie was pushing against my teeth, desperate to be uttered. I simultaneously fought my urge to confess while searching for the right way to answer. I hoped I was handling this correctly.

"Can you please just accept that my friends are completely trustworthy and that I would never dream of jeopardising the case?" My carefully phrased answer did nothing to change Manny's unhappy expression. I rushed on, hoping to distract him. "How much has Phillip told you? Do you know about the dead artists?"

"What dead artists?" He was quiet for a second and I could see the moment his curiosity overcame his concerns. "Don't think that I don't know what you're doing. We will talk about this sooner or later."

My first word of a lengthy explanation was interrupted by a tall gentleman stopping at our booth. I immediately recognised Manny's friend from the photo of the Foundation's gala event. Major-General Leon Hofmann. He was taller than the impression I had from the photo, but had the same close-cropped gray hair, light brown eyes and thin lips. A worried expression pulled at his face. Introductions were made all around and Leon sat down next to Manny. A waiter took our coffee orders and we settled.

"Genevieve, explain about the dead artists." Manny's order did not sit well with me. Nor did the new guest's presence. I hadn't had time to read and to come to my own conclusions about the Eurocorps man. At this moment I only had Manny's trusted friendship with Phillip to go by. That was by no means enough for me.

Leon must have sensed my hesitance. "I appreciate your reluctance to trust a stranger, Doctor Lenard. But I was the one after all who asked Manny to find someone trustworthy to help us figure this whole thing out. It was on my insistence that he asked Phillip. You can therefore rest assured that my only interest is in figuring out who took those weapons, where they are and what they are being used for."

His respectful manner, in such severe contrast to Manny's annoying attitude, went a long way to convince me. But it was his short monologue that gave me some time to start forming a baseline from which I could read him. What I read was deep concern, bordering on desperation. There were no alarms being set off by his non-verbal and verbal cues.

My decision made about Leon's sincerity, I told them about Danielle, her art, the miraculously recovered artworks, the cruises, the ships, the companies owning those ships and the art auctions. I stopped only for a few seconds to allow the waiter to place our coffees on the table. Both men listened with an intensity uncommon to me. Manny even more so. There wasn't much that he missed. Three times he interrupted me to ask a question for clarification.

My throat was scratchy from talking so much by the time I was ready to confront Manny about the charity foundation. After a quick sip of lukewarm coffee, I pulled my work computer closer and brought up the photo of the gala event. I turned the computer so that the screen was facing Manny and Leon. "What is your connection to the Foundation for Development of Sustainable Education?"

Manny gave me a searching look before he turned his attention to the computer screen. "This shindig? This was what? Two, three years ago?"

"Two years," I answered.

"This was some charity evening that I had no choice in attending. Chief Dutoit virtually ordered me to be there. This is neither my interest nor my department, but it was good for PR. Or so the Chief said. I suppose there is a reason you are showing me this?"

"Ten cruise ships have connections to the Foundation. All of those ships have hosted art auctions with suspected forgeries. It is widely publicised that the auctions donate three percent of all money changing hands to the Foundation."

Manny looked back at the photo. I wondered what was going on in his mind. "Isn't it also strange how many important figures are in this photo?"

"Who are these actors and this philanthropist?" I pointed to the man who was hidden by the supermodel's expensive hairdo.

"The stars are just there for the celebrity pull," Manny said. "But Tomasz Kubanov? He's something else. I met him for the first time that night. He's some Russian bigwig. He's also the one who founded this charity."

"He is?" I did not expect this. "Why did I not see this information anywhere? I did extensive research on the Foundation."

"I don't know," Manny said in his sarcastic voice. "Maybe he's one of those private, behind-the-scenes guys."

"You don't like him. Why not?"

"He was too smooth for my liking."

"What do you mean by smooth?"

"He was a real charmer. Never forceful, making everyone feel comfortable and good about themselves. Hell, I even liked the guy while he was chatting to us. It was only after he had moved away that I realised how he was playing everyone like a violin. I'm sure that he could bend anyone to his will just with a smile."

I doubted that, but was too surprised by the detailed impression Manny had shared to express my opinion. Instead I turned to Leon who was leaning over to look at the computer screen. "Does he have a connection to you, Leon?"

"Apart from that evening and another charity function last year, I had never spoken to or had any other contact with this man." He was shaking his head throughout his sentence. "Why are you so curious about him?"

"Genevieve will never, ever say it is a gut feeling, but I suspect that is what is driving her." Phillip spoke for the first time since we started and I was not pleased with his observation.

"It is not a gut feeling." I knew I sounded defensive and didn't care.

Manny narrowed his eyes. "What are you thinking, Doc?"

"I don't know. If Mister Kubanov founded the Foundation and the Foundation has these strong ties to the ships, maybe he is behind all this."

"It's bothering Genevieve that she can't figure out who's behind the murders." Phillip scowled. "And behind her attack."

"I'd be happy to blame a Russian, especially this one," Manny grumbled.

"What is everyone's problem with Russia?" My question was fast and unchecked.

"Who else doesn't trust Russia?"

Answering Manny would require bringing Colin into the conversation. I reached for a creative way to avoid that. Deception was uncommonly hard work. "There are corrupt individuals everywhere. Just because a few Russians are abusing their power doesn't mean the whole country is bad."

"There are unfortunately more than just a few abusing their power," Leon interjected softly and I sighed. An argument about Russia's positive points was forming in my head and I felt a diatribe coming on.

"Let's not digress." Phillip mercifully intervened. "What's our next step?"

"I'll get the Foundation's financials and I'll also look into this Kubanov character," Manny said. "I, for one, would like to see if that three percent made it to the Foundation's bank account."

He massaged his neck and puffed a slow breath out. Was his distress about the added elements to the case or about something else?

I narrowed my eyes and plunged. "What's the problem, Manny?"

Immediately a sneering dimple appeared in his left cheek. I deeply disliked this man. "What do you think is the problem, Miss Face-reader?"

"Are you being sarcastic again?" My question caused Leon to cover his chuckle with a cough and Phillip to inhale sharply. Manny just glared his disdain at me. "I take that as a yes. That means that you are angry, but I doubt that you are angry with me. I'm just an easy target. What is really causing you such concern?"

Manny started to speak, but I interrupted him. "And it's *Doctor* Face-reader to you."

There was a moment of stunned silence before all three men laughed. This case must have changed me into a comedienne. The laughter died down, but it seemed to have broken the tension around the table. Manny had the decency to look contrite.

"I apologise, Doc. Since Monday I've been getting a lot of flack from the Chief. He's giving me hell about this case, demanding reports, telling me that I'm wasting time and resources on something that is of no concern to the EDA."

"Could you please explain the exact position of the Chief in the EDA's organisation?" I asked.

"Right at the top of the EDA's organigram is the Steering Board, chaired by the Head." Manny lowered his voice. "I trust her. The man giving me such a hard time is directly under the Head. Frederique Dutoit is the Chief Executive. Under him is myself as the Deputy Chief Executive of Strategy and another deputy."

"But why is the Chief on your case? Aren't you sending him any reports?" Leon sounded very concerned.

"I've been able to avoid him for the best part of this week, but he's ordered me in for a full report on Friday."

"What are you going to tell him?" Leon asked.

In classic blocking behaviour, Manny closed his eyes in order to distance himself from the unpleasantness awaiting him. On a sigh, he opened his eyes, stress lines visible all over his face. "I don't know."

"Has anyone else shown an interest in this case?" Leon looked intently at Manny.

"No. Why?"

"Well, I've had a few unpleasant conversations with Brigadier-General Nick Crenshaw about the missing weapons. Apart from the Commanding General, he's the only one who knows the true extent of the loss of our weapons. It's been kept under strict confidentiality. Since Brigadier-General Crenshaw was in charge of the weapons, he's been excluded from the investigation. Merely asking about it is breaking protocol."

"Do you think he's involved?"

"A month ago, I would never have suspected him, but now I don't know. I'm suspecting just about everyone."

"I know the feeling." Manny sounded tired. "Apart from the Head, I don't trust anyone. Hell, sometimes I don't even know if I should trust the Head."

I decided to visit Eurocorps' website again to familiarise myself with this Brigadier-General Crenshaw. By now I had formed a good baseline to read Leon and could clearly see his discomfort at having to suspect everyone.

"I have the Head asking for discretion," Manny continued, "but it is Chief Dutoit who's been chewing my ass for the lack of progress. Not that we haven't made any progress. I've just not informed him about it. I don't know if I should. And this is not making it any easier." He tossed the photo of Danielle's boyfriend on the table as if it were a live snake.

Leon leaned in. "What's this? Who's this?"

"This is Piotr Chulkov, the murdered girl's boyfriend." Apparently Manny hadn't wasted any time identifying Danielle's boyfriend.

"Chulkov." I scanned my memory of all the discoveries in the case for the appearance of that surname. "I've heard that name before."

"He's the brother of the thug who killed Danielle," Manny answered just as I remembered who also had that surname.

"Nikolay Chulkov killed his brother Piotr's girlfriend and then himself?" I was aghast. "Why?"

"That is the million-dollar question," Manny said as if to himself. "Piotr's name did, however, set off a few red lights. That is why it was so easy to ID him. Piotr has been on several international law enforcement agencies' radars."

"For what?" Phillip sat up in his chair, looking very concerned.

"Every crime you can imagine. It is his connection to a

private Russian army that caught my attention though."

"Private Russian army?" Phillip sounded like a parrot, repeating everything Manny revealed. I was riveted. I hadn't thought it possible for this case to have become more complex and thus more interesting, but it just had.

"Communism had barely ended when numerous secret military organisations popped up everywhere. Most dissolved within the first year. They were mostly started by discontented communists with strong military influence, hoping to maintain the strength of communism." Manny's top lip lifted as if he smelled something bad. "Unfortunately there were quite a few very rich people who managed to form their own personal armies."

"To what end?" Why would anyone want their own army? I might need one to keep the influx of criminals from my front door. And windows.

"To protect their illegal activities." Manny's strong dislike for everything Russian was evident in his harsh tone. "The arms dealers, drug dealers, mafia bosses and human traffickers all have their own protection. Some are amateurish, but most are former military, trained and skilled."

Immediately I thought of the four men in my apartment. Only two of them had been Russian though. Could there be a connection? It was just too much of a coincidence that the men who attacked me had been scared of Red when the Russian murderer promised, 'Red will end all twenty-seven.' And what was the significance of the 'twenty-seven daffodils'?

"What is it, Genevieve?" As usual Phillip saw that my mind was working on something.

"I was thinking about the men who attacked me." I wasn't yet ready to share my theories on Piros.

"Men attacked her?" Leon's outraged question was aimed at Manny. "Is that where the bruises came from?"

I thought that I had hidden them well with my makeup, but

the way they were now staring at my face proved my skills were not quite up to par.

"Yes, she was attacked in her apartment. And she hasn't told me everything."

"I've told you all the important parts." I was sure he would disagree with me if he were ever to find out about Colin and Vinnie. "I also told you about the insignia on two of the men's uniforms."

"They wore uniforms?" This was the first time since Leon entered the room that he seemed less than composed.

"You'd better tell him the whole story." Manny emphasised the two last words, but I ignored it. I told Leon about the attack, aware of Manny's scrutiny. He was no doubt hoping to catch me in a lie or inconsistency. Since my memory was faultless, I told Leon exactly what I had told Manny. Including the part about the insignias.

"Do any of these private armies have logos or insignias?" I asked.

"Some of them view themselves as legitimate armies and therefore have everything an army would have."

"Including insignias."

"Including insignias. Can you remember what it looked like?" Leon asked.

"If I was any good at drawing, I would've drawn it for you." This was not a skill I had managed to excel in. "But if you show me pictures of insignias, I'll be able to point out the one without any doubt."

"I'll email you the gallery that we have." Leon looked at Manny. "She's still using the EDA computer, right?"

"Yes, and it's totally secure." Manny would surely contemplate throwing me in prison if he knew that Colin had seen and worked on the EDA computer.

"Leon, you said these armies have everything a legitimate army would have. Would that include weapons?" I had all three men's undivided attention. Manny and Leon shared a look heavy with concern.

"Genevieve." Defeat weighed heavily on Leon's voice. "I pray to God that you are not suggesting what I think you are suggesting."

"I'm suggesting that your stolen weapons might have gone to one of these Russian pseudo-armies. There are too many connections now to not consider it a possibility. I don't know if Manny told you, but there are five unsolved murders in the last five years in Europe with SIG 226 nine-millimetre pistols."

"That's nothing strange. SIG 226's are very common weapons."

"In my search, I've discovered that there might be thirteen suspicious deaths of artists."

"I told Manny about this on Monday." Phillip turned to Manny. "Have you found any ballistic evidence?"

Leon leaned forward with a sigh. "I've requested the ballistic reports from the five cases you gave Manny and we're currently looking into all open cases in the EU where the calibre weapons from our list of stolen weapons were used. Unfortunately, I can't give you any indication how long it might take before we get results."

"What complicates this process even more is the SIG's popularity," Manny said. He exhibited no enthusiasm for this line of investigation.

"Do you at least agree that it is strange that all five murder victims were artists?"

I saw the moment all the separate incidences started connecting in Leon's mind. His pupils constricted in high focus and his jaw muscles tightened. A negative conclusion must have been reached in his head. He closed his eyes for a moment, blocking out those thoughts. "This is a nightmare. An abhorrent nightmare."

"Please bear in mind that even though too many things

connect to be coincidence, we still don't have solid physical proof." I needed to find irrefutable paper trails to support all this. "That is why the financials for the Foundation and any information on Kubanov would be a good start to prove any connection."

"I'll get on that ASAP." Manny sighed.

A subtle change in Leon's body language drew my attention. His torso shifted ever so slightly to the door and I was sure that had I looked under the table, his feet would have been pointing in that direction as well.

"You have to go," I stated.

"Unfortunately, you're right. I do have to go." Leon got up. We all promised to stay in touch. Not a minute later I was alone with Manny and Phillip.

"There's more about Piotr Chulkov." Manny took a sheet of paper out of a thick folder in front of him and laid it on the table. It was an organigram. With a lot of empty spaces.

"What's this?" Phillip asked the obvious question.

"The RNT, the Russian Ninja Turtles." Manny held up his hand when I inhaled to question such a ridiculous name. "This is the name that Interpol gave this group when they first started their activities."

"What activities?"

"Patience, Doc. Give me time to inhale while I talk."

I pressed my lips together and nodded.

"Their name comes from the stealth with which they move, their black outfits and the characteristic flat, rounded backpacks they carry when they're on a mission."

"The Spaniard who attacked me had a backpack like the one you're describing."

Both men stared at me, but it was Manny who spoke with genuine worry in his voice. "These guys are cold-blooded, Genevieve. They are not to be trifled with. They operate all over the globe. They've eliminated well-protected individuals. There have also been sightings of them during riots, suggesting that they were the instigators. They are mostly known for their violent solutions to a person posing a problem, be it political, corporate or personal."

"And Piotr Chulkov is involved with the Russian Ninja Turtles?" I could barely say this silly name given to a group of mercenaries.

Manny pointed to a box in the middle of the organisational chart. "It's been guessed that this is where he fits in this organisation. He is thought of as a recruiter. Apparently, he is quite good at charming people into joining with them or working for them."

"Who are they?" I asked.

"Five years ago a man went to Interpol and claimed that he had been part of the RNT." Manny opened the folder and took out a photo. A Caucasian man was sitting in a hotel room and he looked like he had been in a terrible car accident.

"What happened to him?"

"The RNT," Manny said. "According to him, nobody had ever left the RNT alive before. He was beaten to an inch of his life. And then he was shot. Five times. Nobody knows how he survived, but Interpol was very happy he did. Most of what we know about the RNT, we learned from him. He was terrified of what the RNT would do to him and his family if they discovered that he was still alive. His name isn't even recorded on this report. After he was debriefed to exhaustion, Interpol gave him a new identity and sent him to another country. They have not been able to find him for two years now."

"He's dead?" Phillip asked.

"Maybe. Or he decided to take his safety into his own hands and changed identities again to completely disappear."

"It seems to be so easy to do that." I was thinking of Colin and his poets. Never would I have thought that becoming another person could be possible and yet it was apparently very easy. I realised my mistake when Phillip frowned at me and Manny looked at me with renewed suspicion. I frantically searched my mind for an escape. "All I mean is that Nikolay had other identities as well."

"You really are a terrible liar, Doc."

"What else do you know about the RNT?" Phillip brought us back on topic.

Manny narrowed his eyes at me in warning before he relented. "He told them about the RNT's training facility, but didn't know where it was. Apparently, they were all blindfolded before they were taken there by plane, two helicopter rides and finally an eight-hour trip in the back of a darkened truck. He said that by the time he and the other two recruits had arrived at the compound, they were totally disoriented. All he could say was that it was in the northern hemisphere, since it was still autumn when they arrived. Interpol's guys were able to ascertain from this man's descriptions that he had been in Hungary."

"Yet another tie that binds Hungary to this case," I said. "Where did they find him?"

"They didn't. He found them. There wasn't much he was able to remember from his beating. When he came to he was in a hospital in Zagreb. How he got to Croatia, he couldn't remember. He spent three months in a Catholic hospital before he was released."

"Why was he beaten up?"

"The RNT did a job somewhere and a lot of innocent people got killed. He said that it was the last straw for him. He mentioned to one of his team members, his best friend, that he was thinking about getting out. His memory was still intact for the few hours after he had told his mate, but then he said he couldn't remember much after that. According to him, the loyalty that these guys had towards the RNT bordered on that of a cult. They would do anything to protect the secrecy of this organisation."

"So why didn't they kill him?" Phillip asked.

"They thought they had. He had five bullets removed from his body. Each one had narrowly missed vital organs. He was told by the hospital that a farmer had found him on the outskirts of the city. He had lost so much blood that no one thought he was going to make it. But that's not the important part. Lying in the hospital had given him time to think. The betrayal of his best friend and the death of all those innocents were weighing heavily on him. That's when he decided to contact Interpol.

"According to him, the compound trained private armies mostly for rich and important Russians. These are elite armies and only three armies a year have the chance of a six-week training session. For some, it is a refresher course, for others it is full training. All of the soldiers come from a military or law enforcement background. But the six-week training the RNT received every year was the most brutal of them all. They were in the employ of the people who ran the compound. Their jobs were not to protect somebody. No, they were sent to eliminate a politician's opposition or to start a revolt in a country that was developing too well."

"They were being used to manipulate the political arena?" This was amazing. It reminded me of a master chess player thinking seven moves ahead.

"Yes," Manny answered. "These were countries like Georgia, Armenia, Moldova."

"All countries of the old USSR." I shook my head in disbelief. "Wow."

"This ex-RNT soldier said after his first job that he regretted ever joining them. I had to read this twice last night before I believed my eyes." Manny paused. People usually did this for dramatic effect or what they were about to say was of extreme importance. "His first assignment was an assassination. Of an artist. This guy is a sniper, he kills for a living, but killing an innocent artist didn't sit right with him. Especially not after he had seen the beautiful works that this young girl produced. From his descriptions, she was painting Monets."

"Most likely a forger, killed after her skill was exploited." I thought about what Manny had just told us. "Hold on. I deduced that these RNT guys are selected very carefully. How could they not have seen his sentimental side?"

"Aha." Manny leaned forward. "This is also interesting. Apparently they all had to go through a comprehensive psychological evaluation before they were accepted. The recruiter never told them what their work would be. Only that they would be working in one of the most elite, secret armies of the world. On further questioning, Interpol realised that the psych eval was almost exactly the same as the one they use for their recruits."

"Almost exactly is an oxymoron," I said. "Either it is almost or it is exactly."

"Genevieve," Phillip said in a low voice.

"You want numbers, Doc? Interpol estimated it to be roughly ninety percent the same as theirs. And the Interpol evaluation was custom-designed."

"Which means that the trainer had access to Interpol. Who is their trainer?" I asked.

"Interpol is investigating him." For the first time since he had started telling us about the RNT, Manny was not forthcoming. Before I could give it too much thought, he rambled forth. "Given their history, I would like to know what their true purpose was in your apartment, why they attacked you."

"What do you mean?" Phillip asked.

"From what this guy told Interpol"—Manny pointed at the

folder—"they never warned anyone. They just killed."

"And you want to know why they didn't kill me?" My chest tightened. I mentally wrote two bars of Mozart to calm down.

"Yes, and I'll add some more questions." Manny rubbed the back of his neck. This pacifying behaviour showed his growing concern and the need to calm himself. "Why is it that so many weapons could disappear over such an extended period of time without raising any alarms? Why is it that no one has made any connections in almost twenty years? Or that the RNT have not been prosecuted? Leon told me that Eurocorps had in the past looked into them quite a few times, yet no arrests, no incarceration. Why is that?"

"There has to be some connection to higher officials. Someone who could cover up any suspicion reported on RNT activities." I hated myself for sounding just like Colin. He was going to revel in being right.

"This is sadly the conclusion that I have come to. I suspect that the RNT or whomever they're working for has some kind of hold on one or more officials. How far it reaches I don't know. I also don't know whether they're blackmailing, threatening or intimidating these suckers." Manny might look absentminded, but once again he had just proven his mental acuity. "And you"—he pointed accusingly at me—"you're holding out too much on me. I want to know who this person is who is helping you. Finding Danielle's identity could not have been easy. Not without breaking a law or two. I will not have my name, my reputation tainted by some illegal activity. Who is helping you?"

I stared at Manny in horror. For the second time today, the truth was desperately fighting to pass my lips.

"Don't say a word, Genevieve." Phillip's order came fast and strong. He turned to Manny. "I know who she's working with and it's under control. Can't you just accept the progress that we've made and that we are finding enough evidence to put an end to this?"

The two men stared at each other for a full minute before Manny relented. "For now, Phillip. I will back off, but only for now."

I slowly exhaled a breath I hadn't even known I had been holding. Manny grumbled for another five minutes about honesty and openness in this case. As usual, Phillip calmed him with promises that from now on we would have daily meetings to report back with whatever discoveries we made. I started packing up my computer. It seemed like our meeting was finished, and a longing to be in my viewing room, isolated from the rest of the world, overwhelmed me.

I stood up and announced, "I'm going to work." Without waiting for a reaction, I picked up my bags and headed to the door. No sooner had I opened the door to a sunlit street than Vinnie appeared at my side.

"Where to, Jen-girl?"

"The office, please."

We walked to his SUV and got in without saying another word. I really liked that about Vinnie. He knew when not to talk. And if he did and I wasn't listening, he never took offence. It made it easier to tolerate having him around all the time.

We left the seedier side of town behind, slowly making our way through the quaint streets of the historic part of town. The trees lined most of the streets and the ornate streetlamps added a unique charm to the pedestrian-friendly sidewalks.

It was time to get my head back into this case. I had a lot of loose pieces that needed connecting and had no idea where to start. It was beginning to feel like I was running in circles. It was not a comfortable feeling and I hoped that I was going to change that today.

Chapter SIXTEEN

I was still running in circles. I looked at the three computer screens in front of me and wanted to use some of the words Vinnie had uttered when he had burned his hand on the stove yesterday.

It had been an extremely frustrating few days since I had met Leon. Daily meetings with Manny had done nothing to further our co-operation. He had seemed more angered by my lack of new connections and information than I was. Aggravating man.

After four days of fourteen-hour searches, countless data files being perused and combed through, I had nothing. To top everything, Colin had disappeared. He had left a message with Vinnie that he was looking into something and would check in as soon as he could. That was also four days ago. I hadn't heard anything from him since. I was getting increasingly annoyed with agents and criminals alike.

"Your coffee, m'lady." Vinnie placed a steaming mug of coffee on the coaster next to my right hand. "You should really take a break, Jen-girl. It's Sunday morning, for goodness' sake. You should be enjoying a lazy breakfast."

I glared at the huge man hovering over me. He reminded me of a documentary I watched about fowl. Not even the mother hens clucked around their chicks as much as he did around me. I didn't tell him that he reminded me of a chicken though. With a sigh I sat back and reached for the coffee. "Where is Colin?"

Vinnie pulled out a chair and sat down facing me. He was wearing his usual canvas pants and loose T-shirt. I had wondered if he had any other clothes in his wardrobe, but after a week of him living in my apartment, I had come to the conclusion that this was his uniform. His pants and shirts were always neatly pressed, just like a uniform, and he took great care with his appearance. He was also quite fastidious about keeping the kitchen neat. This man was a surprising perfectionist.

"He said he would come as soon as he can, Jen-girl."

"Where is he?" This time I infused much more demand in my voice. This brought humour lines to soften Vinnie's features.

"Busy."

"Is he working on this case?" If I had not been so annoyed by his amusement and watching him so closely, I would not have caught the micro-expression of discomfort. "Vinnie! Is Colin not working on this case?"

"I did not say that."

"You didn't need to. It's written all over your face. What is he doing?"

"Jen-girl," he pleaded, "I can't tell you. Colin will come back soon. Most likely today."

I let out a feminine groan of annoyance, a sound very unlike me. This broke the last of the tenuous hold I had on my patience. I could feel my gaze intensifying and by the alarmed look on Vinnie's face, he had noticed the depth of my ire. At the exact moment I was ready to blast him with four days of built-up frustration, a strange ringing came from my handbag on the chair next to me.

"Your phone is ringing."

"Nobody should be phoning me." I opened my handbag with more force than necessary. I found my phone in its pocket. A glance at the screen did not help me to identify the caller. I slid my finger across the touch screen to answer the call. "What?"

"Is that how you answer your phone, Doctor Face-reader?" The surprise in Manny's voice drove my annoyance level higher.

"Where did you get my number? Nobody is supposed to have my number."

"Phillip gave it to me. You never answer your home phone, so I made him give me this number."

I was going to kill Phillip for this. "It's Sunday morning, Manny. What do you want?"

"I was hoping that you maybe discovered something new. I just got off the phone with the Chief. And he gave me hell. We need to make some headway, missy."

"Doctor," I said through my teeth. "Maybe if I had the financials from the Foundation, I would have been able to give you something new. Where are those financials? You keep promising them to me."

"And I keep telling you that I've requested them. As soon as I get the figures, they will be available to you." He took an audible breath, I supposed to calm himself. He sounded as annoyed as I felt. "Are we done with this hostile greeting?"

Shame pushed colour into my cheeks. Hoping that Vinnie didn't see me blushing was too much to hope for. He was staring at me, listening intently to my side of the conversation. I turned my torso away from Vinnie and sighed. "I'm sorry, Manny. I'm just frustrated that I've not made any new progress."

The silence that left the open line softly buzzing made me wonder if I had shocked Manny with my apology. It made me feel a bit better that I might have surprised the perpetually dishevelled agent. "I understand your frustration. After the Chief's phone call this morning, I threw my cereal bowl against the wall. Now I have to clean the mess up."

I laughed softly at the image of a pyjama-clad Manny cleaning up soggy cornflakes from the walls and floor. At moments like this I almost liked him. "Why is the Chief pushing this so much?"

"Good question. It isn't as if I'm taking time off other projects or neglecting anything important. If anything, this should be given more time and attention. I really don't like being torn another one."

"Another what?"

There was a moment of silence. "Nothing. Never mind. Did you look at the email Leon sent you?"

"I did. And as I said in my email that I cc'ed you on, none of those insignias look even close to the one I saw on the uniform."

"Are you sure?" His question rankled me. Instead of being rude, I chose to remain silent. After a while he got the message. "Okay, that's settled then. Please just tell me that you did discover something new."

"Nothing new. Just more confirmation. Everything I know, I emailed you in the last report." At least writing that report had made me feel productive. I was fast nearing a point of desperate frustration.

"This is how most investigations go. You get a lead, hit a wall, get a lead, hit another wall. Sometimes you happen upon that one thing that brings everything together and answers all the questions." The line was quiet for a long time while both of us were lost in our thoughts. Manny sounded tired when he spoke again. "Have you looked at the file on the weapons theft?"

"I have, but not in depth. I looked superficially for something that might represent a pattern, but got a bit lost in this shipping thing. I'll look into it soon."

"Do that, and let me know if you find something." We exchanged awkward goodbyes and ended the phone call. I leaned back in my chair and wished for some kind of inspiration to start a new search that might lead to more clarity about how everything fit together.

"Telephone skills are not one of your strengths, Jen-girl." Vinnie's voice broke into my thoughts and I turned to him. I had forgotten about his presence. He had an uncanny ability to blend into his environment. Numerous times I had forgotten about him being in my apartment while he sat a few feet away from me reading his newspaper. It would appear that I was comfortable in his presence. "Jen-girl? Come back to me."

"Hmm?" Once again I had disappeared into my head, trying to understand all these new dynamics in my life. "Oh, the phone. No, I don't like speaking on the phone."

"Why not?" He looked genuinely interested.

"Body language accounts for an overwhelming percentage of our communication. If I only have a small percentage to analyse, I don't understand people and can't tell when people are lying."

Vinnie gave a surprised laugh. "You really believe people lie so much?"

"Of course. It is part of social interaction. Saying what is truly on your mind, giving your honest opinion and answering questions truthfully is an overwhelmingly bad thing to do in a social setting. Being polite and diplomatic relies heavily on your skills to twist the truth so it doesn't upset anyone."

"Wow. And you never lie?"

"Not never. I lied last week." I had to stop talking because Vinnie was laughing so hard. He must have seen the look on my face, because he stopped.

"I'm sorry, Jen-girl. I really didn't mean to offend or hurt you. I've just never met anyone like you. And that is a compliment."

My smile thanking Vinnie for his strange compliment froze as a familiar figure walked towards us from the direction of the study. Colin. He had broken in again. Our eyes met and widened in an involuntary micro-expression. This indicated a positive emotional response to a pleasant surprise. It immediately made me irrationally angry that I was as happy to see him as he me. Combined with his refusal to use the front door, it had my blood pressure soaring. "Where have you been?"

"Hi, Jenny. Miss me?" He gave me an arrogant smile and nodded to Vinnie. "What's up?"

I didn't give Vinnie a chance to return the greeting. My voice was hostile at the realisation that I actually did miss the criminal. "Four days. You just up and go for four days doing God knows what. I know that you haven't been working on this case. How am I supposed to trust your commitment to this when you go off without giving me the courtesy of telling me?"

Colin's eyes narrowed and the corners of his mouth moved slightly down. I was making him angry. "Jenny, stop."

"Dude, I didn't tell her anything. I swear." Vinnie sounded worried.

"I know, Vin." He gave Vinnie a half smile. "She read you."

"*She* is here." I slapped my hand on the dining room table. To my disgust, tears were gathering in my eyes. I hadn't cried in front of people in eighteen years. I bit down hard on my teeth, resenting everyone who had caused me to have uncontrolled emotions in the last week.

All signs of anger on Colin's face were immediately replaced with concern. Slowly, as if not to startle me, he pulled a chair closer and sat down between Vinnie and me. How could he look so calm when my emotions were bouncing around like this? Emotions had always been a nuisance to me. I knew that they were messengers, telling me what was happening in my psyche, but having them often interfered with rationality. And now was a time to regain my grip on rational thought. My breathing had become too rapid and I focussed on calming myself and closing my mind to pesky emotions.

I called up one of Mozart's earlier works and concentrated on the blank sheet of mental music paper. It took writing nine bars until I felt normalcy settle in me. I opened my eyes to find Colin sitting close. He leaned a bit closer and gently placed a warm hand on my clenched fists. "I'm sorry I left like that, Jenny. I never meant to upset you."

"I shouldn't have been so upset just now."

"What caused it?" he asked with a concerned frown.

"The realisation that I missed you." The words were out of my mouth before I could stop them. A sense of vulnerability and terror washed over me. I squeezed my eyes closed and frantically started writing a few more bars of Mozart. In over two decades I had not given anyone this much power to hurt me as I had just done. Admitting that I had felt the loss of Colin's company placed me in a position that I had sworn to myself I would never occupy again. I didn't want to need people.

"Jenny, look at me."

It took me three more bars before I opened my eyes and looked in a face completely devoid of malice. I studied him intently for a full minute before I allowed myself to believe that he looked genuinely concerned. To his and Vinnie's credit, neither had uttered as much as a snicker at my uncensored admission.

"I'm okay." I answered the question I saw in his eyes.

"Good." He leaned in even closer to completely invade my space and whispered, "I also missed you."

Relief stole my breath. I knew that it showed clearly on my face. There was no way that I was able to control that intense an emotion from showing. Colin gave my hands a light squeeze before he released them and sat back. "If I promise to never leave you like that again, will you tell me where you are on the case?"

I dismissed his promise with a wave of my hand, thankful to move away from emotions, and proceeded to tell him the miniscule progress we had made in the last four days. The few bars of Mozart that I had written had also served to calm my frustration with the case. As I told Colin about my conversation with Manny, something was pushing in the back of my head, seeking attention. Maybe if I wrote a few more bars, I could allow it entrance and examination. I suspected it was the key to moving forward.

"Have you checked names of the dead artists against the shipping manifests, guest lists, etcetera?" Colin's question blasted through my brain like lightning. That was the thought that had been seeking entrance.

"I was waiting for you." I turned back to the computer and immediately opened that file. "I found five artists who were murdered and you knew of thirteen. You never gave me their names. Without more data the search would have been futile."

One by one Colin recited names. A few he had to spell, their foreignness uncomfortable on the ear and tongue. Two of the names I already had on my list. It was with those two and four others that sadness changed Colin's voice. He had known these people. I turned to him and held his eyes for a short moment. "I'm sorry about this, Colin."

"So am I."

I entered all the names into the software to search against the ships' manifests and pressed enter. "This is going to take some time. Vinnie made coffee. Would you like some?"

Vinnie was already halfway to the kitchen when Colin answered, "That would be great. Thanks, Vin."

"He has completely taken over my apartment."

"Is that a problem?" Colin glanced at the kitchen before studying me.

"No," I answered after taking time to find how I truly felt. "He's neat and non-intrusive."

"Rare qualities in a man." The soft wrinkles forming in the corners of his eyes clued me in that he was joking. I was actually about to agree with him, but answered him instead with a small smile. We held each other's eyes until he shifted his body. A series of minute facial muscle movements warned me that he was going to say something he considered of great importance.

A succession of pings crudely broke the moment. I didn't take my eyes off Colin and saw how he changed his mind. His focus shifted from something internal to the computer. "What was that?"

"Connections." I turned to the computer and looked at the lines of information that the software programme had delivered. I didn't know if Colin understood what all the little white letters on the blue background meant, but found myself too stunned to ask. It was hard to believe what I was looking at. This might just be that one thing that Manny and I had been talking about. The one thing that would connect all the different elements we had uncovered so far.

My mind was working full speed. I turned my internal Mozart to top volume and leaned into the cerebral activity. Nothing else existed at that moment. Not Vinnie placing Colin's coffee on a coaster next to him. Not Colin softly calling to me. What mattered most were the pieces of the puzzle moving to their places on their own volition. At the crescendo in the middle of the second movement, a thought popped into my head and I acted on it.

I entered another search order into the software and waited, all the while letting Mozart lead the way. I didn't hear anything from the two men. Whether it was because I had blocked them out or they were silently waiting for me, I didn't know. Nor did I care. I was rocking back and forth to the music in my head and looking expectantly at the computer screen.

Another ping and a second window with search information popped open. I maximised the window, simply to see this golden find fill as much space as possible. "Oh my."

"Jenny?" Colin's warm hand lightly touched my forearm and slowly brought me back into my skin and into the room. "What have you found?"

I stared at him through the haze of excitement. "An address."

His eyes widened and his jaw slackened. After a silent few heartbeats, both Vinnie's and Colin's eyes moved to the computer screens. Their eyes narrowed and they frowned. "Jenny, tell us what we're looking at."

I inhaled very deeply. I was going to explain. That required simple vocabulary, sentences and focus. I changed windows to the results of the first search and pointed out a few lines in between all the script. "Every single one of those artists was on one of those cruise ships at some point in the last eight years."

"Motherfucker." It was the first time that Vinnie had used such strong language in front of me. It was usually reserved for the kitchen while I was working. He must have been as shocked as I was.

Colin's expletive followed immediately, his head moving from side to side in shocked denial. I changed windows to the result of the second search and tapped lightly on the screen. "I was wondering about romances like Danielle had with her Russian boyfriend. Of all the artists, only two ever shared their rooms. Danielle was one. The other was Karin Vittone. She shared a room with a Mark Smith. His address is on the manifest."

"Where does the fucker live?" The menace in Vinnie's voice reminded me that he was more than just a non-intrusive houseguest.

"Here. In Strasbourg."

"Judas fucking Priest." Colin leaned back in his chair. "I'll go visit the bastard."

"Both of you are jumping to conclusions that he is a guilty party."

"How can we not?" Colin asked. "Just look at everything we've found so far. The fact that Mark Smith shared a room with one of the dead artists makes him at the very least a person of interest, but most likely a suspect. I'll go check out his house tomorrow evening."

"What do you mean 'check out his house'?" A cold feeling crept through me.

"He means break into the fuc... the suspect's house, Jen-girl." Vinnie spat out his disgust at this person. Obviously, innocent until proven guilty was not something he lived by.

"You can't break into his house. It's illegal." The comical look on both the men's faces brought reality crashing around me. "Of course. You are a criminal who breaks into places and steals things."

"Jenny."

"Oh, don't use your warning tone of voice on me. Do you want all the reasons why this is a bad idea?"

"Will you make me a list?" The relaxation around his eyes stopped me cold.

"Are you making fun of my lists?" My voice gradually rose until the last word came out as a squeak.

"A little." He grew serious. "Your lists, however, are what have gotten us this far, so I'm very happy with your lists. But"—he stopped me as I reached for the notepad to start on all the reasons why he shouldn't break into Mark Smith's house—"I am going to look at this house, list or no."

"Let him do this, Jen-girl."

I glared at Vinnie for interfering and then closed my eyes. A few bars of Mozart and I was calmer. "What are you going to do?"

"I'll go tonight and just look around. Check out the neighbourhood, the security and a general look around. Tomorrow evening I will break into his house and look around inside. I want to see who he really is."

"What do you mean?"

"A man is much more than just a name."

"Not that I think Mark Smith is his real name," Vinnie interrupted.

"Neither do I. We'll have to see if it's his real address." Colin shook his head. "Some people are such incompetent criminals. Anyway. We all reveal a lot about who we are by how we live. Our homes give away a lot of inside information on our lives, likes, habits and the like."

Suddenly I was very curious to see Colin's home. And Vinnie's. I already knew what my apartment said about me. I wasn't hard to decode. Then I thought again about Colin's plans for the next two nights. "I don't like it."

"I'll be careful, Jenny."

"If you get caught, don't come back here." I couldn't stop the petulance tainting my voice. Vinnie chuckled and Colin's smile reached deep into his eyes.

"I won't get caught. I'm too good for that." He turned to Vinnie. "Did you get the phones?"

"Oh, yes." Vinnie got up from the table and grabbed a large paper shopping bag from next to the coffee table. I hadn't even noticed him putting it there. He handed it to Colin. "There are three in there. Bought in different stores."

"Good." Colin dug into the bag and took out three different boxes containing cell phones. He handed me one, but I refused to take it. "Take it, Jenny."

"No. I already have a smartphone."

Colin sighed. "I know. This is a phone that cannot be traced to you, Manny, Phillip or anyone else."

"Why do I need this?" I narrowed my eyes when Colin and Vinnie exchanged a look. "What?"

"Someone's been trying to wiretap your phones."

"My phones?"

"Your home phone and most likely your cell phone," Vinnie said. "Two days ago there was an unscheduled visit from the telephone company to your building. Since then your phone has a different buzz."

"And now I need another cell phone? Why?"

"Jen-girl, don't you ever watch any cop shows or movies? Ever?" Vinnie rolled his eyes when I mutely shook my head. "You're strange. If you watched anything other than the news, you would know that we need these phones to communicate without anyone else knowing about it. And it seems like there are a lot of people interested in knowing about this."

I took a moment to process the information and took the box from Colin. "Okay."

"I've already set it up. It has Colin's and my numbers on it."

"Don't use it to contact anyone but us," Colin added.

"I never use my smartphone." I broke off and tilted my head. "Not to phone people anyway."

"Her telephone skills are not the smoothest," Vinnie whispered loudly to Colin, who only smiled.

I took the cheap phone out of the box and looked at Colin. "Will you phone me to tell me that everything is okay tonight?"

He nodded.

I shook the phone at him. "And tomorrow evening? If anything happens, you'll phone?"

"She cares about you, dude." Vinnie smiled. I felt like throwing my new cell phone at his head. He must have sensed my displeasure, because his smile died and he tried to force his face into a neutral expression. He failed miserably.

"Ignore him." Colin moved closer to the computer. "Can you give me the address, please?"

With a sigh I wrote down the address on a post-it note and handed it to him. He looked at it for a few moments and then handed it back to me. Apparently I was not the only one with a good memory.

No matter how much I convinced myself that I didn't believe in gut feelings, a tightness in my torso made me feel very uncomfortable about Colin's plan. A tightness that didn't want to go away.

Chapter SEVENTEEN

"Vinnie, I don't like this." I didn't know why I was whispering. No one could overhear my telephonic discussion while I was in my soundproof viewing room. "I don't care that he phoned me last night and told me that this will be easy. He's still entering someone's house illegally."

"Colin will be fine, Jen-girl. I'm going to say this one more time: he knows what he's doing." He dragged out the last part as if I was slow in comprehension. "Now get off the phone and do your work. I'll be waiting for you when you're done."

"Fine." I didn't wait for a response and just closed the new cell phone to disconnect. Vinnie and I had been arguing ever since Colin left us last night. I wished that I had had more time. Then I could have analysed this bad feeling I had about Colin breaking into Mark Smith's house. But all my time was consumed with finding more connections in this case. And the connections seemed to be forthcoming. With Colin's help yesterday, I had found two more artists who had been murdered. Both had been on cruises.

Now I was ready to look into the financials of the Foundation for Development of Sustainable Education. It had been in my inbox when I opened my email this morning with a sarcastic note from Manny. He was angry again and I didn't know why. I hadn't done anything new to annoy him. Maybe he had received another phone call from Chief Dutoit.

First things first. I went to the music files on my computer and selected the playlist I favoured when dealing with more challenging cases. Once Mozart was floating through the room, filling every available space with its purity, everything in me stilled. Like always, it felt like my thoughts, my life, my entirety snapped into focus. I opened the first financial report and started working through it.

As per usual when I was absorbed in something interesting, time drifted away from me. It was the gentle swoosh of the viewing room door opening and closing that brought me back to the present. I glanced at my watch and was shocked that it was just past four o'clock. I had been working through these financials for the last eight hours. It had been very productive. I turned to my visitor with an elated sense of achievement. Which was promptly replaced with annoyance. I was looking at a very disapproving face.

"Why have you not contacted me, Doctor Face-reader?" Manny pulled a chair closer and sat down next to me. I looked over his shoulder at the door, hoping that Phillip would be following him to buffer this conversation, but alas. The door remained disappointingly closed.

"Why would I contact you?"

"Because I asked you to. On all seven messages I left on your bloody cell phone."

"I've told you that I don't use my cell phone."

"Then why do you have one?" He stopped me when I opened my mouth to give him the lengthy explanation of recording people in public places. "No, I actually don't want to know. Could you please turn that racket down?"

I looked at him blankly.

"The music, missy. The music."

I turned Mozart's Fugue in G minor down to a soft din in the background. Manny continued frowning, so I switched it off.

"Tell me that you've got something new. My boss is riding my arse, Leon is riding my arse because *his* boss is riding his arse, and I'm sick of it."

The way he threw himself back against the chair and closed his eyes in a pained expression prevented me from inquiring about the arse-riding. I made a mental note to remember this new expression and ask Vinnie about it. I assumed its meaning and liked it. I also liked the idea that I could take away the stress lines marring Manny's face. I didn't like other people placing so much pressure on him. Why I would feel this was a worrying mystery.

"We have the names of sixteen murdered artists, most of whom were amateurs. These murders took place in the last eight years."

I had Manny's full attention. He was sitting up in the chair now. Not a single stress line on his face, only interest.

"Every single one of them was on a cruise ship that travelled along the Baltic or North Sea routes. Only Danielle and another artist ever shared rooms on the ships. Karin Vittone, the other artist, shared her room with one Mark Smith."

Manny remained silent for a very long time, staring at the wall behind me. Then he lifted his eyes and gave me a smile. The first genuine smile I had seen on his face. "I could kiss you right now."

My eyes stretched in shock and I pushed with my feet to roll my chair away from him. "Please don't."

His smile was immediately replaced by a scowl. "It's just an expression, missy."

I realised how my reaction must have looked and closed my eyes with regret. "Manny, I'm sorry. I'm not good with this. With relating to people. With speaking to people without giving offence. I'm especially not good with physical contact."

My mind flashed back to the few times that Colin had touched me and Vinnie had ruffled my hair. Vinnie I had wanted to hit over the head, but not because he had touched me. Rather because he had messed up my carefully styled hair. Colin's touch didn't cause any negative reflexes.

"Genevieve!" Manny's annoyed voice broke into my thoughts. "Would you please not get lost in your head. Phillip is not here to help me if you go all weird again."

"And people say I have no diplomacy." I smiled. "It's actually refreshing to know someone ruder than I."

Manny grumbled something about uppity little geniuses and sighed. "Please tell me everything you've found so far."

I did. I told him everything that I had discovered yesterday with the exception of Mark Smith's address. I knew that it was wrong and that at one point I was going to pay dearly for it, but what else was I supposed to do? If I told him about the address, he would send people there and Colin would be discovered.

A heaviness settled in my mind with the thought that I was aiding and abetting a criminal. Even worse, I was withholding vital information from a law enforcement agent. This was going to land me in jail.

"What about the Foundation's financials?"

"They're perfect." I ignored Manny's groan of disappointment. "Too perfect. That is never a good sign. Especially for a charity. In any large organisation there are anomalies in their financials. It is to be expected. But here"—I pointed at one of the monitors against the wall—"everything is perfect. Which made me very suspicious."

"Please tell me you found something else."

"I did." I flinched a little at my admission. I didn't want Manny to want to kiss me again. When he didn't threaten me with such grateful behaviour, I continued. "Yesterday I delved deeper into auctions. I honestly don't know how many auctions there were on the cruise ships since I could only work with those that were advertised."

"Fair enough."

"Everything about the auctions, the marketing, pamphlets, everything was very average. Nothing to raise any questions."

"But something got your attention."

"Would you stop interrupting me?" My sharp reprimand surprised and then angered Manny. His lips disappeared into a thin line. I felt free to continue. "Thank you. Yes, something got my attention. I have established that twenty-seven of the thirty-three companies I've identified used the same legal and accounting firms. Those same two firms are listed on the Foundation's expenditure statements. That connects the ships to each other and to the Foundation."

"That's fantastic. A concrete connection."

"There's more. On every cruise that held an auction, three percent of the profit was promised to the Foundation. So I cross-checked the dates of the cruises. Look here." I aimed my laser pointer at one of the ten monitors. "On the sixteenth of July last year, the *Krolewska* cruise ship held an auction. The *Krolewska* is owned by Zeek, a company owned by Kozlevich. If you look over here"—I pointed at the monitor to the left— "you'll see that on the nineteenth of July, three days later, the *Krolewska* donated fifty thousand euro to the Foundation. The next day, Zeek donated a hundred and fifty thousand euro to the Foundation."

"Holy mother of all that is pure." Manny stared wide-eyed at the monitors. I wished that I could have taken a photo of his face. It was textbook disbelief. "I take it that this is not the only instance."

"Indeed not. This exact system was used with eight other auctions that I've found so far. Three days after the auction was held, the cruise ship donated an amount to the Foundation and the next day that amount was tripled by the company that owns that ship. The combined amount of all these so-called donations so far is over five million euro."

"A lot of money, but in the grand scheme of things, not that huge."

"True, but did you know that the Foundation received over eighteen million euro last year in donations, grants and all other kinds of funding?"

"What?"

"Did you know that—"

"I heard you before. Where did they get that much money from?"

"That is what I want to check next. I'm sure there are some legitimate donations, but I'm going to look deeper. Now that I have a pattern, the first donation and the tripled donation the next day, I'll look for more transfers like that. But I found something even more interesting."

"I don't think my heart can take it."

"I didn't know you had heart problems." Alarmed, I leaned closer, looking for signs of physical discomfort displayed on his face.

Manny leaned back in his chair and frowned at me. "You are sometimes so weird I have to wonder if you are human. I do not have heart problems. It's an expression. Please, just tell me what else you've found."

I put this new expression on the list to ask Vinnie about. A grimace settled around my mouth. I didn't like what I was about to tell Manny. "Since I had the auctions with their dates, I decided to cross-check it with the dates of the deaths of the artists. Shortly after each auction—sometimes a day, sometimes a week, but never more than ten days—an artist turned up dead. I have found five situations like this."

"Holy mother." If there were an analogue clock in my viewing room, I would have heard the seconds tick away the long silence between us. "Send this all to me. Everything."

"I'll write up a report and send it to you early this evening."

"I simply cannot believe that one of the most high-profile charities in Europe, helping tens of thousands of people every year, can be involved in this. This is going to cause an international political situation. Many top officials in Europe lend their support to the Foundation." He exhaled slowly, puffing his cheeks. People did this to calm down after a negative experience, or in this case, a negative realisation. "To top it all, it seems like the Foundation is run by goons."

"Who is this Mister Goons?" I hadn't seen that name anywhere during my research into the Foundation.

Manny stared at me open-mouthed. "Have you absolutely no vocabulary outside of your academic dictionaries?"

"I've never found it imperative to my work." That had most certainly changed in the last two weeks. "What or who is a goons then?"

"Lowlife criminals."

"Oh." I dragged out the sound, wondering how Vinnie and Colin would respond to being called goons. Time to refocus. "What is the connection between the EDA, Eurocorps and the Foundation? I've looked for something, but all I've found are numerous functions attended by officials from the two agencies. There are also many articles mentioning donations, support and involvement from the European Commission, EDA and Eurocorps. Do you know anything about this?"

"Since the beginning of the EDA, the Foundation was its favoured charity. I've been forced to attend more black-tie functions for this charity than I care for." His nose crinkled in disgust. "I always thought having these elaborate functions was such a waste of money. Money that could be put to better use to help more people. But such is the politics of charities."

"What about Eurocorps' involvement?"

"I don't know. Let's ask Leon." He took out his cell phone, touched the screen a few times, held it between us and waited. It rang four times.

"Manny." Leon's voice was even deeper over the phone.

"Leon, I'm with Doctor Lenard and you're on speaker. Is this a good time?"

"Hold on." We heard a muffled order for someone to return in half an hour and a door clicked closed. "I'm back. What's happening?"

Manny looked at me and lifted his eyebrows. I lifted my

eyebrows back at him. His eyes narrowed and he huffed. He rolled his eyes and then spoke towards the phone. "The doc and I were talking about the Foundation's connection between the EDA and Eurocorps. How long has Eurocorps been involved with the Foundation?"

Obviously Leon was up to date with everything so far, because he didn't pause to answer. "The first time I heard about the Foundation was, let me think, about seven years ago. It was Brigadier-General Crenshaw who pushed us to go to that first event. It was the year after I joined Eurocorps. I remember this because he was really making an issue of it."

"The same Nick Crenshaw from the Iron Curtain division? The same Crenshaw asking too many questions about the weapons theft?" Manny asked.

"The same."

I found this conversation interesting, especially the intense dislike for Brigadier-General Crenshaw I heard in Leon's voice and saw on Manny's face. "Could you gentlemen please tell me more about him?"

"Oh, hello, Genevieve." Leon sounded surprised to hear my voice. He must have forgotten about me. "Nick Crenshaw served with Manny and myself a million years ago."

"The three of us floated between agencies, sometimes together, sometimes not," Manny said. "At one point all three of us were in Interpol. Later on Crenshaw was stationed in Hungary, in what we called the Iron Curtain division, the ICD."

"Manny?" Leon sounded worried.

"It's all right, Leon. Doc is privy to quite a bit of confidential stuff at the moment. But I'm definitely not going to tell her anything too confidential." He looked at me. "You have to understand that this conversation is never to become public knowledge."

I just nodded. Would telling Vinnie and Colin be considered making this public knowledge? Since I knew I could never ask

Manny this, I bit my tongue. Literally.

"Good. The Iron Curtain division worked in countries that were previously under communist rule. If the scuttlebutt..." Manny frowned at me and sighed. "If rumours were to be believed, Crenshaw was heading up a unit that was doing all kinds of intelligence work following the collapse of the Soviet Union. After Interpol, he joined Eurocorps. Do you know when that was, Leon?"

"Five years before me. That would be thirteen years ago." There was a short silence. "Why are we discussing Crenshaw's résumé?"

"Because he was the one who insisted that Eurocorps get involved with the Foundation."

"And because he was in Hungary," I added. "Aside from the many times that Russia has come up in my research, Hungary is the one country that has come up time and time again."

"How does Hungary fit into this?" Leon asked. "And where do the stolen weapons fit in?"

"Well, that is for you to find out." I looked at Manny. "Have you still not obtained any information on the other murdered artists? Or the ballistic reports?"

Manny's lips disappeared. Once again I had expressed my frustration uncensored. I was about to explain when Leon's voice sounded strained. "The request that I sent last week to the local police stations conveniently disappeared. Apparently, it never even reached them. I refiled this morning and made sure that each one was received."

Concern settled deep in my brain. Manny's insider had to have enough authority to be following this investigation. I started thinking about all the information that had electronically been communicated between us. With the exception of Colin and Vinnie's presence, there wasn't much unrevealed. Except my thoughts and theories.

"Leon, have you ever heard of Piros?" That name still

bothered me. Those thugs who broke into my apartment had used it with enough fear to awaken concern.

"Why?" The tone of Leon's voice grabbed my attention. A wealth of suspicion and worry was delivered with that one word.

"Because the men who broke into my apartment said that Piros was going to be very unhappy about what had happened in my apartment and he was going to require an immediate report. They also said that he had big plans."

Muffled words came through the phone, loud enough for me to raise my brows in surprise. I had not expected Leon to use such strong language. A look at Manny's face made my stomach clench with dread.

"Why the hell did you not tell me about this?" Manny pushed the words through clenched teeth.

"Because I did not know where it fit in. If it fit anywhere. I still don't know."

"So you withheld information from me?" His face was turning an alarming shade of red.

"She just told you about that, Manny. Shall we move on?" Leon broke the glaring silence between Manny and myself. "Genevieve, Piros is a legend in Eastern Europe. Nobody has ever been able to put a name to the legend or to get close to him. He enjoys the protection of many powerful people in Central and Eastern Europe and apparently also in Russia."

"You remember the armies we told you about last week?" Angry tension pulled at Manny's mouth. "The RNT? Well, Piros is the guy who trains these armies, missy."

"Manny, stop shouting at the girl."

Manny bit down hard and breathed loudly for a few moments. "Doctor Face-reader, are you very sure that those men said Piros? Were they speaking English?"

"They were speaking English and Russian, and before you ask, I'm proficient in Russian. The fear in their voices is what made me take notice. Those guys were really large men, able to do someone serious bodily harm." I suppressed an involuntary shiver. "Yet they were very visibly scared of this Piros."

"Manny, we can't mention this anywhere official. This will open all kinds of Pandora's boxes," Leon said gravely.

"I know." Manny rubbed the back of his neck and looked at me. "The RNT soldier who escaped told Interpol a few things about Piros."

"Was that what you were not telling me when I asked about the trainer of the RNT?"

"Yes. There are a lot of things that you don't need to know, and at that point Piros being the trainer was one of those things."

I had no right to accuse Manny of withholding information that could have proven helpful if I had known it earlier. I was guilty of the same. And more. So I waited for him to continue.

"There is a list of aliases possibly associated with Piros. Some of them are stolen identities, but none were ever confirmed to have direct ties to him. Our guy gave us two more names, but he gave us a lot more about the training. Apparently, Piros communicates with the soldiers during training through earpieces. As far as our guy knows, no one had ever seen him. All of them know his voice extremely well. It used to give our guy nightmares that he would wake up from screaming. Piros would give them orders in four different languages."

"Which languages?" I asked.

"English, Hungarian, Russian and French. They were expected to know all four. It was part of the qualification process. If they passed the psych eval, the training started. They had lectures where they were taught the legal and law enforcement procedures of different Western European countries. This bastard has an extensive knowledge of the internal workings of the system."

"Which only serves to reinforce our suspicions that he's an official in an EU agency," Leon said.

Manny grunted. "Our guy said their equipment was the latest of everything. They lacked for nothing. During training Piros would watch them on the cameras that were placed all over the compound. They used to joke that he could be training them from anywhere in the world. A few of them started hating his voice in their ears all the time. They were never allowed to remove the earpieces, not even while they were sleeping. He said the worst was when Piros used the word red. Like for code red, red alert and some such things."

"Why red?" I asked.

"When he said it in French, he used to draw it out in an awkward sound. Apparently that is where he got his name from."

"Piros is red in Hungarian," I whispered as my heart slammed against my chest. My earlier suspicion had just been confirmed. "How long has Piros been active in Europe?"

"The first time the name Piros was mentioned was about fifteen years ago." Leon answered.

"But according to our guy, he started not long after the Soviet Union was dissolved," Manny added.

"Okay, so two decades ago communism fell." I was thinking out loud. "A lot of countries were suddenly freed from Russia's rule. Many powerful people lost their power. A few of these went on to become involved in criminal activities."

"Most of them were already criminals." Manny's hatred for Russia was wearing me down. I glared at him until he lifted his hands and waited for me to continue.

"They had to protect their enterprises and formed private armies. In comes this Piros person, ready to train these armies. Do you agree with me that it would be a reasonable assumption that this person would have had to have military training himself in order to train these armies?" Both men agreed with me. I cleared my throat nervously. "There is something else. I've been thinking a lot about those three sentences Chulkov shouted.

When I translated it to Russian, his mother tongue, he might have been talking about Piros."

"What?" Manny shot up into the most aware posture I had yet seen him in. "Explain."

I did. When Manny's eyes lost focus, I stopped explaining Russian grammar and its lack of definite and indefinite articles. I was forced to stick to the bare minimum. Such incomplete explanations left me unsatisfied, but it appeared to be enough to clarify things for Leon and Manny. "And before you shout at me again for not telling you sooner, it was and still is a mere guess."

"A bloody good one." Manny relaxed into his chair. "That means that the Russian was shouting that Piros will end all twenty-seven daffodils? What the hell does that mean?"

"If we're going with my hypothesis, then twenty-seven and daffodils may also have different meanings."

"Like what?" Leon asked.

"I'm still working on it." Not that I was getting closer to anything that made sense.

"This might be relevant or not, but our guy told Interpol that there were a lot of rumours about Piros' love for art. Apparently he has quite an art collection. Not that anyone has seen it. Our guy couldn't even remember where he had heard the rumour, but it fits in quite neatly with our case."

I frowned while weighing this bit of information. "It does fit in neatly, but since it is insubstantial conjecture, I will ignore it."

Manny looked offended. "You're the one always saying that even the smallest detail might be the most important key to unlock this secret."

"I know I've never said anything like that." As if I would use an analogy like that. My mind was, however, already going in a new direction. "Leon, you told me last week that you had concerns about Brigadier-General Crenshaw. That you didn't trust him?"

"Did I say that?"

"Yes, you did. Should I tell you exactly what you said?"

"She will. This woman remembers everything word for word." Manny sounded like he enjoyed telling Leon this.

"Oh, dear." Leon sighed. "Well, yes. There was something about Crenshaw's by-the-way attitude that didn't sit well with me. He knew he was not supposed to inquire about the investigation, yet he did. He was using our history to buddy up to me."

"And you told us that he spent a lot of time in Hungary, in Eastern Europe. Is it possible that he could be this Piros person?"

From the look on Manny's face, I might have suggested that vampires existed, psychics were to be believed and the tooth fairy was real. The silence on the other side of the line precluded me from knowing Leon's reaction to my question.

"Holy mother of all the saints," Manny eventually breathed. "Leon?"

"I don't know, this is a lot to think about," came the quiet answer. "I have a meeting coming up. Let me give this some more thought. I'll get back to you."

The line was abruptly disconnected. Manny glared at the phone in his hand and then looked at me. "You certainly know how to kick open a hornets' nest."

I knew this expression, but did not think it fitting. "What do you mean?"

"Genevieve, if what you've just told me is true, it will do irreparable damage to Eurocorps. To have such a notorious criminal as a powerful official in one of the most prestigious agencies in Europe would devastate its credibility. Much more than a little sex scandal. It would destroy all the careful negotiations between Russia and the EU. God, Eurocorps might never recover from this."

"Oh." Whether it was geographical, religious or otherwise, the fragility of politics always amazed me. I gave my mind free rein for a few moments and then gasped at my own brilliance. "Do you have footage of these gala events?"

Manny looked confused and glanced at the monitors against the wall. "You mean video footage of the charity events?"

"Yes. Do you have any footage of the people attending? All those high officials?"

"There should be some footage of it. I can remember last year there was a whole camera crew annoying the hell out of me. They were everywhere, all the time, trying to get as many VIP's as possible on video. They even wanted to interview me." He sneered at the memory.

"Fantastic." Excitement rushed through me. This was it. This was what I was good at. "Bring me as much as possible. From last year, the year before, it doesn't matter. The more I see, the more I can read."

Manny gave me a sideways look, but I didn't care that he looked at me as if I was a newly discovered species. I was thrilled with the prospect of watching the interaction between all these people who had come up in my discoveries. And to have all of them in one room? Not only would I be able to put faces to these people, but I would be able to read their faces. If they were taped by a professional crew, so much the better. The quality would also help a lot. Watching this footage would tell me so much more than a biography on a website.

"I'll phone now to have it put on the network. Give me five minutes." He got up with a groan. Exhaustion lined his eyes. "I'm also going to have to speak to Phillip. I'll pop in again a bit later."

He disappeared through the door and I turned to my computers. I had been so busy with the case, working through loads of data, that I hadn't watched any footage in what felt like months. It had been only two weeks. I loved observing the subtleties of human interaction. People had no idea how much like, dislike, distrust or love they communicated without uttering a single word. Impatiently I glared at the EDA computer, waiting for the footage.

Chapter EIGHTEEN

"Could you please move away from me." I clenched my teeth and glared at Manny. This was the fourth time I had to ask him to respect my personal space. "At least fifty centimetres."

"I'm not even touching you." If possible Manny looked even more rumpled than usual, and had become almost unbearable with his churlishness.

"Fifty centimetres," was my cold reply and I waited for him to shift away.

With a growl he pushed his chair back a bit. "Happy?"

"My God," Phillip groaned on my other side. "You two are worse than toddlers. Maybe it's time we call it a night and go home."

"No!" Both Manny and I responded immediately. It was unsurprising that we were all tired. We had been going through footage of one Foundation event after the other. The two men had been extremely patient with my insistence on watching what they deemed irrelevant footage. Nothing was ever irrelevant, not in a case like this. I looked at my watch and was not shocked to see that midnight was creeping up on us.

"Phillip, why don't you go home? You don't have to be here for this." Manny reached for his cup of coffee and scowled when he found it empty. "I'm the one who knows all the people in the videos and Miss I-need-my-space here knows how to read them. Go home."

"And leave you two to kill each other?"

"I won't kill him, Phillip. Not as long as he stays out of my space." My sincere promise caused exasperation to overtake Phillip's facial muscles. I sighed. "Okay, I promise I will try harder to be nice to Manny. Just go home. You really look tired."

"As do you."

"We will finish this one video and then Doc and I will also go home." Manny's mouth turned down in distaste. "I will stay at least fifty centimetres away from her. Go home."

Phillip frowned. His exhaustion seemed to override his inherent need to be in control and he stood up. "Only this one video. We can continue this tomorrow. Genevieve, how are you getting home?"

"I'll phone..." I slammed my mouth shut and was overcome with relief that Manny wasn't looking at me. He would have seen my face and, as sharp as he was, would have questioned my expression.

"Don't phone for a taxi." Thankfully Manny had come to the wrong conclusion. "I'll take you home."

Phillip broke the stunned silence before I could refuse. "That's a wonderful idea. Thank you, Manny."

I held back my refusal when I saw the warning on Phillip's face. Vinnie and Colin were not going to be happy about this. As it was Vinnie had reluctantly gone home when I told him that I was going to work late. Neither he nor I had heard anything from Colin, and Vinnie had spent another five minutes reassuring me that Colin was fine. I was worried about the infuriating criminal and really didn't want an EDA official driving me home. But, since there was nothing to be done about this now, I shrugged my acceptance. After a few more promises of good behaviour, Phillip was mollified and left me with Manny.

Manny moved even farther away from me. "Shall we look at the video of last year's gala fundraising then?"

"Yes, let's." Work was safe territory and I gladly jumped to it. I had downloaded all the footage onto my work computer the moment it was available on the EDA network. We had looked at it in chronological order. I wanted to see if there had been any significant changes in dynamics between the different people. Opening last year's gala footage with my special viewing software, I watched as the monitors filled with people.

"God, I hate these things," Manny frowned at the monitors.

"Why?" I was curious. This might be the only thing Manny and I had in common.

"All this pomp and ceremony."

"Nothing is real. Everyone is there on display, showing their importance, power and influence."

"Exactly, and I have to go again." His pained groan caught my attention.

"When?"

"This Saturday. Same place, same people, same bullshit."

My mind went into overdrive. It was screaming at me to take a moment, write some Mozart and allow the connections to form. I didn't want to zone out in Manny's presence, so I pushed it back. Later I would give myself over to Mozart and give my mind freedom. "Do you have an invitation?"

"Unfortunately yes. The invitation is actually a book, a full programme for the evening, including the artwork on auction."

"Could I see it?"

That got his attention. "Why?"

"Just something I'm thinking." I tried to be nonchalant. Manny's glare proved yet again I had no future in acting. I reverted to impatience. "Get me the programme. If my suspicions are grounded, the programme will prove it. Until I see it, I'm not going to say anything more on this topic."

"Okay, okay." He lifted both hands. "You can have the bloody programme. It's in my car. Shall we get back to the footage? We're missing the fun parts."

I frowned at his sarcasm, but turned my attention back to the monitors. We watched in silence for a few minutes.

"Pause it." He waited until the monitors showed a still picture of well-dressed people in a room reminiscent of balls held centuries ago. Waiters were carrying trays heavy with champagne or appetisers. Large chandeliers bathed the room in the right kind of light to soften lines and wrinkles. "You see those flowers everywhere? It's awful. This house is in a flower street, the front yard is a jungle of bloody flowers and at these events, they go totally overboard with flower arrangements. The whole house reeks." His top lip lifted in disgust.

"Are you allergic?" It was the only logical conclusion for a hatred of something that gave most people pleasure.

"Terribly," he answered. His eyes narrowed and he leaned a bit closer. "This is actually a good shot. See, there on the left is the Head."

The Head of the EDA, Sarah Crichton, was a short, stout woman who carried herself with an assuredness usually only found in men. Her short brown hair framed a face that seldom smiled. I had watched her at more than half a dozen events and liked her. Even though she didn't wear a social smile like most of the men surrounding her, she showed genuine interest in those who approached her. She spent equal time with everyone, favouring no one.

"Who is that?" With my laser pointer, I aimed at a man who was leaning towards Sarah Crichton. Unfortunately, he was also leaning away from the camera, which made it difficult to see his face and body.

"It looks like him." Manny narrowed his eyes and leaned towards the monitors. "Yup, it's Brigadier-General Nick Crenshaw."

"You really don't like him, do you?"

"No." Manny sat back in his chair. "Fortunately I don't have to work with him."

"If it makes you feel any better, your Head also doesn't like him."

Manny straightened with interest. "She doesn't?"

"No." I played the footage in slow motion. "Look at when he

approaches her. Her torso very slightly moves away from him, even though she looks straight at him and gives him her full attention. We move our torsos away from what we don't like or what doesn't appeal to us." I stopped the video. Using the software to find the exact clip I was looking for, I zoomed in on her face while I played it in slow motion. "Look at her face. She's squinting ever so slightly. We do that when we want to block objectionable things. Her lowered eyebrows tell the same story as does this." I stopped the video to show the corners of her mouth pulling towards her ears. "In real time you might not even notice the movement of her lips. And someone might mistake it for a smile, but this micro-expression uses the *buccinator* muscles on the sides of the face. It is not a smile."

"What is it then?" Manny looked from the image on the monitor to me.

"A sneer." I paused to appreciate the surprise on Manny's face. "Taken in the full context, she most definitely does not like Brigadier-General Crenshaw."

He turned back to the monitors, studying the paused image. "Play it again."

I played the clip again, first in slow motion and then in real time. "Did you see it?"

"I wouldn't have if you hadn't pointed it out. This is really amazing, Doctor Face-reader. What else can you tell about these people, the ones we were looking at earlier?"

"Let's see." I pressed play and watched a few more minutes. I stopped the footage and hesitated. Where was Phillip when I needed guidance?

"What?" Manny must have picked up on my unease.

I decided to take the plunge. "It's you. Look at your body language over here. For most of this clip you lean back to keep your distance, but are socially polite. When this man—"

"That's Frederique Dutoit, the Chief Executive of the EDA."

"I know." I had seen the tall man in enough clips to

recognise the elegant middle-aged man. He was wearing a quality bespoke suit and carried himself with a dignity born from understated power. I studied him as he leaned towards Manny in amicable camaraderie. "When he approaches you, you hide your hands. This is the first time that I've seen you do that."

Manny looked at his hands resting on his thighs and frowned unhappily. "And what does that mean?"

"It means that you are suspicious of the person you are speaking to or you are uncomfortable to speak with him. Why don't you trust him?"

"I do trust him. He is one of the most honourable men I know. He has been awarded many medals for his service to the continent. During the Cold War, he even went undercover in Russia for some time. His selfless actions have saved many lives. Sure, his enthusiasm for attending the Foundation's gala annoyed me, but for him it has always been about charity, about giving back. On their holidays, Dutoit and his wife Irena open their farm in Hungary to unprivileged kids. He takes them fishing, horse riding and Irena teaches them to cook. He even has artists and musicians come to teach them." Manny stopped his rationalisation to frown at my incredulous expression.

"Such an impassioned defence of someone else is often required to convince the speaker rather than the audience. Again I ask, why don't you trust him?"

Manny swallowed his immediate response and took his time to answer. "I thought I did. You've just successfully cast a healthy twenty-year-long working relationship in doubt."

"No, I didn't. I just told you what your subconscious already knew."

"Well, I don't know why I don't trust him." He paused. "I know why I don't like Crenshaw. He likes the Russkies too much and doesn't respect the code."

"What code?"

"It's an unspoken code, Doc. We live by this code through being loyal, honest, respectful and true to something much bigger than us. Crenshaw is only watching out for numero uno." He looked at me and a small smile tugged at his mouth. "Numero uno is himself. He's only watching out for himself. He doesn't care about anyone else."

"Does the Chief not live by that code? Is he also watching out for numero uno?" The expression felt foreign and wrong on my tongue.

"Chief Executive Frederique Dutoit has a reputation of being fair, loyal and demands more of himself than he does of those who work for him."

"Yet you are not convinced."

"You are much too sharp, missy."

If sarcasm was what he used to mask his anger, provocative insults were his way of masking his discomfiture. I decided to not say anything about his offensive form of address. "I didn't mean to make you uncomfortable. It is just what I see on the footage."

"I know. And you are right. Dutoit has been in the EU military scene for longer than Leon, myself and Crenshaw. He's moved around a bit as well, also spending time in Eastern Europe, but he never became as attached to that side of the world as Crenshaw."

"They seem to have some connection though."

"What do you mean?"

I played a few minutes of footage and pointed to the monitor. "Look at how studiously they avoid each other. Apart from the expected social greetings, they never speak to each other. They keep circulating the room away from each other, but visually seek each other out every now and then."

"I have no idea what to make of that. Are you sure they're not acting normally?"

I lifted one eyebrow, tilted my head to one side and gave him a sideways look. Really? After being so impressed with my ability to read people, he dared question it? He sniffed and turned his attention back to the monitors when I continued playing the footage. We watched people milling around, but I kept looking for Leon, Manny, Sarah Crichton, Crenshaw and Frederique Dutoit. It was the dynamics between these people that were important. For the moment.

This was one of the few videos that also had an audio feed. For the most part I turned it off to focus on the body language rather than being distracted by the din of a social gathering. It reminded me too much of my childhood, my parents entertaining high society, expecting me to be normal. On the monitors I watched the same kind of people acting out the same rituals I saw as a child. Some things never changed.

I watched as Crenshaw charmed an older lady, smiling insincerely when addressed by the lady's overweight, middle-aged female companion. If I had to guess, it was the older lady who had either the power or prestige Crenshaw was after. The companion was an obvious annoyance to him. From the left appeared a man in uniform and touched Crenshaw lightly on the shoulder to gain his attention.

My eyes locked on the uniformed man's sleeve and a rush of adrenaline left me gasping for air. All I could do was reach for Mozart in my head and focus on it with every iota of strength I had. It was either that or black out completely.

"Genevieve!" Manny's voice sounded very close to me. He was breaking the fifty-centimetre rule. I was a few bars into writing Mozart's Gavotte in B-flat when I felt him move even closer. Too close. "Oh Christ, missy. If you don't pull yourself out of this funk, I'm going to phone a bloody ambulance. That will mean lots of people touching you."

It was a combination of the panic in Manny's voice and his threat that brought me back into my skin. My throat felt dry and raw, and I was surprised to find my hands clutching my hair in tight fists. I swallowed with difficulty and forced my hands on my lap.

"You don't have to phone an ambulance."

"Are you sure?" Apprehension and worry warred on his face. "Are you okay now?"

I took a few shaky breaths. "Yes. Thank you."

"You have to stop doing that to me. I don't have heart problems, but spending time with you might change that." Like the first day, he looked at me as if I was an alien being, ready to wreak havoc on his planet. "Can you talk about what set you off?"

I glanced at the monitors and was glad to see that I had only blanked out for three minutes. The video was still playing and I quickly stopped it and started working on the screening software. When I got the video to the right point on the timeline, I zoomed in and aimed the laser pointer at the still image. "That is what I saw."

"What?" Manny looked confused. "You are pointing at the soldier talking to Crenshaw. I don't know who the guy is, but from his rank, I can tell you that he is a major in the Polish army and is serving in Eurocorps."

"What about this?" With the laser pointer I circled the insignia on the man's sleeve.

"That is a specialised division in Eurocorps," he answered after a brief hesitation.

"What division? What does this man do?"

"Why are you so interested?" He glanced back at the monitor and his eyes widened. "It's the insignia. Is that the insignia you saw on the uniform of those men who attacked you?" The last word came out as an outraged roar.

"That is the exact one."

"Bloody holy hell." Manny looked from me to the monitor

and back again until he finally glared at the monitor. "Holy mother of God."

I gave him another minute to recover so that he could answer me with words that were not a prayer or a curse. A multitude of expressions played over his tired features, telling me what he was thinking. It was when his face relaxed a fraction that I asked again, "What division does this insignia belong to?"

"The intelligence division."

"I suppose this is not intelligence as in academia."

"Nope. This is intelligence as in the gathering of information about other countries. Intel not available on the internet. While I was working for Eurocorps, their purpose was mainly to be informed about what was happening."

"Like all the other intelligence agencies claim."

"Right." He shook his head. "I can't believe this. I'll have to speak to Leon about it. What the hell were two Eurocorps intelligence agents doing intimidating you in your apartment?"

"Don't forget that they were working in a team with two Russian guys."

"How can I forget that? What a mess."

"At least now we know who those guys were." I switched on the audio and zoomed in on the major's face, hoping that I might hear what he was saying to Crenshaw. The noise of a social event filled the viewing room. I used the software programme to filter out the background noise and was left with voices and a few other indistinct sounds. I rewound the video to where the major approached Crenshaw. Manny and I both leaned forward, frowning at the monitor.

We watched the major tap Crenshaw lightly on the shoulder and give the two ladies a social smile. The companion assessed him with interest in her eyes, but he was completely focussed on Crenshaw. The latter turned his head at the first contact of a hand on his shoulder and did a double-take. A few micro-expressions told me that he was worried.

"Sir?" The major had a deep voice, barely audible above all the other conversations taking place.

Crenshaw excused himself from the two ladies and both men turned towards the camera. "What are you doing here?"

"We have a si…" Loud laughter close by drowned out the rest of that sentence. I would have to get someone who could lip-read to tell me what was said. Only snippets of this conversation were audible. "… they aren't pleased with the situation. But Piros…"

"Fuck. That's not good." Fear cut deep lines next to Crenshaw's eyes. "When does he wa—"

A party of five people moved in between the camera and the two men. They toasted the success of the Foundation's fundraising loudly and congratulated each other on a successful event. Only Crenshaw's gray hair was visible and the major's left shoulder. We couldn't hear a word they were saying. After another fifteen seconds, the major moved off screen. Crenshaw had moved to the other side, once again visible and decidedly worried. He inhaled deeply and masked his worry when a well-dressed man approached him. They moved off camera while talking about an international conference coming up. I paused the video.

"They talked about Piros."

"I heard that. Seems like you were right."

"I'm predominantly right." It was a fact backed up by years of evidence. I didn't see the need to be coy, but Manny's groan made me realise that I should not have admitted such.

"Okay, so now we have Crenshaw and Dutoit avoiding each other. According to you that signifies a connection."

"Especially since they did that in the other videos as well."

"Why didn't you point it out earlier?"

"I was familiarising myself with everyone. I also had to know who comes from where. Things like culture, age and gender all influence our non-verbal communication." I stopped, angry with myself. "It's my process and I won't justify it to you."

"Okay, okay. You've proven to me above and beyond that you know what you're doing, so I won't pick a fight with you now for not saying anything sooner." He bit down hard on his jaw for a few moments. "So Crenshaw and Dutoit are avoiding each other. Crenshaw and the major from the intel division are talking about Piros. What else have you seen so far that you haven't told me about?"

I searched the footage for a specific focal point, zoomed in on it and said, "That."

"What? The painting?"

"Yes, it is exactly the same painting as the one that we saw in Danielle's room. It looks like a Gauguin. I don't know if that is the original, but the one in her room looked just like the original as well. I just wish I had a better visual of it. Do you know someone who could clean up this image?"

"No."

I tried to get as clear a shot as possible of the image and emailed it to myself. Maybe Colin would be able to identify the painting.

"Wait. Hold up." Whenever Manny went into suspicious, interrogation mode, his voice had a sharp edge to it. Like now. "Exactly when were you in the murder victim's room? And who was with you?"

I sucked in my lips and bit down hard to avoid speaking. I knew it. I knew that the time was going to come that I was going to say too much. That was why I hated deception. One constantly had to be aware of what one was saying to not let something slip. Telling the truth at all times was so much simpler.

"Doctor Face-reader, don't fuck with me. Not now."

I had to think fast. If I told him the details about my visit to Danielle's roommate it would only lead to more questions. That would lead to more pressure for me to tell the truth and as tired as I was, I would very likely cave. I was also becoming increasingly more worried about Colin and his imbecile idea of breaking into Mark Smith's home. All that spelled trouble for my deception abilities. Not that I had any.

"Manny, I really don't want to talk about it."

"Too late. You're the one who brought this up. You better tell me everything. Now."

If he hadn't shouted the last word at me, I might have given in. Since I had never reacted well to aggressive orders, I pulled my shoulders back and glared at him. "No. I will not tell you anything when you speak to me like that. Phillip knows everything and he can tell you."

"Are you telling me that Phillip has been withholding information from me?" I had managed to make him even angrier.

"I'm not going to say anything else. You should speak to Phillip first. Phillip should be here to deal with this." He was my buffer and I really needed one now. I folded my arms across my chest. We glared at each other for what felt like an hour before Manny gave up.

"I'm too tired for this. Pack your stuff, we're going home."

It sounded like a good solution to me. We had after all promised Phillip that we would only work through that one video. It didn't matter that we had only got halfway through. There were a lot of new discoveries and Manny and I had reached the end of our truce for the night. "Okay. Give me a few minutes to close everything down."

Manny disappeared while I put a few time-markers on the footage so that I knew where to return to when I viewed it again. I saved everything, switched off all the equipment, picked up my handbag and left the viewing room. We didn't speak as we made our way to his car. He didn't ask me where I lived, but I wasn't surprised when we left the parking area and started going in the right direction. What kind of agent would he be if he hadn't done a background check on me?

We were driving in blissful silence before he developed a need to speak. "We will revisit this issue, Doctor Face-reader."

"I know." I wasn't looking forward to it, but I knew that he would have to know everything at some point. And that point was coming much closer. The new discoveries and how they were all connected were leading up to a conversation that was going to enrage Manny. Of that I was sure.

"The programme for Saturday's event is on the backseat," he said into the loaded silence hanging between us.

"Thank you." I twisted around and saw the elegant glossy book, typical of art auction catalogues. I opened the first page when a cell phone started ringing.

"Aren't you going to answer that?" Manny asked after the fourth ring and I realised the ringing was coming from my handbag. I reached into my bag with a frown. Had Colin changed the ring tone on my smartphone again?

This was immediately followed by another thought. This had to be the extra cell phone that Colin had given me in case of emergencies. My stomach turned as my hand closed around the vibrating device.

Chapter NINETEEN

"Hello?"

"Jenny, it's me." The controlled strain in Colin's voice set my entire system on high alert.

"Are you okay?"

"Yes. No. Shit, I don't know."

"What happened?" I could barely breathe from the fear that he was in danger.

"I was in Mark Smith's house. It was really easy to get in there and that made me suspicious. Jenny, we have a big problem."

"What?" I heard the near-hysteria in my voice and turned away from Manny's worried looks. Colin could not have phoned me at a worse time.

"He's dead."

"Who?"

"Mark Smith. He's dead, Jenny. Dead. Someone shot him. I had been watching the house the whole day and knew that no one was there. At least that's what I thought." In contrast to his usual composure, he was babbling when he wasn't taking shaken breaths. "I got in and went to disable the alarm system, but it was already disabled. That made me suspicious. Why would the alarm system be disabled when he wasn't home? But I knew there was no one there, so I immediately went to his study. He had a very clever hiding place for his safe, but I found it and opened it in less than thirty seconds. I looked through all the stuff in there and saw a few interesting things, but left it all there. Then I decided to go into the next room. And that's when I found him."

I made an encouraging sound, not wanting to respond

verbally. Colin was clearly shaken from finding a dead man. It made me feel better about trusting, working with and worrying about this criminal. He took another shaky breath. "He was lying on the floor of the living room and it looked like there had been a struggle. There was so much blood. It looked like someone had emptied out a gun into his chest. Oh, God."

I waited for him to take a few heaving breaths. "What did you do?"

"I went back into his study and stole some stuff."

"You did what?" I shouted into the phone. Manny's head swivelled to me and I turned my torso even more towards the door. I wished I could ask Colin all the questions going through my head, beginning with why he hadn't phoned the police.

"I had and still have a bad feeling about this, Jenny. Something is not right about this murder. That was why I decided to make sure we have some stuff to find out exactly who this Mark Smith was. No sooner had I taken the stuff and made my way to his back yard when the police showed up. How did they know to come, Jenny? I had been watching the house the whole day and never saw anyone going in or out. I also never heard any gunshots. It took me a good hour to get safely out of the area. I only started looking through the stuff a few minutes ago and already have found a few very interesting things. Get this. The dead guy's name is not Mark Smith."

"What is it?" I didn't know why I was whispering, but it felt like the right thing to do. It only caused Manny to lean closer to me. I could feel him entering my personal space at my back.

"His name is, or should I say was, Brigadier-General Nick Crenshaw. He worked for those bastards, Eurocorps." He must have heard me gasp. "What? Do you know who this guy is, Jenny?"

"Yes."

"Tell me more."

"I can't."

"Why not? Aren't you at home?"

"No, but I'm on my way."

"And you're not with Vinnie? Who's driving you home?" He was angry. "Are you driving alone?"

"Agent Manfred Millard is driving me home." I stole a glance over my shoulder at Manny and saw that he was shamelessly listening to my side of the conversation. Worry had turned into suspicion and his body had gone still with concentration.

Colin swore. "You need to get away from him. Something isn't right, Jenny."

"So you keep saying. Why do you think that?"

"Apart from the obvious murdered Eurocorps man? I'm beginning to think that someone knew that we were going to find him. I don't know anything about violent crimes, but I know how to set up a scene."

"And that is what it looked like to you?"

"Yes." He paused. "Shit, wait. Vinnie is also phoning me. Hold the line."

I held the phone tightly against my ear. This was not good. Vinnie was at home waiting for me to phone him for a ride. I had forgotten to send him a text message that Manny was going to drop me off.

"What the hell?" Manny's irritated question interrupted my musing. I turned in my seat and found him scowling at the rear view mirror. Still holding the phone to my ear, I looked behind us. My heart rate accelerated to an alarming speed. Flashing lights of at least four police vehicles were coming up behind us and the sound of the sirens was becoming overwhelming.

"Jenny, are you still there?" Colin's voice sounded loud against my ear.

"Yes." My voice sounded foreign from the tension raising its pitch.

"Vinnie said that the police just showed up at your place." He was quiet for a heartbeat. "Are those sirens?"

"Yes. I think we are being followed by the police."

"We are being pulled over by the police, Doctor Face-reader." Manny slowed the car down and rolled slowly to the side of the road. He turned to me with dismay all over his face. "What have you done?"

"Jenny, listen to me. Jenny!" Colin was shouting in my ear.

"What?" I spoke into this phone, but looked straight into Manny's eyes.

"Jenny, I think this is a setup. Don't ask any questions. Just do exactly what I say. When I hang up, give Millard this phone and tell him to keep it. I will contact him. Also tell him that you were speaking to me, and that I'm helping you." With that last order, Colin ended the call and I was left with a dead phone in my hand and a staggering number of questions.

"I am so close to leaving you to fend for yourself, missy. What is going on here?" Manny still held my gaze. His dismay was quickly turning into anger.

It wasn't difficult for me to make a decision. I handed him the phone, which he glared at for a long second before he took it. Outside the car, mayhem continued to ensue. Four police cars surrounded Manny's silver Ford and armed law enforcement officers were piling out of their vehicles with their weapons trained on us.

In need of an extra second to build more courage, I carefully put the programme in my handbag. I swallowed twice and looked at Manny again. "I was speaking to Colin Frey. He is the outside consultant who has been helping me with this case. He said that you were to keep that phone and that he was going to contact you on it soon."

Were it not for the aggressive policemen shouting orders at us, Manny's expression might have been comical. "Colin Frey! You've been working with Colin Frey?"

"Yes. I don't think we have time for an argument now, Manny." I nodded meaningfully at the officers still shouting at us to show our hands and exit the vehicle. "As soon as I can, I will explain everything to you."

"You will do that and so much more, missy." Manny lifted his hands above the steering wheel in a universal gesture of surrender and I copied him.

Orders were shouted at us and Manny followed them, proving his excellent grasp of French. I also followed all the orders, but completed it with enhanced gestures of surrender and harmlessness. On the inside of a minute I found myself standing on the street, hands in the air and staring at the barrels of two handguns. They must have thought Manny to be the more dangerous, since he had three guns aimed at his chest.

My parents could never understand why lesser situations would send me into a black space of nothingness, but larger, more intimidating events invigorated me. It was because the larger events provided me with such a wealth of behaviour to observe and analyse that I didn't want to miss a moment. Having more than half a dozen officers shouting at me, treating me like a dangerous criminal was fascinating beyond anything I had ever observed.

With the exception of one officer, they all were confident that they had the situation under control. Their bodies were balanced, muscles ready to act on any change in the situation. It was, more than anything else, their faces that gave away their confidence. Looking straight ahead, they were constantly assessing Manny and me, their mouths drawn in determined lines. They knew what they were doing and trusted each other to do the same.

A shorter officer to the left of me did not share that confidence. He was overcompensating with exaggerated gestures and body language aggressive enough to cause concern. Anger pulled his eyebrows together and lifted his top lip in an aggressive sneer. It wouldn't take much for him to do something that might end with fatal consequences.

I turned to him with my hands lifted even higher, exposing my torso completely. Humans responded to the body language presented to them and I was giving him innocuous. I regulated my facial muscles into a submissive smile which almost turned triumphant when I noticed the muscle tension in his body lighten. This was too easy.

Manny was on the other side of the car, not having as much fun as me. He was shouting back at one of the officers. "Just let me reach into the inside pocket of my jacket. I'll show you my credentials. I'm an EDA official, you arrogant prick."

"Sir, keep your hands where we can see them. We know who you are. Our orders are only to apprehend Miss Lenard."

"It is *Doctor* Lenard to you, sonny." Manny lowered his arms a fraction. "If you only have to apprehend her, why are you aiming your guns at me?"

"Manny." I addressed him quietly, hoping he would hear me above all the commotion. "You're not helping the situation."

"Not helping…" He sputtered and then inhaled deeply. "She's right. I'm not helping. Could we all just stop shouting at each other?"

I didn't want to point out to him that after we exited his car, he had been the only one shouting. Instead I kept my eyes on the insecure officer. "What do you need me to do?"

"Please turn around, face the vehicle and place your hands on the roof." It was the officer next to him who spoke, which brought most of the tension back to the first officer's stance. He was not respected by his peers and he resented it. Team dynamics was a study in itself, but now was not the time for it. I did as asked and lost my focus when cold handcuffs embraced my wrists.

I lifted my eyes, looking for something to analyse so that the panic starting in me wouldn't grow. I didn't have to look far. On the other side of the car, Manny was now in deep debate with the officer who looked to be the team leader.

"What do you mean, you have fingerprints?"

"Miss"—the officer swallowed at Manny's growl and corrected himself—"Doctor Lenard's fingerprints were found at a crime scene and we need her to come in to the police station for questioning."

"So you arrested her?"

"The crime scene is quite incriminating, sir."

"What crime scene?"

"I'm sorry, sir. I can't tell you that. It is an ongoing investigation." The officer was genuinely sorry, but I didn't think it was because of his concern for me. His face told me that he would've taken great joy in telling Manny about my alleged crime.

"It's okay, Manny. I'll go with them. I haven't done anything wrong."

The expression on Manny's face told me that he didn't think that to be the truth. He was furious with me for not telling him about my co-operation with Colin. I was sure that that was the only wrongdoing he could accuse me of. And accuse me he was going to. I could see the promise of it in his eyes. He looked at me for a few more moments and I watched anger make way for concern. "Are you okay?"

I knew what he was referring to. "I'm okay. This is not as bad as that photo."

He gave me a tight smile. "Don't speak to anyone, Genevieve. Do you hear me?"

"Why not? I haven't done anything wrong." I had nothing to hide.

Manny bit down hard on his teeth and turned to the leading officer. "May I please have a minute with Doctor Lenard? Your courtesy will be noted and will be remembered by the EDA and Eurocorps in the future."

The officer's eyes flashed in respect for those two agencies and nodded his agreement. "One minute, then we go."

Manny walked around the car and stopped inside my personal space. Now didn't seem to be the time to remind him of the fifty-centimetre rule. Not while I was handcuffed and surrounded by police. He pushed his face close to mine and I wondered if it was because he wanted me to read how serious he was. "Listen very carefully to me, Doctor Face-reader. This case that we are working on is the most important thing that you should remember right now. As you know, we are working with people who have enough power to ruin you, me, Leon, Phillip and whoever the hell they choose. I do not want you to say anything to anyone. Not even to ask for water or the lavvy."

"The lavvy?"

He rolled his eyes. "The toilet, missy. I will follow you to the police station and sort this out. Then you and I are going to have a very hard conversation."

The officers were becoming restless, glancing uneasily at us. My mind was working overtime and I had reached a hypothesis. We didn't have much time, so I was going to be honest and direct without polite filters. I lowered my voice and leaned very close to Manny's ear. "They're going to say that I killed Crenshaw. I didn't. Colin didn't. Colin thinks it's a conspiracy and that this is a setup."

Manny jerked away from me, looking at me as if I was completely insane. He opened his mouth only to close it again while shaking his head. The officers decided they had waited long enough and walked purposefully towards us. Manny gave me another searing look which I supposed was to reiterate his warning. I nodded at him and then turned to the officers. They had holstered their weapons, but I had no doubt that they would reach for them if I posed any threat. I made sure that my body language and facial expressions communicated harmlessness.

The drive to the police station happened too fast for me. I wanted more time to observe the dynamics between the officers.

The short officer was driving so aggressively that his partner commented on it. That only put the insecure man more on edge. I was willing to stake my reputation that this officer's behaviour was going to spiral into something problematic within the next three months.

Too soon we were at the police station and I was escorted to a small room with a wooden table and three steel chairs. Nothing else.

Since I wasn't an expert on police procedure I didn't know what to expect. What I didn't expect was the handcuffs to be taken off, to be told to sit down and then to be left on my own. The sudden solitude was a welcome change. Being in constant close proximity to people these last few days was wearing me down. At least I knew that I had nothing to worry about. Between Phillip and Manny, I had respectable and solid alibis. It would have been impossible for me to have killed anyone. Not when I had been with either one or both men for the larger part of the day.

After fifteen minutes, I got up and tried the door. It was locked. I placed my ear against the door and imagined that I could hear Manny's annoying voice. Only now it didn't sound annoying to me. It calmed me. I went back to my seat at the table. A few minutes later an officer came in, rudely dropped my handbag on the table and left without saying a word. Maybe Manny had convinced them to give this to me. I didn't know. I grabbed my bag to make sure nothing had been taken. It was all there. Including the programme of the Foundation's annual gala event. I stared unseeingly at the cover.

I glanced at my watch and saw that only another fifteen minutes had passed. If I were going to be detained like this, I might as well make use of the time. I studied the programme from cover to cover, absorbing everything. The niggling in my subconscious started up again and wouldn't relent. There was a connection to be made. I sat back in the steel chair and called up the Mozart Gavotte that I had started earlier.

When next I looked at my watch, it was ten minutes to six. I had mentally written the Gavotte and two Minuets and it had only taken me five hours. My mind felt energised and my soul centred. And I was jittery with excitement. The connection I had made was so obvious, I almost felt embarrassed for not seeing it earlier. It was only a theory, yet it was the overwhelming evidence that had my heart racing. I needed one or all of the annoying men in my life as sounding boards.

As if on cue, Manny burst through the door, followed by the leading officer who had stopped us. The other man looked exhausted yet furious. He leaned against the wall close to the door and pulled his lips into a thin line. His eyes kept resting on the back of Manny's head, narrowing with what laypeople would call a murderous look. Manny had not made any friends during the early-morning hours.

"Are you okay, Doctor Face-reader?"

"Yes, thank you."

Manny studied me intently for a few seconds. Apparently he decided that I looked fine and he sat down in a chair next to me. "Do you need anything?"

"The lavvy."

He smiled at my use of the word I had not earlier understood, but quickly sobered. "This is a mess, Genevieve. A big mess."

I could count on one hand the number of times Manny had called me by my name. This was obviously as bad as I had expected. "Is this about—"

"Not now." Manny interrupted me before I could finish my question. He looked at the policeman hovering by the table. "They didn't arrest you?"

"I don't know." How did one know if one was arrested? Surely being handcuffed equalled being arrested.

"Did they explain your rights to you?"

"What rights?" My eyes widened with the memory of a few Hollywood movies I had watched in my student years. "Oh, those rights. No. Nobody told me anything. And I didn't speak to anyone."

Manny turned to the police officer and glared at him before giving me his full attention again. "They should never have handcuffed you. You were never under arrest. They just wanted to bring you in for questioning."

"Why? No one has questioned me all night, so why have I been here at all?"

"Brigadier-General Crenshaw was murdered last night." Manny waited for my response and I realised that I was supposed to look shocked for the benefit of our audience. I was a millisecond late, but quickly manipulated my face into the appropriate expression. He lifted an unbelieving eyebrow at me, but continued. "Your fingerprints were found at the crime scene. They were on a glass of whiskey and also on the coffee table in the room where he was shot."

This time I did not have to pretend to be shocked. "My fingerprints? How—"

The memory of my hand being forcefully held against a device rushed through my mind. Had those thugs taken my fingerprints? Was it possible to take my fingerprints from a machine and put it on a glass? I wanted to ask Manny this, but didn't know if it was a good idea. Not with the police officer showing such intense interest in our conversation.

"Your fingerprints were taken when you started working at Rousseau & Rousseau and were placed on a few databases. That is how they managed to identify the prints so quickly." He had misunderstood my shock and hesitation, but had also answered a question that I was going to ask. Manny noticed the police officer moving closer and shook his head. "We'll talk about this later. You are not under arrest, which means that you can go home."

"I can go home?" Relief rushed through me. Not wanting to spend another second in this place, I got up and felt the effects of sitting in an uncomfortable chair for five hours. My legs were a bit shaky and the muscles in my back were stiff. I took my handbag and turned to the door. I couldn't wait to lie down in a tub of steamy hot water. "Is there any paperwork or something that I still need to do here?"

"I've taken care of all of that." Manny got up and followed me. He gave a dismissive nod towards the police officer and together we walked down a long corridor. I heard some commotion up ahead, but kept my focus on Manny.

"Thank you."

For a second, I thought that he hadn't heard my quietly spoken recognition of his help. He stopped next to me, reached for my elbow and just as quickly withdrew his hand. Lowering his brow just enough to look me straight in the eye, he spoke just as quietly. "I did what was necessary. I did this because I know that you don't have it in you to do anything remotely criminal. But I also did this because I want answers." He straightened. "Honest, complete, full, *detailed* answers."

My comment on his overuse of adjectives died when Phillip came barrelling down the corridor. He looked as if he was on his way to a meeting, dressed in one of his bespoke suits, smoothly shaved and looking much fresher than I felt. It was the tightness in his face that belied the image of a man in full control. His steps faltered slightly when he saw us and that was when I noticed the empty music sheets he was clutching in his right hand.

He stopped in front of us, indecision making him rock back and forth on the balls of his feet. As a rule it was not something that I liked, needed or allowed, but I knew that Phillip needed more than verbal reassurance. With a slight smile, I opened my arms and immediately found myself in a tight embrace, surrounded by his arms and the scent that was uniquely him.

Phillip's intense concern and now relief meant more to me than I wanted to admit. People were starting to show their care for me and that made me feel uncomfortably vulnerable.

"Enough of this. Let's get her home." Manny's gravelly voice broke the emotional moment and I stepped out of Phillip's arms. "And before you ask, she's okay."

"You brought me music sheets." I looked at the papers now crumpled in his fist.

"I thought you might need them."

"I was okay. Am okay."

"I told you that. Now can we please leave this hell-hole?" The agitation in Manny's voice and on his face was all we needed to follow him to his car.

He and Phillip agreed over my head that I was to go with Manny and that Phillip would follow us in his car. The trip to my apartment was done in complete silence. I thought it prudent to wait for Manny to initiate the dreaded conversation. For now I was just content watching the activities of the city waking up. A few people were jogging, but mostly the streets were still deserted.

Manny found a parking space a block away from my apartment building and we waited for Phillip in the foyer. The two men talked quietly while we rode up to my apartment. With a sigh I accepted that the hot bath I was so looking forward to was going to have to wait. At least I had the new connection. I placed an inordinate amount of hope that it would placate Manny's unavoidable fury.

Chapter TWENTY

As soon as I inserted the key in the front door to my apartment, the door burst open. I barely had time to register Vinnie's presence filling the door before he picked me up in a hug so tight I had difficulty catching my breath to complain. My feet were dangling at least twenty centimetres above the floor, my arms encased by his. I felt like a rag doll.

"Jen-girl. You're okay," Vinnie mumbled into my hair. It was the slight thickening in his voice that surprised me more than anything. The intimidating man was close to tears. This caused a foreign desire to comfort him. I stopped fighting his hug and rested my head against his shoulder.

"I'm okay, Vinnie. You can let me go now."

"You heard the lady. Let her go."

It was like someone had flicked a switch. All the muscles in Vinnie's body tightened at the hostile order Manny uttered. Still holding on to me, he turned me away from the two older men behind me, presenting them his muscular back, which in turn made him much more vulnerable to attack. His instinctive protectiveness was much stronger than I had thought.

I started squirming. "Vinnie, it's okay. You know Phillip and that is Manny."

Over his shoulder Vinnie glared at both men. "What are you doing here?"

"Vinnie." All this physical closeness was becoming too much for me to handle. The strained tone in my voice evidenced it. Fortunately Vinnie picked up on it and slowly put me down. He moved a strong arm across my chest to keep me behind him as he turned. He was much stronger than I, so I didn't even attempt to fight his manoeuvre. Instead I walked deeper into my apartment, turned around and sternly addressed all three men.

"This has been a very long evening. We are all tired and I don't have the patience to deal with the three of you. Unless you are willing to accept my honesty without any niceties, I suggest you go home and come back after I've had a long, hot bath and slept for at least eight hours."

I was really hoping that all three of them would be loath to be with an undiplomatic me. It was not to be. I saw it on their faces.

"Honesty would be a nice change." Manny pushed past Vinnie and walked straight to the kitchen. "A cup of coffee would also be very nice."

"I'll make it." Vinnie was not only being overprotective of me, he was also being territorial of my apartment. Vinnie left Phillip at the door and stalked to the kitchen. Phillip closed the door quietly and walked past me with amusement in his eyes.

"This is going to be interesting," he said and then also walked to the kitchen. "Manny, why don't we all sit here by the dining room table? Vinnie can make us coffee and we can talk."

Phillip was facing the two men who both were showing power displays. He unquestionably was a master at mediating difficult situations and I was exceedingly grateful for his presence. Manny and Vinnie were staring at each other, measuring the other's strength. Vinnie might beat Manny when it came to physical strength, but the older man had experience and the law backing him up.

It was he who first stepped back. Not that it made him any less of a threat. Without another word he walked to the dining room table, pulled out a chair and sat down heavily. The night's events had really taken their toll on him.

After a quick visit to my bathroom, I joined Phillip at the

table. We sat in uncomfortable silence while Vinnie moved around the kitchen.

"Who is he?" Manny pointed with his chin to the kitchen.

"He is—" Phillip started to answer, but stopped when Manny started shaking his head.

"No, Phillip. Little Miss Face-reader here is going to answer all my questions today. You are not going to help her. Not any more." He looked at me. "Now answer me, who is he? And I want the full truth."

"Vinnie. He's a friend of Colin's and is also helping with the case. He knows everything I know." It looked like I had slapped Manny in the face. He bit down hard on his teeth and I rushed on. He had asked for the full truth and I was going to give it to him. "He has helped a lot to get us this far in the investigation."

"And I'm Jen-girl's bodyguard." Vinnie placed a tray with four large steaming coffee mugs on the table and sat next to me.

"Do you have a record?" Manny addressed Vinnie through his teeth. I assumed that Manny was referring to Vinnie's relationship with law enforcement, not the Olympics.

"No."

"But you've been investigated?"

"Maybe."

"He's not stalling or lying. He's telling the truth. Had he lied, his eye contact would have changed. When Vinnie lies, he actually engages in greater eye contact, not less," I quickly explained when anger pulled Manny's face into a tight scowl.

"Hey." Vinnie looked offended as if I was sharing a secret he had trusted me with.

"His face would've become slightly flushed," I continued, pointing at Vinnie's cheeks. "Also his breathing would've increased and usually his lips tighten just a bit. We can control only a few of the deception cues, but never all of them. His whole body is congruent with what he said."

Manny was still clenching his jaws and I could see him

struggling for control. "I'm going to need your full name."

"You can need all you want." Vinnie shrugged.

"I have a suggestion." Phillip spoke in his mediating voice. "Why don't we accept the situation for what it is? Manny, we can't do anything about Vinnie knowing everything about the case."

"Or about bloody Colin Frey being in the middle of this." The way Manny said Colin's name did not bode well for co-operation. He did not like Colin. I really wanted to know what the history was between the two men.

"So," Phillip continued, "we are all here. Let's work with it. I think we should start with what happened tonight and get that out of the way."

"Yes, I would like to know why Jen-girl was at the police station for such a long time." Vinnie moved his torso towards me, again showing his protectiveness.

"Vinnie," Phillip warned. "We're going to have to get past all this posturing and work together. Let's just all give full disclosure on what we know so far."

Neither Manny nor Vinnie liked this suggestion. Fortunately they accepted Phillip's guidance. I was fascinated by this struggle for male dominance. So much so that I didn't mind them talking as if I were not in the room.

"I first have to have my say." Manny's tone was still very argumentative and Vinnie bristled next to me, but remained silent. "I don't like being made a fool of. And that is what you have been doing by withholding information from me. In my opinion it equals lying and I won't stand for it. This is it. From now on you will tell me everything, and I mean everything, that you discover. You are not to use your own discretion and not tell me something because you consider it of lesser importance. Do you understand?"

"What if I discover that all the ships were manufactured in different years or one thousand one hundred and forty-seven Picasso artworks are currently missing? Or that the Foundation spent over eighteen thousand Euros last year on powdered hot chocolate to distribute to children's homes or—"

"Genevieve." Phillip had a very specific tone he used when he was warning me. He drowned my name in that tone. "Let's agree that you'll tell Manny everything relevant to the case."

"Oh. Yes, of course." Why hadn't he simply asked for that? Everything meant everything. Right? "I hope I didn't upset you."

"Upset me? That does not even begin to describe how I feel at this moment. On Phillip's recommendation, I trusted you. I had to convince the Head of the EDA and Chief Dutoit that you were beyond reproach and that I would stake my reputation on your discretion. Now I find out that you have been working with not one, but two criminals. Telling them more than you've been telling me. Sharing confidential bloody information with criminals." His ranting ended loud enough for me to wince.

"They're good guys."

"Really? That is what you are going with? This is your great argument? And here I thought you were a genius." He leaned towards me. "I don't care if they are bloody saints. They're criminals."

"Hey, watch it, pops." Vinnie's warning rumbled deep in his chest.

"No, Vinnie. He's right. I should have told him everything. But you are wrong, Manny." I pulled my shoulders back. "They really are good guys. Vinnie and Colin have helped me a lot in this case. Phillip knows me well enough to know that I would never have allowed them in my home if I did not believe or trust them. Things are very black and white for me, but at the moment you seem to be much more intolerant than I am."

Phillip covered his laugh by coughing discreetly. "Now that we have that off our chests, can we move on?"

Manny closed his eyes and breathed deeply a few times. "Fine, let's talk about what happened tonight. Doctor Face-reader was in the police station for such a long time because I considered it to be the safest place for her at the time."

"The safest?" Why would I need to hide in a police station?

"Yes, missy. When we got to the station, the police still didn't want to tell me anything. I thought you were lying to me about Crenshaw until Leon phoned me, rather frantically. It was—is—all too suspicious for me. I mean, the same day that we talked about suspecting Crenshaw to be Piros, he's murdered. Your fingerprints were found at the scene even though I knew that you could not have done it. Very convenient. According to preliminary reports, he was murdered around nine o'clock. At that time both Phillip and I were sitting with you in your viewing room. It was very obvious something was off with this case, but I wanted you to be safe. I went with one of the detectives to the crime scene. They said that someone had broken into the house and some things were stolen. While I was talking to them your buddy phoned me."

"What buddy? I don't have buddies."

"Colin Frey, your criminal buddy. He phoned me and shouted at me." These were two men who stood at opposing ends of the law and societal norms. I did not need much imagination to predict how hostile that conversation must have been. "He wanted to know if you had been arrested. Something you should keep in mind, Doctor Face-reader, is that your co-operation with criminals does not bode well for you."

"Children, children." Phillip sounded simultaneously tired and amused. "Let's stay on point here. Manny, you were saying that Colin phoned you. Did you learn anything interesting?"

"Hmph. He did not tell me much. Only that when he entered Crenshaw's house, the man was already dead. He also thought that the whole thing seemed staged and he thought that the doc might be someone's target. He did not say who that someone was, nor did he say why he was in Crenshaw's house. What he did was threaten me. Me! An officer of the law."

"What did he threaten you with?" Phillip asked.

"That he was going to destroy my career, my life if he found out that you"—Manny looked at me the way I looked at messy kitchens—"were treated badly in any way. Looks like your buddy is sweet on you, missy."

Vinnie chuckled and Phillip simply looked horrified.

"I don't exactly understand the meaning of 'sweet on me', but it leads me to infer that you mean Colin is attracted to me. That is ridiculous. He is a highly intelligent, intuitive individual who is also extremely loyal. What you misunderstood for attraction is loyalty." The human race and their silly romantic notions. I placed the blame completely at the door of fairy tales and Hollywood.

"On point, people. Genevieve, why was Colin at Crenshaw's house?"

I had no doubt that Phillip would give me one of his fatherly talks later on, warning me against Colin. For now I was happy to stick to a less personal topic. "He didn't know it was Crenshaw's house."

"Whose house did he think he was illegally entering?" Manny emphasised the two last words.

"Mark Smith's. When we found his name on the manifest, that he had shared a room with the artist Karin Vittone on one of the cruises, there was an address with his name. He had bought a piece of art at the auction on the cruise and it was to be shipped to him to that address. Colin went to check it out."

Blood was flowing to Manny's face, indicating fury.

"How did the police know to go to Crenshaw's house?" Phillip's question seemed to reduce Manny's ire. Marginally.

He answered in a tight voice. "Apparently the police received an anonymous phone call telling them that there was someone in the house. When they arrived, there was no one there, but they found Crenshaw in the living room with eleven gunshot wounds to his chest and torso. None of the neighbours had heard any gunshots, so they're thinking that a silencer was used. As you know, they found Doctor Face-reader's fingerprints on a whiskey glass and also on the coffee table in the living room."

"Did they find her fingerprints anywhere else?" Vinnie asked.

"No, but they were still processing the rest of the house when I left." Manny looked at me strangely. "I might not have a gazillion degrees in face-reading, Doc, but your face is telling me that something is bothering you."

"Do you know if someone can steal my fingerprints and put them on a glass?"

Manny lifted his eyebrows and then frowned. "When did this happen?"

"When those guys broke into my house, I think they took my fingerprints. Just before I passed out from the drugs, the Spaniard pushed my fingers against what looked like a tablet computer. I saw it scan my hand, but didn't know what to think of it."

"It's possible and very easy to do, Jen-girl." Vinnie stopped explaining when he noticed Manny's interested look. "Or so I saw on Discovery Channel."

I laughed. "Now he is lying."

"Jen-girl, please don't give my secrets away." Vinnie squirmed next to me.

"Vinnie is right. Planting fingerprints is not exactly rocket science. It seems like someone is trying to set you up, Doc."

"Which means that someone is feeling very threatened by what Genevieve is discovering."

"But how do they know what I'm discovering?" I started counting people on my fingers. "Phillip is not telling anyone. Neither are Vinnie and Colin. You and Leon are the only ones with bosses and other people asking about this. Since Crenshaw has been murdered, it can't be him, so who else might be connected to this whole thing?"

Manny's shoulders slumped. "It has to be someone within the agencies. Either the EDA or Eurocorps. As it is, Eurocorps is going to have troubles with Crenshaw's murder. Most likely they will be able to spin it into something much less malevolent."

"First the attack and warning in your apartment and now this. Why is this happening?" Phillip asked Manny.

"My gut tells me that someone wants to discredit the doc. She doesn't have much else to lose except her reputation."

"That's harsh, Manny." Phillip was defensive and I wondered why he thought Manny had insulted me. It was all true.

"If they manage to cast enough doubt on her integrity, whatever she uncovers can easily be made inadmissible in court. And they will win again. Now that I've shown you mine, show me yours, Doc."

"Show you my what?"

"Oh, God, this is going to drive me insane." He actually grabbed and pulled at his short hair. "It is now your turn to tell me everything that you've kept from me."

It took me only fifteen minutes to fill him in on all the bits I hadn't told him about. "See, I wasn't withholding that much from you."

It was the wrong thing to say. Manny's lips thinned and his pupils constricted. Now was the right time to use my insights to win his favour. I blurted, "Piros is going to kill all the artists on Friday."

All movement stilled. I might as well have been looking at a paused scene of a video. Manny blinked slowly and leaned towards me. "Explain to me in easy, short sentences how you know this."

I reached into my handbag hanging on the back of the chair and took out the programme. I placed it on the table and pointed at the front page. "What does it say?"

Manny glared at me. Phillip, who knew my methods well, answered me. "Should I read everything?"

"Yes."

"The Foundation for Development of Sustainable Education's sixteenth annual gala fundraiser. Twenty-seventh June, seven o'clock. La Maison Russie, 213 Rue des Jonquilles." Phillip looked up from the programme. "Interesting."

"What is interesting?" Manny's impatience indicated I had to explain.

"Jonquilles is the French word for daffodils. Rue des Jonquilles is Daffodil Street."

"No fucking way!" Vinnie stared at me with open awe. "That whole thing the Russian murderer was shouting, the red will end all twenty-seven daffodils? This is it? He was saying that Piros will end everything on the twenty-seventh at Rue des Jonquilles?"

I had planned a more eloquent delivery, but Vinnie's excited questions were equally effective. Manny's eyes bulged. He slammed his hand on the programme. "You think it's going to happen at this event?"

"This is merely an educated guess," I said. "But it makes perfect sense. Despite the lack of irrefutable evidence, the Foundation is linked to the deaths of all these artists. In conjunction with what we've learned so far about Piros, the RNT and the auctions at sea, it seems a logical conclusion. Add to that the thugs who broke in here, saying that Piros had something big planned for the flower house. You told me how flower-rich La Maison Russie is. And it's on Daffodil Street."

"It's not a far reach to conclude that La Maison Russie is the flower house," Phillip said thoughtfully.

"Given what you've told me about Piros, the probability of him being there is very high." I nodded at Manny's alerted look. "Not only is he a master strategist, he exhibits symptoms of megalomania. The delusions of grandeur, of having great social and political power are evident in the role he is purported to have played in some riots and revolts. There is also the violence and manipulation for which he has a reputation. Megalomaniacs often suffer from poor self-esteem. His need for validation would dictate his presence for this action. He would stand somewhere, from his position of power, and watch his plan come together."

"That's all nice and dandy, but Chulkov said that the red will end all twenty-seven. We're assuming it doesn't mean that Piros will destroy twenty-seven paintings or close twenty-seven businesses, right?"

"Even in English we talk about ending someone when murder is on the table, arsehole." Vinnie, always so gentle with me, looked like he wanted to crush Manny.

"I'm not a linguist, but I'm fluent in English, Russian and French," I said. "Looking at it from numerous angles, this is the only interpretation that reasonably makes sense. The red will end all twenty-seven very possibly means that Piros will end the artists on the twenty-seventh."

"How do you know it will be the artists?"

I took the programme, found the right page and laid it open on the table. I pointed to the text. "In this article, it says that the auction will be preceded by an awards ceremony for young accomplished artists. The Foundation has invited sixty-seven artists from all over the world. Awards in seven categories will be given and after the auction they will be treated to a weekend in the French Alps. I posit that they will not reach or return from the Alps."

"Sixty-seven young artists?" Manny's eyes were huge. "This is worse than I thought. I'll have to run this by Leon."

"Can't you cancel this event?" I asked. "That would prevent Piros from ending anything."

"That's a hasty option and maybe not the best. I don't have the guest list, but I can assume that the place will be crawling with important EU officials. Cancelling the event without, as you called it, irrefutable proof is not an option. We need an alternative plan. Continue doing what you do best. Find us some more connections, more evidence. Leon and I will plan operational strategies."

We sat in pensive silence for a few minutes. The excitement of the last twenty-four hours was weighing heavily on me. I really needed that hot bath and my bed. Then I would be able to analyse this again. Usually I didn't need to take time off when I was working through challenging problems. That was because it was exclusively a cerebral exercise. This time it had involved being taken to a dirty, messy police station in a disgusting police car. And all the physical proximity during this case had my mind begging me for a reprieve.

I was just about to excuse myself when Phillip broke the silence. "What are we going to do to keep Genevieve safe?"

Manny turned to me, narrowed his eyes and tilted his head a fraction. "Would you agree to not leave your apartment until this thing is over?"

"What if it takes months?"

"Oh, dear God, I hope not. My health would not survive that." He rubbed his hand hard over his face. "Let's hope we find Piros, the art forgers, the weapons and the bloody traitor so this can end. Very soon."

"I'll agree to one week." Staying in my apartment was not going to be punishment. It had taken me years, but I had surrounded myself with things that made me feel safe and at home.

"And I'll be here." Vinnie folded his arms in a gesture not to be argued with. It took almost a full minute before the three men grunted their agreement on my safety. This might have pointed to some kind of truce, but it was resentful, reluctant and without any mutual trust.

"Phillip, could you please bring all my computers later on? I'll need them by"—I looked at my watch and did a quick time calculation—"three o'clock this afternoon."

"I'll bring them around. You just make sure that you get enough rest."

"We're not done yet." Manny looked put out that Phillip and I were making arrangements for later. He clearly wanted to continue this discussion. "Who killed Crenshaw? If you're so sure it wasn't Frey."

"Of course it wasn't Colin. What would be his motivation? Really, Manny, I thought you were more intelligent than that." I held up my hand at the three different reactions. Vinnie chuckled, Phillip inhaled to undoubtedly mediate and Manny, well, he just looked angrier. "I'm too tired to censor myself, so you'll have to accept this or go." I really wanted them to go. I waited, but no one left nor did they say anything. I sighed. "I'm not a murder investigator, but if I look at it logically—"

"How else would you ever look at it?" Manny grumbled. I ignored him.

"— I would have to start my suspect list with Piros. I wouldn't suspect him of actually pulling the trigger. He most likely ordered his private army of mercenaries to do his dirty work. They did steal my fingerprints and planted them at the crime scene. Logical deduction leads me to the conclusion that Crenshaw's murderers are the same thugs who broke into my apartment and manhandled me."

"Yet once again nothing would be traced back to Piros. The guy is a strategic planning genius. In the almost two decades that his name has been floating around Europe, nothing ever pointed to anyone specific."

"Then he most likely is a very good chess player," I said absently. The change in Manny's breathing made me look at him. "What?"

"Chief Dutoit is a good chess player. And he's been breathing down my neck about this case. I'm sure I have at least five missed calls from him by now." He stopped himself with a humourless laugh. "I'm talking utter hogwash. It wouldn't be the Chief. I think we're all just tired and are reaching now."

"Talk for yourself, Manny. My mind is clear. Tired, but clear. I do, however, think that you should leave so that I can rest."

Vinnie moved next to me, pulling himself up in his chair and so making himself look bigger than the giant he was. "Yes, I think it's a good idea to let Jen-girl rest. You should leave."

Years of dealing with all kinds of criminals must have made Manny immune to intimidation, but Phillip looked perturbed. "I think it's a good idea. Manny, let's go."

It took another five minutes of reassuring Manny that I would not keep anything relevant from him again. But it took only a scowl from Vinnie to reassure the men that I would be safe at home, under his protection. The moment my front door closed and Vinnie locked all five locks, I almost cried with relief. I didn't think I would be able to stay awake through a hot bath. Maybe just a quick shower before I gave my body the rest it was screaming for.

Chapter TWENTY-ONE

I walked out of my bedroom and was met with the wonderful aromas of coffee and caramelised onions. Vinnie was cooking.

"Good afternoon, sleeping beauty." Vinnie placed a heavenly mug of coffee on the counter and I grabbed it. He also placed a plate with oatmeal cookies on the counter.

"Vinnie, if there is only one reason why I am happy that you live here, it is for the coffee that always awaits me when I wake up. How do you know when to start making it?" I brought the mug up to my face and inhaled the strong aroma. I took a careful sip of the hot brew.

"You're a rather loud shower diva, Jen-girl."

"A what?"

Vinnie turned away from the food cooking on the stove. He was able to mask the smile, but he didn't have control over the muscles of his eyes. They cause laughter lines to deepen. "You sing really loudly, and I must say not too badly, when you shower. That is enough warning for me to get busy in the kitchen. You're also quite easy to time. You spend ten minutes in the shower, ten doing whatever you're doing before the hairdryer comes on and you're out of your bedroom ten minutes after that. All in all, I have about thirty minutes to get myself going and your coffee ready."

I stopped drinking my coffee and stared at Vinnie. "I'm that precise?"

"I don't know if you should sound so proud about this, Jen-girl." He turned back to whatever was cooking in the pots, picked up a wooden spoon and stirred the contents of the larger pot. "But you certainly are scheduled. Nothing wrong with it, of course."

"Of course." If it hadn't been for Vinnie's non-caring shrug, I knew that I would've felt the same tightness in my chest as when my parents always condemned my peculiarities. With Vinnie there was no censure, only fresh coffee.

In the week that Vinnie had been staying with me we had never talked about anything other than the case. I suddenly wanted to know more about the gentle giant who so unobtrusively was sharing my space. Leaning against the kitchen counter, I tried to come up with a conversation starter but came up empty.

So many years of studying psychology and writing papers on human interaction had done nothing for my own skills. I realised that I was sorely lacking in the skill of making friends. A skill that came naturally for the vast majority of people. Staring at Vinnie's back I decided that I could worry about this gap in my skill-set at a later stage. There were more pressing matters to attend to.

"Did Phillip bring my computers?"

"Yup. He came about an hour ago. They're on the dining room table."

"Were you rude to him?"

Vinnie glanced over his shoulder at me with a wide grin. "He's not the one I have a problem with. It's that filthy fed who grinds my gears."

"He grinds your gears? Does that mean he irritates you?"

Vinnie snorted. "To put it mildly. The guy irritates the hell outta me."

"Manny? What's your problem with him?" I walked to the dining room table and placed the plate of cookies at a safe distance from my computers for a later snack. The computers I arranged for optimum usefulness with the notepad in the centre. The way I liked it. When Vinnie didn't answer me, I looked up to see him watching me. "What?"

"You're amazing, Jen-girl. The way you know exactly how things should be." The wistful look on his face matched the tone of his voice. Before I could tell him that I was only using logic to streamline everything, including the placing of my computers, he shook his head. "Never mind that. Millard is just a big bad wolf trying to intimidate anyone he can."

"I actually think that he is very intelligent but prefers to hide it. That way he gets a lot more out of people."

"Whatever." Clearly Vinnie did not agree with me. He returned to his cooking. "You do your thing over there, Jen-girl. Dinner will be ready in an hour."

It didn't take long for me to get lost in the new information waiting for me on the EDA server. Manny had kept his word and I had the full financials of the charity foundation for the last ten years waiting for me. There was also an email from Manny. He sarcastically asked me whether I would please lower myself from up high and take a deeper look at the weapons theft file. Why he was angry with me, I had no idea. I snarled at his email and wondered if his anger stemmed from his Chief pressuring him. It still gave him no right to be sarcastic.

"Don't kill it, Jen-girl." Vinnie's voice next to me made me jump.

"Huh?"

"You're looking at that computer as if you plan to kill it. Slowly."

"It's Manny."

"Aha." A wealth of understanding was communicated with those two syllables. Vinnie pulled out the chair next to me, moved it farther away to give me more space and sat down. "What's he done now?"

"He's angry with me about *his*"—I strongly emphasised the possessive pronoun—"lack of progress on the inquiry into the weapons theft. It's not even his inquiry. The case belongs to Leon. He should be angry with Leon."

"So what does he expect you to do?"

"Find out who stole the weapons, I suppose." I sighed at Manny's irrational demand.

"Jen-girl?" Vinnie waited until I looked at him. "I... uh... know this dude who knows a lot about weapons."

"An illegal arms dealer?"

"That is one way to describe him." Vinnie looked decidedly uncomfortable. "Anyway, I could ask him if he knows something about these weapons. But that means you'll have to give me everything you know about these weapons."

"I'm not so sure that's a good idea." Manny's sarcasm would increase exponentially if he found out.

"I promise it will never come back to you. I've been doing this for a while and know how to get information. Trust me with this. I'll get you info."

I took a deep breath and held it while I analysed the pros and cons of taking this action. The cons mostly revolved around Manny's wrath, but also included the fact that such highly confidential information would be put out into the criminal sphere. I exhaled, took another deep breath and thought that on the other hand those weapons were already in the criminal sphere. It led me to a few more pros and I exhaled with a puff of air.

"Will you be careful with how you share this information?"

"Like I said, it will never come back to you."

"Okay."

"Email me the list of the weapons. It has all the specs, right?"

"Yes." I emailed him the list from my computer, not wanting Manny to know that I was sharing anything with Vinnie. Had I emailed it from the EDA computer or even my work computer, all those cons would have rained down on me like a hailstorm. I had no illusions that Manny was now keeping an even closer eye on my activities. He would find out about this, I had no doubt, but I would prefer it to be later rather than sooner. After Vinnie had spoken to the guy he knew. "There. It should be in your inbox."

"I'll get on that now." He got up. "Oh, yes, Colin phoned. He'll be here later. Is it okay for us to wait with dinner until he comes? Then we can all eat together."

"No problem." I would just make myself another coffee to keep my energy up until dinner. I also had the plate of cookies Vinnie always seemed to keep in stock.

He disappeared to his room to contact his criminal cohorts. I was not going to allow myself to once again think and worry about the gray areas these people moved in. Then I would have to think how my association with these guys kept pushing me deeper into these gray areas.

I needed to get my mind off this and it wasn't difficult. I decided to take another look at the Foundation's financials, more specifically the previous year's grants. Eighteen million euro from the EU was a significant amount and I needed to understand how one charitable organisation could receive so much.

No matter how I looked at it, the Foundation for Development of Sustainable Education came by their money in a legal manner. It was all above board. But it couldn't be right. I checked their income. All legal donations, including the donations from the shipping companies. The donations were technically legal even if the money had come from auctioning off forged artefacts on a ship in no man's land where the enforcement of laws was dubious at best. If it weren't the donations, the income, it had to be their expenditure.

Their financials had been audited by an EU-appointed forensic accounting team, so I didn't spend too much time looking for the misplacement of funds. Instead, I looked for patterns. Some people said that the devil was in the details. I always found the devil in patterns.

First, I looked at their activities to get an overall perspective. Despite my suspicions of this charity organisation, I was impressed. In the last decade they had built homes, sent numerous youths to university, started a music centre, opened thirteen food distribution centres and much more. Every project involved several participants, all seemingly well organised and efficient. I moved to the numbers.

I looked at the amounts spent, the projects the money was spent on, the companies subcontracted to complete the work for these projects. Nothing was amiss. It was all above reproach. But the pattern was there, I knew it was there. It was as if my brain had recognised it, processed it and now relaxed with that knowledge. I just needed that insight to move from my unconscious mind to my conscious mind. I walked to my sound system and programmed it to play Mozart's Horn Concerto No. 3.

Seated again at my computers, I stared at the monitors while allowing the music to weave its magic over and through me. Nothing. I closed my eyes and stilled my mind. Nothing. It was there, I knew it was there. I crossed my arms tightly around my torso and focussed solely on the music. That was the only way my unconscious and conscious minds would connect. With Mozart.

"Jenny?" A familiar, safe voice kept calling me, pulling me back into reality. For a short while I resisted it, but he would not desist. "Jenny, come back to us."

I opened my eyes to find Colin sitting next to me, his warm hand resting gently on my arms. Both arms were still tightly wound around my torso and I realised that I was rocking. I stopped, rather surprised that I had been doing that. "How long have I been rocking like this?"

"Vinnie says you've been like this for about two hours."

"Oh." Damn. I was only going to give my brain a short reprieve. Seemingly it had needed more time. But it was time well spent as connections started flooding my consciousness. "Oh!"

"What?" Colin jerked at my sudden exclamation.

I looked at his hand still resting on my arms and then up at his face. "You're here."

"Yes, I am."

I shook off his hand and turned to my computers. "I will tell you later how angry I am with you, how worried I was and how happy I am to see you. But it will have to wait." My hands were moving from one computer to the other and back while I was talking absently. I registered what I had said when Vinnie huffed his amusement from the kitchen. My fingers froze above the keys for a second, but I shook off the embarrassment that I had admitted to my emotions. The revelations coming with each file I was opening took precedence over my tight hold on all emotions.

The more files I opened, the more I was proving myself right. "It is so obvious. So very, very obvious. Why do people ever think that it won't be obvious?"

"What is so obvious?" Colin made himself comfortable next to me and waited. He proved to be quite patient when it took me more than thirty minutes to get my facts straight. I had just made another list. Absently I noted that Vinnie brought him coffee and placed a fresh cup by my right hand. Colin was finishing off the last of the cookies that I had forgotten about.

"It's all the same office. It's statistically impossible for all of them to be at the same office." I turned to him, beaming. I could not believe how easy it actually was. My moment of glory was short-lived when Colin leaned forward and waited until I not only looked at him, but was focussed on him, not still lost inside my own head.

"Jenny, you're going to have to explain. I wasn't here for your whole thought process."

"Oh. Of course. Sorry." I turned back to the computers and started pointing things out. "Here is the list of all the shipping companies. Included in the information I had about them was their company registration information. Here on this computer I have all the information and it states the office where the company was registered. Volosovo is a smallish town eighty-five kilometres from St. Petersburg.

"Now, look at this. I was looking into the financials of the Foundation and found nothing wrong with the donations or their expenditures. For every project that they received EU funding for, they had subcontracted companies to complete these projects. These companies were named when the Foundation requested payment for the different legs of their projects. Nothing hidden and all above board. Look at my new list with those companies."

"You made another list."

"I did and you will not mock me when you see what I've discovered. Each of these companies was also registered at the same office as the shipping companies. What is the probability of eighteen of the thirty-three shipping companies we have listed and twenty other companies, including catering, interior design, engineering and construction companies, all being registered at the same office?"

"None?" Colin moved in closer.

"None," I confirmed.

"Have you put them in chronological order? I mean from the first registered company to the last?"

"Not yet." I realised what he was aiming at. "Oh my! You think that if we get this in chronological order, we can find the first company."

"Yup."

Vinnie appeared in front of us with light brown oven mitts on his hands. They were most certainly not my oven mitts. I did not own oven mitts that looked like happy dogs, complete with ears flopping around. He pointed an oven mitt at the computer. "But wouldn't that also mean that the first company registered might lead us directly to the asshole who started this?"

My lower jaw went slack and I stared at the muscular,

scarred criminal wearing happy-puppy oven mitts. "You are just like Manny!"

The anger that radiated from Vinnie made me realise that I had said something very insulting. It took me only a second to realise my latest faux pas. Colin's laughter fuelled Vinnie's anger and I sighed. I was going to have to explain myself. Again. "Colin, stop laughing. Vinnie, I'm sorry. I know you despise Manny. What I meant was that just like Manny you hide your true intellect and insights. Knowing that people will underestimate you gives you an advantage. It is an excellent mechanism to get more from people than they would generally be willing to give. I'm the complete opposite. The moment I open my mouth, people give me less. Usually they just avoid me."

"Aw, Jen-girl. You're not that bad. Maybe you are a little bit blunt, but I like it. I just don't like being associated with Millard."

"Understood." I shuddered. Talking to people required so much forethought. "I just want to clarify that I was actually paying you a compliment. Not many people would've followed that path of reasoning to the person who might be behind all this."

"Why, thank you, ma'am." He looked uncomfortable with the compliment. His eyes moved around looking for something. Most likely a change of topic. "Dinner is ready. Do you guys want to eat now or later?"

The moment Vinnie mentioned food, my stomach rumbled and I realised how hungry I was. "Now is good."

"What about your lists?" Colin nodded to the computers.

"I don't have all the companies' registration information. I would need to look into each company associated with the Foundation. I would also need their registration office and the date of registration to confirm the connection. Then I can put them in chronological order."

"Can you access that info?" Colin asked.

"I doubt it. At least not for all the companies, unless their information is publicly available on the internet."

"You never try alternative ways of accessing info?" Colin asked.

I gasped. Horrified. "I never do anything illegal on my computers. All the data I retrieve are on public sites. If people only knew how much information is publicly available. You just need to know where to look." I got up and walked to the kitchen. Colin followed me. Vinnie had dished up something that smelled heavenly. There were three trays on the kitchen counter, each with a plate of food, a glass of wine and cutlery resting on a folded red serviette. It looked like we were going to eat in the living area.

"And you know where to look." Colin took his tray and walked with me to the living area.

"I've been doing this for long enough to know where to look for corporate information. If that fails, there are always social networking sites, online job-hunting sites where people post their lives in the form of résumés, and let's not forget about companies advertising their services. A lot can be learned from that as well."

Vinnie picked up his tray and joined us. I marvelled at the gnocchi on the tray on my lap. It looked and smelled more appetizing than a similar dish I had had in a Michelin-recommended restaurant.

"So, what do you do when you run out of publicly available information?" Colin asked as he lifted the fork to his mouth. I thought we were done with the conversation. Apparently not.

"That has not yet happened." My fork clattered onto my plate as a realisation hit me. "It has happened."

Both men looked up and waited for me to continue. I didn't, not until Colin asked, "When?"

"This week. With Danielle. I haven't exactly asked for your help, but have used it. Oh my." I covered my face with both hands. There was no doubt in my mind. I was going to have to draw up a new list of guidelines for myself. Guidelines that would unblur the lines that used to clarify my strict moral and ethical codes.

"Jenny, stop arguing with yourself. Nothing would be done tonight in any case. Maybe I shouldn't have asked you. I should just surprise you with the info." Colin lifted his hand to stop my response. He pointed at my plate with his knife. "Leave it for later. Eat. You're missing out on Vinnie's great gnocchi."

My stomach rumbled again. Later tonight I would work on new guidelines. I had no idea if I could rationalise the illegal gaining of information. With the mouth-watering aroma wafting up from my plate, I decided that physical needs took precedence. I had to eat.

"So," Colin said after a few minutes of silence, "Vinnie told me everything that happened at the station."

"Everything?"

"Everything I know, Jen-girl."

"Did he tell you that I didn't speak to anyone?"

Colin smiled. "He did. Was it difficult?"

"Not really. Nobody came into the room once they put me there."

"But you were treated right?"

"I don't know the protocol for treatment when in an interrogation room, so I can't answer that. I was left in a locked room for five hours. I was fine. What were you doing while I was held at the police station? No, wait, first tell me about Crenshaw's house."

"Nothing to tell, really. Everything happened like I told you. I watched the house the whole day. No one went in and no one came out. By the time I went in, the house had been dark since nightfall. It was obvious no one was home."

"Which means that he was killed in the dark?"

"Must be. The drapes were closed, so the neighbours wouldn't have seen muzzle flashes even if they were looking at the house."

"And no one heard anything."

"I most certainly didn't. As soon as I got in the house, I was suspicious. I first went into his office to find some clues and get out as soon as I could. That's when I found the safe. I got in, saw what was in there and took everything. It turned out that only the flash drives might be of use. There were five identical-looking flash drives. All the documents were just personal stuff of no particular interest. I had just finished sorting through this when I started smelling it."

"What?"

"The blood. I was so focussed on listening for anyone coming in and at the same time getting something out of the safe that I never paid attention to my nose."

"His nose is legendary," Vinnie said. "He will smell a painting and tell you what mix was used."

"It's not a mix, Vin." Colin closed his eyes for a second. A shudder shook his shoulders. When he opened his eyes, they looked haunted. "There was so much blood. Crenshaw was lying at an awkward angle and it was very obvious that he was dead. The wooden coffee table was overturned and that is when I got suspicious. Well, more suspicious."

"About the coffee table?" I asked.

"Yes. It is one of those low, long tables. Not easy to topple over. It would move across the floor if someone bumps into it. So I reckon that someone must have picked it up and laid it on its side to make it look like there had been a struggle. Also, the sofa cushions were messed with. If the struggle was violent enough to have the cushions displaced, surely the sofa itself would've moved from its original position. It had not."

"That sounds like someone was looking for something rather than setting up a crime scene." Vinnie seemed captivated by this.

"If they had lifted all the cushions, yes. But only a few were displaced. Vin, I've seen your aunt's living room after you and your cousins had a wrestling match in there. This looked nothing like that. It looked too neat, too arranged. And the whiskey glass that was so conveniently on the side table? I'm no crime scene investigator, but I know when something looks off. I still can't place my finger on exactly what was wrong, but I didn't have more time to look around."

"Because the police arrived?"

"Yup. That was another suspicious thing. If I didn't even know something was amiss in the house, how did the police know to come? I had been watching the house the whole day." He took a sip of his wine. "Soon as I heard the sirens, I made my way outside, but decided to watch."

"You stayed there?" Was this man totally insane?

"Not at the house, no. I was watching them from the balcony of a neighbour's house. I would really like to know how the police knew to bring their crime scene guys. They stopped their van five minutes after the patrol cars arrived and cleared the house. From the time I left until the first crime scene investigator walked into the house all suited up was a total of fifteen minutes." Colin and Vinnie looked at each other with an understanding I didn't share.

"Dude, that's just wrong."

"Why?" What did they know that I didn't?

"Jenny, the police simply are not that well organised. Their response time is hit-and-miss. Sometimes it takes them three minutes, sometimes fifteen minutes to act on a call. If there is a call for the forensic guys, it could take hours to get those guys to leave their labs, get their vans ready to roll. It's only with high-profile cases that they act that fast."

"But Crenshaw is… was… high-profile."

"True. But I still want to know how the police knew to be there in full force."

"So that must be why they got my fingerprints so quickly."

"And why is it that your fingerprints are on file?"

"I work for an international insurance company. I deal daily with fraud cases. I never asked Phillip why it was important, but they wanted my prints on file and I didn't have a reason to say no."

Colin stared at me incredulously for almost a minute. "Okay, I'm not going to touch this one. So, after watching the police for a while, it was a bit tricky to get out of the area. By the time I wanted to leave, they were everywhere."

"And you couldn't get out?"

"Of course I could get out." He looked insulted at my sincere question. "It just took me a little longer. The moment it was okay for me to phone, I called you. And the rest you know."

"No, I don't. You haven't told me where you've been the whole day."

A cluster of expressions fluttered across his face. "You're not going to like this."

"Colin, I can see on your face that you don't want to tell me. Get past that and tell me."

He hesitated. The internal conflict was as clear on his face. "You have to know that I really did try to do this myself, but it's too sophisticated for my skills. It took me hours, but I got nowhere, so—"

"Just tell her, dude." Vinnie groaned in annoyance.

"I met with Francine."

"Francine? Your friend who found Danielle?"

"Yes. She's going to help me"—he cleared his throat—"help *us* with the code."

"What code?" I placed my tray with the empty plate and wine glass on the coffee table. Leaning towards Colin, I placed my hands on my thighs. "Stop talking in circles and tell me what you're so blunderingly trying to avoid."

Colin stood. "I'd rather just show you. Let's go to the computers."

Chapter TWENTY-TWO

"And this is from Crenshaw's safe?" I stared at the computer screen. "Five flash drives with this on it?"

"Yup."

"It looks like those 3D pictures that were popular when I was a teenager," Vinnie said over my shoulder.

"Yup."

"And you tried to open this?"

"Yup." Colin shrugged. "This is far above what I can do. It's not any kind of encryption I've ever seen."

Silence fell between us. I stared at the computer screen, at the dots forming an optical illusion. It looked like they were moving around the screen.

Colin had given me two of the five flash drives he had taken from Crenshaw's safe. Each one looked the same when I inserted it into my computer. A screen of dots appeared. When I clicked on the external drive, a password request popped up. I was not a hacker. Apparently Colin was, but not a good one.

That brought me to the other issue. I inhaled deeply, trying to find rational calm. "Who exactly is Francine?"

"A trustworthy friend."

"If she's so trustworthy, why does your face and body tell me that you are worried about her?"

Colin sighed a laugh. "I'm not worried about her. I'm worried about your reaction to her helping us."

"What did you tell her?" Vinnie asked.

"That this is a government cover-up and if she is able to get into those files a huge conspiracy will be revealed." Colin's answer caused Vinnie to laugh. I didn't understand why it was funny. Colin turned to me. "Francine believes that there is a conspiracy behind every government decision, action. Aw, hell, I'm sure she believes her birth was a conspiracy."

"And you trusted this crazy person with something that might potentially solve this case? With something that was stolen from a murdered Eurocorps Brigadier-General's private safe?" I shoved my chair back and glared at him. "How, please tell me how, am I supposed to explain that to Manny?"

"Why would you explain anything to him?"

"Because I told him that I would give him full disclosure from now on. I'm not keeping any more secrets. It's exhausting."

"Well, that certainly takes the fun out of this."

"The fun?" My shocked exclamation echoed through my apartment. I inhaled deeply and modulated my tone. "What fun? Oh. You enjoyed keeping Manny in the dark about these things. My God. You must really carry an enormous grudge against him. Whatever did he do to you?"

"Oh, dear," Vinnie said and quickly walked to the kitchen. Colin's jaws were clamped so tight, I feared for his teeth. In the kitchen Vinnie was making coffee again. I did not give in to the temptation to look when I heard a cup clang against something. I was not looking anywhere but at Colin's face.

"Stop reading me."

"What else am I supposed to do when you're not telling me everything?"

He swallowed. "Manny and I have had a few run-ins. I'm not a big fan of his, and I'm sure he feels the same way about me."

"And you're not going to tell me what happened."

"I would prefer not to."

I narrowed my eyes when I heard Vinnie expel air loudly. As if he had been holding his breath. Why was Vinnie worried about Colin telling me about his history with Manny? It was most inconvenient to have yet another mystery added to this already complicated day.

"Well, then tell me about Francine. Please tell me why I should not kick you out of my apartment for bringing another criminal into this mess."

"Firstly, you can't kick me out. Vinnie will protect me." He smiled when Vinnie chuckled. "Secondly, Francine is not a criminal."

"But…" For once I was able to stop my runaway mouth in time.

"But what? She's my friend, therefore she must be a criminal? Or is it her distrust of the government that makes you jump to these conclusions?"

"Okay, okay. I'm sorry. But you can't blame me for thinking that."

"Forget it." He shifted in his chair.

"Colin, please." Asking plainly didn't work. Maybe begging would. "I really need to know who this Francine is. It will make me feel safer. Please?"

His face softened. "I've known Francine for fifteen years. She is a computer genius. One of those people governments fear. And employ. Francine has very strong objections against anything to do with government. According to her, they're all just puppets being controlled by some unseen force, playing geopolitical games with the world. She also believes that the only way she can keep herself safe from all government conspiracies is to work for them. She is formally contracted by the EC to keep their online systems safe. Informally she works for the British and American governments as well. All of them think that she is working exclusively for them."

"She is just like you." This amused me so much, I almost missed the annoyance on Colin's face. Oh, dear. I was insulting everyone today with my comparisons. "What I mean is that she likes to beat the system. She likes to play with the authorities. Just like you."

Colin took a few seconds to think this over. "I suppose

you're right. Anyway. Now you know something about her that could destroy her. She gave me permission to trust you with this, so that you will feel more comfortable trusting her with breaking this encryption."

"Do you trust her?"

"With this? Implicitly." He showed every marker that he was telling the truth. I had come to trust Colin and his intuition. It would seem that Francine was another individual moving on the fringes of society to be included in this case.

Colin shifted in his seat. His expression changed.

"What?" Suspicion was heavy in my voice.

"You're running out of places to look for the registration details of these subcontracted companies. Let me help."

"How?"

"Francine—"

"No." I knew it. His face had told me he was going to say something annoying. "I can find this. I just need time."

"But Francine can find it much faster." He must have seen my revulsion at the outright lack of faith in my skills. "I don't mean it like that. She is really good at finding information that is hidden."

"Illegally." I turned away from him.

"Not necessarily. Okay, maybe, but at least you'll get it. How else are you going to find anything on a small catering company that doesn't even have a website?" He squeezed my forearm lightly until I looked at him. "Come on. What do you have to lose? When we have all the data, we can put it into chronological order. Like you said, we need all the facts. She will look into this for us and maybe even find more companies."

"She doesn't know what to look for."

"You can tell her."

"No," I almost shouted. With a frown I cleared my throat. "I don't want to speak to anyone else."

"Then I'll tell her." He took out his smartphone and silently waited for my permission.

The moment I closed my eyes in resignation, I heard him tapping on the phone's screen. I listened to the one-sided conversation. Colin was telling Francine just enough to give her clear parameters for finding the necessary information. There was no conceivable way she would be able to draw any conclusions from this little information alone. I was impressed, but still worried.

"Now I'll have to tell Manny about this too," I groused as soon as Colin ended the call. No sooner had I spoken than the doorbell rang.

"Expecting anyone?" Colin straightened, his body coiled.

"No." I glanced at the door, not knowing what kind of trouble was waiting there. Vinnie came from the kitchen, laced his fingers, reversed his hands and stretched them far enough to pop his knuckles. With this non-verbal announcement of battle readiness, he walked to the door and looked through the peephole. Every muscle in his body tightened.

The doorbell rang again, followed by banging on the door. "Open this door!"

Vinnie's fists tightened and he looked over his shoulder at Colin. "This dude is cruising for a bruising."

I had no idea what that meant, but I knew what his body language indicated. With a sigh I got up and walked to the door. It took an insistent tug to get Vinnie to move away from the door so that I could open it. Manny was standing with his fist raised for another pounding when the door swung open.

"Manny."

"Doctor Face-reader." He nodded to me and then to Vinnie. "Criminal."

"Asshole," Vinnie returned the greeting without missing a heartbeat. I laughed.

"You two are the most wonderful subjects to study.

Textbook territorial displays, verbal abuse to show superiority, and the lowered tone used to intimidate." It didn't seem like either man appreciated my observations. "Manny, please come in."

I stepped aside to allow Manny entrance to my apartment. He walked past me and the moment his body tensed, I realised that he had just noticed Colin. I swung around wondering if I should have given Colin the chance to first leave my apartment before I had opened the door to Manny. Now it was too late. Colin had moved and was sitting on the sofa facing the bookshelves.

"Colin Frey, as I live and breathe."

"Colonel Millard." Colin remained seated, lounging on the sofa. His legs crossed at the ankles and his left arm rested on the back of the sofa. All signs of not feeling threatened in his territory. An obvious ploy not allowing Manny the upper hand. "You missed dinner with us. Would you like a glass of wine?"

Oh, this was better than sneaking video footage of people in cafés. I wished I had had the foresight to set up recording equipment. It would have given me hours of joy replaying this. Analysing the dynamics between three alpha males. Heaven.

"Oh, so this is your apartment where you offer the guests wine, is it?"

"Just being hospitable, Millard."

An interesting bit of information entered my mind. "Did you know that the *Saccopteryx bilineata*, or more commonly known sac-winged bats, adjust the frequency of their territorial songs? When another male enters their territory they sing lower and more often to scare off the intruder. It has also been shown that the more often and the lower the male sings, the more offspring he produces." All three men stared at me with slack jaws. "What? They do. That is how they prove their male superiority to an opponent. And make more babies."

Colin got up from the sofa. "I don't think we're going to start singing, do you, Millard?"

Manny stared at Colin with great animosity.

"Come on, Millard, surely we can be civilized."

"Like in Prague?" Manny looked doubtful.

"Ah, Prague." Colin crooned. His posture belied his tone though. He was ready for an altercation. "If I didn't know any better, I would say our colonel was suffering from a case of sour grapes."

"What happened in Prague?" I asked.

"Nothing." Both men answered simultaneously without looking at me, still staring at each other in challenge. Often men did this, waiting for the weaker to lower his gaze in submission. I did not think either of them would submit to the other soon.

"Well, if none of you are going to sing, can we try to solve this case?"

A smile tugged at Colin's lips and he turned to me. He did not break the stare in submission; he did it out of respect for me. It won him a few points.

"Jenny tells me that you should now be told everything," he said, still looking at me.

"That must really gall you." Manny looked happy at that prospect. "The only way I can protect Doctor Lenard is if I know who is involved in this case. Unfortunately, that includes you and the gorilla over there."

Not for the first time, Manny insisted that I was Doctor Lenard. Knowingly or unknowingly, he had revealed his opinion of me. This behaviour could often be observed with siblings. Within their own relationship they could tease each other, insult, banter and call each other names. Outside of that dynamic, they would declare war on anyone abusing their siblings. Such behaviour was exclusive to and only acceptable within that circle of trust. Manny had just shown me that I was included in his circle of trust. Interesting.

"Let's sit by the computers. I have something to show you, Manny." I walked to the dining room table, knowing the men would follow. Not doing so would give the others reason to beat him down for disrespecting me. This situation was a first for me. The level of civility and co-operation depended entirely on me. All three men felt responsible for me and would do anything to keep me safe. Even co-operate. It was a position of power I had not held before.

We settled around the table. Colin sat to my right, Manny to my left. Vinnie brought a tray with coffee and settled across from us. I brought Manny up to date with my discoveries about the Foundation's extraordinary income in the last fiscal year. He looked disappointed at the lack of irregularities in their income and expenditures. But he did pale slightly when I showed him the list with all the companies registered at the same office. We spent about twenty minutes in a relatively amicable discussion. I postponed telling him about the registration dates. Or to be more precise, Francine's involvement in finding the dates.

"I understand the eighteen shipping companies registered at this office. Where did the other twenty companies come from?" Manny frowned at my list.

"The Foundation receives funding from the EU for projects. These projects are part of a programme that has the EU working in partnership with Russia. That means that the EU pumps money into this programme and Russia puts in an equal amount. This programme focuses on specific needs that were determined by the EU. Entities can apply for funding to enable them to run projects that will meet these needs. Somehow the Foundation received funding for eleven separate projects.

"Each project needed to subcontract companies to complete the work. These companies included carpenters, caterers, engineering companies and the like. I have not had time to analyse the projects, but it seems that they are varied. Which makes it great for the bad guys. They could register many different companies. Each company gets paid for their services. I don't know how yet, but all the signs are here that the Foundation used this to launder money."

"What money? From the art auctions?" Manny asked.

"Most likely. I have no way to determine how much money had come from the art auctions. Which means that I don't know what money comes from where."

"Would you be able to find out how they did this?"

"I'm good at spotting patterns. I usually get to this point and then hand it over to the forensic accountants."

"Is there any way to determine what money came from where?" Manny asked.

"We would need to look at each company's finances individually. Who knows what condition their books are in. Or whether we would be able to get access to their books. You have to keep in mind, some are small companies." I pursed my lips. "Frankly, I don't think it will be possible."

"Bugger," Manny grunted. "Okay, what else do you have?"

"This." I changed screens with a click and we were all looking at dots. Colin sat back and folded his arms. Classic blocking behaviour. I did not care that he wasn't pleased with me telling Manny everything. He just had to accept it.

"What's this?" Manny frowned at the screen.

"We don't know. Colin got this from Crenshaw's safe. There are five flash drives that open to this screen when you insert it in the computer." I lifted my hand to stop Manny. "Don't start shouting yet. Let me tell you everything first. Then you can yell."

Despite Colin and Vinnie's disapproving glares, I told Manny everything about the flash drives. To his credit, he did not arrest Colin. He did, however, exhibit increasing degrees of fury. I swallowed my nerves and continued. "Colin couldn't open the files, so he gave them to a trusted friend. She has three and we have two."

Manny surprised me. He sat quietly for a long time processing what I had told him. His glare moved between Colin, Vinnie and myself while a myriad of emotions moved across his face. He went from shock to anger to fury to an internal struggle. Finally he nodded his head and looked at Colin.

"How long before your *friend*"—he spat out the word—"will have results?"

"Hours? Days? I really don't know. She owes me one, so she's making this a priority. As soon as she's in, we'll know."

"She's... um, also helping with something else." My voice cracked under the strain. Manny lifted an angry eyebrow. I forged on. "We have a theory that if we put all the companies' registration dates in chronological order, we might be able to determine where it all started. Who started it all. I have not been able to find the registration dates for six companies and Colin's friend is going to find this for us. She might also be able to find more companies connected to the Foundation and the ships."

I sat back and looked at Manny. He just grunted and was quiet for a while. I took the time to observe. Even lacking the context of the history between Manny and Colin, I came to some interesting conclusions. These two men disliked each other intensely, but respected each other too. It was an interesting contradiction. They seemed to value the other's knowledge, experience and input. Yet every sentence was tinged with sarcasm. Unlike Manny's sarcasm towards me indicating his anger, this was defensive. It was a protection mechanism people used to not allow their opponent the insight into their begrudging respect.

"I want her name and contact information." Manny straightened himself. "You three have been working behind my back and I don't like it. Frey, I don't care who you have by the short and curlies in which agencies, you will not manipulate me.

If either you or the gorilla step out of line, I'll arrest Doctor Lenard."

"Hey. I will not accept responsibility for their criminal actions."

"No, Doc. You're the one who lied to my face."

"I didn't lie. I just didn't tell you everything."

"Same difference. I can get you arrested for breach of security. From the beginning you knew how sensitive this information was and that it was not to be shared with any outsiders. And now you've included yet another person. You're going to carry the burden." When no one spoke, he nodded. "Good. Glad we understand each other. And while you're giving me the name of your gal, you might as well tell me your full name, gorilla."

"Why don't you suck my—"

"Vinnie, please. We're all working together here to prevent more artists from being murdered with guns stolen from Eurocorps. This is so much bigger than Colin's ego, your fear of being labelled or my dislike of social niceties." In one sentence I had just summarised each one of us. And all of a sudden my obsessions and neuroses seemed petty. I must have been saying something right, because all three men were still listening. "Let's put our own issues aside and be totally open with each other until this thing is over. Then you can get back to your grudges and distrust."

"Well, I'll be damned, Doc." Manny smiled wryly.

"Damned?" I waved the silly expression away with a flick of my wrist. "Let's get back to the case. What don't we know?"

"Have you looked at the weapons' theft reports?" Thankfully, Manny was all business again.

"Yes. I couldn't find anything out of the ordinary, so Vinnie offered his help."

"I'm not giving you my name," Vinnie stated. "I will help. I will protect Jen-girl, but you will not have my name."

Fortunately the stare-down between Vinnie and Manny didn't last long. Manny closed his eyes and sighed. "Fine. What do you have on the guns?"

"Nothing yet. I hope to hear something by tomorrow."

"I suppose I don't want to know who you'll be hearing from."

"You suppose right." Vinnie folded his arms across his muscular chest, effectively ending the topic.

We were waiting for Francine to break the encryption. We were waiting for registration dates. We were waiting for Vinnie's gunrunners to share information about stolen guns. I hated waiting. So I started thinking of any other loose ends.

"Oh, Colin." I spoke so quickly that he started next to me. I smiled. "Sorry. I was wondering if you could look at something for me."

"What?"

I moved to my personal computer and looked for a specific email. "Manny and I were looking at footage of a gala event and I saw something familiar. Ah, here it is. Do you recognise this?"

Colin moved closer to the screen to look at the blurred image of the Gauguin painting I had noticed in the ball room. His eyes widened. "It's Gauguin's Still Life, The White Bowl."

"This is his Still Life, The White Bowl?"

"Yes. Why?" Colin sounded worried.

"The canvas strip found on the dead girl came from this painting." Manny said absently.

"This is the Gauguin painting that was found on Danielle?"

"Yes. I'm familiar with Gauguin's work, but I'm not an expert," I said. "I knew that Rousseau & Rousseau insured that painting, but I've never actually seen it. This painting was hanging in Danielle's room. It was the second painting from the left next to her bed."

Colin closed his eyes, seemingly accessing his visual memory. His eyes shot open. "You're right. It was there. Which I suppose we can assume was a forgery. It didn't have any piece missing, no strip taken off it."

Manny pointed at the computer screen. "Does that mean this one is real?"

"There is no way to tell," Colin answered. "I would have to see it. Even then I might need more than just a look. Danielle was really good with her forgeries. The one hanging here might be the painting that strip was torn from, it might be a forgery, it might be the original."

"Can't you tell if this painting is missing the strip?" Vinnie asked from behind the screens. I was secretly glad he wasn't curious enough to come around to our side to look at the screens. As it was, there were too many men sitting close to me.

"I tried to get a better view, but there is a man's head is in the way throughout the short view. And it is possible that the frame might hide the missing strip."

"Only one way to tell and that is to see it," Colin said again. He lifted an eyebrow. "This photo was taken at an event at La Maison Russie, right?"

Manny's eyes widened. Then they narrowed and he glared at Colin. "No, Frey. You are not going to break in anywhere. I will see what I can arrange for us to see this. I'll get you more information about the place."

"I wasn't planning on breaking in, you ass. I was simply asking to find out if it was a public or private place. I thought if it were public we could go on an excursion." Colin was exhibiting cues of deception. I didn't say anything.

Manny inhaled angrily. I put my hands out towards the men sitting next to me. "Focus. Common goal."

Both men grunted and slumped back in their chairs. I rolled my eyes and snarled at Vinnie's grin. God, I hated working with people. Especially alpha males. It was so much easier observing them.

"Is there anything else you need to know?" I asked Manny.

He thought for a minute. "Not for now."

"Then this meeting is over."

"Yes. Go to your cave. Jen-girl will let you know when we get anything else." Vinnie got up, ready to escort Manny to the door. A few more threats were grunted between the three men. I chose to ignore them. I had done enough mediating for one evening. It was not part of my job description.

By the time Vinnie closed the door behind Manny, it was close to eleven o'clock and I was ready for bed. It seemed that I had not caught up enough sleep during the day. And playing the referee was exhausting. My respect for Phillip's natural ability to mediate rocketed. I turned off all the computers, turned to my bedroom and stopped. "What the hell do you think you're doing?"

"She cussed." Vinnie sounded breathless from shock.

"Colin?" I glared at him, waiting for his answer.

"What does it look like?" He shook the overnight bag in his hand towards the study. "I'm going to sleep."

"Not in my apartment."

"Jenny." He softened his tone. It was too soft. The thief was trying to manipulate me with smooth words. "I'm tired. I'm also worried about you. After what happened yesterday, I would sleep so much better knowing that you're safe."

"Vinnie is here." And one overbearing criminal in my apartment was more than enough.

"Now there will be two of us to protect you."

I breathed past my fury, past my rebellion against another presence in my apartment. It didn't take me long to read the two men in front of me. I briefly closed my eyes in resignation. "You are not being fair to me. There are two of you and only one of me. And I don't have the energy to fight you."

"I won't be in the way." He waited until I looked at him. Honesty and concern lined his features. "Only until this is resolved. Together we will be a much stronger force."

"Fine." I sounded petulant. I felt petulant. God, I really hated working with people. And now I had to live with them. With a huff I walked to my room. Tomorrow I would fight these men again. Now I was too tired.

Chapter **TWENTY-THREE**

Forty-eight hours. Apparently that was the time limit on my ability to share living space with two bickering men. What made it worse was that I hadn't seen Phillip since they brought me back from the police station. I missed his calming, buffering presence. I missed his natural, easy knowledge of working with people. I missed him.

It was early evening. I had planted myself in front of the computers again. Vinnie was stacking the dinner dishes in the dishwasher. Colin was glaring at the television. They had just had another argument about Vinnie's contact taking his time to get back regarding the stolen weapons. I did not understand it at all, but they seemed to enjoy the bickering. It was driving me insane. I wanted them to leave. I wanted my old life back.

"What about your girlfriend Francine?" Vinnie asked loudly from the kitchen. "It's not like that chick got into those files in the first ten minutes. And what about all the info on those companies? Huh?"

Colin ignored Vinnie's provocation. I had come up empty on my searches for more details on the companies. I had been convinced that their registration particulars would be public information. It wasn't.

"Francine is your girlfriend?" I asked. The status of their relationship was news to me.

"She's not my girlfriend." Colin turned his glare from the television to Vinnie. He had been quiet most of the afternoon and evening. I suspected that he was regretting his insistence on staying here. I regretted giving in so easily. I turned back to my computers and left the men to their juvenile arguments.

The last two days I had spent watching every second of footage that Manny had been able to send me. My saving grace had been the headphones that I put on to listen while I watched. That way I hadn't heard most of the bickering. At first I was concerned that their friendship was in danger. Their non-verbal cues, however, totally contradicted the insults they were hurling at each other. The only conclusion I could draw from this was that they found this to be an entertaining outlet for the tension that was building in all of us.

Colin had kept his promise. He hadn't been in my way. Not in the sense of him intruding on my space. The two of them never ventured close to my bedroom or bathroom. The rest of my apartment had been completely taken over though. I sighed and focussed my mind on the footage of last year's event. Every time I watched it, I saw something new. I couldn't wait to show it to Manny. He had phoned a few times, but had spent the last two days with Leon and the investigation into Crenshaw's murder. Not even under the most severe torture would I admit that I missed Manny.

"Dude." Vinnie's shocked exclamation pulled me out of my zone. "This is wicked sick."

Vinnie had moved from the kitchen to the sofa. They were watching the television in fascinated horror. I heard feminine grunts and suction sounds that widened my eyes. Of all the audacious things they could have done, this was too much.

"What are you watching?"

"Oh, Jen-girl. You have to come and see this." Gone was the quarrelling. Vinnie sat next to Colin, no argumentative body language on display.

I slowly got up. "If you two are watching porn in my apartment, I will notify every law enforcement agency of your whereabouts."

Both heads swivelled to me in shock. Just then the doorbell

rang. I started moving towards the door, but Vinnie stopped me with a head shake. He got up, made some hand signals to Colin, who nodded. Vinnie walked to the door and I to the sofa where Colin had lost interest in the television. I was still curious about the sounds filling my apartment.

On the television screen were two women wrestling in mud. At least it wasn't porn. I had nothing against people watching porn. I simply didn't want two men watching it in my apartment. The two women were trying to grab hold of each other, but the mud did not allow for that. They were in a large square tub, knee-deep in mud. A large male-dominated crowd was cheering them on. I frowned. "Why would they do that?"

"Because the men think it's sexy, Doc." Manny spoke next to me. I hadn't heard him come in, and turned. He looked oddly amused. And typically rumpled. Vinnie stood behind Manny and had lost all traces of laughter. Colin's mirth also disappeared and I sighed. Great. Now I was going to have not two, but three men bickering. On the television screen one of the women had the other face down in the mud. Loud male cheering filled my apartment. I almost asked again about the mud-wrestling, but decided that I really wasn't interested.

"Hello, Manny. Please tell me that you have new information." I grabbed the remote control off Colin's lap and switched the television off. I ignored their protests. "I have all those lists and would be grateful to have something new to compare them against."

"Ah, you and your lists." Manny shrugged out of his suit jacket and threw it over the back of one of the wingback chairs. I swallowed, picked up the jacket and draped it over a hanger and hung it on the coat rack by the door. I walked back and nodded pointedly towards the computers. All three men followed me to the dining room table.

"So, do you have something new for me?" I asked Manny again. A bit less patient this time.

"I do." He pulled out a chair and placed himself in front of the EDA computer. "What about you?"

"We haven't heard anything about the guns or the files or the registration details yet." I was not ashamed to admit that I was pleased when Manny gave Vinnie and Colin a disapproving look. They shrugged it off and everyone took their usual seats. I pulled my shoulders back a bit and lifted one eyebrow in arrogance. "I, on the other hand, have discovered something very interesting. But you must show me yours first, then I'll show you mine."

There was a pregnant silence for a millisecond. Long enough for me to realise that I had said something to bring surprised looks to their faces. I remembered Manny saying something similar once. It only took another millisecond for me to conclude how they had interpreted my word. I threw my hands in the air. "You are unbelievable. You're thinking of sex? Really? Can we please focus on work?"

Manny cleared his throat. "Of course, Doc. Let me start with the Crenshaw case."

"Have they found anything else to connect him to Piros?" Colin asked.

"As a matter of fact, they did. In one of the bedrooms was a black and white photo of Budapest's parliament. On the back of the photo was written, 'to Piros, congrats on the divorce', with the date next to it."

"What date?" I asked.

"We already checked it. The date written was October 1996. During that time Crenshaw was stationed in Hungary."

"So he was Piros?" Colin didn't sound convinced.

I also couldn't believe this. On the video where I had recognised the insignia, the soldier had talked about Piros in conversation with Crenshaw. Or had he? I had never heard the full sentence. Maybe he had addressed Crenshaw as Piros. Had I missed something?

"Miss what?" Manny asked.

I blinked at him a few times before I realised that I must have been thinking aloud. "I don't know. Let me check something."

I turned to the EDA computer and mentally patted myself on the shoulder for my obsessive nature. The time-stamped markers that I had placed on the video made it easy to access that clip.

"What are we looking at?" Colin asked next to me.

I didn't answer him, just played the clip. Then played it again. I played it for a third time in slow motion.

"Crenshaw is not Piros." Once I knew what to look for it was easy to see.

"How can you tell?" Manny asked.

"Crenshaw's reaction when the soldier mentions Piros." I played the clip again, pausing it at a specific moment, and zoomed in on Crenshaw's face. "Look at the tightening of his jaw muscles, his neck is stiff, his nose wings are flared and then there is the lip occlusion. All indicators of a negative emotion causing great tension. There are no other cues showing it to be anything but fear. And he only displays this on hearing Piros' name. Crenshaw is not Piros."

"But we have a photo with a date," Manny said.

"I heard a but in there. What is wrong with that date?" I asked.

"Sharp, Doc, sharp." Manny nodded his approval. "Crenshaw was stationed there during that time. He also got divorced around that time."

"But?" I wished he would get to it.

"But"—Manny smiled at me—"at that time Crenshaw was involved in some diplomatically delicate proceedings. Those details are still classified. All I know is that he told me years later that he and his wife had to pretend to still be married long after the divorce had gone through. Apparently their divorce would have ruined years of work. So they got all the legalities done, but nobody knew about their divorce until two years after the fact."

"Nobody?" Colin pressed his index finger to his eyebrow. Classic eye blocking. He disagreed with Manny. "There is always someone who knows."

"Granted," Manny said. "Leon swears that Crenshaw loved the cloak-and-dagger stuff. He would never have told anyone. He liked knowing things no one else was privy to. That limits it to his superiors. Leon phoned around and none of them were on real friendly terms with Crenshaw. They respected his work, but would never have sent him a congratulatory photo."

"So the photo was planted?"

"That is the general consensus. The crime scene investigators also determined that the frame that originally hung in that specific space had been smaller. There is a faint shadow on the wall, which means that the previous frame had been there for a long time. All the other frames in the house had a thin layer of dust on the top. The photo's frame didn't. So yes, I think that photo was placed there recently."

"Any fingerprints on the photo?" I asked. After my recent experiences I had become very aware of fingerprints.

"None. That is equally suspicious. No fingerprints anywhere on the photo or the frame is simply impossible. Unless it had all been cleaned." He leaned back in the chair. I wondered what Manny would look like if he was rested, shaved and wearing pressed clothes. "Leon and I spent most of today looking at Crenshaw's employment records. I compared it to your lists, Doc. There was record of him living or travelling to most of the places where the artists were murdered. Maybe not at the exact date, but around that time. There were some places he had not been to though. At least not in an official capacity. Leon and I realised that the problem with that is that Crenshaw was not the only person connected to some European agency or military to have visited those places."

"Making a list of all those people and placing them there would require a staggering amount of data." I was doing the calculations in my head. "Is there any way that we can narrow it down?"

"Let's not worry about that list, Doc." Manny pulled the EDA computer closer to him and I groaned. He was moving it out of place. "I have another list for you."

"What list?" The wrong angle of the computer was forgotten.

"All the art that is in the house where last year's gala event was held. La Maison Russie. Look at this." He worked the computer and then turned it towards me. Again at a wrong angle. Every cell in my body screamed at me to align the computer as it had been. I forced myself to focus. On the screen was a badly organised list. It didn't make sense.

"What am I looking at?"

"A list of all the artwork in La Maison Russie." He smiled when he saw my eyebrows lifting. "Quite something, yes?"

"It's a terrible list." I frowned angrily at the screen. "Nothing is in order. It's not organised at all. Not alphabetically, by artist, era or even medium. Who drew up this list?"

"I did, missy." The words were clipped. I looked away from the screen and saw Manny's face pulled tight in anger. Oh, dear. "Not everyone systemizes things as anally as you do."

"What does my anus have to do with being organised?" My question elicited different responses. Vinnie chuckled, Colin groaned and Manny stared at me incredulously. Nobody answered me. "Well?"

"Jenny, it's an expression people used to describe obsessive perfectionists," Colin explained.

"It doesn't make sense," I said, discounting the expression. I had first encountered this ridiculous expression during my psychology studies. It had never conveyed any rationale, no matter how many times it had been explained to me. I turned back to the computer. "I'll organise this list and compare it to the lists I have of the miraculously recovered art and suspected forgeries. Do you have the name of the owner of the house?"

"It belongs to a Russian investment firm." Manny looked relieved to talk about the case instead of anatomical euphemisms. "The name of the company is on the bottom of the list."

"You included irrelevant information in this list?" Did people have no concept of list-making? I scrolled down the page. "P&S."

"P&S?" Colin asked.

"It's short for Posiet and Somov ZAO."

"Another closed joint-stock company," Colin said. "Does this Posiet & Somov mean anything to you?"

"Nothing aside from both names being Russian surnames. It would be safe to assume that those are the surnames of the people who founded this company. I wonder if they also registered in Volosovo."

"Give me a moment," Colin said. He picked his smartphone off the table. After a moment of tapping the screen, he put it to his ear and smiled at me. "I was hoping to surprise you with this."

"With what?" Manny growled next to me. Colin lifted a finger to indicate silence. This seemed to anger Manny further, if his breathing was any indicator.

"Hallo, sexy." Colin smiled into the phone. Who was he talking to? There was silence around the table. We were all watching Colin. "No, I'm well, thanks, love. Listen, do you have the registration details yet?"

"I want the details for that friend of his," Manny said next to me. I ignored him. The only person Colin would ask about registration details was Francine. That information interested me much more than Manny's displeasure.

Colin was making agreeing sounds. "Fantastic. You're a doll. I have one more company for you to check. Posiet & Somov ZAO... Yes, I'll wait." He looked at me and smiled. "She's just making a quick call. And she's going to email me the details for those companies. She got all of them."

"Francine?" I asked.

"Yes." There was a full minute of silence in my apartment. I glanced at Manny and could see his mind working. He was busy building up a righteous fury. Just as Manny inhaled angrily, Colin lifted his finger again. "Yes, hon, I'm still here… yes? Super. Thanks, doll. Can't you tell me anything more about those codes?" More agreeing sounds. "Hon, I really appreciate it. Yes, yes, I know. It will be a larger bottle than last time, I promise."

A few more promises and Colin finished his call. He turned to us. "Our Francine has some interesting friends. She knows somebody who knows somebody who works in the Russian bureaucracy. That person has been able to get her everything we need. Not only were all thirty-three shipping companies registered in Volosovo, but P&S as well."

Vinnie shook his head. "This seems like a huge criminal enterprise that has been running for many years. How could they have made such a fundamental mistake?"

"Says the expert on criminal activity." Manny was sarcastic. He was angry.

"I'm not in prison, am I?" Vinnie was halfway out of his chair when his cell phone started ringing. He glared at Manny for two more rings, answered the call and walked to his bedroom.

"Please tell me this Francine is your trusted friend you talked about. My ulcer won't be able to handle yet another criminal knowing everything." Manny looked pained.

"Yes, she is the same person," Colin said. "She said that it should take her programme another few hours to get into those files. She's very impressed with the coding."

"Okay then." It looked like Manny was having just as much trouble as I co-operating with criminals. For a man like

Manny it would be working with people who did not work within the same honour code as he. Both of us were challenged outside of our clearly delineated beliefs. I supposed for Colin and Vinnie, they were having difficulty being forced to work within parameters.

This was a totally mismatched team and it made for fascinating observations. Contrary to all indicators, we were tolerating each other pretty well. A common goal did that to people. We were inclined to forget race, religion, politics, even personal beliefs if our goal was commanding enough. Ours was. Stop the people who were using, then killing artists.

"Show me what you've got, Doc." Manny brought me out of my musings.

"The video footage you sent me." I moved my computer back and aligned my chair. Moved the computer again. Tilted my head and narrowed my eyes. Another five millimetres to the right and I sighed contentedly. Movement caught my peripheral vision. Manny and Colin were shaking their heads at me. At least they agreed on one thing. Even if it was at my expense.

"Watch this." I clicked on a clip and played it once.

"Is this last year's gala event?" Colin asked.

"Looks like it," Manny answered. "Yes, there is that White Bowl still life painting."

"Still Life, The White Bowl," Colin sighed. "What are we looking at, Jenny?"

"Group dynamics are interesting to observe, to learn from. Watching a group of people, whether they are teenagers, female friends, gangsters or a police team, can teach us a lot about the dynamics in that group."

"That's how you knew that the German was the leader of the group that broke into your place."

"Yes." My hand moved involuntarily to my left eyebrow. Most of the bruising was gone. The memory was still very fresh. "When watching people who know each other in a group setting, you can see who's considered the alpha, the leader. The other's eyes will constantly stray towards him or her to check in."

"Check in?" Manny asked.

"For approval, permission, acknowledgement. Even if they are not standing together in the same group, there will constantly be eye contact between them. Millisecond eye contact. If someone's behaviour is off, the others will have disapproving looks and might even intervene. But it all depends on the leader."

"And every group has a leader," Colin stated.

"Even in a group of friends there is a stronger personality that the others will follow. It doesn't mean that it is like a military outfit where everyone follows the officer blindly. They would just imitate that person's habits, from choice of drink to relating to people. The leader would not seek out acknowledgement. He or she would give it. Now watch this clip again. Watch Crenshaw." I replayed the same clip and turned down the sound. Sometimes we see better without auditory distractions.

The formal part of the event had taken place and people were mingling. Business cards changed hands, social smiles were abundant and eyes were roaming constantly for the next contact to be made. Crenshaw was standing next to a pillar with a glass of red wine in his left hand. He was talking to an elderly couple. His body language was submissive, which led me to believe that this couple held enough power for him to want to impress them.

"Doc," Manny said while the clip was playing. "I can watch this all I want, but I don't know what to look for."

"He's not acknowledging anyone." Didn't they see it? It was so obvious.

"How would that look?"

I demonstrated with an elderly gentleman who Manny said

was the European Commissioner for Trade. Quite a few people at the event were connected to him. It was visible from how their eyes were seeking him out. If they made contact, he would nod slightly or lift his eyebrows. That pacified and pleased those people, relaxing their facial muscles and body language.

"Okay, so what does this mean?" Manny asked. This was going to be more difficult than I thought.

"Crenshaw did not give acknowledgement, but rather sought it. I then made note of where he was looking. Then I looked for other people also looking in that direction. That included the guys from the intelligence division of Eurocorps. They were definitely submissive to Crenshaw, but they only made eye contact with him when they needed to talk to him."

"So who were they looking at?" Manny was studying the screen.

"I don't know. That person is off screen. This is the only footage that I have of this part of the event. Were there any other cameras? Any possibility of any more footage?"

"I'll have to check," Manny said. "So how do you interpret all this, Doc?"

"From watching this and other clips, I don't think that Crenshaw was the brains behind the operation."

"We already agreed he wasn't Piros," Manny said. "Leon and I talked a lot about Crenshaw. I'm no profiler, but he doesn't sound like he could plan a thing like this. He was an operations guy. He made things happen; he didn't plan them. He was also good at the diplomatic stuff, but never took initiative."

"And this would need initiative," Colin said.

"A chess player, like I said before," I stated.

"Leon said that Crenshaw couldn't play chess if his life depended on it."

"Enough said." That was it for me. I was convinced.

"Unfortunately this isn't concrete evidence. It's just reasonable doubt." Manny looked very tired. "I'd rather we now focussed our energy on finding the person behind it all. I would also love to know what Crenshaw's part in all this was."

"Hopefully the coded files will give us insight into that." The need to comfort Manny surprised me. I wasn't an empathetic person.

"First they tried to intimidate Jenny from working the case, then they set her up for Crenshaw's murder. At the same time we are given clues making Crenshaw look like a master criminal. Who has the power to do this, Millard?" For a change Colin didn't sound argumentative. Just very concerned.

"I don't know, Frey. And that worries me."

"How sure are you about Chief Dutoit?" Colin asked.

Manny hesitated. "Sure."

"I don't need Jenny's skill to know you're lying, Millard."

"Until this case I was very sure of him," Manny admitted after a minute of glaring at Colin.

"What changed?" I asked.

"His uncommon interest in this case. Doctor Face-reader's observations." Manny's cell phone started ringing with a most annoying disco ring tone. His eyes widened. "Talk about the devil."

I frowned at yet another expression that I didn't understand. He cleared his throat nervously, pressed something on his phone and said, "You're on speakerphone, Chief Dutoit."

"Thank you, Colonel Millard. Good evening, Doctor Lenard."

"Um... Good evening." I had no idea how to address this man. And I did not want to speak to him. Next to me Manny was gesturing to Colin to keep quiet. Colin lifted his middle finger in a vulgar gesture, but sat back in his chair. Vinnie folded his arms and glared.

"Colonel Millard's been telling me what a wonderful asset you've been to this investigation. I appreciate all the work you've done so far as well as your discretion. I can't stress enough the importance of keeping this as confidential as possible."

I took a moment to find the safest answer. "I understand, sir."

"Earlier tonight I spoke with Phillip Rousseau. He kindly agreed to remove himself from this investigation."

"He what?" Phillip would never leave me on my own with all these people. All these men.

"The Commanding General of Eurocorps headquarters, Lieutenant-General Barreiros, and I had a lengthy conversation with Colonel Millard and Major-General Leon Hofmann. We decided to limit any other eyes on this case. Mister Rousseau completely understood our position. He did, however, sound very concerned about you spending time with Colonel Millard. Are there any problems I should be aware of?"

"No, there aren't any problems. Not yet." There were so many things I wanted to address. I started with the most disturbing. "I don't understand your rationale for removing Phillip from this investigation. He knows everything."

"And I have his word that all that information is safe."

"So what's your problem? I need Phillip." Next to me, Manny gasped at my irreverence. I didn't care. I was feeling the loss of Phillip's presence and interpersonal skills in my life very strongly.

"Doctor Lenard." Chief Dutoit's voice turned hard. "We are focussing on a much larger problem here. Not to take away from the horror of the deaths of those artists, there are the stolen weapons from Eurocorps. The political impact of all this alone could be staggering, as could the long-term damage to the agency's reputation and credibility. And I really don't want this to touch the EDA."

I was tempted to tell him I didn't care about his stupid politics, but I breathed through it. It would seem that we all needed reminding to stay focussed. "I understand."

"We will keep all information limited to us here in Doctor Lenard's apartment. It will not leave here, sir." Manny needed commendation for that brilliant sentence. It was not a lie. Simply an ingenious manipulation of the truth. He had successfully included Vinnie and Colin without Chief Dutoit being any the wiser.

"Well, that's good. Colonel Millard, I want you to focus on this investigation. It needs to be done with."

"Yes, sir."

"In the meantime, Lieutenant-General Barreiros and the Head of the EDA decided that we'll issue a statement that Crenshaw's death was a bungled burglary. Mister Rousseau agreed to spread the word that Doctor Lenard is on extended sick leave."

"I'm not sick."

"I know that, Doctor Lenard. If anyone else wonders why you're not at work, sick leave makes much more sense. Especially if it is due to overwhelming stress."

"I'm not stressed." Although my voice sounded very stressed at that moment.

"I know that too, Doctor Lenard." A sigh came through the phone. "Mister Rousseau is very concerned about you. He agreed to this because I reasoned that the people who had tried to intimidate and set you up for murder might back off a bit if you are at home, too stressed to work."

That made sense. "Okay then. Can I at least phone Phillip?"

"No. The only people you will be in contact with are Colonel Millard and me. Understood?"

"I understand," I said. I was under house and phone arrest.

"Good. I hope that we have this wrapped up very soon. And once again, thank you for all your help, Doctor Lenard. I'll be keeping an eye on you."

I blinked at that. Was it a threat or was it supposed to make me feel safe?

The phone call ended and we sat in silence. Every day we seemed to unearth more pieces to a puzzle that had only revealed background until now. I needed more prominent pieces to start making sense of it all. I needed something more concrete. Something that could start filling in the huge gaps and create a better picture.

And I needed Phillip. I rued the day I had agreed to get involved in all this.

Chapter **TWENTY-FOUR**

"Dudes, y'all are going to love me." Vinnie stormed into the living area waving a piece of paper.

"Did he just call me dude?" Manny asked me, but I was too stunned by the change in Vinnie's accent to respond. When did he start speaking like a Texan native?

Vinnie slapped the piece of paper down in front of me. "Who's your daddy now?"

"The same man as before. My father is Gerard Leonard Lenard." My factual statement was met with stunned silence. Manny gaped at me. The moment Colin and Vinnie saw his face, they laughed. Soon all three men were shaking with mirth.

Manny was wiping tears from his cheeks. "Why would anyone name their child like a Doctor Seuss character?"

"I don't know who this doctor is."

"Never mind that, Jen-girl." Vinnie's voice was still thick with laughter. He leaned over, crowding me and tapped on his notes. "Look at this."

I did. On the piece of paper was one of the neatest lists I have yet seen. In such contrast to the scarred, slang-speaking muscle-man. "Your gun guy got back to you."

"He did. He is one of the most pedantic dealers I know. I think he's a bigger list-maker than you. Every single transaction he's ever made is recorded. Maybe that is why he has a controlling interest in this part of the world in this market." The excitement of the information in front of me had made him lose his cautiousness around Manny. His eyes widened with regret when Manny inhaled sharply.

"You are in contact with Hawk?" The muscles in Manny's cheeks bunched, he was biting down so hard on his jaw. "He has been on the radar of every agency since forever and no one can get anything on him."

"I can neither confirm nor deny any knowledge of such a man," Vinnie said.

"What's your relationship with Hawk?"

"I can neither confirm nor deny any—"

"Yeah, yeah, I get it," Manny said. "You do realise that you know a man who is wholly evil. He provides weapons to Third World countries that use children as soldiers. The fifteen automatic guns used by the extremist group who killed all those children in Spain two months ago were traced to him as well."

"So why have you not put him away yet?" Vinnie was denying knowledge of this man, but I could see the truth. He knew Hawk and he did not like him. No, it was stronger. Vinnie didn't like Manny, but he despised Hawk.

"Because he is smart. All we have are rumours, circumstantial evidence and gut feelings. Nothing that can be taken to court."

A loaded silence filled the air. I studied Vinnie's face and thought how hard it must be to carry so many secrets inside oneself. Manny must have seen something on his face as well. He dropped his chin and looked at Vinnie from under his eyebrows. "If you know anything, if you can give us anything, point us in a direction to put a stop to this man—"

"I can neither—" Vinnie looked worried.

"Just listen to me, asshole! No one will ever know where I got the intel from. Look, I really don't like you, but Doc here seems to trust you. That means something. You can't be all bad. You have the opportunity to do something really good here. Do it, man. Give me enough to put that man away forever." Manny cleared his throat. "I will owe you one."

It must have been an appealing proposition, if Vinnie's eye-flash was anything to go by. He maintained his nonchalant attitude. "Whatever."

Manny moved forward to push harder, but was interrupted by his ringing cell phone. "We're not done with this," he said before he answered his phone. "Millard. Yes. I'm here. She is."

"Is that Phillip?" I asked. Manny turned away from me and continued listening. I was not put off. "Manny, if that is Phillip, I want to talk to him."

Manny glared at me when I tugged on his sleeve. He put his hand over the bottom of his phone. "You heard what the Chief said. You can't speak to him."

"I want to speak to Phillip." I reached for his phone, but he pulled away. "Give me the phone. I want to speak to him."

A deep voice sounded through the phone. Manny glared at me, placed the phone on the table and spoke towards it. "You're on speakerphone."

"Genevieve?" Phillip's voice came through Manny's phone. It sounded tinny and like home.

"Phillip. They say I can't speak to you."

"That's right. How are you? Are you okay? Do you need anything?" The questions came out in a rush. Phillip was worried.

"I'm fine, thank you."

"Who else is with you?"

I looked at the three men around the table. Colin and Vinnie were frowning at me, shaking their heads. "Vinnie and Colin."

A snort turned into a polite cough before Phillip spoke again. "So which one of you is the referee?"

"Jenny is," Colin answered in a none too friendly tone. "What do you want?"

"I knew you could do it, Genevieve," Phillip said softly after a moment. "Are they treating you well?"

"We're treating her fine. Now answer the question." Two things were clear. Colin did not like his presence known. And he did not like Phillip's question.

"The results are back from the tests that were done on that canvas strip found on the girl," Phillip said.

"On Danielle?" I asked.

"Yes. The strip that was found in her coat comes from the original painting."

"Why did she have that strip sewn into the coat?" I wondered.

"Maybe she realised her life was in danger and she wanted to use it for her own protection," Phillip said. "I don't think we'll ever know."

"Have you managed to contact the owner?" Manny asked.

"We tracked him down in India. He's on some kind of yoga or meditation retreat and has no interest in rushing home to check if his painting is still there. He is an eccentric man. Rich, but eccentric. He believes that he's made enough money. Now he needs to find himself."

"Then why did he buy the painting?" Vinnie frowned.

"I believe the words he used were, 'It is pretty'. That is how he buys everything. He has a vault full of artwork that is never showcased, but only there for his enjoyment."

"What kind of vault is it? Does anyone have access to that vault?" Colin asked. Manny looked at him, but he ignored the interested stare.

"I would breach confidentiality if I shared security information. What I can tell you is that no one else has access. He's eccentric and paranoid. That is why he is in no rush to get home. He's convinced that with his security system, no one will ever be able to get in there." Phillip stopped when Colin and Vinnie snickered. "He also refused to believe that the strip was authentic."

"But you are one hundred percent sure that the painting he bought is the original?" I asked.

"Yes. With his paranoia we had to test his pretty painting in all possible ways before he was happy. There are seven authentication certificates in his insurance file."

"Yet we don't know if the painting is in his vault or if it is hanging in La Maison Russie." I was frustrated. "Does this man not care that his painting might be stolen?"

"Like I said, Genevieve, he's convinced that it's an impossibility." Phillip groaned. "This is an insurance nightmare. That painting is worth a lot of money."

"If we can see that painting in La Maison Russie, we'll see if that strip is missing. If the frame covers that part, I might still be able to ascertain whether it is a forgery," Colin said.

"By visual inspection only?" Phillip said. "It is a very unreliable method of authentication. One that only a handful of people can accomplish with any degree of accuracy."

Vinnie's lips thinned and he leaned towards the phone. Colin stopped him with a shake of his head. Vinnie's loyalty towards Colin was fascinating.

"Without sounding arrogant," Colin said, "I'm quite good at spotting forgeries. Even really good ones like Danielle's. And now I know her work. I saw it in her room. I'll be able to see if it is her work hanging in the La Maison Russie. Or if it is the original."

"I told you before, you won't be able to get inside that house, Frey." Manny said. "I'll get the doc in, but you can't go."

"What do you mean, you'll get Genevieve in?" Phillip asked loudly.

Manny cleared his throat. He should never play poker. He had too many tells. Clearing his throat was only one of them. He was nervous about the reception of what he was about to say. "Leon and I discussed your theory that Piros will be at the gala. Because there is a high probability he will be there, we contacted the local police chief."

He held up both hands. "Let me finish before you start arguing, Frey. We presented him with the opportunity for the local GIPN team to plan a rescue at La Maison Russie. He's quite a smart guy and I'm sure that he didn't believe our ruse that it was merely hypothetical. But he agreed to have the team on standby tomorrow. This morning he told me they had run through numerous possible scenarios and he deemed them ready for almost anything."

"GIPN is going to be at the event?" The challenge brightened Colin's eyes. His words on the day we met came back to me. It really was about the outwitting, not the crime, for him.

"Who is this GIPN?" I asked.

"The French version of a SWAT team. They're very good." Manny didn't take his eyes off Colin. "And that is another reason why you should not be there, Frey."

"It still doesn't mean Jenny will be safe."

Manny sighed heavily. "I don't like this either, but Leon and I came to a dead end with options. There is no way that the two of us can observe the guests without it being noticed. It will be too obvious if we change our behaviour from the last few years and suddenly take an intense interest in everyone. We also can't have more of our people there, since that would have the same effect."

"It will alert Piros," I said.

"Yes, and we'll lose the opportunity to catch him red-handed. That is a sure-fire way to put him behind bars for a very long time."

"But you're playing with people's lives here." Phillip sounded disgusted with the idea.

"We hope it won't come to that. That is why GIPN will be there, to prevent anything serious from happening." Manny turned to me. "I found this interesting book on body language and micro-expressions. It says that one can spot premeditated and spontaneous action before it happens."

"You read a book on body language? Why?"

"It doesn't matter." Manny shifted in his chair and cleared his throat. "Is it true? Would you be able to spot something like that and point it out to us?"

"Of course," I said. "It's impossible to hide complete clusters of non-verbal cues indicating intent. For example—"

"You don't need to give examples, Doc. I just need to know that you'll be able to point us in the right direction. My invite includes two tickets and I thought that you could be my date for the evening. You could do that observation thingie you do while we check out the artwork there."

"No!" Vinnie's voice drowned out Phillip's. Neither liked the idea.

"Manny, how can you even think of putting Genevieve in a situation like that after what's happened?" Phillip was angry.

"And who's going to protect Jen-girl? You?" Vinnie's top lip curled.

"I'll go." I wasn't particularly eager to put myself in any kind of danger. I was even less inclined to attend the kind of event I had promised myself many years ago I would never go to again. "Firstly, nobody gets to tell me what I can or can't do. Secondly, and more importantly, it would be a crime if we don't use this opportunity to catch Piros."

"But we don't even know who he is," Vinnie said.

"He'll give himself away, Vinnie. People always do."

"I still want to know who's going to protect you." Vinnie folded his arms and jutted his bottom jaw.

"She's not going to need protection. There will be so many people around, she'll be completely safe."

"You don't believe that." I waved my hand at his face. "You touched your lips, your eye focus was fixed and you blinked rapidly. All cues that you were not comfortable with what you were saying."

"Holy Mary, I hate this." Manny pushed his chair out and rushed to the kitchen. Only to immediately turn around and come back. He pointed his finger in my face. "You irritate me."

"Manny?" Phillip couldn't see what was happening. It was no surprise that he was concerned.

"On second thought," Colin said, "I think it could work. Provided that Jenny never leaves your sight."

The sudden change was conspicuous. Colin was not the kind of person to change his stance on something so quickly. He definitely would never trust my safety to Manny. I watched him closely. An almost indiscernible nod towards Vinnie gave him away. Colin and Vinnie were going to gain entrance to the event no matter what Phillip or especially Manny said. I thought about it and decided I liked the idea of their presence. I decided not to say anything to give their plan away. Maybe I was beginning to learn the art of deception.

"But"—Vinnie glared at Manny—"you must give us your word that you will not let Jen-girl alone for one second."

"What if I need the washroom?" I asked.

"Then he will walk you there and wait outside the door," Phillip answered. It would seem that we had reached an agreement. "I still don't like it, but if that is what you think best."

"I think it is," Manny said and sat down again. "Doc doesn't have to do anything except watch the people there and point out anyone suspicious. Is there anything else, Phillip?"

"For now that is all." He hesitated. "Genevieve?"

"Yes?"

"If you need me, you know where I am." The heaviness in his voice gave the statement much more meaning. I just didn't know what I was supposed to read into it.

"Okay," was the best answer I could come up with. Nothing more was said that interested me. Soon the phone call ended.

"Tell me more about the information you have on this list," Manny immediately asked Vinnie. When Vinnie's lips thinned, Manny sighed. "No more questions about Hawk."

"For now, you mean." Vinnie snorted. "Whatever. Like I said before, he records every transaction, whether it is buying or selling. All details are written down—names, dates, specs of products, everything."

"My kingdom for that list," Manny muttered. Vinnie's calculating expression stopped me from asking about Manny's kingdom. Did Vinnie truly have access to something so incriminating? Was he planning on giving it to Manny?

"Whatever." More avoidance. Vinnie pointed to the paper in front of me. "On this list are some weapons from Eurocorps' cache. The specs are the same. All of them come from the same supplier."

Manny took the piece of paper. "Where is the name of the supplier?"

Vinnie massaged his neck and exhaled slowly with puffed cheeks. He was uncomfortable.

"What is it going to cost you?" I asked softly. He was already in debt to this Hawk-person. Of that I was convinced.

"I'm sorry, Jen-girl. The price for the name of the supplier is too high." He closed his eyes briefly and shook his head. "Just look at what we do have."

"The date of purchase, date of sale, calibre, serial numbers," I said.

"They didn't remove the serial numbers?" Manny asked.

"Nope. Hawk removed them before he moved it. He also took the time for bore-lapping."

"Oh, no." Manny groaned. "Bastards."

"What is bore-lapping?" I asked.

Vinnie looked at Manny. When Manny closed his eyes, Vinnie explained. "It is a method used to kind of polish the inside of a barrel. If done correctly it can improve the performance of a barrel."

"And it removes the rifling." One corner of Manny's mouth lifted in a smile. "That means, Doc, these guns can't be identified. Guns can be traced to the owners by the serial numbers and also by the striae. These are the lines formed on a bullet by the rifling on the inside of a barrel when it travels through the barrel. Each barrel creates its own unique striae."

"The gun's fingerprint." I was very proud of my comparison. Especially when all three men nodded their heads in agreement. "So, by bore-lapping and removing the serial number it is impossible to trace the weapon anywhere."

"Well done, Doctor Face-reader." Manny waved the paper in his hand. "This, however, gives us a direct link to the weapons' case. Leon will be delighted. There are just a few things that do not make sense at all."

"Like why the Russian Ninja Turtles would steal guns to stock up their supplies, but then sell them on the black market," I interrupted.

"Exactly," Manny said.

"It wasn't a Russian who sold Hawk the guns," Vinnie said. "This is why the price for this info was so high. He must have bought the guns from someone very important, else he would've given up the name. The price he's asking for this name tells me a lot."

"Crenshaw," Manny said. "Hawk could've recognised him. Did he know the guns came from Eurocorps?"

"He didn't say, but a guy who knows a guy told me that everyone knew there were Eurocorps guns on the streets."

"I suppose Crenshaw decided to make a bit of extra money for himself on the side. I'm sure if Leon compares this list to the stolen weapons from Eurocorps, the remaining weapons might be the ones in RNT possession. I will give this list to Leon. Thank you, Vinnie."

Vinnie responded with a half-nod. This was helpful, but not for me. I needed that one piece of the puzzle that would connect it all. I needed something that would help me solve the mystery of Piros. But most of all, I needed this case to end.

It would seem like nothing was close to ending. The short lull was rudely broken by the doorbell. I was the only one at the table who did not go into fight mode. The testosterone levels in the room heightened.

"I'll get it." Vinnie was already halfway to the door. Manny moved his torso a few inches towards me. Unconsciously he had just moved himself half in front of me. This time I didn't remind him about my personal space. Colin followed Vinnie, but stopped a few feet behind him.

Vinnie looked through the peephole, straightened and looked again. Then he turned to Colin with a half-smile. "You're not going to like this."

Colin took the few steps to look through the peephole. When he straightened, his jaw was clenched. He opened the door just wide enough to step through. Vinnie followed him and closed the door. I didn't get to see who was on the other side of the door. I only heard the surprise in an unfamiliar female voice.

"Who's that?" Manny asked me. He had moved back to slump in his chair.

"I don't know."

"Don't you want to know?"

"Manny, I've grown weary with all these secrets and deception, and I don't want to be bothered with this."

He started to respond, but loud voices made their way through the closed front door. I could not hear exactly what was being said, but Vinnie did shout the word 'agent'. That was followed by a female 'oh' and then I could only hear the murmur of their voices. My curiosity was now piqued. Before I could act on this, the door opened and the two men stepped in. No woman.

"Who was that?" Manny asked.

Colin's nostrils flared. They walked towards us. "You know, Millard, for all Jenny's faults, she is much less offensive than you. You really need to work on your tone."

"Oh, thank you, Colin." I was touched. There was only truth in his statement. Never before had I received a compliment in reference to my social skills. If it was a compliment.

"You're welcome, Jenny." Colin handed me a flash drive. "Francine opened the first drive."

"That was Francine by the door?" I asked. "Why didn't you let her in?"

Colin glanced at Manny. "She doesn't like law enforcement types."

"But she works for—"

"Us," Colin interrupted me with a pointed look.

"Ah. I see. You don't want me to say anything about her in front of Manny." She had after all entrusted me with her duplicity. Or was it triplicity? I didn't know how many entities she was working for. I could only hope she worked exclusively for the good guys. "Why didn't she just email the documents?"

"She wanted to meet you." Vinnie smiled. "You intrigue her."

"Oh." I didn't consider myself intriguing. I took the flash drive from Colin and inserted it into my personal computer. There were two folders. I opened the first one and got a well-organised list of companies that were registered at Volosovo. My face must have given my surprise away because Manny moved closer to look at the computer monitor.

"Fifty centimetres." I turned my head to glare at Manny. And waited until he moved far enough. Focussing again on the computer, I zoomed in so that the text was large enough to read from where he was sitting. Colin's arm brushed mine, but it didn't feel like an intrusion of my personal space. I didn't ask him to move away. "This is amazing. She found more companies. And all of them registered at the same place. She even managed to get all the dates."

These companies could wait until later for me to compare it with the lists I had. I also wanted to check for any connections they had to the Foundation's financials. Also later. I closed the folder and opened the second folder.

Vinnie was standing behind us. All attention was focussed on the computer monitor. The folder held three documents. Each one had a date on it. The first was from 1999 until 2003, the second from 2004 until 2008. The last one was until last year. I opened the first one and gasped.

"Jackpot," Manny said after a stunned moment. I hardly heard him. My mind was processing the information on the screen. It was more than I had hoped for. Neatly laid out on the screen was a complete list of all the people who had been on cruises. Listed were cruise ship names, dates of cruises, people, addresses, room numbers, number of people per room, amount of money spent by each person, items bought, even the smallest glass of water was listed. It was an immensely detailed list.

"Is this enough information for you, Jenny?" Colin asked very close to me. I turned my head to find his face almost next to mine.

I frowned and pulled away. "This is perfect. With all of this information I'm sure that we will find something to connect a few more things. This is fantastic."

"This is from only one of the flash drives you found in Crenshaw's safe?" Manny asked Colin.

"Yes, there are four more. Francine is working on those as well."

"Why do you think he had all this?" Vinnie asked.

"Assuming that he's not Piros, that he is not the mastermind behind all of this?" Colin said. "I think that he kept this as insurance. Maybe he didn't trust Piros. Maybe he expected to one day be forced to use this to get himself out of a tight place."

"I really don't care why he had this," I said. "I'm just glad he did. And now we have it."

The three men speculated some more, but I had lost interest. Their conversation receded until it was a distant drone. Already I had a search running between one of my lists and the names of people on the cruises. I vaguely heard Manny say his farewells and leave. I waved my hand impatiently and once again lost myself in the search.

Only when Colin threatened to shower in my bathroom did I agree to turn the computers off and get a few hours' sleep. I had to give my body some rest before I continued looking for new connections. Tomorrow was going to be a very exciting day. I just knew it.

Chapter TWENTY-FIVE

"Aw, Jen-girl, have mercy." Vinnie's plea stopped me mid-sentence.

"What?"

"I can't take all this information anymore. Can't you please just give us the highlights?"

"But then you lose the context."

"Screw the context. My brain is on fire." Vinnie dropped his head in his hands. I would never have thought of him as melodramatic. Maybe he really didn't want to hear the finer and immensely exciting details of my discoveries.

"Just the highlights?" I asked, disappointed. I loved the details. And these were exhilarating details.

"It might be quicker, Jenny," Colin said.

"Fine." I turned away from the computer. On the screen was a wonderfully laid out list. What a waste. "The first list that Francine accessed didn't bring me any closer to finding out who Piros is or who has been killing the artists."

"Oh, God, I need coffee." Vinnie went to the kitchen. I could also do with another cup of coffee. It had been a long morning comparing all the lists I had on my computer.

When I had woken up Vinnie hadn't been in the apartment. He had returned less than an hour ago, carrying bags of groceries and curious about my discoveries. Until I started laying it all out.

"I found so many exciting connections. I've been trying this whole week to find out who owns Kozlevich."

"You're still looking into the company who owns all the shipping companies?"

I took exception to Colin's tone. "You might consider it a waste of time. I do not. It is an oddity that the owner of Kozlevich isn't listed anywhere. That makes me suspicious. Especially when, after a week, I couldn't find anything."

"I didn't mean to offend you, Jenny." He was genuinely contrite.

I accepted his apology with a nod. "I know who owns Kozlevich."

"What? Who?" Colin leaned forward.

"Francine found the owners." I consciously chose not to ponder too much on how she had obtained this information. "Three entities own Kozlevich. A Simon Brun owns thirty-three percent, P&S owns thirty-three percent and a private holder owns thirty-four percent."

Vinnie stared at me with a slack jaw. Colin shook his head disbelievingly. "P&S? The bastards who also own La Maison Russie? Judas Priest."

"Who's Simon Brun?" Vinnie asked.

"I have no idea. Francine emailed me and said she tried to find out who he is, but hasn't been able to get anything yet. She's busy with the decoding of the flash drives, but she promised to find out about Brun and also the mysterious private holder." I thought of my earlier clock analogy with all the parts. I whispered to myself, "Wheels within wheels."

"You can say that again," Vinnie said.

"Wheels within wheels," I repeated and was rewarded with broad smiles from both men.

"Did you get anything else from the list?" Colin asked.

"Which one?" I asked.

"Let's start with the list of companies."

"Francine did an amazing job. There are companies that I had not uncovered. I now have quite an extensive list of shipping companies and other companies working for or with the Foundation. Not all of them are still active, but all of them at one time were connected." I was itching to show them the details. With difficulty I resisted the urge. "I took Vinnie's idea and looked for the first of these companies to register in Volosovo. I think it is not one hundred percent correct to deduce that it would be the very first company. I mean, I can only work with what I have. Maybe there are more companies."

"Jenny," Colin interrupted me gently.

"Oh. I'm rambling. Sorry." I inhaled deeply. "Just for the record, this is a calculated assumption."

"Noted." Colin smiled.

"The first company that I have here is P&S." They looked as shocked as I had been when I first saw this. "Posiet and Somov seems to play quite an important role in this mystery."

"Dude, we are so going tomorrow evening." Vinnie looked at Colin with excitement flushing his cheeks.

"Vin," Colin warned.

"Don't worry, Colin. I know you are planning to go there tomorrow evening," I said.

Vinnie leaned forward, closer to me. "Jen-girl, isn't it difficult to always know everything people are thinking?"

"No." What a silly notion that it might be difficult. "It makes my life easier. That way I don't have to guess at people's intentions and meanings and try to read between the lines. And in case you were wondering, I don't mind that you will be there tomorrow evening."

"Why haven't you told Millard?" Colin asked. Curious.

"Because I'll feel safer if both of you are there too."

Colin smiled. "Do we know who owns P&S?"

"No. I have all the information on P&S, but can't find the name of the owner of this company anywhere."

"I'll ask Francine to look into that."

"Okay." It was becoming easier to accept help from people

functioning on the fringes. "Um... could you also ask her if she could find out who the private holder is?"

"Sure. She'll enjoy that challenge. What did you find with the other list?"

"I compared all the names of the cruise guests with the lists I have of Eurocorps employees, EDA employees, those fictional private investigators and the dead artists. All the artists were on the guest list of the cruises. I was also not surprised to find Crenshaw there. As well as Mark Smith. Other interesting people are Chief Frederique Dutoit and a lot of the VIP's that we saw on the footage of last year's gala event. And the enigmatic Tomasz Kubanov was also a frequent guest."

"I suppose that makes sense," Colin said. "He's the founder of the Foundation and on the receiving end of a lot of donations from these cruises. Not to mention the millions they get from the European Union."

"I simply can't reconcile myself to the notion that he is not involved in this. It is after all his charity organisation. A charity organisation with close ties to a lot of dead artists, forged artworks and apparently money laundering. He must be somehow involved."

"But look at all the good things the Foundation has done." Colin pointed towards the computers. "Everything I've read points to him only being the face of the Foundation. I agree with you that he is shady, but we have nothing connecting him personally to this. It only implicates the Foundation. And of course Piros."

"Manny needs to tell us more. He promised a week ago already to find out more about Kubanov. Until we know more, it is only speculation."

"Millard will just tell you all the official stuff."

"And that is bad?" I asked.

"Not bad. Incomplete," Colin answered.

"Yeah," Vinnie said. "They don't even know my surname.

Not very efficient investigators, are they?"

"Don't underestimate Millard." There was a strong warning in Colin's voice. "He's sharper than most people think."

I refrained from insisting on an explanation. Hopefully, when Colin was ready, he would tell me about him and Manny. We were lost in our own contemplation for a few minutes until Colin asked, "Did you have time to look at the stuff Francine emailed you this morning?"

"Yes. She apologised for crashing my party yesterday. What does that mean?"

"It means that she came here uninvited."

"But I didn't have a party here."

"If there are more than three people, Francine sees it as a party."

"Or a conspiracy," Vinnie said.

I thought for a second. "So, you will be crashing the gala event tomorrow evening?"

Vinnie laughed. "No, Jen-girl. We won't be crashing."

"We have invitations," Colin said when he noticed my frown. "Just don't ask where and how we got them."

"Okay," I said slowly. I turned back to the computers. "Francine managed to decode the second flash drive. It has a list of all the young artists and the works we can assume they had forged. At first all the names and artworks next to it didn't make sense. Then I recognised names."

"What? Why didn't you tell me? Why didn't Francine tell me?"

For an uncanny second I had the desire to put my hand on Colin's arm to calm him. I didn't. "Maybe she didn't tell you because she knew you would be this upset. You really care about these artists."

"Of course I do. Jesus, at last count, sixteen have lost their lives because they were good at what they did."

"It's thirty-seven," I said.

"Thirty-seven what?"

"The list I have here has thirty-seven young artists on it and all the works that they've reproduced. Eleven names were the same as our list of sixteen murdered artists. Francine posits this is a list of all the murdered artists."

"Thirty-seven?" Colin's lips disappeared and he swallowed hard. I hated being the one to give bad news. "Thirty-seven gifted people. The bastard had a list of all the murdered artists? Were they all students?"

"Most of them, yes. It seems to be a pattern. Find an extraordinarily gifted young person, get them to forge a few masterpieces, then kill them. I just don't understand why they would all be murdered. It's really sad." I shook my head. "To use impressionable young people like that."

"Were most of them killed with handguns?" Vinnie asked.

"I don't have access to police reports of their deaths, so I can't say. From what I got on the internet, some of them were killed with handguns. Others apparently committed suicide. It's not difficult to believe that artists suffer from depression and commit suicide. Some of the other artists jumped from buildings and bridges."

"Or were pushed," Vinnie added.

"I wouldn't know. But those who didn't jump killed themselves with handguns."

"Same calibre—"

"As the stolen guns, yes," I finished Vinnie's sentence. "Not that it can be used as concrete evidence."

"Thirty-seven," Colin said softly and shook his head.

It was quiet while we thought about this. The doorbell followed by Manny's demanding voice broke the silence. Three minutes later he was seated at the table. The tension in the room had risen to uncomfortable levels. I ignored the resentment on all three faces and told Manny everything about the companies.

"So, it all started with P&S?"

"This is only an assumption," I said. "A fact, however, is the names of the three owners of Kozlevich. P&S owns thirty-three percent, Simon Brun owns thirty-three percent and an unknown entity owns the remaining thirty-four percent."

Manny frowned and leaned forward, resting his elbows on his knees. "Simon Brun?"

"Yes. We don't know who he is. This is the first time his name has come up."

"I know that name from somewhere." Manny pointed at the EDA computer. "Hand me that thing. I have to check something."

I took a bracing breath before I moved the computer from its careful placement. We sat in silence for a few minutes while Manny grumbled at the computer. He surprised me with fast fingers and a comfort with technology.

"I knew it!" He jabbed at the screen. "Simon Brun is one of the two aliases for Piros that our guy gave to Interpol."

"Simon Brun is Piros?" I was breathless. All the lists, all the cross-checking and we had a name. Vinnie's bottom jaw had gone slack and Colin's eyes were wide. We were all in shock. "But who is this Simon Brun?"

Manny did something on the computer before he turned it to us. On the screen was an enlargement of a driver's licence. "He's an eighty-two-year-old retired teacher, living in the Belgian city of Turnhout."

"This can't be right," Colin said. "This must be a forged identity."

I clenched my teeth to not say a thing about Professor John Dryden, the professor who took me to Danielle's apartment. Colin would know all about forging identity documents.

"That much we knew, Frey," Manny said. "Nobody has been able to track Simon Brun down to verify his age and identity though."

"Francine will find him," I said and quickly continued. "No, don't fight with me, Manny. She's the one who gave us the three owners of P&S. And she offered to find out who Simon Brun and the private holder are."

Manny's lips disappeared, but he nodded.

Colin turned to me. "I have a question for you."

Why did people say that? Why didn't they just ask the question? I didn't encourage Colin to ask his question. After some time I did lift my eyebrows, though. It would seem that he needed permission to ask.

"It's hypothetical, so don't focus too much on facts. I'm wondering about the many people, prominent people, who bought art at these auctions. Only to discover that they had bought forgeries. Would they ever report it?"

I thought of people like my parents. "Knowing the importance these people attach to never looking foolish, I can't imagine that anyone would admit to buying a forgery at an auction on a ship."

"There would also be the speculation on whether these people preferred to buy art at sea because of its legal gray area," Colin added.

"And that would not be acceptable to anyone in a prominent position. Just the speculation could destroy careers, reputations and social standing."

"Especially since quite a few of the names that we saw on those lists are people in high political positions in the EU." Colin grinned. "This is delicious."

"What is?" I asked.

"This scandal." His smile widened. "If this ever comes out, it will rock the European high-flying world and destroy years of building EU relations and PR."

Manny rolled his head on his shoulders as if to ease the tension in his neck muscles. "So I've discovered a few things about Tomasz Kubanov. He started three charity organisations before he founded the Foundation for Development of

Sustainable Education. The theory is that it took him three tries before he got it right.

"The Foundation to date is the largest of his charities and also the most active. The second biggest is an education fund. Fifteen years ago Kubanov lent his personal support and that of the Foundation to a trust fund for artists. The limited information I've been able to get tells me that the trust fund is there to give talented young people opportunities to become masters."

I jerked. My brain felt like it had received a lightning bolt's energy. Something Manny had just told us fit perfectly with something I had seen, read or heard previously. I closed my eyes and in my head I switched on Mozart's Clarinet Concerto in A major.

"Jenny?" Colin touched my arm lightly.

I opened my eyes to notice that the light in my apartment had changed. Once again time had floated away while I was in my head. A glance at my watch confirmed that thirty minutes had gone by. I turned to Colin. "Give me a moment."

"Okay." He leaned back in his chair and nodded at Manny as if he had just won an argument. Vinnie wasn't at the table.

It didn't take me long to find what I was looking for. It was so exciting that I was bouncing in my chair.

"Jenny, you have to tell us what has you so excited." Colin sounded pained.

"Connections."

"What connections, Doc?" Manny's silence while I had been working impressed me. As did the lack of hostility around the table. Vinnie had returned and was lounging in his chair. I wondered how long the patience and peace would last.

"What do these artists have in common?" I asked.

"They're all dead, and they were all on the cruise ships owned by companies whose major shareholder is another company," Colin answered.

"Right. There is one more connection. Look." I pointed at the computer screen. "I came across this when I was researching art students. A scholar wrote this academic article about scholarships. His focus was on the arts and here are a few students he interviewed. Seven of these names are on Francine's list."

"Bloody holy hell," Manny said.

"The name of the institution giving the scholarships is not mentioned in this article," I continued. "But it is mentioned that the students were awarded a holiday on a cruise ship as a reward when they excelled in their studies."

We stared at the article in silence for some time, each lost in their own thoughts. I turned to Manny. "Did Kubanov start the trust fund or is he only a patron of it?"

"He's only a patron," Manny said.

"Then who started this trust fund?"

"I don't know."

"Do you have the name of this trust fund?"

"The Michaelangelo fund. That is unfortunately all I got. Since I was focussing on the event, I left this line of inquiry for later." He sounded regretful. "After this event, I'll definitely be looking at Kubanov more closely."

Colin leaned back in his chair and started tapping on the screen of his smartphone. I frowned at his rudeness and focussed on Manny again. "What we found on Kubanov was only positive. He has really helped a lot of people. From the many articles adulating him, it would be impossible to think anything bad about him. If it weren't for the evidence accumulating against him, I would never have suspected him. It is such a dichotomy. The funding and the true purpose for his charity organisations have been at the expense of many lives. Yet he has given an unbelievable number of people aid. Through the Foundation alone, two villages have homes for around nine hundred people, including children that he gave better lives to.

"His personal residence in Russia is quite modest for a man of his means. That endears him only more to the masses. He's not like many politicians talking about coming from poverty, understanding their constituents, but living in mansions. He is in public view, but always comes across as modest and humble. Nowhere on the internet could I find any direct connection between him and a remotely negative situation or a singular scandal."

"But we already have so much evidence," Vinnie said. "Isn't it enough to get rid of him, his Foundation and Piros?"

"There is no doubt in my mind that Kubanov and Piros are connected," Manny said. "I can take this to an EU court, but with the right lawyers, Kubanov could still get away. We need indisputable, concrete evidence."

"Like what?" Vinnie sounded like a five-year-old.

"Bank accounts, anything on paper connecting him to Piros, to the Eurocorps weapons, to the artists, to anything. People aren't guilty by association." Manny's eyes locked on Vinnie. "Just because your dad was a governor who got his housekeeper pregnant doesn't mean that you're also going to go into politics."

A breath of charged silence was the only warning I got. The next moment Vinnie was in front of Manny. The large man's body language gave every indicator that Manny might not live through this. Colin jumped up and pushed himself between the two combative men. Vinnie's fists were bunched as was his jaw. Manny was still seated. A smug, knowing smile played around his mouth.

"What did you do?" Vinnie screamed at him and lunged forward. Colin was no match for the large man and moved with him. His hands were ineffectively pushing against Vinnie's chest.

"Vin, dude." Colin pushed harder, but didn't budge Vinnie an inch. "He's not worth it. Let it be."

"No." He didn't tone down his voice. I felt very uncomfortable with the promise of such violence in my apartment. It might make an interesting study in male behaviour, but I preferred such studies on the screens in my viewing room. A few thoughts flew through my mind, including the fact that I didn't know how to remove bloodstains from my lovely wooden floors, so I stood up.

Vinnie pushed against Colin to get to Manny. "The bastard investigated me."

Manny leaned forward as if he wasn't baiting an enraged bodybuilder. "Are you really surprised that I investigated you, Carlton Venneri-Smith?"

"No!" A tortured scream roared through my apartment. Vinnie shoved Colin out of the way, stepped forward and picked Manny up by the collar of his rumpled jacket. Something of great importance was happening and I didn't know what to do. But I didn't want to clean blood off my floors. Vinnie walked Manny backwards to the kitchen, threatening him with all types of bodily harm in a voice that chilled me. He stopped in front of the long counter and bent Manny backwards. I walked to them as fast as I could. Colin tried to grab my arm, but I sidestepped him.

I stopped next to Vinnie and put my hand on his forearm. This did not come naturally to me. Powerful muscles strained against my palm. Vinnie's strength and size were unnerving. "Vinnie, please don't do this."

"Stay out of it, Jen-girl." He didn't even look at me.

I put my other hand on his shoulder. Never before had I tried to calm anyone down. Nor had I ever tried to do it by touch. I didn't know if I was doing it right. All I knew was that Colin's dislike of Manny would make his attempts to calm

Vinnie down a moot exercise. That left the job to me. I leaned closer to the man I had come to like and respect.

"Vinnie, I feel very uncomfortable right now. Your behaviour is scaring me." That got him to glance at me. I looked him straight in the eye and allowed him to see my discomfort. "I don't know what to do and that makes me scared. Please don't do this to me."

His features softened as well as the muscles under my palms. He took a few slow breaths through clenching teeth. I wondered if I should say anything else. In psychology I had learned all the placating phrases, but they weren't coming to me now. All I could do was stand there, too close for my own comfort, and hope that Vinnie would let go of Manny's collar. The older man was showing signs of pain and flashes of concern.

Vinnie pushed Manny away like trash and turned to me. Hands that a second ago were ready to inflict pain curled gently around my shoulders. "I'm sorry, Jen-girl. I never want to scare you."

"I know." I didn't know what to do with my hands. I didn't want to touch him anymore, but I knew he needed it. I awkwardly placed my hands on his chest. "You're my friend. I trust you."

Only on video footage and in textbooks had I seen the expression of such deep gratitude. A simple touch, two short sentences and I had just given Vinnie a priceless gift. To my horror, tears were forming in my eyes. I pushed against his chest as I blinked rapidly. But Vinnie wouldn't let me go. He pulled me closer and wrapped his arms around me. I stood stiffly in his embrace, rueing my impulsive action. Until Vinnie whispered, "Thank you," into my hair. It softened me. I gave him three more seconds before I stepped away.

Colin was leaning against the counter with an expression I did not want to evaluate. Going from rational emotional safety to this overwhelmed me. Analysing the deep affection on Colin's face might send me into hours of writing Mozart. Not only was I feeling bombarded with emotions, but this new insight into Vinnie's past was also proving to be very distracting. So I did what I was best at when confronted with emotions. Compartmentalised. If later I wanted to analyse, I could look into it. Now I wanted to get back onto safe territory. I walked back to the dining room table and placed the EDA computer in its usual place.

Vinnie and Colin were quietly talking in the kitchen. Colin was telling Vinnie that he wasn't to be surprised that Manny had looked into his life. Manny had returned to his chair as if nothing had transpired. That annoyed me. He had purposefully been provocative and it had caused an overload of emotions I would have to deal with later. This behaviour was not to happen again in my apartment and he was going to hear my thoughts on it.

On my inhale, my personal computer pinged. I glanced at the screen and swallowed my diatribe. "Francine's just sent the third and fourth decoded flash drives."

Chapter **TWENTY-SIX**

Forgotten were all personal agendas. Manny straightened in his chair and by the time I opened the email, Colin was sitting next to me and Vinnie was standing behind me. Everyone leaned in to read the email. My breathing shallowed. After the last ten minutes, this was too much for me.

"Move away from me." I lifted my hands wanting to push them away. "I'll read the email to you. Just move away."

The men must have heard the strain in my voice. They responded immediately by giving me the space I needed. Vinnie walked around the table and sat down across from me. I didn't complain when Manny scraped his chair on my wooden floors. He was moving away from me and that mattered more. Colin remained where he was, only leaning back in his chair. I could breathe again.

"Thank you. I'll read what she said before I open the attachments." I had the urge to clear my throat. I didn't. "Francine listed everything so neatly. By number. Why does she ask at the end if it is English enough?"

"I asked her to not use tech talk when she sent you emails. It's worse than euphemisms and slang," Colin said. "What did she say?"

"Well, in number one she states that P&S is owned by two companies. One owns ninety-nine percent, the other owns one percent. In number two she says that she's still searching, but couldn't find the names of the owners or founders of the companies anywhere. Oh my, she is quite rude here. She says that she'll find the motherfuckers. And that I should not worry.

Why would I worry?"

"It's just an expression. She's obviously pissed off. It is not often that Francine can't find something or someone." Colin smiled.

"Oh. Okay. Number three states that she found out who was behind the scholarships for those unlucky students." I confronted Colin. "How did she know about these students having scholarships?"

He waved his smartphone at me. "I sent her a text message. She works really fast."

I frowned my displeasure before I returned to Francine's email. I read a few sentences in silence. My eyes widened, followed by rapid blinking for a few moments. I looked at Manny. "Guess who paid for their tuition?"

"The Michaelangelo fund?" Manny sounded hoarse.

I read from the email. "'This Michaelangelo education fund is rather enigmatic. I didn't find much publicity for it. Once or twice it came up in a search, but the mention of it was too vague to catch it in a general search. I checked all thirty-seven students listed on the flash drive. So far I've found fourteen who were on scholarships from this fund. What is this? Why didn't you tell me these artists were dead? My search created a pattern and I found more students with financial support from this trust fund. I will do more checking and send you a complete list. What is going on here? Genevieve? Colin?'"

Manny frowned deeply, the corners of his mouth turning down. "Frey, what did you tell this woman?"

"I didn't tell her anything. I only gave her search parameters."

I was also frowning. "What is her IQ?"

"What does that have to do with anything?" Colin folded his arms and frowned back at us.

"From the little that I've seen of her work"—I glanced at the computer screen—"she has an above-average IQ. It wouldn't be difficult to take the information from the flash drives, combine it with the other things she's found for us and reach a conclusion."

"Who is this woman?" Manny wanted to investigate her as well. It was in his voice, his body language, his eyes. Vinnie's relaxed posture changed. Clearly he had not forgotten Manny's propensity to dig into people's lives.

"She can be trusted," Colin answered. "That's all you need to know."

I was trying to think of the best way to retain our focus on the email when an uncanny realisation dawned on me. "Do you guys realise we are a team? I've never worked in a team before."

Three different postures—one of defiance, one of offence and one of fury—all changed to horror.

"What? Why are you looking so disturbed by this thought?"

"Jenny, look at your team members," Colin reminded me gently. Once I had made up my mind to trust Vinnie and Colin, I had grown further and further away from the knowledge of their skillsets. It shocked me that in the last few days I had stopped thinking of them as what they were. Criminals.

"Oh, no," I whispered.

"And now you've scared us all." Colin's smile didn't look scared. "Don't worry about me. I'm sure my reputation will survive."

"It's not only my reputation I'm worried about." Manny muttered something unintelligible under his breath. "A whole lifetime of service and this is who I'm working with?"

In all honesty, I had never given Manny's predicament any thought. It was disturbing enough for me to work with two criminals. I could not imagine how Manny had to be feeling co-operating with the very people he had spent his life keeping off the streets. Deep regret for voicing my observation settled on my shoulders. If I hadn't said anything, maybe no one around the table would be looking as agitated as they did. I had exacerbated an already volatile situation.

Never before had I missed Phillip's presence as much as at

this very moment. He would have known exactly what to say or do. This situation was far beyond my purview. Yet I tried. "Manny, Colin told me something about Francine. Enough for me to feel comfortable to let her be part of this team."

"Have you met her?" Manny asked.

"No," I said. "I hold Colin responsible for her."

"Hey," Colin complained.

"No," Manny interrupted. "It's a good idea. You're the one who brought her in, Frey. You will be the one paying for any misstep on her part."

Colin relaxed. "That won't happen."

"You better pray it doesn't. I still want to know who she is."

"You can ask her if you ever meet her." From Vinnie's vindictive smile I surmised that Francine didn't introduce herself to too many people.

Manny stifled a yawn and nodded at my computer. "What else does she say?"

"That the third and fourth flash drives were easier to decode, now that she has cracked the first two." I looked at Colin. "I presume she didn't physically break them."

He smiled and just shook his head.

I returned to the email. "She says that the third flash drive holds details about all auction and private sales. The fourth drive has financial data. It also has a long list of other numbers that she says are all weapon identification numbers. Oh. Oh, my. She's really, really rude here." I leaned closer to check Francine's spelling of a number of creative swearwords.

"Oh, she knows," Vinnie said proudly. "She's figured it out."

Manny looked down at his hands, not saying a word. His eye muscles moved, indicators of internal dialogue. Another yawn brought him out of his contemplation. He dug the heels of his hands in his eyes and rubbed hard.

"The old man is tired," Vinnie whispered meaningfully out of the corner of his mouth.

"What's the time?" I asked as I looked at the bottom of the computer screen. "It's past eleven already."

"Time flies when you're having fun." Nothing on Colin's face indicated the muttered sentence held any truth.

"Okay." The resolve in Manny's voice led me to conclude that he had come to a decision. "Doc, email me those numbers. But email them from your private email to my private email. I'll give them to Leon to cross-reference with their weapons inventory. How many numbers are there?"

I opened the appropriate file and flinched. "There are two sets of numbers. Together they add up to seventeen hundred and eighty-six numbers. That is more than double the quantity of stolen weapons Leon knows about."

"Not good, not good at all," Manny said.

"Should I email this to Leon?" I asked.

"No. Email it to my private email and I'll forward it to Leon's private email. It's better that everything stays off official places." He pushed himself up with a groan. "I'm going home."

My bottom jaw slackened and my eyes stretched. "You cannot be serious."

"As a heart attack." No heart condition could be pertinent to the case, so I assumed Manny was using a euphemism. He had to be exhausted to regress from the proper English he had been speaking. "Look, it's late and I'm tired. We're not going to crack this nut wide open within the next few hours, so I suggest we all get a good night's rest. Then we can do this again tomorrow, just a bit fresher. Doc, do you think you'll be able to hold off going through those flash drives for the night?"

I stared at him. How could anyone expect that of me? It was said that every morning, Mozart's mother used to play a scale up to the seventh note. Mozart's compulsion to finish the octave was what got him out of bed. He simply had to press the last, the finishing note. What Manny was asking me was worse than

Mrs. Mozart's methods.

"You're serious." I could see no deception cues.

"As a heart attack," he repeated.

It took a mere millisecond and then I understood. I giggled. "It's not funny, but it's actually funny."

"Glad to be of some entertainment value." Manny walked to the front door. "I'll be here early in the morning to check out those drives. Try to get some sleep."

He didn't wait for any response, just walked to the door with slumped shoulders. I stared at my front door as it closed. "I can't do it."

"Of course you can, Jenny." Colin took my personal computer away from me and started shutting down all running programmes.

"Don't do that!" My demand came out louder than intended. It didn't slow Colin down though.

"You need your beauty sleep. Tomorrow is the big event and you need to be fresh and alert for it. God only knows what will happen there." He was still distressed about me going to the charity function. It was clearly depicted on his face, his body language, his voice.

Not to my recollection had I ever had the desire to please people. Too early in my life I had learned that no matter what I did, people—more specifically my parents—were never pleased with my actions. I adjusted my behaviour to avoid conflict, but never to make people more comfortable. The concern burning lines on Colin and Vinnie's faces was changing that. I did the unthinkable.

"Fine. I'll wait until the morning."

"And you'll sleep." An order.

I sighed. "I'll sleep. But I'll be up early to work on this. It is your choice whether you want to be here for it."

"I'm not going anywhere," Vinnie said as he got up.

"Same goes for me." Colin smiled when I winced. "Until you are out of danger, you're stuck with us, Jenny."

I decided not to reply. I only gave them the most condescending look I could muster. "Make sure everything is where it should be. Including the computers."

Colin frowned at where he had placed my personal computer. Obviously he couldn't see that it was at least two centimetres to the left. It was with greater restraint than I had known I possessed that I got up and walked to my bedroom.

A few quiet moments alone and I realised how tired I was. It had been two and a half weeks of emotional, informational and tactile overload. I needed to sleep, but would not be able to. There was only one thing that could prevent insomnia. I sneaked back to the dining room table, aligned the computers and the chairs, and returned to my bedroom smiling. Relieved.

Surprisingly, I slept well and woke up Saturday morning feeling refreshed. But that eighth, final note of the scale needed to be played. The increasing discomfort of not having looked at the flash drives sent me through my morning routine much faster than usual. So much so that I made it to the kitchen before Vinnie. I smiled while preparing the coffee. He was going to be unhappy about this.

"You're too fast." Vinnie stormed into the kitchen, pulling a T-shirt over his head. I was afforded a glimpse of his muscular torso. Long, ugly scars zigzagged across his left side from his collarbone to below his pants. The soft T-shirt flowed down and covered it up too quickly. I knew so little about this man. There was not only the question of his origins and his name, but also these scars that I wanted to ask him about. But the expression on his face did not invite any questions. He stomped towards me and pointed to the dining room.

"Morning, Vinnie." I smiled at him.

He grunted a greeting and shook his pointed finger. "Go do your thing on your computers. I'll bring your coffee."

Since it had been my impatience for the new information that had driven me into the kitchen so early, I didn't argue. I sat down in front of the computers and switched them all on. In the two minutes it took all three machines to whirr to life, I glanced at my notepad. The page with all the connected parts was mocking me.

I frowned at Piros' name in the box with extra angry lines surrounding it. His connection to this case was tenuous and it was easy enough to find him. Piros, on the other hand, was exceptionally adept at remaining an enigma. Even as Simon Brun he was an unknown entity.

I pulled my mind away from the riddle of Piros' identity and opened my email. My stomach tightened in anticipation. I loved this part. The new information. The possibility that this might be the key. Francine had attached two zip files, one for each flash drive. I opened the first one.

"Jenny." Colin spoke rather loudly. And he was touching me.

I glared at the long fingers curled around my wrist and looked up. There was more sunlight in the room. I glanced at the bottom right corner of my computer. It was just past eight. I had sat down at half past five. Colin was sitting next to me, Manny at the head of the table nursing a mug of coffee and Vinnie across from me. It surprised me to see Leon sitting between Vinnie and Manny. Next to my right hand was a mug of steaming coffee. I sighed on a shrug. "Good morning."

"Morning, Doc. What have you got for us?" Manny looked better after a night's rest.

"A lot. Oh my, have I got a lot." I reached for the coffee and smiled my thanks to Vinnie. A quick look at Leon and I was simply too curious. "You also have something. What is it?"

"Morning, Doctor Lenard." Leon shifted in his chair. "I took all the data that you had on the murders of the artists and did a lot of legwork. Quite a few of the police departments under whose jurisdiction the murders fell do not have adequate equipment or manpower. That means that the crime scenes and evidence were not processed as well as they should have been. Upon my request, they sent the evidence and we used our resources to rush it through a few tests."

"The point?" I asked. This was taking too long. People and their annoying need for a long run-up.

Leon frowned. "The point is that we were able to find ballistic evidence that seven murders were committed with stolen Eurocorps weapons. The other bullets were too damaged to test their striae."

"Is there a direct link to Crenshaw and these weapons?" Colin asked.

"There is. Manny sent me all those numbers." The corners of his mouth turned down. "All thousand seven hundred and eighty-seven numbers are a match to Eurocorps weapons. This goes back nine years, all within the time that Crenshaw worked for Eurocorps. My guys are digging deeper and with this information I'm convinced they will find evidence linking Crenshaw to the thefts."

I wondered if Leon had worked through the night. I had come upon my new findings this morning. "I ran a comparison with those numbers and the ones that Hawk had given Vinnie. They're an exact match for the second set of numbers on the flash drive. From what we know so far, I would postulate that the second set of numbers are the weapons that Crenshaw took for personal gain. The first set of numbers would be much more of an uninformed hypothesis."

"Just tell us what you're thinking, Jenny." Colin shifted in his chair.

"I would dare hypothesise that Crenshaw had a close connection to Piros and that he procured those weapons for Piros and his private army." I swallowed and pushed out the words. "The Russian Ninja Turtles."

"And I would dare agree with you," Manny said softly.

"Okay, great." Colin bit off the words. His breathing was harsh as he pushed his fists into his thighs. "We have all these theories, but artists are still in danger. How does this help us stop the killing?"

"I suppose it doesn't." Leon's face showed indicators of his own frustration.

"I have something that might help." Pride raised Manny's voice. He placed folded sheets of paper on the table. "The guest list."

Colin, Vinnie and I lunged for the list. Vinnie got to it first, almost knocking Leon off his chair. Once he had it, he handed it to me. "Do your thing, Jen-girl."

I glanced at the names and a thrill rushed through me. I handed the two typed sheets to Colin. "Read the names to me."

As he read, I put the names on the computer. It took ten minutes before I could run a comparison to all the other lists I had accumulated in the last three weeks.

"This will take about fifteen minutes. Let me tell you now about the information on the flash drives." As one, the four men leaned towards me. I leaned away. "The one drive consists solely of details of all the auctions and private sales. All the dates, the artworks, who bought what, where it was shipped. Very detailed."

"And of little to no help with the murders." Sneering dimples formed on Colin's cheeks. "Unless you found something in that?"

"No, I didn't. There was some duplication of the other lists, but nothing new."

Leon put both hands on the table. "Surely this could be enough evidence to present to a prosecutor."

"Of course," Manny answered. "They can go after these stupid rich people buying forged artworks. I don't care about them. I want to stop the killing."

"The fourth flash drive might help us get closer," I said.

"It's all the financial details of the Foundation."

"But we already have the financials of the Foundation," Manny said.

"The official version." Vinnie rolled his eyes.

"I compared it to the official version and it actually is consistent. This version only gives more information."

"Like what?" Leon asked.

"In the official version, payments to consultants are shown. These consultants look legitimate at first glance. On the flash drives these consultants are specified. For example, payments were made to customs officials. Each official's name, his position, the date, everything is here. There is a lot of payment information like this."

"Interpol, Europol and a few other guys are going to love this." Manny smiled as if he had won an award. "Something tells me there's more, Doc."

"There is," I said. "What interested me most were the payments to so-called security firms. A few searches on the internet and on the EDA computer did not give me one hit on these firms. As far as I could find, they don't exist."

"Not even registered in Volosovo, thirty-three percent owned by P&S, Simon Brun and a private dick?" Vinnie asked. I silently congratulated myself on recognising his sarcasm.

"No. They simply don't exist. This list only has the names, the amounts and the banks that the payments were made to. Unfortunately, no account numbers. There are five security companies on this expenses list and they all used the same bank, same branch."

"We need to get that information," Manny said.

"On it." Colin held his smartphone against his ear. He winked at me before his attention was drawn to the phone. "Hi, doll. Yes, we're looking at it now. Great job. Yes? No, I can't. They're here. Listen, I'm sending you five company names and the bank they use. Could you please get their account numbers and anything else on them? You are?" Colin's eyes widened. "Interesting. I'll tell them. Thanks, doll." He ended the call and turned to me. "Could you please email Francine that info? She'll check it for us."

"Who's Francine?" Leon asked. I was growing bored of that discussion, so I ignored it and sent Francine an email. Leon, Vinnie and Manny were in a loud disagreement when I turned to Colin.

"What did she say that you found so interesting?"

Colin smiled. "She wasn't surprised that I wanted more information on bank-related stuff. She's working on the last flash drive and she says that it seems to be loads of numbers. In her opinion, they're all bank account numbers and she'll send us the names of the account holders. For her finding the five companies' bank details won't be much of a challenge."

"This is so illegal." Manny dropped his face in his hands. I knew he was right. We were circumventing legal protocol put in place to protect people's rights, their privacy.

"Let's not focus on that now," I said. "I found something else that was very interesting about the payments made to the security firms. The dates of these payments coincided every time within days of the murder of an artist."

"Blood money." Vinnie swallowed and stared out the window. I wondered about his chequered past. Was I under the wrong impression that he had been an assassin? The Vinnie I had come to know was not the kind of person to fit that profile. Yet another layer to this man.

"Jenny?" Colin brought me back to the present. "What does your computer say about the guest list?"

"Oh, yes." I turned to my computer and worked through the results. "There are a lot of important people here. The Head of the EDA will be there, as will your Chief."

"I'm not surprised Chief Dutoit will be there. He loves these high-profile events," Manny said.

"Kubanov will be there, but that is to be expected. It is after all his charity organisation. Wait a moment." Something had caught my eye. I spent a few minutes doing a cross-reference and smiled. "Francine emailed me a list this morning with thirty-four students who are currently at universities on scholarships from the Michaelangelo fund."

"Alive?" Colin asked.

"Yes," I said. "And all thirty-four are on this guest list. There are sixty-seven artists on the guest list. I don't know who the other thirty-three are."

"Around six hundred people were invited. Of these"— Manny pointed at the list—"four hundred and eighty-two have confirmed their attendance."

A cold shiver went down my spine. My parents' parties were never that big and I always felt an onset of panic with the sensory overload. Dread for tonight's event sent my heart racing. "That's a lot of people. It must be an enormous place to accommodate such a large crowd."

"It's only called the Russian House, Doc. It's more like a hotel," Manny said.

"You mean a mansion?" Colin lifted his lip in disdain at Manny's lack of sophistication.

"No, I mean it is more like a hotel, you arrogant arse. The ballroom doubles as a conference room and can easily host seven hundred people. Put in a few works of art, tables for everyone and there is still room for a dance floor. There are twenty-four guest rooms, each with its own bathroom. There is even an underground parking area for guests. A hotel." Manny narrowed his eyes at Colin.

"A mansion," Colin said, lifting his eyebrow. "You need to get out more, Manfred."

"Mansion or hotel, we still have to talk about safety tonight." Vinnie's grave statement brought stillness to the table. He looked at Leon. "Is Jen-girl going to be safe?"

"Everyone is in place for tonight," Leon said. "GIPN is getting into place already. They are completely covert and will surround the perimeter. Not one street is uncovered. Apart from Manny and myself, we've managed to get four of our best guys inside. Manny and I will keep an eye on you, Genevieve, and four GIPN guys will be at hand to protect the artists or apprehend Piros, whichever comes first."

"Tell them about the bus," Manny said.

"Oh yes. Our sources were able to find out that La Maison Russie rented a bus for tonight," Leon said.

"The bus that is supposed to take the artists to the Alps?" I asked.

"Yes. We took control of the bus arrangements. Our own driver will be taking the artists to a place of safety as soon as they leave the premises."

"And do what with them?" Colin asked softly.

"We're not going to arrest them for forgery, Frey," Manny said. "That is for another time. Their safety trumps arresting them for painting pretty pictures."

I couldn't help but smile when Colin gasped. "Colin, Manny is baiting you. Look at his orbicularis oculi muscles."

Colin bit down hard on his jaw before he looked at me. "I don't even know what those muscles are."

"They're the muscles around our eyes." The frown drawing Colin's brows together stopped my explanation. I didn't understand why Colin and Manny needed to irritate each other so much. "Never mind."

Leon explained in excruciating detail the security detail for the evening. Vinnie challenged all the plans with conspiracy theories of underground tunnels, secret allies and helicopters. It bored me. I turned to my computer and left the men to annoy each other.

I opened my email in the hopes that Francine might have sent me something. I was not disappointed. Her style was most satisfactory. She didn't waste time on the silly social niceties most people required. The email was concise and very interesting.

"Jenny?" Colin's gentle touch made me aware of the silence around the table. All eyes were on me.

"Yes?"

"What are you looking at?"

"Simon Brun, who we are pretty sure is Piros, started and funded the Michaelangelo trust fund."

"Doc, back up." Manny sat up in his chair. "Give it to us slowly."

I was tempted to repeat my previous sentence much slower, but didn't want to add to Manny's stress levels. "Francine sent an email. She discovered that P&S, Simon Brun and those five security companies all used that same bank, the same branch."

"Which bank?" Colin asked.

I looked at the email. "The DBS bank in Singapore. I think Francine might have broken a few laws here. She hacked into those accounts."

Leon and Manny groaned, Vinnie and Colin smiled. I was looking at the black and white of law enforcement and I didn't know anymore where I fit in. I ignored the disconcerting cognitive dissonance.

"There are a lot of transfers between Simon Brun and the five security companies' accounts. Most of the transactions are transfers to Brun's account. The security companies have similar transaction histories, transfers to Brun and three companies in Hungary."

"Hungary?" Manny lifted his eyebrows and turned to Leon. "What do you think?"

Leon was quiet for some time. "I think we need to ask this Francine to get us the names of all the account holders Brun and the security companies sent money to. If possible, she should find out who the bloody hell this Simon Brun is."

Manny's lips disappeared completely. All the muscles in his body tightened until I thought he might get up and hit someone. Instead he looked at me with angry resentment. "Email that Francine woman and tell her to do this. Holy Mother, I can't believe I've come to this."

"Manny, we don't have to do it like this. Surely there is another way," I said.

"With court orders and a long list of legal procedures that will take days to go through. No, Doc, this is for the best. I'll just take the punches as they come."

I studied Manny, looking for any sign of doubt. I did not wish for this upright man to regret his decision. I was taken aback by the unfamiliar empathic consideration evident in my thinking. In Manny's demeanour there was no sign of uncertainty though, only anger.

I turned to my computer and composed an email to Francine. Only my typing broke the heavy silence in my apartment. We had all crossed a line from which there would be no return.

Francine replied immediately, promising to have something before the event. I didn't even bother to question how she knew about tonight's event. Things had rolled out of my control. The prospect of having to be around hundreds of pretentious people tonight did nothing to help my disposition.

A heaviness had settled between us. There wasn't anything else to discuss, so Manny and Leon took their leave. They wanted to double-check the security and other things that didn't interest me. Vinnie left for the kitchen to prepare a late lunch for us and I stayed in my chair, staring at the computers. As much as I tried, I couldn't stop myself from thinking about the throng of bodies, the demand of social politeness and the probable danger tonight would bring.

Chapter **TWENTY-SEVEN**

"I can't do this." I took a shaky breath. "I just can't do this."

Colin and Vinnie looked up from their reading material. They were lounging on the sofas in the living area. While I had been in my room getting ready, they had also changed. Colin looked handsome in a way that made me think of my first description of him. He looked suave, James Bond suave. Vinnie looked even more like a Mafia enforcer than before. The tuxedo pants, blinding white shirt and a bow tie did not soften his look at all. He looked dangerous.

Their eyes stretched as they took in my attire. I frowned when they continued to ignore my declaration. They were not only blatantly looking at my ankle-length sapphire dress, but their eyes lingered where the dress flowed around my hips and hugged my torso. It was when Colin's eyebrows lifted and his eyes rested on the tailored bodice hugging my cleavage that I put my hands on my hips.

"Don't look at me like I'm a painting you want to steal." It felt good to speak in annoyance rather than the panic threatening to cripple me.

Colin stood up and walked towards me. "Jenny, if you were a painting, I would steal you and look at you all day, every day. You are breath-taking."

"Oh."

Vinnie smiled and also got up. "Colin is right. You look beautiful, Jen-girl. You'll steal the limelight tonight."

I cringed. "I really don't want that."

Vinnie looked at Colin as if asking for his help. When Colin only smiled at him, he sighed. "I'm going to say the wrong things, so I think it's best I go."

"Where are you going?" I asked.

"To pick up my date for the evening." He took his tuxedo jacket from the coat tree and shrugged it on. I didn't know much about men's wear, but I was convinced that Vinnie's tuxedo had to be tailor-made. No off-the-rack suit would fit over his muscular thighs and broad shoulders. "I'll leave Colin to do the talking. But you must know, Jen-girl, you are a beauty and I'll be watching your back the whole time tonight."

His sincerity calmed me, even though his words reminded me why I couldn't do this. I blinked a few times, trying to smile. I couldn't. "Thank you, Vinnie."

He opened the door. "See you guys later."

"See you, Vin." Colin was standing next to me. We watched Vinnie close the door behind him. I couldn't help another sigh escaping my lips. Immediately Colin gently took my hand in his. "What's bothering you?"

I turned to him, with my hand still in his. It surprised me that I drew strength from his touch, but at the moment I needed it more than my need to understand it. I curled my fingers around his hand and held on tight. "I can't do this, Colin. I can't go in there with all those people looking at me."

He pulled on my hand and led me to the sofas. Once we were seated, he enclosed my hand in both of his. "What would happen if people looked at you, Jenny?"

I shuddered. "They will know."

"Know what?"

"That it's all a lie." I waved my other hand around. "That I'm a social disaster."

Colin was quiet for a long moment, studying my face. "No, I don't think that is what is worrying you. What is really worrying you?"

My eyes flashed in surprise. Colin was much more astute than

I had thought. It took me three false starts before I had enough courage to speak. "I'm scared."

"Of what?"

"That I'll be attacked again. That you, Manny and Vinnie will get hurt. That I won't be able to do anything about it. That I won't be able to identify Piros. That I won't—"

"Whoa, Jenny. Slow down." Colin squeezed my hand and leaned a bit closer. "You are not responsible for protecting us. It's the other way around. We will be there to protect you. Leon and the GIPN team have the safety of the young artists under control. All you have to do is study people. You know, like you do in cafés, or in your viewing room, or when I don't give you the answers you want."

His last comment elicited a small smile. It didn't stay very long. "But there will be a lot of people. They'll be touching me."

"I'm touching you now." We both looked down at my hand between his.

"It's not the same."

"No?"

"No." I looked for a way to explain this. "There's no logic to this. I don't know why, but I feel safe with you. I trust you. When other people touch me, it feels like they're attacking me, like they're draining my energy. Your touch calms me, it makes me feel protected. It really doesn't make sense. You're not as strong as Vinnie. He could protect me better. No, this feeling really has no rational grounds."

Colin laughed softly. "It's only because of your extreme rationalisation that I won't take offence."

"Why? Did I say something wrong?"

"No, Jenny, you didn't." His soft smile held hints of affection. He was quiet for some time. "I have an idea. How good are you at dissociation?"

"I excel in that. Sometimes that is the only aid I have when I find myself in a social setting."

"Great. So here's my suggestion. When we are at La Maison Russie, you could hold my hand or my arm and only focus on that touch. You can think of it as an anchor."

I considered it, playing possible scenarios in my mind. "I like it. An anchor. You will be my anchor."

It was only a glimpse, but Colin's pupils dilated a moment before he closed his eyes on a pained chuckle. When he opened his eyes, I only saw friendship. I had been so absorbed by this case that I had never considered the emotions I experienced around Colin. A frown pulled my brows together when I realised I would have to spend time identifying the individual emotions to see if attraction was amongst them.

"Jenny?"

I shook my head to clear it of irrelevant thoughts. "Yes?"

"I asked you if you're feeling better now. Are you ready for tonight?"

"No."

He was surprised by my answer. "Why not?"

"You will make me feel safe from the crowd. But you can't protect me from Piros and his army."

"You're right, I alone can't protect you. But we have Vinnie, GIPN, Leon and even Millard." His lip lifted as if smelling something bad. "He is very good at his job and won't let anything happen to you."

"You consider him competent, but you don't trust him. Why should I trust him?"

"God, I hate saying this," Colin groaned. "Millard is one of the finest detectives I know. He's also a good person. And I do trust him. Just never tell that asshole I said this."

"Why not?"

"First he'll gloat and then he'll take advantage of it." Colin must have seen the confused look on my face. He was contradicting himself and I needed clarity. Colin sighed and shook his head. "Our history is long and not pleasant. We have a kind of love-hate relationship."

"That doesn't make sense."

His hands tightened around mine while he seemed lost in thought for a few minutes. I gave him time to gather his thoughts. Maybe I wasn't the only one who needed an anchor. Resolve tightened his lips and he took a deep breath. "I used to, um, appropriate art."

"Steal?"

"Shit. All right, yes, I was stealing. That was a long time ago."

"Before the poets?"

"Long before the poets." A small smile lightened the seriousness around his eyes. "I was good, very good. But I was fast going down a very bad road. I was an arrogant young shit, thinking that I was above the law. There were, of course, quite a few law enforcement agencies trying to capture me, but I was too good. But there was one detective who got close a few times."

"Manny?"

Colin grunted. "He was good, but I was better. He was on my tail for four years and almost got me three times. As much as he studied me, I also studied him. I think he still hates me for knowing so much about him."

"You respect him. I can hear it in your voice."

"He is an asshole, but a very good detective. And fair. I have a lot of respect for that." It fascinated me that Colin would be angry to admit this. "I usually worked alone, but during one particular job I met Vinnie and we just sort of clicked."

"An instant rapport?"

"Yes, that. He was... no, that's his story to tell. Anyway, I used to work alone, but Vinnie came in handy a few times when I needed an extra set of hands or eyes." His hands tightened around mine again and he took a shuddering breath. "I was contracted to steal a Rembrandt from a museum's conservation centre. It wasn't a one-man job, so I asked Vinnie's help. I had the painting and was ready to leave when I got to Vinnie. He was standing over the body of a museum security guard."

"Oh my! Vinnie killed someone?"

"I thought so at first, until I saw the devastation on Vinnie's face. The guard wasn't supposed to be in that area, but for some reason appeared out of the blue. Vinnie didn't expect it and when the old guy showed up, Vinnie did his intimidation thing and the old guy had a heart attack."

"That's awful."

"Vinnie was in shock. He took full responsibility for the man's death, but I knew that he would never survive prison."

In a flash a few things became clear to me. "You sent Vinnie away and phoned Manny?"

"How do you know this?" Colin looked suspicious.

"Vinnie's loyalty towards you and the way you care for him. I knew that there had to be something very strong to bind the two of you together like this. But I must admit, I didn't expect something so dramatic. Phoning Manny would be in character for you. He was someone you respected, albeit reluctantly, and you knew he was fair."

"I really should never get on your bad side, Jenny. You see everything. Yes, that was the reason I phoned Manny. One of the reasons I can't stand the man is the way he gloated when he arrested me. But I had my revenge." He grinned. "He had interrogated me for only an hour when he was called out. When he returned three hours later, he was furious. His bosses had ordered him off the case. I think he's still got a bug up his arse about that."

I let the last comment go unexplained. "Why did they order him off the case?"

He sighed. "They were the devil and offered me a deal."

"Are you referring to the metaphor?"

"Yes, I am. I made a deal with the devil that night." His gaze intensified and I knew that the next sentence was going to be significant and extremely confidential. "The price of my freedom was to work cases for Interpol in an unofficial capacity. They had intel on a lot of artefacts stolen during conflicts, but officially couldn't do anything about it. They needed someone to get those pieces back without any connection to Interpol. And I fell into their laps."

"You are Robin Hood."

Colin laughed. "Trust you to use the one metaphor I abhor."

"Does Manny know that you work for the good guys?"

"No. Only three people at Interpol know about my work. Most of the cases were so politically sensitive that a hint of this could've caused wars." He grew quiet for a moment. "It was the best thing that could have happened to me. I don't want to think about where I could be today if I hadn't started thinking about my actions. These cases also opened my eyes to a lot of humanity's inhumanity."

"Why don't you tell Manny?" It was only a glimpse, but the micro-expression on Colin's face made me utter a shocked laugh. "You enjoy him not knowing. You are outwitting him."

"And I'm trusting you with this."

"Of course. And four other people."

"Hmm?"

"Five people know about your work. Three people at Interpol, Vinnie and I. Five people."

Colin nodded soberly. My breath grew short with the importance of what Colin had just trusted me with. We sat in silence, lost in our thoughts. It took a few moments for me to identify the emotions pressing on my chest. Respect, admiration and a curious tenderness for the man next to me overwhelmed me.

For once I gave in to my impulse, leaned over and gave Colin a soft kiss on his shaved cheek. "You're a good man, Colin Frey. A very good man."

His shock at my atypical display of affection was interrupted by my doorbell, followed by a loud knock.

"That would be Manny." I pulled at my hand, but Colin didn't let go.

"I'll get the door. Stay here." He got up, walked to the door with strong steps and opened it only enough to peek through. "Wait here. Don't argue, Millard, just wait here."

I blinked at Colin's tone. He had always been mocking and condescending towards Manny, never commanding. That must have been the reason why I didn't hear Manny argue as the door closed. Colin walked back to me and took his place next to me again.

"Jenny, if you don't want to go, I will support you in this. Millard is waiting for you, but I'll deal with him." He leaned in and made sure I was looking into his eyes. "If you decide to go, I will not allow anything to happen to you."

"Oh, Colin, you can't make that promise." I closed my eyes, breathed deeply a few times and reached inside myself to analyse my feelings. "I'll go. If Manny is as good as you say and I can hold your hand, I will feel safe enough."

A smile pulled at his lips, but he swallowed it away. He got up and held out his hand to me. "M'lady?"

I put my hand in his and let him pull me up. He weaved his fingers though mine and walked to the front door. He briefly let go to put on his jacket, but immediately took my hand again before opening the door. A scowling Manny was leaning against the wall across from my front door. "What's going on?"

I was too shocked at the sight of a cleanly shaved Manny dressed in an immaculate tuxedo to answer.

"I'll be Jenny's date for the evening."

"Not going to happen, Frey. You're not going. There is no way that you have an invitation and I'm not getting you inside. Not happening."

"Au contraire, my dear Millard." Colin pulled an envelope

from the inside pocket of his jacket and waved it at Manny. "My invitation."

From one second to the next, Manny's expression changed from annoyance to suspicion. "Is that invite real? Where and how did you get that?"

"I'm not without my resources."

It was his quick glance at me that made realisation crash through me. He had acquired the invitation through Interpol. I bit my lips to refrain from saying anything and tried to focus on something else. It wasn't difficult. Manny's transformation was very distracting.

"You look fifteen years younger," I blurted. "And you're actually handsome."

"Oh, for the love of all that is holy, Doc." Manny's scowl was back. "You're not going to distract me from refusing to allow Frey to join us."

"I wasn't trying to do that. You really look younger." I decided to stop this line of conversation when Manny's lips turned into an angry thin line. "If Colin doesn't go, I won't go. He's my anchor. And his invitation is real and legitimate."

"What is she talking about?" Manny asked Colin.

"She needs me." Colin squeezed my hand. "I'll be by her side the whole night. Now if we're done with this conversation, our transport is waiting."

Without waiting for Manny's response, Colin led me to the elevator. Angry footsteps followed us after a moment.

"We're going in my car." Manny started an argument on why we should go in his car. I lost interest in his diatribe and went over the details of what I knew about Piros in my head. I didn't pay attention to the arriving elevator car and blindly followed Colin when the doors opened to the ground floor. I needed to make sure that I hadn't overlooked anything concerning Piros.

A shocked silence brought me back to the present and I found myself between the two men at the entrance to my building. Parked in front of us was a limousine.

"There has to be something illegal about this." Manny stared at the long vehicle in disbelief.

"Nothing illegal or wrong with a bit of style. Don't you agree, Jenny?"

I lifted a shoulder. "Will it get us to the event?"

"Yes."

"Then let's go before I change my mind."

Manny continued to grumble, but he followed us to the car. His arguments about using his car forgotten. The driver was standing at the open passenger door and received a scowl from Manny when he greeted him. I was too nervous to allow rudeness or the lush interior of the limousine to have any effect on me. It was awkward, but I didn't let go of Colin's hand when I entered the vehicle first. With conscious effort I relaxed my panicked grip on his hand, but he immediately tightened his hold. I truly hoped that I would have some time tomorrow to analyse the relief and feeling of safety I drew from Colin's touch.

I leaned back against the seat and allowed Colin and Manny's conversation to wash over me. They seemed to have reached a truce and were talking about the security procedures taken by GIPN. Colin seemed to understand all the coded police jargon. I didn't care to ask. My only concern was to put an end to this case.

Too soon we stopped. I looked out the window and saw a circular driveway with a line of limousines dropping off elegantly dressed couples. We waited our turn to reach the entrance and the doorman opened the passenger door. Manny got out first, followed by Colin. Still holding my hand, he assisted me until I stood between him and Manny. When the latter uttered an inelegant groan, I glanced at him and then followed his line of sight.

Waiting by the door was Vinnie, looking marginally less

dangerous because of the woman next to him. She was the most beautiful woman I had ever seen in real life. Tall, with the exotic looks of a few races mixed in one, she looked like she had walked off the front page of a glossy women's magazine. The kind of magazine I never read. Vinnie said something out of the corner of his mouth and she laughed without any inhibitions. I liked that.

"Who's that?" I asked Colin as we moved towards them. Vinnie glanced at our entwined fingers and narrowed his eyes for a second before he gave me a genuine smile.

Colin didn't answer me until we were within handshake distance of the couple. "Jenny, I would like you to meet Francine. Francine, this is Doctor Genevieve Lenard."

"Oh my God, you're gorgeous." Francine took a step closer. "I would love to hug you, but I won't. These guys told me a lot about you, but they never told me that you were so beautiful."

"You are Francine?" I stared at her in shock. "You are not the only one from whom such knowledge was withheld. In a classic sense you are much more beautiful than I."

"Should we start a mutual admiration club for you two?" Manny was angry. He was being sarcastic. When he wasn't glaring at Vinnie, he aimed his hostile gaze at me. Why he was furious with me, I did not know.

"And who is this delightful gentleman?" Francine fluttered her eyes at Manny. I was sure she was being acerbic. His scowl intensified.

"Francine, this is Manny Millard. Millard, Francine," Colin said.

"You're the one who—"

"Works very hard for good people, and you are the law," Francine interrupted him with a sharp edge to her words. Manny narrowed his eyes and then nodded in acknowledgement of something unspoken. I didn't know what that something was. Before I could ask, Francine pointed at the front door. "The party has already started. Shall we go in?"

Chapter TWENTY-EIGHT

"I thought you would have the names for us before the event." I looked up at Francine to see a brief frown. We were in one of the front rooms, surrounded by throngs of designer-dressed bodies. Feigned interest, false laughter and idle chatter threatened to distract me. I focussed on the warmth of the palm touching mine and waited for Francine to answer.

"I also thought I would have them." She picked a champagne flute off the tray, which a bulky waiter politely offered to our group. Vinnie and Colin also took flutes. Manny declined and I did not have a free hand. My left hand had a death grip on Colin's and my clutch bag was in my right hand. Alcohol was not something that I considered wise at this time. What I needed more was information.

"So you have nothing?" I asked. Everyone looked at me with widened eyes. Maybe my tone had been too displeased.

"I think I'm angrier about this than you are," Francine said. She elbowed Vinnie lightly and he took a tablet computer from his jacket's interior pocket. Big pockets for a big jacket. "But I don't have nothing." She swiped the tablet a few times, tapped a few more times and smiled triumphantly. We followed Manny to a mantelpiece and stood close enough so no one could overhear Francine. "This flash drive is the mother lode."

"Francine, English," Colin said.

Francine glanced at me. "Oh, yes. Okay. This flash drive has all the account numbers of anyone who ever had any dealings with the shipping companies. It is divided into the art auctions, the artists, the security companies, which by the way is helping me get the real names of the owners of these accounts. The banks' encryption is really good, but—"

"I really don't want to know this," Manny said.

"Ah, of course. You can't be party to anything that is not strictly by the book. Hypocrite." Francine rolled her eyes.

"Would you stop interrupting Francine so she could tell y'all what she's found." Vinnie glared at Manny. I wondered why he had the Texan accent again.

"Thanks, Vin." Francine leaned into him, her eyes on her tablet. "I did a lot of search work on your Mister Brun. He has a few accounts all over the world, but his Hungarian account is the oldest. It was opened twenty-five years ago. I checked the photo ID's he gave when he opened his numerous accounts and each is different. Never the same person's photo. It's most definitely a cover identity."

"It isn't logical that he would use the same name over and over again. It makes it so much easier for him to be discovered." I huffed. "Not a very intelligent move for a criminal."

"Maybe he has some sentimental attachment to the name," Manny said.

"He also owns property in all these countries where he has his accounts. In Croatia he has a large villa and there he insured some artwork to the amount of"—she checked her tablet—"seven million US dollars."

"Does it say which pieces are insured?" I asked.

"No, but I can find that for you if you need it. Something that bothered me was the lack of family that I found with all his identities. Except for Hungary. There he listed his wife as Irene Brun."

"Irene?" A connection was tugging at my consciousness.

"Jenny?" Colin squeezed my hand. "What is it?"

"Somewhere I came across that name. I just can't remember where." I needed a quiet place and Mozart.

"Irene is a very common name," Manny said. "It is also very possible that it is a false identity."

"Don't worry about it now, Jen-girl," Vinnie said. "It's more important that you check out the people here."

"Do you have anything else on Simon Brun?" Manny asked.

"No, but I'm also working on that." She waved her tablet computer at us. "This tablet connects to my work computers and will let me know as soon as the decryption is complete. I've set it up to immediately compare the names of the owners of those five accounts to all the other lists of names that I have. It will also do a general search on those names, which should give us more."

"We're running out of time, people." Stress tightened Manny's throat so that his speech was strained.

Tension pulled at my back and shoulder muscles and I wished that I was more comfortable with other people touching me. A deep tissue massage would be wonderful. I turned my attention away from the group towards the door and froze. Colin must have felt my reaction. He rubbed my forearm. I glanced at him and he smiled at me. "Wild horses couldn't keep him away."

Emotion placed a huge lump in my throat as Phillip made his way through the crowd towards us. Not once did he take his eyes off me. If one could've chosen one's parents, I knew who I would've chosen as my father. A wide smile lit up his face as he reached us.

"Genevieve, you look well." He lifted his hands and let them drop before he touched me. "Actually, you look beautiful. How are you?"

"Coping," I answered honestly. "This is not something I'm prepared for."

"I don't think anyone was prepared for this." He smiled at me and for the first time looked at the people forming a protective circle around me. "Good evening, everyone."

Greetings and introductions were exchanged. Phillip didn't insist on knowing any more about the case. He was just there to make sure of my safety.

Manny glanced at his watch. "Most of the guests should be here already. Maybe we should start mingling. Do you all have your cell phones?"

"I have my smartphone." I pinched my clutch bag under my arm and proudly lifted my phone.

"Will you answer it?" Manny lifted one eyebrow.

"If I must."

"Tonight you must, missy."

Manny asked for Vinnie, Colin and Francine's numbers. A brief argument about invasion of privacy and someone's big brother was interrupted by Phillip reminding everyone of the bigger picture. I observed a lot of resentment when the exchange of numbers happened. Just then we were joined by Leon. Another round of greetings and introductions followed before I pulled lightly on Colin's hand.

"They're arguing again. Can we please start analysing people?"

"A very good idea." He looked relieved. "They're stomping on my last nerve, so I can't imagine how you must feel."

As soon as we left, Vinnie and Francine followed us at a distance. Throughout the welcoming and award ceremony at least two of our group were within view. I started relaxing into the feeling of being watched and protected. We were approaching the bar for a much-needed glass of water when Manny intercepted us.

"Seen anything?"

"Relevant to the case?" I asked. I had observed a lot of interesting behaviour, but didn't want to hear Manny's sarcasm again.

"Yes, missy."

"I've seen a few men with similar posture and movement as the thugs who broke into my place."

Colin stiffened. "Why didn't you say anything?"

"They just walked and behaved in a similar manner. It's not evidence of anything. They're mingling, but are much more observant than any of the other guests."

"Some of them might be our guys," Manny said. "Have you seen anyone who might be Piros?"

"No."

Manny sighed. "Okay, let me borrow you for a while. I want to introduce you to my boss."

"Which one?" I asked.

"The Head of the EDA and the Chief Executive. They're in the other room." Manny looked at Colin. "I don't think it's a good idea for you to tag along."

"Amen to that." Colin blinked twice and suddenly looked concerned. He turned to me. "Jenny, will you be okay?"

I looked at our hands and for the first time in hours took my hand out of his. The imprint of his hand felt ridiculously permanent on my palm. I rubbed my palm against my thigh and took a bracing breath. "If it's only ten minutes, I'll be okay."

"Millard, you heard the lady. Ten minutes or I'll come looking for her." There was no ambiguity in the threat delivered. Even I heard the unspoken implications.

"You don't get to threaten me, you lowlife. It will be ten minutes because of Doctor Lenard, not because of you." Manny gestured for me to go ahead of him and said over his shoulder, "Arsehole."

"I have a theory," I said as we made our way through the crowd. Manny leaned closer to me and nodded that he was listening. I phrased what I was about to say very carefully. "You think you are old and settled in your ways. It is not true. You are an exceptionally open-minded person, for some reason reluctant to let anyone see it. I also think that you like Colin, respect him and even like Vinnie. What I don't know or understand is why you can't admit to this. Why you think it is shameful."

Manny was quiet for so long that I glanced up at him. An angry vein was throbbing on his forehead and he was continually swallowing. I had failed to phrase myself carefully. He stopped and breathed as if he had just run up a few flights of stairs. A waiter passed us with a tray and Manny grabbed a glass with an amber-coloured drink in it. In one gulp he emptied the glass and closed his eyes. I waited, watching as his breathing slowed and his face returned to its normal colour.

"Doc, you would drive a man to do and say things that could land him in prison."

"Technically, I don't have that kind of power. We are each responsible for our own—"

"Doc." Manny held up his hand as if stopping traffic. "Now would be a good time to not speak. I'm going to forget the last five minutes and introduce you to my bosses. You are going to be your best social self and you are going to observe the hell out of them."

He didn't wait for my response, but turned away from me and walked with measured steps to a small group of people. I followed him, immediately recognising the Head of the EDA and Chief Dutoit from the footage I had watched. They made their excuses and broke away from the group to face us.

"You must be Doctor Lenard."

"And you must be the Head of the EDA, Sarah Crichton." I was ready and produced a warm smile. I even allowed her to shake my hand without flinching.

"Doctor Lenard," Frederique Dutoit said. "It is a pleasure to finally meet you in person."

My smile faltered and it took work to not react when we shook hands. In deference to our different nationalities, we spoke English. Chief Dutoit's English was perfect and without accent. His voice deep and smooth. I needed a moment to ascertain what it was about his voice, his non-verbal communication that was troubling me. Very likely it was just his social pretence. And I always found social pretence grossly abrasive.

I answered a few polite questions about the event. When questions about the case were aimed at me, Manny smoothly interrupted and answered untruthfully or with half-truths. I allowed him to lead this strange interaction, aware of how important it was for him. It was also invaluable for me. I was reeling with the revelations of what the Head and Chief were loudly projecting. I wondered if Manny knew how much the Chief hated him, or the Head distrusted the Chief, but valued Manny. Office politics. I couldn't stand it.

"Genevieve, there you are." A soft hand rested on my shoulder blade. I turned to be air-kissed by an enthusiastic Francine. "When I heard that you were here, I just had to find you."

"Um, hello." Her strange behaviour led me to surmise that she was pretending. I didn't know if I was allowed to use her name or not. Or what my role in this ruse was.

"Oh, honey, look at you. You look fantastic. I just have to hug you." I was pulled into an embrace that I forced myself to return. While holding me close she whispered into my ear, "I'm sorry for all this touching, but I need you to play along. You need to go to the ladies' room with me."

I straightened when she let me go and managed a happy smile. "It's wonderful to see you too. I didn't know you would be here."

"Yet here I am." She turned to a slack-jawed Manny and smiled brightly at him. Her acting skills were admirable. "If you'll excuse us, us girls need to freshen up."

Francine didn't wait for a response, but grabbed my hand and started pulling me away from the group. I sent an apologetic smile to Manny and his bosses. The cluster of facial muscle movements indicated Manny's intense anger. Oh, dear. I turned my attention to Francine. "What's happening?"

"Colin got impatient." She let go of my hand and led us out of the room. "And I needed to go to the washroom, so I thought it was a good plan to get you away from those stuffy suits."

"Are we really going to the washroom? I thought it was all a ruse."

"After two glasses of bubbly, my bladder is killing me. So yes, we're going to the loo."

"What about Colin and Vinnie?"

"They're following us and will keep an eye on the doors."

"Oh." I followed her to restrooms more elegant than any of those in the top hotels and mansions I had been in. An anteroom with lush carpets and designer sofas led to a room that looked like it had been carved out of marble. A middle-aged lady passed us on her way out, preceded and followed by an excess of perfume. I looked at Francine and she rolled her eyes.

"Rich old ladies." She nodded at our surroundings. "Stunning, isn't it? I have only seen this kind of crazy opulence in Moscow and St Petersburg. This is so Russian."

"It is beautiful," I said. It was not my taste though. It was cold, impersonal and would take far too much time and specialised products to keep clean.

Francine disappeared into one of the cubicles. I made use of the facilities and met Francine at the marble basins with gold-finished taps. I dried my hands on a small hand towel and dispensed of it in a small wicker basket.

An electronic ping sounded next to me and I glanced at Francine. Her eyes widened in pleasure and she grabbed her tablet computer out of her bag. "Results. We have results."

"What results?" I lowered my voice when three women entered the room chatting about someone's weight gain. Francine was tapping and swiping the tablet screen without any awareness of our surroundings. I lowered my voice even more. "Maybe we should leave."

"Hmm?" She looked up and then focussed on the sofas by the entrance. "Let's go sit there. I need a moment to check this out."

I followed her there and sat down next to her. The sofas were not only beautiful, but surprisingly comfortable. It took less than a minute before I became impatient. "Speak to me, Francine."

"In a moment." She swiped and tapped a few more times. When she looked up, her eyes were bright. "Who exactly is Kubanov?"

"He's the founder of the charity organisation hosting this event. Why?"

"Simon Brun is married to his cousin." She tilted the tablet towards me and pointed at the screen. "I followed the bank accounts like I said earlier. His Hungarian account where his wife is registered also required photo ID of her. There are two more bank accounts with her photo, one as Irene Brun, the other as Irena Kubanov, born in Volosovo, Russia."

I closed my eyes for a heartbeat, then opened them on a deep inhale. "When you first mentioned her name, I knew I had seen it somewhere. It was on the Foundation's website. Kubanov said there that his inspiration came from a few people in his life, one of them being his cousin Irena. So, that is the connection between Kubanov and Piros. We need to tell Manny and the others."

"That's not all, Genevieve." Francine changed screens on the tablet. It showed a scanned form of sorts. "I checked the name Simon Brun on Interpol's database."

"You can do that?" Understanding hit me when she merely raised her eyebrows. How many agencies was she working for? "Oh, okay. Sorry. Go on."

"His name was set to send a red alert when searched. I circumvented it." She waited for two ladies to exit the room before she continued quietly. "Simon Brun was the name used by an undercover agent during the eighties. There is a list here of places he worked, but nowhere does it say who the agent was."

"We have to tell Manny now." I got up and took my smartphone from my clutch bag.

It took only two rings before Manny answered. "Where are you?"

"Meet us in front of the ladies' room. Francine found something," I said. The rude oaf didn't even answer me; he just disconnected the call. Francine and I left the restroom and found Manny, Colin and Vinnie huddling next to a large flower arrangement. They were leaning in close in what seemed a heated discussion. I sighed. They were arguing again. It would seem that Manny had already been close by when I phoned him.

I narrowed my eyes on a realisation. When we were close enough, I interrupted Manny. "Why aren't you sneezing?"

"I beg your pardon?"

"You said that you suffer severely from allergies to flowers. Why aren't you sneezing?"

"Because I have really good medication, missy. Now can we get to business?"

"Okay," I said. "What were you talking about?"

Colin took half a step to the left and nodded at the wall. "What do you see?"

I looked at the beautiful flower arrangement. It held no clues. I raised my eyes and blinked in shock. "Gauguin's Still Life, The White Bowl."

"And it's the real thing," Colin said. "I'm willing to stake my freedom on it."

"You still haven't convinced me." Manny glared at the painting. "How can you be so sure?"

"While you were arguing, I studied the painting," Colin said. "Look close enough at the frame and you'll see that I'm right."

I stepped closer and focussed on the bottom left corner.

"He's right. You have to look carefully, but I can see where the strip was cut from the painting."

"I still can't believe that Danielle would've desecrated a masterpiece like this," Colin said.

"Desperation makes people do strange things, Frey," Manny said. He looked at me. "Care to share what big new revelations you two ladies got in the restroom?"

I left it to Francine to fill them in and show them the new information on her tablet. For a few precious moments I allowed Mozart to dominate my mind. I took two steps backwards to gain a minimal distance from all the outraged expressions bouncing back and forth within our small group. As it was, I hoped that we could find Piros tonight and end his reign. Not only was he a megalomaniac tyrant, he was also a traitor. And a serial killer.

My gaze drifted away from our group, over the crowd of pretentious people competing to improve their social standing, yet unaware that their presence here put them in association with murderers of the worst calibre. A familiar voice pulled my attention to the left.

About three meters from me stood Manny's boss, Chief Dutoit, who was deep in discussion with another man. His tailored suit and manicured hands gave him the look of a pampered businessman. Not quite the kind of company a man of Chief Dutoit's character would seek out. This anomaly interested me. I paid closer attention. They were conversing in French, arguing about a delayed delivery that could have disastrous financial repercussions.

Next to me, Vinnie and Manny were trading insults, Vinnie about the depth of the corruption in government agencies, Manny about simpleminded criminals. I smiled. They liked each other. Colin and Francine were focussed on her tablet.

My amusement at my group and interest in Chief Dutoit's discussion were brought to a brutal halt. All it took was one word. A word so softly spoken I could barely believe I had heard it, yet I was convinced that I had. In my mind all the separate elements of this case moved into perfect alignment. One word combined all the loose bits of information to a state of completion where all my observations, analyses and theories into one single conclusion. The answer to all the questions. The innermost gear powering, driving all the others.

Still arguing, Chief Dutoit and the other man started walking away. Without thinking I followed the voice that had uttered that crucial word. Overcrowding, people touching me and my own personal safety no longer mattered. Hearing that word again was all I could think about. Getting it recorded would be even better. With a start I realised that my smartphone, still resting in my palm, enabled me to do exactly that.

I followed them through two rooms. The crowded rooms made it easy to keep some distance between us. It also provided me with an irrational sense of safety. That last thought made me gasp. Colin. Manny. I should not have left like I had. The sudden vibration of my smartphone in my hand nearly had me screaming in fright. Adrenaline pumped through my system, causing me to answer the call with a shaking hand.

"Hello?" I whispered unnecessarily. I was surrounded by conversation and laughter.

"Jenny, where are you?" Colin sounded winded and worried.

"Um, I don't know. I went through two rooms. They've turned left. It looks like a corridor to the back of the house. Maybe to the right side of the house. I really don't know. I'm following Piros."

"You're what?" Manny's loud voice made me cringe.

"Am I on speaker phone?"

"Yes."

"I know who he is," I said just as I broke free of the crowds. I glanced into the long corridor. I took three steps back into the crowd. "I don't think it would be prudent to continue talking to you. The corridor is rather quiet and they might hear me. I'm switching on my video app and streaming it to your phone. Find me."

I ignored three male voices yelling all types of orders at me and tapped the mute button. It took only a moment before I connected Colin via video to what I was seeing. Another tap on my smartphone and it was recording. I took a moment to examine my situation and decide on a course of action. First things first. I kicked off my shoes for comfort and stealth. One calming breath and I walked down the long, dimly-lit corridor, my smartphone leading the way.

Chapter TWENTY-NINE

The men disappeared through an open door into what looked like a library. I stopped next to the door and peeked around the corner. They were standing in front of a solid wooden door against the far wall of the library. Chief Dutoit reached up and took a key from on top of the doorframe. He unlocked the door and returned the key to its hiding place.

"Let's go," he said and followed the other man through the door. The door closed behind them and locked with an audible click. I waited until I thought the men might have moved far away from the door. Still holding the phone in front of me, I walked to the door and reached up. I was too short. An impatient growl escaped my lips as I looked around for something to aid me.

Most of the furniture in the room looked antique and undoubtedly too heavy for me to drag to the door. Except for the small footstool next to a beautiful nineteenth-century wingback chair big enough for me to curl up and sleep in. I dragged the stool to the door and retrieved the key. I pushed the stool away and stared at the key. I didn't know what would greet me behind that door, but I didn't want to waste any time waiting for Manny and Colin.

As quietly as I could, I pushed the key into the lock and turned. I winced when it clicked and held my breath. No one came storming through the door, so I pulled the door only a centimetre away from the lock. I left the key under the stool, aiming my phone at it so that Colin would know where to find it. My forte was in the safety of my viewing room, not sneaking around. The shaking of my hands, tightness in my throat and shallow breathing were evidence of that.

It required three deep breaths before I had enough courage to open the door wide enough to look beyond the opening. I was looking at the dark-blue walls of a staircase. Most likely it led to the basement or to a wine cellar. As I slipped through the door and the lock clicked behind me, it felt like I was standing at the top of a staircase leading me to my doom.

The sounds of the party were now mostly muted. The two men's voices floated up the staircase, which looked uncommonly long going down. I held my phone in front of me like a shield and carefully went down the stairs towards the argument. Two-thirds of the way down, I could distinguish their words.

"This is a disaster," the other man said. "How did they know our plans?"

"Someone must have talked," Chief Dutoit said. Visual cues were my strength, but it was easy to hear the contained rage in his words. "It was not anybody on my team. Which leaves only you and your trusted right-hand man."

I had reached the bottom of the staircase. I stood on the last step and leaned against the wall, hoping that they were not close enough to see me. Straight ahead of the stairs were rows and rows of shelved wine bottles in a softly lit room. The visible plumbing and ventilation pipes running along the ceiling did not take away from the muted elegance of this space. It was a well-maintained cellar. There were even paintings against the walls. Expensive paintings. They probably were all forgeries.

"Sir, it wasn't us. I would never betray you." The other man's thin answer came from the right. I dared a look around the wall and saw them. Chief Dutoit was standing close to the other man. He was leaning forward, almost nose to nose, his one hand on his hip, the other tightened in a fist. The other man's shoulders were slightly hunched, his eyes wide.

"Sir, I've been with you for ten years. I believe in what you do. I would never—"

"Who else could it be?" Chief Dutoit interrupted the other man's stuttering. "Who else would know what we were planning after the award ceremony?"

"Sir, it was on the programme that the artists would go to a retreat after the ceremony."

Moving only my arm, I pushed my smartphone past the corner of the wall, aiming it at them. I hoped that the lack of background noise would aid the limited capabilities of the phone's microphone. The bad lighting most likely would not result in good footage.

"That means nothing." Chief Dutoit's voice was growing softer and more menacing. I swallowed my nerves away, hoping that Colin would show up soon. What was taking them so long? I glanced at my phone's screen. Chief Dutoit was towering even closer to the other man now. "I would like to know what led the police to take all the artists into protective custody. That was—"

A hand clamped on my shoulder and I yelped. Loudly. My smartphone fell to the ground in a clatter, but I had no time to worry about my phone. All I could focus on was the terrifying awareness of a sharp blade against my throat.

Not again. Please, not again. I swallowed, too late realising that it would move the blade against my throat and possibly cause damage. All conversation in the cellar ceased.

"What have we here?" the man behind me asked. I blinked in surprise as I recognised the voice of the German thug who had terrorised me in my apartment. He still had his hand on my shoulder and pushed me forward. "Come, let's introduce you."

A thousand fragmented thoughts fluttered through my mind. Thoughts of Manny's anger about me not waiting for them, that I would miss him calling me 'missy' when he was annoyed with me. That I would miss Colin's touch, Vinnie's protective presence and Phillip's guidance. I was also growing angrier with myself for being so focussed on the conversation between Dutoit and the other man that I had never even considered paying attention to the staircase. The curse of my single-minded focus.

I was prodded by the hand on my shoulder and the knife to my throat until I stood in front of Chief Dutoit and the other man. My self-aimed anger and the enormity of the situation were far too significant for me to succumb to panic. If only I would live to tell this story, to face Manny's anger. I didn't want this to be my last day on earth. I wasn't ready to die.

"Doctor Lenard, we meet again." Chief Dutoit studied me through narrowed eyes.

"Chief Dutoit," I answered in French. I wanted us to speak in the language that would give me that word again. "I can't say that this is a pleasure."

"I found her lurking at the bottom of the staircase, listening to your conversation," the thug said in accented French. I wondered if he had not seen my smartphone, or whether he considered it broken and thus harmless when it had hit the floor. Was it still streaming and recording?

"You will have to forgive my colleague's right-hand man for his tactics." Chief Dutoit nodded at the knife against my throat. "It is only for the safety of the event."

I considered lying, telling him that I had lost my way. Only for a moment though. My lack of deceptive skills would only anger a man who looked close to the edge. His nonverbal cues were alarming. I had to do something to bring him back from his rage.

I forced my muscles to relax, conveying as little threat as possible. I focussed on calming my breathing so that my voice would be controlled, soothing. "It is quite a large selection of wines here. I'm not a big white wine drinker. Only in summer, maybe with a good salad would I indulge."

Chief Dutoit stilled, frowned, then smiled at me. "What do you favour? A merlot? Cabernet sauvignon?"

"My palate prefers a good Pinot noir. I like its purity, its freshness. The notes of damp earth make me feel one with its origins." I could not believe I was talking about wine while very possibly facing death.

"I also prefer a good red wine." The tightness in his face and posture lightened a bit. "I prefer a Cabernet sauvignon though. It goes well with my preference for red meat."

"You really are him," I whispered. "You are Piros."

We stared at each other. There was no mistaking his pronunciation of the word red in French. I was in an eye-lock with one of the most notorious criminals in Europe. I was sure that Manny would be able to align Chief Dutoit's career-tracks with Piros' activities. Where was Manny?

"Ah, Doctor Lenard, you've just earned yourself a death sentence." Chief Dutoit looked disappointed. He nodded at the German who let me go, but stayed close to me. I couldn't resist the need to touch my throat. It was unharmed. Chief Dutoit, aka Piros, walked closer until he stood a foot away from me. "You've been the most fun I've had in years. A worthy adversary. All these years and no one got even close to me."

"They couldn't get close to you if you were the one leading the investigation, or the one closing it down."

"True, true. It pays having worked one's way up the ladder, making friends along the way. It's always who you know, not what you know." His smile sent an uncontrollable shiver down my spine. "Tell me, how did you figure it out? I know it wasn't that idiot Millard."

I wanted to, but I didn't defend Manny. I counted on him not being an idiot so that he could find me and save me from this terrifying ordeal. My hesitation to answer him unfortunately lasted a moment too long. Piros lost his patience and slapped me hard across my left cheek. My head snapped back and I almost lost my balance. When I looked up at him, all I saw past the tears in my eyes was ruthless cold menace.

"How did you figure it out?" His shouted question was as violent an assault on my senses as the slap. I flinched before I could control my panic and my responses with a measure of Mozart.

"Red," I said past the tightness in my throat. "I heard you say red."

I focussed on the micro-movements of his facial muscles to keep me grounded. I could see his mind computing what I had just told him until he reached a conclusion. I saw his intent, but it didn't prepare me. He slapped me viciously across the same cheek as he screamed at me, "Who was it? Who told you where my name came from?"

I tried, but it was too much for me. The picture of Danielle lying in a pool of her own blood flashed across my consciousness followed by disjointed flashes of financial spreadsheets, shipping manifests, flash drives, Vinnie's smile, Manny's frown, Francine's tablet computer. I sank to the floor of the cellar. If I allowed the black void to suck me in, I wouldn't feel any pain, I wouldn't fear for my life. It was beckoning me and I was tempted.

But then I wouldn't be able to tell Manny who Piros was. On a painful breath I imagined Colin holding my hand while I listened to Mozart. The darkness receded and I opened my eyes. I had my arms wrapped around my waist, keening softly and rocking myself. I must have been like this for a few minutes, because Piros was a few feet away from me, barking orders into a cell phone.

The other man was watching me with hatred and disdain on his face. His steady hand was pointing a gun at my head. I looked at my own shaking hands. I wanted to be in my viewing room, not here. If not my viewing room, any other place would suffice. I just wanted to not feel so damned terrified.

Out of the corner of my eye, I noticed the German making his way to the staircase.

"What's wrong with you?" The other man's disgusted question brought my attention back.

"I was slapped. Hard. Twice." I tried to stand up, but he stepped closer and just shook his head. The gun was close enough for me to see into the barrel. I imagined that I could see the tip of the bullet. I swallowed a few times.

"Your weakness sickens me. People like you should not be allowed in public."

"For once I agree with you, Pierre." Piros slid his cell phone into his jacket pocket and walked closer. "It's arranged. I will leave through the back, my transport will pick me up. You can deal with her. You'll have to keep it quiet though. The place is crawling with police. Just find out what she knows first."

"It will be my pleasure." His smile told me what kind of sick pleasure he would get from following Piros' orders.

"Doctor Lenard." Piros looked down at me with all the arrogant power he thought he had. "It truly was a pleasurable few weeks watching you work. You've caused me great inconvenience, but a new challenge. I will have to regroup, but it is a long-overdue necessity."

"You won't get away." I said it with more conviction than I felt. Surely Manny and Colin should have found me by now. Where were they? Was Piros really going to get away?

"I will." He smirked. "You won't."

Powerless, I watched as he turned away and walked to the back of the basement. Presumably to another door that would lead him to freedom to continue his evil work.

I had to do something. I had to stop this, but I didn't know how. I wanted to howl with frustration, but didn't dare do anything with that gun so close to my head.

Suddenly my senses were overwhelmed by the loudest sound and brightest light I had ever encountered. All my frustration, thoughts and desperate plans made place for panic. It felt like a bomb had exploded in the cellar, but I was still alive. I looked for damage, debris flying about but I couldn't see anything. The loudness of the bang left me totally disoriented. I fell back on the floor, my hands slammed over my ears, screaming soundlessly. My ears were ringing, nausea causing me to curl into a foetal position. An irrational thought crossed my mind that I had never felt more alive.

I forced Mozart into my mind as it threatened to shut down. When strong arms lifted me against a solid chest and gently carried me away, my breathing became erratic. Bile rose in my throat from the fear of being touched. The fear of being carried to a place worse than where I was. I started squirming, but the hands held me tighter. We were climbing the stairs, away from the cellar. Shouted orders barely superseded the ringing in my ears and I felt even more disoriented and scared.

"Jenny, you have to calm down." Colin's voice rumbled where he held me against his chest. I opened my eyes. My vision was back. The bright flash of light must have only blinded me momentarily. We were in the library. Colin sat down in the large wingback chair, still holding me to his chest. "I've got you. Just calm down."

"Piros." I managed to push the word past my lips.

"GIPN has him." From his breathing I knew he was speaking louder than usual. I was glad. The ringing in my ears was terrible. He touched my face and I leaned into his palm. "God, I nearly died waiting for those arseholes to get their shit together. I thought we were going to lose you. Why didn't you wait?"

"I was scared we were going to lose the opportunity to catch Piros red-handed."

Colin bit down hard on his jaw, not taking his eyes off me for one moment. "Never, ever again. You will never put your life in danger like this again. Promise me."

I stared at the agony on his face, in his eyes. "You care."

"Of course I fucking care!" He took a few calming breaths. "Jenny, promise me."

It wasn't a hard promise to make. I never wanted to experience the last ten minutes again. "I promise."

"Jen-girl!" Vinnie's voice boomed across the room. He ran to us and slid to a stop on his knees at our feet. He looked at Colin. "Did you make her promise?" He looked at me. "Did you promise? Your word, Jen-girl. We want your word."

"I promised Colin that I would never put my life in danger like this again."

"Did you promise that you would never go into another situation without one of us next to you?"

"Vinnie, that is an illogical promise to make. You can't always be with me." I pushed myself into a more upright position. "Why didn't you guys come to my rescue earlier? Didn't you get the video I was streaming to your phone?"

"We got it," Colin said. "Manny and Leon decided that it would be better to send the professionals in to control the situation. We had to wait ten minutes for GIPN to get themselves organised over here."

"Ten minutes of hell." Vinnie's groan barely rose above the ringing that was still loud in my ears.

"Doctor I-read-fucking-faces Lenard!" Manny's angry voice drew my attention to the cellar door. He stormed to us and Colin's arms tightened around me. Vinnie stood up, but strangely didn't put himself between me and Manny. Instead he moved to the side. Manny stopped in front of us, glaring down at me long enough for my heart rate to increase. "What the fuck were you thinking?"

"Manny," I said softly.

"Don't fucking Manny me! I can't talk to you right now. I'm so fucking angry with you." He was short of breath from rage. On a growl he glared at Colin. "You talk to her."

I blinked in astonishment as Manny swung around and stormed back to the basement. What happened to the dynamics between them while I was in the cellar? There was a sense of co-operation between them that I had not seen before.

"Jenny, are you okay? Really okay?" Colin asked when I looked at him.

"There's a loud ringing in my head."

"It's the stun grenade they used," Vinnie said. "It produces a loud blast and a flash of light to disorient the enemy."

"It worked on me," I said. "Did it work on the German, Piros and the other man? Oh my, do you know who Piros is?"

"We figured out that Dutoit is Piros while you were playing Nancy Drew," Colin said.

"I don't know who she is." I shrugged off another meaningless name thrown at me. "How did you figure it out?"

"Manny phoned one of his old friends at Interpol to ask about Simon Brun. Seems Manny's old friend is one of the big guys over there. Big enough to have answers to highly confidential questions. Apparently Simon Brun had made quite a name for himself in the covert world at that time. Enough for this friend to remember the alias and the agent. Bloody Chief Dutoit."

My response died in my mouth as three men, dressed in black like the thugs who had broken into my apartment, escorted Piros through the cellar door. His face was beaten up, but he looked like he had won a prize rather than being caught. Behind them Manny followed, shaking his hand. My eyebrows lifted as I looked from Manny's bloody knuckles to Piros' battered face. I didn't say anything until they left the room. "Why does Piros look so arrogant?"

"He probably thinks he is too valuable for any law enforcement agency to send him to prison," Colin said. "He reckons he's an asset who will be valued and given special witness protection status."

"How do you know this?" I asked.

Colin stared at me until I realised his work for Interpol must have taught him a lot about these kinds of situations. My understanding must have been evident on my face. He shook his head at me when I opened my mouth to say something about this. I closed my mouth and bit down on my lips for good measure. Colin smiled for the first time since I had opened my eyes to find myself in his arms.

I was still in his arms. I tried to sit up, but he held on to me.

"Colin, let me up. I can't sit on your lap."

"Why not?"

I frowned. "I don't know."

"Well then. Stay here until you feel better."

"I feel fine."

"Not light-headed?"

"A little."

"What about your cheek?"

My hand floated up to touch the sensitive swelling where I had been slapped twice. "I don't think anything is broken. It really hurts though."

"You will get checked by the paramedic." Manny's gruff order caught me by surprise. I hadn't seen him come back into the library. He was standing with his hands on his hips a scant few feet away, the corners of his mouth pulled down. "What are you doing on Frey's lap?"

"She's lightheaded," Vinnie said as if it would answer more than just that one question. He had seated himself in the adjacent chair. He looked exhausted.

"He's touching you." Manny looked totally put out by this. Colin looked smug. I wanted to change the topic.

"What about the German and the other man? Who is the other man? Where are all the guests?" I asked.

Manny studied me for a while. At least this time it wasn't with intense rage twisting his facial muscles. I only saw inflexible determination. "This is how it's going to be, missy. You will first allow the GIPN team doctor to check you. If, and only if, he says that you are okay, I will answer all your questions. You will not complain when he needs to touch you to determine that you are okay. Understood?"

There was only one correct answer. "Yes."

Fifteen minutes later I was still on Colin's lap, but had endured being prodded and touched by a dark-skinned doctor with dreadlocks and gentle hands. Colin's hand rubbing small circles on my back had helped me focus on calming my breathing when the doctor pressed against my cheekbone. As soon as he said I was okay, but might consider x-rays just to be sure, I leaned away from him. Vinnie stood up and scowled at the doctor until he left. All the while Manny had been talking on his cell phone. As soon as the doctor left the library he dragged an antique chair closer and perched on it. He looked uncomfortable on the spindly-legged chair.

"Phillip will visit you at your apartment tomorrow. He sends his regards." He gave a crooked smile. "He knew we weren't going to leave you and he didn't want to overwhelm you with too many people around."

There were still a lot of police-type people walking around the house, but mostly we were alone in the library. I didn't feel overwhelmed sitting on Colin's lap, Vinnie less than a foot to my left and Manny sitting right in front of us. How my life had changed in less than a month.

"Will you answer my questions now?" I asked.

"Doc, you're not good for an old man's mental and physical health." He ignored Colin and Vinnie's snorts. "Okay, here's the rundown. The other man was Piros' lawyer. Had been for the last fifteen years. A crooked lawyer to boot."

"Like all lawyers," said Vinnie.

"His name was on the list of payments on the flash drives," Manny continued as if Vinnie didn't exist, their co-operation a thing of the past. "He's in custody as is the German. Both of them immediately asked for legal representation."

"Will they get it?" Colin asked.

"Maybe not immediately. This is an international case with terrorist roots. Piros and his associates have only the most basic of human rights after what they have done. Piros thought he would be able to cut a deal, but there is no chance of that ever happening. Not with the crimes he has committed."

"And we have evidence," I said proudly.

"That we do, Doc. That we do."

"What about the artists?" I asked.

"After the ceremony they were put on a bus. GIPN intercepted them and took them into protective custody. They are all young people, at first arrogant, but started talking very quickly when they realised their freedom was at risk. We should get even more evidence from them."

"And they're safe," I said.

"They are. If only you had enough sense to keep yourself safe, missy." He frowned at me. "You, the rational, logical, level-headed, intellectual genius, followed a known mass killer into a basement. Have you no sense of self-preservation?"

Manny was getting agitated again, so I refrained from commenting on his habitual redundant use of adjectives. "You talked so often about catching him red-handed, I didn't want to lose the opportunity. To be honest, I didn't really think much about my own safety."

"I swear to all that is pure and holy, Doc. You need a keeper."

"I do not." All three men made disagreeing noises. I was deeply offended. "I do not need a keeper."

"Anyway," Manny continued. "While you were busy giving us heart attacks with your mindless behaviour, the GIPN team moved all the guests to the other side of the house. They're still vetting all the guests and have so far detained twelve men."

"Those men I noticed to be military types?" I asked.

"Possibly," Manny said. "I'm quite impressed with the GIPN team and the police helping them. They're good. The whole cellar takedown was fast, efficient—"

"And saved my life," I said. We were silent for a few moments. I didn't know what they were thinking, but I was still trying to tie up loose ends. "What about Kubanov? We know that he has to be involved with this."

"We have no evidence, Jen-girl," Vinnie said.

"That doesn't matter now," Manny said. "He got away."

Colin tensed. "What do you mean he got away? We know he must have been bankrolling Piros and this whole operation."

Manny's answer got interrupted by his cell phone's annoying ringtone. He glanced at his phone and grimaced. "Give me a moment." He walked away from us as he answered his phone. The call didn't last very long. There was purpose to his steps as he moved back to us.

"What's up, dude?" Vinnie sat up in his chair, looking concerned.

"Don't call me dude. You have to leave."

"Because I called you dude?"

"No, you simpleton. All of you have to leave now. Take Doc home."

I pushed away from Colin. "Why?"

"I've kept most of this investigation under wraps and I think I'm going to pay for this within the next ten minutes. The Head of the EDA just told me that the Secretary-General from Interpol, the Chief of Police and a few other head honchos are all on their way here. I have no doubt that they are going to ask me about the help I received. Doc might be okay admitting to working with me, but I'm sure you two wouldn't want all these guys seeing your faces."

Vinnie jumped up from his chair. I wasn't ready to leave yet, but didn't have a choice when Colin stood, picking me up. "Hey! I still have questions."

"They're going to have to wait, Doc. I'll come around tomorrow morning for a debrief."

I wanted to argue, but Colin and Vinnie were already moving to the back entrance. Only when we left the house did Colin listen to my near-panic pleading. He gently lowered me until my feet touched the ground. But I didn't need to walk anywhere. We were next to the limousine that had brought us here, the driver patiently waiting for us by the open back door.

Chapter THIRTY

I woke up to the heavenly smell of roasted coffee and breakfast. A glance at the antique clock on my dresser made me groan. How could it possibly be three in the afternoon? I seldom slept in, but to sleep more than half the day away was a first for me. I left my room half an hour later, showered and feeling refreshed.

"At bloody last." Manny stood up from the dining table with a welcoming frown. "I thought you would never wake up."

"Leave her be, Manny." My gaze swung to Phillip lounging on a sofa with the Sunday paper spread out around him. He got up and walked towards us. "You only got here fifteen minutes ago."

"And he's already eaten three servings," Vinnie said from the kitchen. He picked up a mug of coffee and a plate laden with food and brought it to the table. "Here you are, Jen-girl. We've already eaten. Except for Millard. He's still stuffing his face."

"Oh, give me a break. I've been under the microscope for the last sixteen hours." Manny sat back down. He was still wearing his tuxedo pants and white shirt. It looked like he had been wearing it for more than twenty-four hours. Manny looked worse than his shirt. His skin was gray from exhaustion, his stubble making him look even more bedraggled. We sat down at the table. The men stared at me.

"Well, aren't you going to say something?" Manny asked me.

I took a sip of coffee. "Where is Colin?"

"In his room, taking a super-secret call," Manny said.

"Why are you angry about it?" I asked.

"He just pisses me off." He sighed heavily. "And I'm really tired, so everything is pissing me off. Except the food. It's really good."

Vinnie wasn't fast enough to hide his surprise at the compliment, or his pleasure. "Um, thanks. There's more."

I spent the next five minutes assuring them that I was feeling okay, despite the horrid bruise on my cheek. Phillip needed extra convincing. I spent another five minutes reassuring Colin when he joined us.

"Enough." I raised my hands in a blocking motion. "Tell me what happened after we left, Manny."

He pushed away his empty plate with a satisfied grunt. "There was almost a riot with all those VIP guests. They didn't want to be vetted. A few were even under the impression that La Maison Russie was part of the Russian embassy and thus not under French jurisdiction. That was soon cleared up. Altogether fifteen men were taken into custody for questioning. It seems that they were all working either for Piros or for the lawyer.

"Piros is being held in extra-secure holding and very likely will be tried for war crimes, amongst others. The bastard quickly lost his smile when he realised that no one was interested in cutting a deal with him. Interpol will launch a thorough investigation together with the law enforcement agencies of all the countries involved. Another investigation will be undertaken into all the forgeries. I swear that the head of the art crimes division was giggling like a teenager when I told him about all the evidence we have. I wouldn't want to be someone whose name is on the cruise list or art buyers' list. The Foundation is also going to be investigated and, of course, Kubanov."

"What about him? Has he been found?" I asked.

"He landed in Russia today, claiming that he has no knowledge of any wrongdoing. He issued a statement at the airport that he was going to demand a full investigation into the Foundation and find the culprits who used his charity to fund their illegal activities."

"Son of a bitch!" Vinnie slammed his hand on the table. "He's behind it all and he's going to get away?"

"We have nothing to tie him directly to anything. It disgusts me, but we will need concrete evidence before anyone would even consider going after a man as powerful as Kubanov." Manny waved his hand to change the topic. "That can be a fish we catch on another day. As it is, we've caught a whale. After so many years reigning in terror, Piros will pay for his crimes. And I've been fired."

"What the fuck?" Vinnie was the first to react after five seconds of stunned silence. "They can't do that. Can they?"

"Why, Manny?" Phillip asked. "Is it because of co-operating with us?"

Manny smiled. "You mean co-operating with these criminals?"

"Watch your mouth, old man," Vinnie said.

Colin was strangely quiet.

"No, it was not about working with you," Manny said to Phillip. "Or working with them. It's actually a decision that the Head and I had been discussing since the beginning of this case. The EDA is not the type of place to be involved with investigations like this."

"But this is what you do," I said. "This is what you are good at."

"I thought that a change in career at the EDA would be good for me, but I can't seem to get away from the detective in me."

"Now what?" Colin asked.

"First I need to get back to Interpol's headquarters. We only took a break after the sixteen hours of discussions about the case. It will take a while to tie this up and hand all the different investigations over. Then I'm going fishing." He scowled when Colin and Vinnie laughed. "I need to get away for a while. I've had a few offers and need to decide what I want to do. What about you two criminals? Ready to change your ways?"

"Not in this life, dude." Vinnie took obvious pleasure goading Manny. True to form Manny responded with an insult and it took ten minutes before Phillip stepped in to calm everyone down. I simply sat back and enjoyed the familiarity of the personalities around my dining table.

"I will miss this," I said softly.

"I think we all will, Jenny." Colin touched my forearm. "This was a unique time for me."

"For all of us," Phillip said. "Genevieve, would you like to take some time off?"

"Oh, no, please. I need to get back to work. To my viewing room." To safety.

Phillip stood up. "Then I'll see you tomorrow. I have to go to a family dinner and need to do a few things before then. Colin, it was a strange experience meeting and working with you. Vinnie, the same."

We all stood up and walked to the front door. Phillip left and Manny took his tuxedo jacket from the coat tree. "Doc, I'll be in touch about some of your lists, but you should be rid of me soon."

"I don't want to be rid of you, Manny." I felt sad. This seemed so final. "I've grown quite fond of your disapproval and frowns."

He gave a tired laugh and took a cautious step forward. "I'm going to kiss you on your cheek, but I don't want you to go all weird on me."

"I won't go all weird on you," I said and offered my cheek. He placed a gentle hand on my shoulder and pecked me softly on my cheek.

"Look after yourself, Doc." He stepped back and shook Vinnie and Colin's hands. "Crime really doesn't pay. Next time we meet I might have to arrest you."

"In your dreams, Millard," Colin said.

"I've done it before, Frey," Manny said as he stepped through the door. "I will do it again."

The door closed and it was just me, Vinnie and Colin.

"Jen-girl, I'm going to abuse your hospitality for a few more days before I fly to visit my auntie Helen in New York. Is that okay?"

"It's very okay, Vinnie. Stay as long as you like." I couldn't keep the relief out of my voice. I had grown used to having people in my space. Not just people. These two men. Vinnie walked to the dining table and started cleaning up. Colin and I stood in silence looking at him work.

"Jenny," Colin started, but stopped when I raised my hand. I took a few deep breaths to enjoy this moment before the inevitable took place. Change. Life was all about change. Something I didn't like. I sighed my acceptance.

"You have to go," I said.

"Yes."

"Was it the phone call earlier?" I asked. "Just after I woke up?"

His lips lifted in a half smile. "Did you see it on my face?"

"No, your shoulders. They were tense."

He took my hand in his and played with my fingers. I thought of a documentary I had watched about specialists who work with traumatised or sensitive animals. Through touch they desensitised the creatures until they were able to function normally in their environment. I wondered if Colin's touch was desensitising me. For the first time in my life I enjoyed another person's touch.

"Jenny?" Colin squeezed my hand to get my attention. "Are you listening?"

"Sorry. Yes, I'm listening."

"I don't know how long I'll be gone, but it shouldn't be longer than a week. Maybe two."

"It's okay. We all have to get back to our lives." I sounded sad. I was sad. I pushed my shoulders back and raised my chin. "When you get back and Vinnie is back from New York, he can cook dinner for us and we can catch up."

"I might be back before him."

"Can you cook dinner?"

Colin laughed. "I'll bring a pizza. Is that okay?"

"I prefer Chinese takeaway."

"Good to know." He pulled at my hand. Slowly, with enough time for me to pull away, he leaned closer. I took a shaky breath and closed my eyes. Soft lips gently rested on my forehead for a long moment. I opened my eyes as Colin pulled back. "Till next time, Jenny."

I did not respond. I just stood back while he picked up a black travel bag next to the sofa and opened the door. One last smile and Colin closed the door behind him.

I didn't know how long I stood there looking at the door. Thinking. About life, about change, about touch, about people.

I had new people in my life. New people who would complicate my life, but also enrich it. They might leave, but they would be back. I knew I could trust them. I knew I could trust Colin. Even though he was a reputed thief, known for breaking and entering.

On this thought I frowned at my front door and said, "He used the door."

~ ~ ~ ~ ~

*Be first to find out when Genevieve's next adventure will be
published. Sign up for the newsletter at*
http://estelleryan.com/contact.html

~ ~ ~ ~ ~

*Listen to the Mozart pieces, look at the paintings from this book
and read more about Gauguin:*
http://estelleryan.com/the-gauguin-connection.html

~ ~ ~ ~ ~

The Dante Connection
Second in the Genevieve Lenard series

Art theft. Coded messages. A high-level threat.

Despite her initial disbelief, Doctor Genevieve Lenard discovers that she is the key that connects stolen works of art, ciphers and sinister threats.

Betrayed by the people who called themselves her friends, Genevieve throws herself into her insurance investigation job with autistic single-mindedness. When hacker Francine appears beaten and bloodied on her doorstep, begging for her help, Genevieve is forced to get past the hurt of her friends' abandonment and team up with them to find the perpetrators.

Little does she know that it will take her on a journey through not one, but two twisted minds to discover the true target of their mysterious messages. It will take all her personal strength and knowledge as a nonverbal communications expert to overcome fears that could cost not only her life, but the lives of many others.

The Dante Connection *now available as paperback and ebook.*

The Dante Connection
Second in the Genevieve Lenard series

Excerpt

Chapter ONE

"Genevieve, you have to help me. I killed two men."

"Francine?" I cringed at my redundant request for confirmation of identity. The sight in front of me shocked my sleepy brain into full alert. My hand tightened around the front door handle and I stared at the grievously injured woman in the hallway.

"Help me, please." Her voice was hoarse as if she had been screaming. Her left eye was swollen shut and her face freshly bruised.

I could not read her expressions. My throat tightened with that realisation. My connection to other people depended on my world-renowned ability to read nonverbal cues. But Francine's face was too damaged to allow much muscle movement. A cut on her cheek was still oozing blood, and she was bleeding from other places too. There were rust coloured splatters all over her clothes. I couldn't see if it was from her injuries. Maybe it was her victims'. A shudder rolled down my spine.

When the insistent ringing of my doorbell had woken me at two in the morning, I had not expected to find the woman who had been avoiding me for two weeks on my doorstep. The exotic beauty I knew to be a computer genius, an exceptional hacker and an enthusiastic proponent for conspiracy theories was weaving, looking ready to lose consciousness. I had only ever seen her looking like a supermodel. The hunched-over figure at my doorstep did not resemble that at all.

"Please?" Her whispered plea brought my attention to her swollen lips.

"But you killed two people." How could I let a killer into my home?

"It was in sel—" A gurgling cough punished her body and she reached out to me. Instinctively I recoiled, but she didn't notice. Her breathing was becoming laboured and it didn't take my three doctorate degrees to know that she needed medical attention.

"Oh, for goodness' sake." I stepped away from the door and opened it wider. "Come on in then."

"Colin," she wheezed as she staggered to my expensive sofas. I closed the door, made sure all five locks were secured in place and hurried over before she reached the living area. With an internal groan, I spread the beige mohair throw over the sofa and watched her lower herself in obvious agony. "Please get Colin here."

"You of all people know that I can't get a hold of him." I had met Colin and Francine five months ago when working on an art crime case. My life had been in danger while investigating the murders of art students. Francine had proven herself to be an invaluable asset when she offered her computer hacking skills. Skills she used for a few government agencies.

Colin, on the other hand, was a criminal. He was an accomplished thief, infamous, and honourable. In that trying time five months ago he had proved himself to be one of the good guys—a concept I had learned from my boss. Not only was Colin a thief, but he was a thief who worked for Interpol. At last count only five people knew of his unconventional job. His cooperation with the law was something neither him nor the powers that be in Interpol wanted to be known. After working side by side with him, I had thought he was my friend, but he had disappeared out of my life a month after the case had closed. That had been four months ago.

At first I had thought he had to be working on some assignment, but after not being able to contact him on the number he had given me, I had become concerned. Three weeks ago I had asked Francine if she could track Colin with her computer skills. We had met only once after that before she too started avoiding my calls. All this rejection did not sit well with me.

"How am I supposed to get Colin here if I can't reach him?" I asked.

"Send him a 911 text to the number you have. He'll phone you."

"How can you be so sure?"

Francine's facial muscles tried to draw together into a pleading expression. "Please, Genevieve. We need him. Just send that text."

Apart from my boss, Francine was the only one who called me Genevieve. Mostly, people called me Doctor Lenard. Three other people used different names for me, but that was in the past.

For a moment I studied her. As usual she was dressed in the best designer clothes, now torn and ruined by bloodstains. She favoured her left side and I wondered if she had been stabbed. There wasn't a large bloodstain in that area, so it was most probably broken ribs. I had a lot of questions about her presence on my sofa. Including the suspicion that her injuries had something to do with her reason for avoiding me. Now she was telling me that we needed Colin. I balked at the 'we'.

A pained groan and tears streaming from her swollen eyes drew me out of my thoughts and put me into action. I stomped to the kitchen, grabbed my smartphone off the counter and swiped the screen. Within three seconds I sent the text message and was staring at the little screen, waiting for Colin to call. My smartphone's screen lit up and a silly ringtone filled my apartment. I swiped the screen.

"Yes?"

"Jenny, what's wrong?" Worry raised Colin's voice from its usual deep rumble. Hearing his voice again for the first time in four months made me happy, sad and angry at the same time. But mostly angry.

"Francine killed two men."

"She...wait...what?" He took a deep breath. "Is she with you?"

"Yes." The more he spoke, the angrier I was becoming. It limited my social vocabulary.

"In your apartment?"

"Yes."

"I'm on my way."

"I'll phone the police."

"No!" Again he took a breath audible enough for me to hear. "Let's first hear what happened."

"She killed two men, Colin. There is nothing more to it. She told me so herself. I should phone the police." My words were clipped.

"Wait a moment."

I heard some clicking noises and narrowed my eyes. Those noises not only came through the phone, but also from a window in the back of my apartment.

My lips tightened and I turned around. "I have a front door."

"That you always lock." Colin smiled as he walked to me in long strides. Something was not right. His usual confident walk seemed impeded in some way. Seeing him after such a long time overwhelmed me with all kinds of emotions which distracted me from my observations. "Hello, Jenny. Did you miss me?"

The Dante Connection now available as paperback and ebook.

Other books in the Genevieve Lenard Series:

Book 1: The Gauguin Connection

Book 2: The Dante Connection

Book 3: The Braque Connection

Book 4: The Flinck Connection

Book 5: The Courbet Connection

Book 6: The Pucelle Connection

Book 7: The Léger Connection

Book 8: The Morisot Connection

Book 9: The Vecellio Connection

and more…

~ ~ ~ ~

Find out more about Estelle at
www.estelleryan.com
Or visit her facebook page to chat with her:
www.facebook.com/EstelleRyanAuthor